BLACK
COFFEE

VILLARD / STRIVERS ROW / NEW YORK

To Corie,

Hey Bro! Thanks so much for supporting me & Black Coffee!

BLACK COFFEE

It's always a pleasure to

A NOVEL

see brothers enjoying Black literature!

much love,

TRACY PRICE-THOMPSON

Tracy Price Thompson.

Copyright © 2002 by Tracy Price-Thompson
Reading Group Guide copyright © 2002 by Random House, Inc.

All rights reserved under International and Pan-American
Copyright Conventions. Published in the United States by
Strivers Row, an imprint of Villard Books, a division of Random House, Inc.,
New York, and simultaneously in Canada by
Random House of Canada Limited, Toronto.

VILLARD BOOKS is a registered trademark of Random House, Inc.
Strivers Row and colophon are trademarks
of Random House, Inc.

Library of Congress Cataloging-in-Publication Data
Price-Thompson, Tracy.
Black coffee: a novel / Tracy Price-Thompson.
p. cm.
ISBN 0-375-75777-5
1. African American women—Fiction.   2. Women soldiers—Fiction.
3. Single mothers—Fiction.   4. Adultery—Fiction.   I. Title.

PS3616.R53 B57 2002
813'.6—dc21   2001035967

Villard Books website address: www.villard.com
Printed in the United States of America on acid-free paper

2   4   6   8   9   7   5   3

First Edition

Book design by JAM Design

This work is dedicated to the memories of my devoted mother, Frances M. Carr, and my beloved father, Edward M. Johnson. If not for your character, wisdom, and loyalty, my life would be a mere fraction of what it is today. Thank you. The power of your love courses on chart, ever steady, gently flowing through my veins.

I may not have you in my life,
but your spirits live in my heart. . . .

Acknowledgments

There have been many kind souls who've helped pave my literary path, so forgive me if I get a bit "long-winded," but by the grace of God I've been fortunate enough to be "long-friended."

I'd like to start out by giving all praise to God, the beneficent and merciful Creator of the universe and Master of the day of judgment, for His infinite mercy in guiding me along the straight path and blessing me in abundance.

This work is dedicated to the memories of my sister and brother, Laverne D. Hansome and Bland J. Carr, whose fighting spirits and loyal love will forever live on in my heart, as well as the memories of my parents, Frances M. Carr and Edward M. Johnson, who were wise enough to fortify me with confidence, grace, and esteem, and to teach me a philosophy of life that enables me to blossom wherever I am planted. Because of my parents, I've learned to look to God for my strength, to dig deep inside for my courage, to count my blessings on grateful fingers, to roll with the punches and land on my feet, and to weather adversity like a true soldier. Thank you for preparing me to appreciate the beauty in every sunrise, and to meet the rigors of this life on *my own* terms.

My deepest thanks go to Greg Thompson, my honest-to-goodness "do-right" man, my anchor and my wings, my bridge over troubled waters, my husband, my lover, and my friend. (YGSGDMD!)

A ka-trillion thanks to my sister, Michelle Carr-McClain, for your unfailing support and belief in my work (especially for reading versions 1–99 of the same chapter and oohing and aahing as though reading it for the very first time!). You have my greatest appreciation for your endless loyalty, sister-love, and untiring efforts on my behalf, and for having more faith in me than I sometimes had in myself. You do a great job filling Mommy's shoes, and she and Daddy would be very proud of you. I love you.

A heartfelt roar of thanks and every drop of my love to Kharim, Kharel, Kharyse, and Khaliyah (my heart, my soul, my pride, and my joy) for being loving, mild-mannered, self-sufficient children, and for putting up with the quirky environment while Mommy got her writing on. (What do you mean you have no clean underwear? Borrow a pair from your brother! What? He has none? Then borrow a pair from your sister!) Lots of love to Erica and Greg Jr., for being two wonderfully intelligent children with brilliant futures on your horizons. I love each of you bright stars from the depths of my soul, and every single thing I do is for you!

Endless love to my special nieces, Toi, Traci, Courtney Rae, Courtney Mae, Ciara, and Angelle, and to my wonderful nephews, Damon, Jerel, Cornell Jr., Brett, and Darius Demetri. In our family, a nephew and a niece warrant the same love and devotion as a son and a daughter. Family is forever, and my love is with you wherever you are. P.S. Toi, don't forget to take your medicine!

To my beautiful godchildren, Eddie Davenport, Shaleek Jamel, and Janise Shanell. I've loved you all since the day you were born, and will continue to love you for all the days of my life. Congrats to Mel and Jamillah! Lots of love to precious baby Isis!

Lots of love and appreciation to my Michigan family, Janice Thompson, George "Tippy" Thompson, Papa George and Mama Ann, Cornell and Delena Grantham, Rick and Dena Jones, Aunt Roz, Fran, Eric, Chrissy, Uncle Sonny, and Aunt Evelyn, and to the entire Johnson clan.

Much love to my very special uncle, Buster Robinson. I love you!!

To the people who know me best, and yet still manage to love me well: my best friends, Kim "come and get me" Kendrick and her wonderful husband, Jimmy Kendrick (I love you, man!), Tawana "Wannie" Harrington, Yvette "No-No" Williams-Gogin, and my entire Tilden family. Thank you for being there for me and my family through thick and thin. Hot peas and butter! I love you all!

A special thank you to TaRessa Stovall, for being a wise counsel, a comfortable shoulder, a trusted confidante, and a wonderful friend. Your spirit is filled with warmth and energy and I value you far more than you know. I love you!

Big thanks go out to Timmothy B. McCann, for your support, allegiance, insight, and constant encouragement. You took great interest in an up-and-coming newbie and guided me through choppy waters that were often teeming with sharks. I pray to be able to do the same for someone else someday.

Much thanks to Renee Martin Shahid, my progressive-minded, upwardly mobile, long-time sister-friend who has doggedly stayed the course of friendship for the last thirty years. (Honey, third grade was a *long* time ago!) Much love to you, girl!

A great big hug and a bundle of love to Tracey M. Davis-Williams, one of my staunchest supporters and a reading motor scooter! So many of my accomplishments would have been impossible without your friendship and loyalty—my college degrees, for starters.

Thank you to Sergeants Rhonda Faye Tatum and Phyllis Nell Primus, for your long-standing friendships and for opening your hearts and homes and making your families my family. Home is wherever the two of you are. I love you both!

A huge shout-out to Robin D. Oliver, for her dedication to my every cause and for proving herself to be the literal definition of a true friend. Your eagerness to see my work in print was second to none. (No need to talk about that two hundred dollars, but thanks for always having my back!)

Thanks to my literary sister-friends, Kimberly Stanley, Camika Spencer, Kimberla Lawson Roby, Lolita Files, Evelyn Coleman, Kieja Shapodee, Pat G'orge Walker, Linda Dominique Grosvenor, Trevy McDonald, Hunter Hayes, Karen E. Quinones Miller, Tonya

Marie Evans, Susan Borden Evans, Venise Berry, Vicki Andrews, Robyn Williams, Delores Thornton, and Pamela Crockett. Each of you awesome writers has encouraged me, supported my efforts, and contributed to my vision in a major way. Much love.

Big thanks to Christine Young-Robinson, my literary partner and future tour companion. Chris, you are good people all the way down to the bone, and I wish you all the best this literary world has to offer.

Big thanks to Pat Houser, my Brooklyn buddy and my dear girl-friend. We have stood the tests of trials and time, and come through unscarred. Thank you for everything, much love.

To Rhonda Gibson, a steadfast supporter and a loyal friend. I love you, my fellow Brooklynite!

Much love to my literary brothers, Blair Walker, Scott Haskins, Gregory "argue for your limitations and you get to keep them" Simpson, Carl Weber, Marcus Major, Brian Egeston, C. Kelly Robinson, Brandon Massey, Edwardo Jackson, Earl Sewell, and William Frederick Cooper.

Many thanks to an expert, tireless publicist and a wonderful woman, Felicia Polk. You had great vision and took notice of me from the very beginning. Your selfless efforts on my behalf are most appreciated. All the best to you!

A great big shout-out to Mondella Jones, for her kindness and support. My daughters love you, and so do I.

Thanks to my book club readers, Sisters With a Vision, Busara Nayo, Unity Sisters One, Sisters With a Purpose, Novel Women, BlackBooks.com (Hey Sister Yasmin and Brother Marlmack!), F.R.O., BlackBooks, and R.A.W. Sistaz (Hey Sister Tee!). Special thanks to Orlanda Thompson, Candy Gill, Venetia Hayes (my good traveling buddy! You know we gotta get that ghetto fish!), Cheryl Charity, Ruby Thomas, Thomas "Teej" James, Michelle Ellison, Sheila Brewer, Jeanette Milliner, Lorraine Byrd, Renee Thompson, Belinda Franklin, Claudia Bell, Nikki Stout, Dawn Collier, Audrey Walker, and the Novel Women: Patrice Brown, Talya Shirley, Charlene Rock, Tracey "Eagle Eye" Thomas, Tracy Bullet, Melanie Ferguson, Tara Harrison, Monica White, and Ebony Dawkins.

All of my appreciation goes to the many independent booksellers who supported *Black Coffee* when it was a self-published novel by an unknown author. You guys treated me like royalty—no, like family. Many thanks go to Ruth Bridges of Atlantic Bookpost, who gave me my first opportunity for a signing and introduced me to some of the most wonderful writers I know; Sandra Evans of Panache Ethnic Collectibles (thanks to Brenda, too!), who supported *Black Coffee*'s launch celebration and made me feel like kinfolk in her store; Fanta Mutota of African Spectrum Books, the toughest book critic I've ever met, who was kind and gentle with me and who looked into my potential and delighted me with what she saw. You and Brother Mutota were gracious and understanding regarding the nightmare dealing with you-know-who, and I will never forget your kindness. To Marcus Williams of Nubian Bookstore, who was always ready to accommodate and host me; Gigi Roane and Willie D. Jennings of Drum and Spear Books, thank you for opening your home and breaking bread with me and my family. We had a great time! To Melissa Lee of Mind and Soul Bookstore, thanks for having me and for taking the delivery snafus by you-know-who in stride; Robin Green-Cary at Sibanye Inc., a beautifully gracious sister inside and out. What can I say? You're the best, Robin. Thanks for everything. To Shunda Blocker, thank you for all of your efforts on my behalf, and for always going the extra mile to take care of me and to promote *Black Coffee*; Andre and Kim at Our Story Bookstore, the warmest and coziest store I've ever signed in. You guys sure know how to make folks feel good. Being in such a relaxing atmosphere makes readers want to prop their feet up and stay awhile. Big thanks to you! To my brothers Kevin and Lloyd at the Black Library, you two wonderful black men possess vision and style, and I see great things on your horizons. Thanks for supporting me without reason or reservation, and big thanks for hand-selling *Black Coffee* to the masses. Much love.

Thank you to Clara Villarosa, Frances Utsey, Emma Rodgers, and Carla Allison. Your acts of kindness and support will always be appreciated.

A special thanks to Pat and Twanda from WJZS Jazz Flavors in Atlanta for your support and promotions.

A big shout-out to my wonderful classmates in the Rutgers

University School of Social Work. You ladies (and you, too, Craig) are a real class act! It was my pleasure to learn in an environment where friendship and compassion were boundless. Thanks to Sherrie L. Respass, Carlyn Hard, Sandie Jones, Kay Soltero, Kim Cremer, Roberta Vlearbone, Sasha Classe, Sarah Hawkins, Sara Figueroa, Jennifer Konen, Nefessa Wiggins, Evelyn Flowers, Alicia Ojeniyi, Stacey Lee, Andrea Damiani, Wendy Cunningham, Sabrina Kane, Bessie Tomlin, Rosie Figueroa, Nicole Muniz, Janette Ramos, and Craig Cole. Very special thanks go to Dr. Ann Abbott for being a calm port in the midst of our storms, and for having a soft voice that is always filled with reason. With your endless wisdom, support, and encouragement, you are the epitome of a social worker, and I am proud to have been your student.

Thanks to my stage buddy, Dheeaba Donghrer, for being talented and nobel enough to play a king. You are a wonderful actor and did great justice to Romulus Caesar!

My deepest gratitude goes to my wonderful agent, Djana Pearson Morris, whose tireless efforts, encouragement, and advocacy on my behalf will always be appreciated, and to my talented editor, Melody Guy, for your keen insight and for making the publishing process virtually painless. You ladies make me feel very special and I am extremely blessed to have you both in my corner.

A huge shout-out to my battle sisters in boots and uniforms in all branches of service. Your hard work and sacrifices may go unsung, but without you, there would be no story to tell. This one is for you!

To Dee Gilbert Woodley, Irma Royster, Dawn Marshall Williams, Latonia Peterson Parks, Michelle Smith Woodley, Staci Silberman, Edie Hall, Stephanie Howard Easton, Yvette "Pat" Mullet, Sheryl Hinds Hayes, Bertha Storey Turner, Vicki Crenshaw, Deborah Torres, Twanda Byrd, Jennifer Myers, Darlene Foye, BG Clara Adams-Enders, Doreen Crook, Dana Hearns, Barbara Wortman, Denise Lane, Retrinda Certain McCoy, Martestene Gray McClendon, Wanda Webb, Vanzetta Wyatt, Regina Kincey, Christine Crumbley, Deborah Nash Nibblins, Linda Henry, Kim Smith, Betty Taylor, Georgia Morgan, Verneatha "Pat" Washington, Jewel "Ann" Myers, Carlyn Ashford, Jerrod Hightower, Chevelle Biles Thompson, and Jean Cox Turner, and to my OCS sisters, Carmella Scott-Skillern, Robin Bowman, and Donna "Smitty" Smith, and in loving memory of two of the sweetest sister-soldiers I've ever known, Irma Mosley and Doris Jones, thank you for enriching my life with your love and friendships. May you both rest in peace.

Last but not least, thank you to my wonderful readers and fans whose e-letters of support and encouragement flooded my mailbox and made my days brighter. Feel free to hit me anytime at tracythomp@aol.com or visit my website at www.TracyPriceThompson.com.

Peace and balance,

Tracy

BLACK COFFEE

SANDERELLA'S SONG

I may be a supersoldier, but I sure as hell ain't no Superwoman. Yes, it's true my hand is steady, I have the eye of a marksman, and I can hit a moving target dead center at four hundred meters, but when it comes to making clever love decisions, I'm not the sharpest knife in the drawer.

While I look pretty lofty in my spit-shined combat boots and razor-sharp battle dress uniform, like a lot of young sisters from the 'hood, I've taken a few wrong turns down the back alleys of life. I've tooted my share of reefer, popped the ring on many a cold brew—I've even dropped a tab of acid during a brief moment of insanity, but I must have been out of my mother-scrunching mind the moment I let crackhead Sonja Reed talk me into reaching for that twenty-dollar heart attack wrapped in tinfoil.

"Damn, Sandie!" Sonja poked me in the ribs with her pointy elbow. "Why you always so uptight, gurlfren'? Here." She passed me a tightly wrapped silver package. "Have a treat. It'll help your square ass fit in—you know, relax!"

Sonja and I were sitting at the vinyl-covered bar of the Sugah Shack, a smoky blue-lighted hole-in-the-wall for the local indigents. Neon strobe lights blinked intermittently from far corners of the room before ricocheting off a shiny silver ball that dangled from the wood-beamed ceiling. Outside, Jack Frost was busy duking it out with Jay Hawk, but inside it was moist and warm, courtesy of the one hundred or so of "us" crammed into the tiny joint.

I'd just completed my final-semester exams and decided to check out the party scene, a luxury I seldom enjoyed since enrolling in night classes at City College. The house music pumped with a thunderous beat, and although I was feeling pretty mellow, shaking my bones and jitterbugging with the fellows, I still flirted along on the fringes of the real action.

"C'mon, chile," Sonja coaxed. She curled her tongue around the tip of a white plastic straw as the metallic disco lights rearranged her features into an erratic jigsaw puzzle. "Come on over here and get your head right so you can relax!"

Relax? I was twenty-two years old with a three-year-old daughter, a part-time job, and a full college load! *Relax* just wasn't in my vocabulary. But Sonja had one thing right. When it came down to drugs, the sistah was a straight-up parallelogram with four equal sides. Aside from social stimulants like marijuana and that dumb encounter with acid, I'd never really been tempted. Real drugs cost real money, real pride, and real self-respect, and with no hope for a return on my investment, I was *real* slow to give up any of those treasures.

But on this particular winter night I was feeling my Wheaties. Mama Ceal had offered to baby-sit, I'd studied like crazy and would graduate with straight A's, and my boyfriend had just dumped me for my best friend's sister.

Relaxation was just what I craved.

So when prompted by Sonja with a sure nod and a half smile, I lowered my head to the shiny black counter and did as I'd seen her do. I inhaled two thick lines of prime white ghost straight into my malfunctioning brain.

"*Yeahhh.*" Sonja giggled as I puckered up my face. "That's it. Now relax."

I relaxed all right. Kicked back so far you would've sworn I was in a coma! Slouching all over the barstool, my body went limper than Michael Jackson's wrist!

For a moment.

Suddenly my heart started pounding like a funky bass drum and my hands got to trembling like a set of wayward brass cymbals. Then I got hot. *Real* hot. Like I was being steamed like a lobster—but from the inside out!

My mouth went Sahara and my nose went numb.

I dashed out of that lean-to of a firetrap and ran the entire two miles to the projects without stopping.

And then I ran back!

Shaking and heaving, I collapsed in the dirty snow behind the Sugah Shack and listened as the bass thump-thump from the music inside competed with the wheeze-bang-*whomp!* in my pulsating chest cavity.

Right then and there I swore off cocaine.

That was *it* for the sistah. Damn if I would be the same fool twice. Cocaine caused too many bodily changes and left you with absolutely no self-control. It just wasn't worth it—all that drama for a sore throat and a postnasal drip! But the experience scared me. My own stupidity appalled me. My judgment was suddenly suspect. Six million coke addicts couldn't all be wrong. Would I someday graduate to bigger and better highs? The mere thought gave me the shakes. Paranoid, petrified, and perplexed, I pondered my chances of survival in my Brooklyn ghetto.

They looked slimmer than an anorexic on crack.

In a desperate attempt to veer off the path of self-destruction before I backslid and sampled any more of Sonja's "treats," I fled my drug-induced demons and rushed headlong into the waiting arms of my favorite relation.

Uncle Sam.

"Act in haste and repent in leisure!" is what my granny used to say, and you know she was right, because from the moment I raised my right hand and swore to defend my country from all enemies foreign and domestic, I've been repenting on a daily basis.

During my early years in the Army I billed myself as a harder-than-a-rock native New Yorker. I was rough around the edges, and my personal motto had been: "Don't start no *S-H*, won't be no *I-T*!" Gradually, I assimilated into the military community and its socialized way of living. Bit by bit the harsh edges of my project demeanor softened, and I managed to shake the ghetto chip from my shoulder; but if you backed me into a corner, I could still go homegirl on you in a New York minute!

But I had a slight problem with protocol.

I was an enlisted soldier, and everyone who outranked me was, in effect, my boss. Now, they don't tell you that mess when you sign up, and they sure as heck don't show it to you on those slaphappy "Be All That You Can Be" commercials. As a lowly buck-private-E-nothing, any Joe Blow in a pair of boots could basically tell me what to do and when to do it. That didn't sit well at all with the sistah. I hated being the low man on the totem pole.

"*Hey you! Mop that floor! Hey you! Hump that rucksack! Hey you! Dig that ditch!*"

Private Benjamin I was not.

I didn't see why I couldn't flip my collar and become an officer, then *give* the orders instead of taking them! Army Officer Candidate School became my one burning mission, and I swore on a stack of Bibles that someday I'd get there.

By hook, or by crook.

But in order to get within a country mile of an OCS application, I had to really humble myself, show my teeth to the powers that be. I had to play lots of political patty-cake, and I played it to a T.

Despite the odds that were stacked mile high against me.

As any fool can tell you, the large-and-in-charge in this great country are typically male and white Anglo-Saxon Protestant, and you can search that acronym from Texas to Timbuktu but you will not find a description of me. Although all women in the armed forces have a tough row to hoe, the black woman has it toughest.

Simply put, a female soldier had to have a pair of balls.

A *black* female soldier had to have a pair of balls that were heavily structured, riding low, and swinging in the breeze—yet big enough to block the sun!

She had to be a survivor. And I am.

Yet, as astute as I've been in my professional life, there have been times in my love life when I've been as dumb as dishwater. Too gullible! And for the life of me I can't figure out why. I mean, there's just no excuse. Lord knows Mama Ceal taught her girls better, but we still went out and bought our own sense.

While I can't speak for my sisters, Ladelle and Bunchie, I know what my problem is: I make pitiful life choices. Take birth control. I've had three children by three different men, only one of whom I married. Now there's not a drop of shame in my game, but if it were you instead of me, I'd be the first in line to tell you about yourself. I'd probably say some raw shit like, "Girl, if you're gonna give it up out of *both* drawers legs, at least have sense enough to use a condom!" So if my expert advice is good for you, why hasn't it ever worked for me?

It started with Kevin. My first love. Too fine, boo-black, and always broke. A so-called actor whose starring role was that of a dimple-faced, together brother with a good head on his shoulders. Kevin said he worked in the lab at Harlem Hospital, when actually he swept that mother and took out the trash! He was responsible for three of my pregnancies: my daughter, Jamillah, and two "whosits" that I deposited at the Women's Health Clinic.

Talk about fertile Myrtle?

Jamillah was just three months old when I bought one of those at-home pregnancy tests and killed another rabbit. Mama Ceal took me down to the Women's Health Clinic, and I don't know what hurt worse, getting rid of that baby or climbing off that table and facing my mama. Well, ten months later, dizzy me had another chance to ponder it. This time I rode the subway down to the clinic alone and deposited "whosit" number two, then cried like a baby and kept my mouth shut about it to Mama.

After that I swore to Jesus and all twelve of his disciples I'd never kill another baby, so help me. And I haven't. I've pushed out the rest of my children on a delivery table, and they've all come home with me. To this day, Mama Ceal doesn't know about that second abortion. Or does she?

Five years later, while stationed in California, I met my ex-husband, Maurice. A fine-ass red bone with sticky fingers and shit for brains. I must've been feeling fine on cloud nine when I took that short trip down the aisle. I didn't even know the guy! Not three months passed between us saying our first "hello"s and our final "I do"s. It was six months before I figured out my new husband could steal the oink off a pig.

Talk about impulsive!

I guess that's part of my problem. I don't take enough time to figure out what I can and cannot stand about a man before finding myself knee-deep in his crappola. And somehow Maurice managed to knock me up when I wasn't looking. Just when I was ready to bet my last dollar that he was shooting blanks, tah-dah! Out rolls my youngest, Kharim. Light, bright, and damn near white. Just like his daddy. I don't regret it, of course. It just amazes me that our final round of marital copulation produced such a stunningly beautiful child. Go figure.

And in between the liar and the thief, there was Antoine "Two-tongue" Thommson.

I will never forget him.

Antoine was a cute dark-chocolate 'Bama slammer, my afternoon delight and midnight snack, my ever-ready Freddie whenever I was inclined to step out on Maurice. Built like he chopped trees for a living, Antoine's body seemed chiseled from stone or maybe even granite.

There's something about a soldier!

But Antoine was a superfreak. Always talking about how he wanted to "sop me up wit a biskit." Those country boys are a mess! He'd have kept me barefoot, pregnant, and spread-eagle on the kitchen table if I'd let him, because to Antoine, sex was a national pastime.

And talk about a tongue? I could've sworn he had two!

That boy could work his tongue six ways to next Sunday.

Antoine popped poontang like it was a delicacy, which, of course,

I thought mine was. I tell you ole boy had such an outstanding technique he should've been granted an honorary doctorate in the Art of Good Head!

But believe it or not, you *can* get too much of a good thing. All of that tonguing can work your last nerve. My stuff must have been like sweet black Maxwell House coffee — good to the last drop — because I couldn't keep him off me! Every time I turned around he was lapping at me like a half-starved kitten at a bowl of warm milk! So I got paranoid. Thought he was trying to steal my love juices, like they were superenergy power crystals or something. I finally had to cuss him out and then call the military police and request a base transfer.

That boy had my kitty cat bone-dry!

Antoine gave me my first son, Hanif, a brilliant and wonderful replica of his daddy, who got out of the Army last year to buy a dairy farm. Yep, a dairy farm. On the fifth of every month I receive a postal money order with an Alabama return address, some little rinky-dink town way back in plumb nearly. Plumb out the state, and nearly out the country! Milk them cows, honey!

But on the real tip there have been many nights when I've wished for a dresser drawer chock-full of disposable Antoine tongues, because I have yet to meet a vibrator *or* a man who could match his pace. So although my head may be a bit too hard, my behind a tad too soft, and I run about a quart low on men sense, my shit is still straight.

Even when it's crooked, it's straight.

I just haven't had any luck making the right love connection, that's all. I've been through many love affairs, like sorting clothes on laundry day. Sometimes I wish I could relive those loves of mine. Just shake them out like the wrinkles in a blanket and erase the slate. Like everyone else, I'd do a lot of things differently, but maybe I'd leave a lot the same, too. Although I've been through some risky changes, I've also learned a lot about myself. These days I know my own worth. I don't need a man to empower me or to motivate me. I'm self-motivated, and my mama empowered me with the strength of a lion.

Can you hear my roar?

I think I'm ready to try again. Ready to learn how to trust, just step out on faith. I could use a warm embrace from a pair of strong, honest arms. My body is dying to explode from something other than my own probing fingers, but I'm scared. I still believe in good old-fashioned relationships. I was blessed with positive examples in my father, Franklin, and my brother, Bailey, so I still have faith in black men. Hell, it's us black women who raise them! I'll just have to give some mother's son a chance. Like I said, step out there naked. High on faith. But I can tell you this, the sistah is *straight*, and never again will I settle for less than what I'm worth.

What I deserve.

I don't need no half-stepping, half-a-man-looking-for-a-woman-to-make-him-whole man. I'm already a whole woman, a whole lot of woman. And I need a whole lot of man. Someone who knows where his head is, and preferably not stuck in a mirror or up his own ass. Someone who won't feel threatened by my accomplishments, by my spirit.

By my *funk*.

A man who is self-confident enough to view my fortitude as an appreciated asset instead of an enviable liability. I need a man who loves himself. A man who loves his mama, his sisters, and his life. Someone who will love my children as much as he loves his own. Someone whom my kids can love and admire, too. I need a brother with a bank account—not overflowing, but rainy-day solid. A financially fit brother who is cognizant of the term *future needs*. I need a man with his own car, or his own bike, or his own skates—just as long as he has his own ride. My days of climbing out of my warm bed at the crack of dawn to chauffeur a grown man home are over!

And he has to be clean.

I don't want no nasty man or no man who has bad bites. Certain flaws are simply unpardonable, and bad breath and body odor are two of them.

And I can't *stand* no mama's boy. No man who's still on the titty. My man must be as self-reliant as I am, if not more so. And my man must be decent in bed. A gentle, tender, and considerate lover. Not the kind of lover who, when you whisper, "Baby, you came too fast," hollers back, "Naw, baby! You came too slow!"

Last but not least, my man must be single, uninvolved, disengaged, and disenfranchised. Let the church say "Amen," because I don't want *nobody's husband* and that's the God's honest truth. None of that if-lovin'-you-is-wrong-I-don't-wanna-be-right crap. That's a dead-end road for sure, because the only things a married man can offer you are his poor wife's headaches and heartaches. Been there. Done that. Thanks, but no thanks!

I guess I need that "Whatta Man" Salt-N-Pepa are always bragging about. Someone dignified. Mighty and exalted.

Hell, with my grandiose expectations, high standards, and endless laundry list of qualifications, I'm gonna need to look for more than just the average bear! My man's gonna need an imperial lineage, a royal genealogy. He's gonna have to be a prince.

No, bump that. A king.

I need me a king.

THE RHAPSODY OF ROMULUS

I, Romulus Caesar, am a king!

But nobody seems to know it.

Especially the evil-assed woman who happens to share my bed. I know, I know. You're probably thinking the same old, same old. "Fornicating husband plus frustrated wife equals fucked-up marriage." But this is different. My situation is totally different.

I'm trapped. Being trapped in a bad marriage is hell, but being trapped in a malicious hail of hate is another matter. I should know. I'd thrown up my hands a long time ago, and, if not for my sons, I'd be one of those husbands who took out the trash and kept right on stepping.

But I'm a king. And a king has responsibilities.

And sometimes he even lives up to them.

Louise and I have been married for eight years, and we've been miserable for the last seven. High-school sweethearts, we both tried the college thang until Lou decided it wasn't for me. Especially when she popped up pregnant during my junior year at Morehouse. Lou was enrolled at nearby Spelman, and those weekend ball-busting love jams had yielded a mighty surprise. Mama was right. I should have kept Mr. Bobo tucked safely in my pants. A hard head certainly makes a soft ass.

And a soft Mr. Bobo, too.

"So, what are we going to do?" Lou demanded after seeing the doctor at the university's free health clinic. We were pregnant, all right. Right nice and pregnant.

"I don't know, Lou. We both have school and all, and no jobs. . . ."

"And? What the hell are you saying, 'We have school'? We have a baby coming, too!"

"Calm down, baby. . . . I know, I know! I just don't know what I should do right now." I was trying to play it cool, but my balls had been reduced to two tiny little periods at the end of a sentence.

"Well, you knew just what to do when you were having fun making this baby! You weren't acting all helpless then!"

Lou had the look of a small ferret, cornered and fixing to bite. She stared at me and hunkered down, prepared to launch. Lips curled. Hair everywhere.

Especially on her chin.

Suddenly, I realized why I had that sinking feeling way down in my gut. Not because I'd gotten her pregnant and didn't know what to do. Uh-uh, that wasn't it. It was because I'd knocked her up and I no longer liked her. Forget about loving her. The love had been factored out of our equation a long time ago.

Put a hat on that willie! Slap a helmet on that soldier!

Big Daddy Jenkins tried to warn me before I left my hometown of Philly, but I'd been too young and dumb to accept his good advice. I made one last weak-ass attempt at saving my life and perhaps hers as well. "Lou, sweetie. We don't have any money . . . how are we gonna provide for a baby? Besides, we're both almost finished with college—"

"*We're* not almost finished with anything! It's not like you're passing anyway! The only reason you're still around is because of the track coach! I'm the one who's nearly finished. I'm the one who has a shot at graduation! You're the fuckup who's ruining my chance for an education, for a future, for a decent freaking *life*!"

Then she began to cry as if her entire world had been a sand castle and I was a turbulent tidal wave.

I was doomed. I was fucked. I was ruined.

But I was a king.

And a king had to do what a king had to do.

Louise had one thing right. I was flunking almost every class, except music and track. Leaving college would be no big loss.

So I did the kingly thing.

I showed up on time at the church where Lou said we were getting married and reported to Army Basic Combat Training the very next day. Boy did my mama cry. "You're ruining your life," she wailed, "your *only* life!"

And you know Mama ain't never lied.

Lou and I lived the typical lower-enlisted military life. Rented furniture, a roach-infested apartment so small that when you took a shit in the bathroom, you had to run the water in the kitchen sink. I stayed gone a lot, too. Out on maneuvers and field exercises that Lou never even knew I'd volunteered for. I'd do almost anything to get away from her ugly ways and that my-shit-don't-stink attitude. I'd even volunteered for drill sergeant duty, which was the kiss of death for most marriages, but was the flame-resistant ladder I used to climb straight out of hell.

Like the stump of an umbilical cord left dangling from a healthy infant, our fragile relationship just withered and died. Love just sorta packed up and walked out on us. But what did we expect? I guess at one time or another we must've had that kind of fairy-tale love thang going on, but truthfully, all I remember is that I was a great big ball of raging hormones and she was light-skinned with long hair and had a sho'nuff Venus flytrap!

Lou used to be my best buddy, but just because a girl looks like a dream and can buff a mean Mr. Bobo doesn't mean she's got your best interests at heart. First she whipped the brother, then she used the old knocked-up, drag-out number on my horny ass and made me pay for it.

Twins!

Twin sons. One looked like me and the other favored her. I loved them equally. They were my only sources of happiness. Lou found her happiness both in writing and in her lopsided relationships with her girlfriends, who were mostly Caucasian and mostly drab and un-attractive. Not too many sisters or happening white chicks would put up with Lou's lousy temperament and bossy ways. She dominated nearly every conversation, chattering away nonstop to anyone who could breathe and nod a bit. That girl could talk her little ass off!

And I do mean little.

I guess carrying the twins had given her some breasts and stolen her behind, because you couldn't tell where Lou's back ended and her butt began.

And here I was a certified leg and ass man!

So I took my refuge on the track. Although my testicles were chained, my mind ran free. I ran with the birds, dusting demons and regrets with the force of a gale wind. I ran to forget, I ran to remember, I ran to forgive.

I ran to live. I ran for my life.

I *ran.*

And while I ran . . . Lou tipped.

Tipped out in the middle of the night and sometimes, so I've heard, during lunch. Small, cozy restaurants, maybe? Hot, juicy passion on cool, tangled hotel sheets, perhaps? Then she tipped back home with her shoes in her hand, creeping across the floor like a goddamn cat burglar! I didn't care enough to kill her, but every dog has his day. And I could feel my day a'coming.

Now I'm no Don Juan by any means. You couldn't even hurt your imagination bad enough to see me as a lady's man. I mean, I look aaiight. Six-two, one ninety-four. A little buff. I hold my own. I'm just not a Casanova or anywhere near it. I was brought up in the church, so I have a lot of love and admiration for women.

Especially black women.

I have a mother and four sisters, and I heard what Aretha hollered about R-e-s-p-e-c-t! Although I get no propers at home, I stay in my marriage because of my boys. Big Daddy Jenkins, my stepdads, did a helluva job working with what he had, but growing up without my real father had been pure hell. To hide my pain, I became one of those incorrigible stepkids who fought, rebelled, and generally gave my stepdads grief for not being who I wanted him to be. Who I needed him to be.

I needed my real father.

But that bastard had left me.

In my twelve-year-old mind daddies were supposed to lead the pack. Parents were supposed to stay *together*, and I swore all out I'd *never* tear my kids' hearts up like that when I got married.

But God bless him, Eddie Jenkins hung in there! Hung like a wet rag!

No matter what I did or how often I tore my drawers, he and Mama stayed together. Deeply committed to each other, they figured they could hang in there until I was eighteen and out of their lives. That's what marriage and parenthood are all about, right? Hanging? Right? Well, not always. I'm turning in my hangout card before my marriage costs me my life. Actually, I don't feel I have a marriage. I have twin sons and a situation.

And I have needs Lou just won't meet.

I need to come home to the comfort of a loving woman every now and then. I'd love to come home from a hard day's work and smell dinner cooking—or, better yet, share the closeness of cooking dinner with my wife. To have a sweet woman melt into me as I wrap her in my arms, inhale her essence, and kiss the sky. I want to compose melodies and pen lyrics that testify to the world how deeply I worship and revere my wife, Mrs. Caesar, the queen of my heart.

But not with Lou.

If I even make like to hold her hand, she jumps back like I have the dreaded goongamoonga! Lou's a distant, cold, get-your-slimy-hands-offa-me icebox, and I'm a passionate, affectionate, rub-you-down-with-some-hot-oil-baby teddy bear! Don't get me wrong, I have my faults. I'm totally wrapped up in creating my own music and have been known to ignore an earthquake when there's a song inside of me trying to get born. I'm also a runner, and I spend a lot of time on the track, and yes, I drink a six-pack or four every weekend and chase it down with a taste or two of scotch. Hell, I sometimes leave the toilet seat up just so she can fall in—but I'm no son of a bitch! I'm just a hardworking, supportive black man who needs a strong, honest, loving, and supportive sister.

But unfortunately I messed around and jumped the broom with the wrong woman. And the sex is unspeakable. I don't even want it anymore. The next time Lou gets some of this, she'll have to tie me down to the bed, strap a tongue depressor to Mr. Bobo, and take it! Yeah, Miss Lou is gonna have to *rape* me 'cause I ain't bustin' a grape up in here no more! Since she's so damned capable, a know-it-all Superwoman, always figuring out how to make a dollar out of fifty-nine cents, let her figure out how to get it on with herself!

Not that she has to.

With all of that tipping, she better hope she don't mess around and tip up on some baaad shit!

Ball of a shag nasty!

It's a damn shame when you have to don a raincoat and rubber gloves just to touch your own wife, but hey, you only have one life. And right now I'm trying to figure out how to save mine. How to make myself happy. A lot of guys would've run out of here a long time ago. They wouldn't have put up with half the shit I've put up with. Like that sanctimonious-ass attitude when she's really the devil's daughter. Tipping out on Friday, slow-grinding in the club on Saturday, then doing back flips in the pulpit on Sunday!

Please!

And you should hear the way she's all the time bragging about her college degrees, like she got them all by herself. I'm the one who had to drop out of school and join the Army while she sat home all day! Plus, she made me keep the babies while she completed college at night.

I didn't mind though.

I wanted my woman to be forward thinking, educated.

I wanted her to succeed.

But I have dreams, too! Goals I'd like to reach. I consider myself an ambitious and progressive-minded black man, so when will I get a chance to do my thang? And to top it all off, I still pay all the bills, including her student loans. I pay the bills, and she banks her paycheck. Now ain't that a bitch? I mean, damn, how much does a man have to give? I offer her my blood, and the woman wants bone marrow!

Sheeiit. Lou has it made in the shade but won't even admit I helped drag her out of the hot sun. So I have to go. I just can't stay. I love my sons and I want to be the man who raises them, but the brother gots to *go*.

Or ain't no telling what'll happen.

I'll support them—I'll even keep on paying all the bills. I don't want my children to suffer just because me and her can't get it on. I'd die for my sons! I would literally die for them. I've been living for them for so long, I don't know how to live without them. I'll have to figure out how to get custody away from her because she's not going to let me just up and take my boys. Lou would die first—or kill me dead.

So I'm just laying in the cut. Chilling.

Watching and waiting.

I'll know when the time is right.

I'll know!

And when it is, I'm gonna be one *running* motherfucker!

I'm gonna run out of here so fast, I leave a raging inferno in my tracks.

A *raging* inferno.

Because let's face it. I'll be running for my life.

1

THE BROWN ROUND

*D*rill Sergeant Caesar, Drill Sergeant Romulus Caesar ... Please report to the Orderly Room."

The crackling static blared from the ancient speakers and sent an icy chill racing down my spine. Especially since today would be the last day I'd ever hear it.

Drill Sergeant Caesar.

Silently the rhythm ran over my lips, my mouth trying on the words like a well-tailored suit. I stretched my six-foot two-inch frame behind the small metal desk, then laced my fingers behind my head and smiled. Ordinarily I hated to hear my name emitted from the public address system, but today I savored the syllables, reveled in the sensations as they greeted my ears, tossed them around like a football as they crashed against my tongue, nibbled at them greedily as they played upon my grin.

"*Drill Sergeant Caesar. Please report to the Orderly Room at once.*"

I glanced at the green-and-white GO ARMY! calendar suspended from the wall. A series of small black X's snaked down the page and led to a bold red X, which marked the spot and confirmed that today was, indeed, the day.

"Drill Sergeant Caesar?"

A sturdy young soldier with a Scandinavian profile filled my doorway and blotted out the light spilling in from the hall. His beefy hands dangled awkwardly at his sides, round as baseball mitts and strong enough to squeeze apples into apple juice.

"Uh—Private Beasley requests puh'mission t' speak."

I couldn't bring myself to respond. My eyes were locked on that carefully printed red X, wishing I could wiggle it just a little farther down the page, praying for a strategy to somehow postpone the inevitable.

"Drill Sergeant!" The brawny private stamped his foot and raised his tone a notch. "Private Beasley requests puh'mission ta speak!"

I rocked back in my chair.

A corn-fed boy from the high mountains of Tennessee, Private Beasley boasted that prior to joining the military he'd never even spoken to a black man, let alone taken orders from one. And he wasn't too keen about starting now.

"It's been weeks, Beasley." My voice was tighter than a Chihuahua's nuts. "Four whole weeks and you haven't learned a damned thing about military courtesy and bearing." I shook my head, then barked, "Speak, Private!"

His cobalt blue eyes raked over me before gawking at the mounted display behind my desk.

"Private Beasley," I repeated. "You may speak."

"Y-yeah," he stammered. Beasley was having a hard time pulling his eyeballs off my wall and aiming them at my face. "Well—er, I mean—umm . . . Yes, Drill Sergeant! Sergeant Williams called in to report a flat tyah. He said fer you to cover fer 'im." Beasley's lips folded into a sneer, and he wiped his nose with his sleeve. "He said you gots to march the company to training area four and blow while we practice drill 'n' ceremonies."

I surveyed the young man, my gaze direct and unwavering. Private Beasley was proving to be a tough nut to crack, but that didn't bother me. Over the past three years I'd cracked both bigger and better, and like the rest of the two-thousand-some-odd privates I'd trained, I could break this dirty white boy down like a shotgun. . . . It was just a matter of time. But right about now, breaking him was the last thing on my mind. I studied him, intently wishing him gone, and he studied me in return, examining me like I was something he'd stumbled upon squirming in a trap. Something he'd just love to free.

And then eat.

I cracked the knuckles of my left hand.

"Tell him no. I can't cover for him today."

I cursed inside. Jared Williams just couldn't run with the big dogs. He'd probably been in the club last night getting his gin on, and now, two sheets to the wind with his head bad and too hungover to move—he was claiming a flat tire. It was bad enough I'd landed duty on today of all days, but I'd be damned if I would pull his load again.

Not today.

Williams drank to escape the stress of this lifestyle. I willingly embraced it.

"Just tell him no," I commanded the private again, and sat up straighter in my chair, "then report his absence to the First Sergeant. Top can assign his detail to the duty drill sergeant."

Let Top put out this fire. That's why they paid First Sergeants the big bucks.

Beasley shook his head. "Uh-uh, Drill Sergeant Caesar. Ah cain't." He counted off on his thick fingers. "Sergeant Williams done hunged up, the company is waitin' outside in fo-mation, and the First Shirt just took off in a Jeep with the Command Sergeant Major."

"First Shirt?" My palms snaked out and cracked against the desk. "Private! What the hell are they feeding you in that mess hall? Dog food? *First Shirt!* So now you're a jarhead? Is this the Army or the goddamned Marines? First Shirt? There's no such animal in this man's Army, and after four weeks of me riding your ass like a mountain goat, you oughtta be aware of that!"

I pulled back a little. Eased off. Ordinarily I would have leaned on an insolent trainee like Beasley until he snapped, but today I shook my head and reminded myself to chill. Riding Beasley was like riding a three-day-old corpse, but after today he wouldn't be my problem. Nah, after today none of the 238 privates of Bravo Company Third of the Fifteenth Infantry Basic Training Battalion, Fort Eustis, Virginia, would be under my command.

"Uh—hey, Sarge." Beasley motioned past me to the array of awards and plaques hanging from the wall behind my desk. "Jes' how much d'you hafta pay to get your name put on one a dem dere certificates?" Although his tone rang sarcastic and flippant, I saw a hint of begrudging admiration flash in his cool aqua glare.

I swiveled around and faced the wall.

"Not a dime, Private Beasley," I replied. "Some things can't be measured in terms of money. Professionalism and dedication are actually priceless." I didn't expect Beasley to understand the depth of my commitment at this stage of his career, but perhaps if I showed him how much my job meant to me, then maybe someday when he stood in my position he'd embrace a young soldier and lead by good example. You know? A sorta each-one-teach-one thang.

"And maybe one day," I continued, "when you've worked your way up the ranks and earned your Noncommissioned Officer stripes, you can apply to the Airborne, Air Assault, and Ranger academies and display your own awards and decorations."

His eyes became slits of pure frost.

"Shucks! I done betta stuff than that when I was knee-high to a goddamn chicken! 'Sides, I hear NCO stands for 'No Chance on the Outside'! I ain't staying in long enough for that! I'm jest gonna do my time an' get the hell back to Tennessee!"

"Is that right?"

"Ya damn skippy that's right—and if *that*"—he slapped his thigh and motioned toward an enlarged issue of *Soldiers* magazine, which bore my smiling face on the cover—"ain't the shit-eatin'est grin I ever seen, well I'll jest be my uncle's son!"

The hearty sound of his laughter set my teeth on edge. On any other day I would have ripped his lips off and stuffed them up his nose, but not today. Today I wanted peace. Despite myself, I sighed.

"You're dismissed, Private." I initiated a hand salute and terminated the conversation while I was still in a decent mood.

Beasley moved toward the door.

"Next time," a cold steel crept into my voice, "if I want any shit out of you, I'll squeeze your fucking head. Now get out."

"Aaiight, boss!" He thrust his hands deeply into his pockets and backed out of my office. "I'm gone!"

I wasn't sure if his failure to return my hand salute was out of defiance or just sheer ignorance, but I let it go. Private Beasley was a wagon I was no longer required to pull. I rose to my feet and scanned the tidy office that had doubled as my part-time home. Every single thing I'd done worth mentioning over the last three years lay embodied in the spirit of these walls. The creamy scent of Kiwi boot polish and Johnson's floor wax soothed me like a lullaby. I executed a sharp about-face and stared into the floor-to-ceiling mirror that covered the opposite wall. The sparkling reflective glass shone spotless, and its brass-framed border was polished to a golden hue.

As a troop leader your physical appearance was ninety percent of your credibility, and this standard piece of Army-issue equipment was as vital to the drill sergeant as the M16 rifle was to the infantry soldier. I examined my reflection, from the glossy spit-shined size-eleven Corcoran Jump Boots planted on my feet to the chocolate-colored Brown Round balanced upon my head. My camouflage battle dress uniform had been specially laundered at my favorite Chinese cleaners, and for the last year the extra-heavy starch had been provided at no additional cost. My gaze touched upon the six-inch-diameter patch glued to my right shirt pocket.

This We'll Defend.

1996. United States Army Drill Sergeant School, Fort Jackson, South Carolina. The small circular patch representing the men and women who were responsible for indoctrinating the future military leaders of America. For thirty-five months, three weeks, and four days I'd worn the coveted patch with pride while living under the brim of the Brown Round and transforming the Army's raw materials into lean, mean, highly trained, combat-ready fighting machines.

Yes, today was my last day as a member of an elite group of soldiers who had persevered not only through the notorious Drill Sergeant Training Academy but also through endless days and nights of what some might call hell but to me had been heaven on earth.

Memories welled in my mind, causing a lump to form in my

throat. My image blurred and shifted before my eyes. I blinked hard and swallowed fast.

Duty called. The soldiers were waiting.

I rechecked my appearance from my blousing rubbers to my gig line. Satisfied, I snapped on my pistol belt and adjusted my head-gear.

I'd cover for Williams all right.

I'd cover his ass one last time. Folks always said I could blow. Hell, the awards and certificates proved it, right? Well, I'd blow for them. I'd blow one last time. I'd lead Bravo Company in marching drills and cadence like they'd never seen before. Today I'd wrap that cadence in music and send melodies charging like lightning across the Sunday-morning sky. Today I'd march and blow cadence until my eardrums popped and my jawbone shattered. Today I'd march and blow cadence until wisps of smoke billowed from my lungs and scorched my lips. Today I'd march and blow cadence until I ruptured an artery and blood seeped from my pores.

And when I recovered, I'd march and I'd blow cadence some more.

Because today would be my last day in heaven.

Come tomorrow I'd be right back in hell.

2

FRESH OUT

One-two-three, *now gimme your LEFT!*"
"*You got it!*"
"*Yo' left-right, o'left-right, o'left-right, o'LEFT!*"
"*Hey!*"

The rhythmic explosion of the singsong cadence drifted crisply from the east and shattered my nerves right along with the peaceful hush of the early July morning.

"*Your MAMA was home when you LEFT!*"
"*You're right!*"
"*Your DADDY was home when you LEFT!*"
"*You're right!*"
"*Your-CAT-your-DOG-your-CHICKEN-your-HOG they ALL were home when you LEFT!*"
"*You're right!*"

The cadence caller bellowed his lyrics in a strong, clear voice, and although his marching formation was well out of view, I could tell by the thunderous roar of the answering calls that the group he led was unusually large. I stood outside of the Fort Eustis Consolidated Troop Pickup Point smelling the green grass grow and waiting for my ride. It was a Sunday morning, and I was anything but easy. Actually, I was pissed to pisstivity and as tired as hell. My stiff new combat boots pinched my toes while the starch in my camouflage uniform bit into my skin, and even at this ungodly hour the Virginia heat— along with my temperament—was beginning to rise.

New to the installation, I was expecting the six A.M. escort the in-processing battalion had promised to send me. Judging by the Casio hugging my left wrist, he was already late. Although it was customary for all new soldiers to process into the base soon after arrival, most commanders postponed the dreaded chore for a few days in order to allow the soldier to become acclimated to the unfamiliar surroundings.

But not my new commander.

She was rumored to be hard-edged and straitlaced, a real bitch on wheels, and my assignment orders directed me to begin the in-processing procedure immediately upon arrival. It didn't matter that I'd arrived on base late Saturday night. In the Army every day was a workday, and while a privileged few were allowed to sleep in on weekends, some unlucky Joe had to get up bright and early on a Sunday morning just to indoctrinate a few unfortunate newbies like me. Yes, some soldiers had it good and some not so good, and if today's orders were indicative of what was yet to come, then Sergeant Sanderella D. Coffee was about to have it pretty damn bad.

I'd just completed a three-year overseas tour in northern Germany (with my sister Ladelle as a semipermanent houseguest), and instead of receiving an authorization to take ordinary leave en route, I was ordered to report directly to my gaining installation: sunny, warm Fort Eustis, Virginia.

"But I sent my children ahead to New York City!" I shrieked at my soon-to-be First Sergeant. I'd called Virginia and raised him on the phone line two seconds after reading the leave restriction clause inserted in my orders. "How in the hell am I supposed to report to Virginia without my kids?"

"Don't worry, Sergeant Coffee," he answered in a tired little voice that was barely audible over the German Bundest Post telephone lines. "Just get yourself here and in-process, and when you're done I'll personally authorize your leave time."

I had my doubts about that. He sounded weak and resigned, not at all confident and authoritative the way a First Sergeant should sound. It was obvious the wicked she-demon of a commander was riding the entire company, including him.

"How much leave time?" I asked suspiciously. I pushed for a verbal commitment before hanging up.

"At least a week. Maybe two. That's the best I can do."

I was skeptical that he could do even that, but without any other recourse, I had to settle for his word and pray that it was good. The whole situation had a major depressing effect on me, and to make matters worse, my ancient Honda Civic—a whooptie if I'd ever seen one—had coughed, sputtered, and died as I waited at the port of Bremerhaven to have her inspected for stateside shipment. Since there was no way in hell I could afford to pay a car note and simultaneously feed three kids, I was forced to rely on my good old Leather Personnel Carriers, better known as "left boot" and "right boot."

I'd risen at precisely o'dark-thirty and humped a bitter country mile from the base's guest housing to this desolate pickup point. Alone on the semidark winding road, I'd foamed at the mouth and marched like a madwoman while my "beasts" did their damnedest to escape from their size 36-D cup cages and my behind performed a funky forbidden dance. And now, forty-five minutes later, jet-lagged and sweaty at the crack of dawn on the Sabbath and still mouthing the mantra "Feet don't fail me now," here I stood.

Alone, hot, hungry, and homesick.

"Sound OFF!"
"One-two!"
"Sound AGAIN!"
"Three-four!"
"Bring it on down now!"
"One-two-three-four!"

The cadence was louder, resonant and full of life. I fished around in my Army-issue black leather purse until I found my compact case. With a snap of my wrist I flipped open my small makeup mirror and peered critically at my wavy reflection. Annoyance arched my thin brows while slanted almond-shaped eyes gave my face a slightly Asian cast. Although I'd recently had my thick hair cut into a chic short style, I still hated it. I needed a style that was even more low maintenance.

Like a wig.

"STOMP your left and DRAG your right!"
"Boots cost money! Boots cost money!"
"Bravo Company's outta-sight!"
"Boom shaka-lacka-lacka! Boom shaka-lacka-lacka!"

The formation was closer and moving fast. No less than company-sized by the sound of it: a minimum of two hundred troops.

And the cadence caller!

Boy did he have a set of lungs on him! His mama had probably caught all kinds of hell when he was a baby. The hearty timbre of his bass roar made me quiver in my bra; the rumbling vibrations shot clear through my aching feet and pierced my very core, while the answering calls of his troops caused the early-morning birds to flee their perches.

It wouldn't be long before they marched straight down the narrow road directly to my front, and since I was the only fool waiting around to in-process on a Sunday, I felt a bit silly standing there egging the grass on and holding up the wall.

I lit a cigarette and struck what I hoped would pass for a casual pose. My body relaxed as I sucked on the Newport and exhaled tons of tension along with the twin clouds of toxic waste. I looked down at the smoldering stick of death. Just what I'd needed, some good clean smoke in my lungs!

As much as I puffed, you'd never guess that I was dying to quit. I'd chewed the Nicorette gum, worn the Nicotrol patch, gone under hypnosis, and did everything else—including four attempts to go cold turkey. Yet through it all, I smoked like a chimney. The truth be told, I was a slave to tobacco; yet my professional dream was to become a commissioned Army officer. I'd never make it at this rate. Officer candidates did not have addictions, and they sure as hell didn't smoke. I couldn't even be considered for the supertough fourteen-week course until I mustered up enough willpower and intestinal fortitude to kick the habit.

To the outside world, I pretended to be strong-willed. Stoic and in control. But in reality I was a wimp. A straight-up tobacco junkie. I might as well admit it. If I were half the woman I pretended to be, I'd shake that tobacco monkey off my back.

And sling him on his ass where he belonged!

"Coon SKIN and alligator HIDE!"
"Ohh yeah!"
"Makes a pair of jump boots just the right SIZE!"
"Ohh yeah!"
"Two old ladies were laying in BED!"
"Ohh yeah!"
"One rolled over to the other and SAID—"

I felt the heavy rhythmic stomping of hundreds of leather combat boots and suddenly the formation was in view. They rounded the slight bend in the road four abreast; the squad leaders marched in the front file at the position of attention, heads and eyes fixed straight ahead. Midway through the mass formation and centered on its right flank was the cadence caller. The troop leader with lungs of iron and pipes of steel.

Great gooka-mooka!

I rubbed my eyes. Bruh-man stood well over six feet tall. A classic soldierly sight: lean, mean, and Army green. Like an infantry Iron Mike statue dipped in deep dark chocolate. Just how I like them. Or rather, how I used to like them before swearing off of them six months ago. I put my hands on my hips and stood a little straighter as I watched the precision-timed green bodies marching so thick you couldn't stir them with a stick.

The cadence caller wore a brown Smokey the Bear type hat, the standard headgear of a drill sergeant. The closer he came, the better he looked, and talk about pipes! The brothah could blow better than Teddy, Barry, and Smokey all wrapped in one! His voice had a soulful, bottomless kind of bellow that drizzled black honey down my spine. The kind of low, mournful cry that had rolled through slave quarters carrying so much pain and sorrow it had "church choir" written all over it.

And his marching style was almost as expert as his cadence. He marched from the waist down, perfectly symmetric, his fingers curled into a semifist, his thumbs pressed against his forefingers and lightly brushing the seams of his pants. His arms swung naturally, nine inches to his front, six inches to his rear. The heels of his boots struck the ground first; then he propelled himself forward onto the balls of his feet.

Perfect!

It looked liked somebody other than me had been studying the Drill and Ceremonies manuals, and if I were in the market for a headache I would definitely shop for a specimen like him, but since I wasn't, the very sight of him annoyed me. Suddenly, he cut loose with a howl so earsplitting and soul piercing—I clenched my cigarette between my lips and jammed my fingers into my ears. The brothah was deafening!

"She said—I wanna be an AIRBORNE RANGER!"
"I wanna be an Airborne Ranger!"
"I wanna live a life of DANGER!"
"I wanna live a life of danger!"
"Rough, tough AIRBORNE RANGER!"
"Rough, tough Airborne Ranger!"
"AIRBORNE!"
"Airborne!"
"RANGER!"

"Ranger!"
"DANGER!"

He was almost in front of me. I wanted to stick out my foot and trip him because while his carriage was excellent and his bearing erect, I detected a slight swagger beneath the surface, a cocky bop in his step, a prideful dip in his stride. He strutted and swaggered under that big brown hat with his chest poked out like a buffed-up Mighty Mouse.

He was showing off!

That was all I needed to see. And hear. Some fine-behind desperate-for-attention drill sergeant wreaking havoc on my eardrums bright and early on a Sunday morning.

But wait! He caught me peeping him and went *up* another octave! Yes, he did!

"COUNT cadence, DELAYED cadence, SKIP cadence, COUNT!"
"ONE!"
"BRAVO COMPANY!"
"TWO!"
"You'd better keep in step . . ."
"THREE!"
"Before you find YOURSELF—"
"FOUR!"
"In the LEANING REST!"

I knew exactly what was coming next. His eyes had strayed from the narrow road before him and were now prancing up and down the spacious avenue of my physique. He gawked at me as though he'd never seen a woman before, when there had to be at least a hundred of them in the formation he led. At this close range I could tell they were a company of basic trainees, and while I personally didn't agree with gender-integrated training, the powers that be had decided that Molly should be trained right alongside Joe.

"COMPANY HALT!"
"Half-Left FACE!"
"Front-Leaning Rest Position — MOVE!"

The entire formation, with the exception of the squad leaders, obediently faced left and dropped down into the push-up position. The standard position of torture.

"Squad Leaders take charge."

I stood stock-still as he left his puzzled soldiers beating their faces and briskly approached me. That was a big no-no. Abandoning untrained troops. Strictly against Army regulations, and he of all people should have known better. He strode across the gravel road with a definite purpose, almost like he was coming over to ask for directions or to bum a cigarette, mine of which still hung loosely from my lips. I could tell by the stripes on his collar that he was an E-7, a Sergeant First Class, two grades above my rank of Sergeant. As he drew closer I squinted to read the name tag embroidered on the right breast pocket of his uniform.

Caesar.

Well, no wonder he pranced around like a proud little pit bull! The brothah probably thought he was a royal somebody! Well, LuCeal Vann didn't raise no fools. I lowered my hands from my ears to my hips, cocked my right leg into a fighting position, exhaled a puff of smoke through my nostrils, and braced myself, because whatever it was Sergeant First Class Caesar was selling, I wasn't about to buy, and whatever he may have been rushing over to bum — the sistah was fresh out!

3

GLORIA

I knew I was making a mistake the moment my right foot left the ground. For a man who had weighed and contemplated his every action for three long years, I was suddenly struck dumb and left without a rational thought. I'd caught a glimpse of her in my peripheral vision as we rounded a small bend in the road and immediately my self-imposed blinders fell off with a crash and a bang. Like a computer, my love-starved brain calculated her data: five-foot-one, 120 pounds of fun, a sweet glistening pool of bubbling brown sugar all decked out in woodland camouflage!

During my stint as a drill sergeant I'd prided myself on using good judgment and doing my best to stay within the parameters of a good leader. Even the top dog himself, the Sergeant Major of the Army, had been brought up on charges of misconduct, but not once had I been derelict in my duties. Not once had I overslept, mistreated a soldier, abused my rank or authority, or taken advantage of a trainee under my command.

Self-preservation had dictated that I didn't even *look* at a female soldier "that way." Not even the time Private Conchita Melendez — a superfine, superfreak Puerto Rican brickhouse — stepped into my office and slammed the door, then spread her legs and showed me her cho-cha. I simply ushered her out, had the entire door removed from its hinges, and had her fine ass discharged.

Juicy cho-cha and all.

At first I had to envision the female privates sporting mustaches and goatees to get the point across to Mr. Bobo, but eventually he chilled. After a while he seemed to understand that privates were poisonous and females were fatal, but now it seemed as if my psyche had a mind of its own. Like a damn fool I was setting myself up for a court-martial on my last day of drill service, but what was a starving brother to do? This sister looked clean shaven and nontoxic and, from where I was marching, stacked as well!

In a flash, I halted my surprised privates for some imagined infraction, ordered them into the push-up position, placed my bewildered squad leaders in charge, and before you could say "your black ass is going to jail," I found myself deserting my soldiers and hauling ass in her direction. That move alone was enough to earn me five years of making little rocks out of big rocks, but I had no choice. The girl was like a radar, and my brain was locked in on her position!

Not only was my reaction to her totally out of character, it was also surprising as hell. Although my thang with Lou was shabbier than a hobo's socks, in the last few years I'd never even thought about approaching another woman. I'd survived without any real intimacy by burying my desires in my superheavy workload, but now even that outlet was about to end.

She was standing in front of the troop pickup point, and as I started across the narrow road, I furiously racked my brain and searched for the right words to say. I'd been out of the game for so long that my rap was nonexistent. I had no idea how to approach her. I could just feel the slap as it whipped across my face.

ME: Hey, baby, what's your name?
HER: Puddin' Tame—ask me again and I'll tell you the same!

Or better yet,

ME: Hey, Miss Lady! Whatcha doing out here so early?
HER: Minding my business and leaving yours alone!

Nah, I knew neither of those lame lines would work, yet my boot-clad feet took giant strides in her direction as though I were suave, sure, and confident. Sheepishly, I chanced my first close-up look into her nutmeg-colored face, and dig this: Her hands were clamped over her ears, and the girl had a stogie dangling from her lips!

Ahh-shit! Mr. Bobo screamed.

I was going to jail for the Marlboro Man!

Just like in a John Wayne movie, a long slim cancer stick dangled from the corner of her mouth. Its business end emitted a thin trail of noxious chemicals. I did a quick double take.

Her right eye was squinted shut as she tried to avoid the billowing cloud of smoke, and she peered suspiciously at me from her left. Suddenly she took both hands from her ears and placed them on her bow hips, and I swear, she stood back on her legs, snorted hard like a bull, and two short puffs of smoke burst forth from her nostrils!

El Matador!

I thought for sure she was about to lift her left leg, paw the ground, and charge me! Damn! *Why'd she have to be a cigarette smoker?* Do you know how bad that stuff tastes on a woman's lips? As fine as she was, I just wasn't all that anxious to sip out of an ashtray. I wanted to turn around. Just turn around, foot it back to my formation, and order my disgruntled privates to get up and move out. I wanted to walk right past that smoking sister and rap to the oak tree behind her, but did I do any of those things?

Hell naw!

I did the only thing a brother could do in a situation like this, I said the first words that touched my mind. I stepped right up on the sister, opened my trap with a stupid grin on my face, and blurted out, "Hey, baby! Is your name Gloria?"

Now I've been called a whole lot of things in my life, but Gloria ain't never been one of them. I had a hunch brother-man was crazy when he left his poor troops sweating and groaning in the middle of the road, but once he let loose with that corny pickup line—I knew he was asinine for sure.

Gloria! I've been taken for a Brenda, a Stephanie, and once or twice even a Debra or a Jackie. But a Gloria? What kind of name was that for a sistah like me? "*Gloriaaa . . . Things ain't been the same since you went awaaaay. . . .*" Gloria made you think of harps and angels, lilies and periwinkles—all sorts of fragile, delicate things. I was more like an orchid or a dandelion: cute and vibrant but tough and able as well.

Like a Sanderella.

Solid and homey, but definitely unpretentious.

I bucked my eyes at him and replied out of the unoccupied corner of my mouth, "Uh-uh, baby, no. My name is *not* Gloria!"

Then I stared from him to his troops and then back to him, hoping he'd get the hint and get back to his trainees, many of whom were sprawled across the pavement weak and spent from upper-body muscle failure.

"Whew, I got you mixed up with someone else," he replied with a small chuckle, apparently satisfied with my answer. He almost looked glad that Gloria wasn't my name, and his diction sounded just like that Oreo-ass Bryant Gumbel trying to perpetrate like he was from Compton.

"Well . . . er," his big boots kicked at the grass, and the powerful muscles in his legs were visible even through the camouflage pattern of his uniform, "I'm sorry for bothering you, sister. My mistake. Enjoy your day." He touched the brim of his headgear, spun around, and took about ten giant steps away from me. Once again he was standing on the asphalt road. He shot me a parting glance before resuming his place in front of the formation and called out over his broad shoulder, "Just for the record, Sarge. What *is* your name?"

I threw my cigarette down and cupped my hands around my mouth. "Puddin' Tame!" I yelled and purposely let a little Brooklyn slip into my tone. "My name ain't no *Gloria*, it's Puddin' Tame! Now ask me again so I can tell you the same!"

4

SKIN TIGHT!

As the last traces of SFC Caesar's marching formation faded from view, a large military vehicle screeched into the parking area, spraying sand and loose gravel in every direction. Almost before the wheels rolled to a stop, a young black woman emerged and trotted toward me with long, confident Naomi Campbell strides. As I watched her approach, I couldn't help but hear the baseline from that funky Ohio Players jam, *"You're a bad-bad missus, in those skin-tight britches . . . runnin' folks in ditches. . . ."*

She smiled brightly and held out her hand. "Hey, I'm Staff Sergeant Sparkle Henderson, and on behalf of the command group, welcome to the 515th Transportation Company."

I took my sweet time checking her out from head to toe. The lines of her uniform were fiercely creased, and her black combat boots glinted like Texas tea in the bright sunshine. I accepted her outstretched hand and shook it. Briefly. Sparkle Henderson appeared to be about my age, and we had roughly the same length hair. Outside of that we were physical opposites.

Everything about Miss Sparkle, including her name, screamed, "Notice me!" She sported a honey-blond dye job that instantly drew your attention to her eyes, and her emerald green contact lenses combined with the cornbread hue of her skin gave her the angular features of a sassy house cat.

She was tall but shapely, and her battle uniform fit so snugly it could have been spray-painted on. As she apologized for being "tardy," Sparkle spoke distinctly and concisely—as if she were reminding herself to pronounce each and every syllable. I sucked my teeth. Not only was this sultry soldier late—with her Bausch & Lomb contacts, Maybelline lashes, and Miss Clairol hair—she was also fake as hell! And she could just save that highfalutin English, because I knew jungle boogie when I saw it!

"So," she breathed in an excited rush as we climbed into the truck, "where are you coming from? Do you have any children? Are you married?"

"Germany. Yes. No." My clipped-off answers sounded like rottweiler barks. We rode in a rugged military pickup painted in the same brown, black, and green pattern of the camouflage uniforms we both wore. As Sparkle Henderson twirled the steering wheel and backed out of the lot, I noticed her manicured nails were painted a soft, glimmering iced coffee, which perfectly adhered to the Army's regulations on length and color.

She smiled again. "Well, it's my fault we're late, so buckle up. I'll get you there in no time." She drove like a professional race-car driver. Weaving in and out of traffic lanes, she handled the heavy vehicle as if it were a mere Pinto. I was impressed with the sistah's driving skills. They matched my own.

I said, "You drive like a native New Yorker." Admiration softened the sarcasm in my voice.

"That's because," Sparkle responded as she cut the steering wheel and rounded the corner on two wheels, "I am."

"Oh, yeah?" A tiny thread of interest wove itself around my thoughts. "What part of New York?"

"Brooklyn, why?"

I smiled inside. Her defensive posture was so typical!

"No reason . . . it just figures you would be from Crooklyn—I mean Brooklyn." I said the word *Brooklyn* in typical Brooklynese fashion: *Bruwk-lin.*

Sparkle's cheerful face suddenly underwent a complete transformation. I watched in fascination as my homegirl metamorphosed. Claws, teeth, horns, and hooves emerged. Her golden skin glowed kryptonite green, and her body began to swell.

She cut her eyes sideways as she approached a stop sign and brought the heavy truck to an abrupt halt. This time homegirl slammed the brakes so hard I lurched forward, then snapped back sharply from the vehicle's momentum.

Dayum! Ole heffah tried to jerk a knot in my neck!

I crooked my head and eyeballed her like she was crazy. If I hadn't been locked snuggly in the seat belt, I would have gone sailing through the truck's windshield. Headfirst!

Sparkle fastened her cat eyes on mine and hissed, "Do you have a problem with the residents of Brooklyn, or an overall disdain for New Yorkers in general?" Her tone was clipped and measured as she enunciated each word in perfect diction. Without waiting for my response she rolled her eyes and zoomed through the intersection. Her foot was suddenly extra-heavy on the gas pedal.

Like she was standing up on it.

I reached up and grabbed hold of the oh-shit strap before answering. "No, not at all. I've been fortunate enough to make the acquaintance of several colleagues who hail from New York. Although," I faltered as we swerved abruptly around a slow-moving Honda, and my brake foot tried to stomp a hole through the floorboard, "although I must say none of them speak in their Oreo voices nearly as eloquently as you do!" I said this as perfectly as a white commercial broadcaster denouncing the dreaded Ebonics.

Sparkle's bottom lip crashed to the ground.

"And just what the fuck is that supposed to mean?"

Girlfriend had dropped all pretenses of refinement, elegance, and cultured speaking. I was having a ball!

I distinctly pronounced each syllable and replied, "Oh, my! You can take the girl out of the ghet-to, but you can't take the ghet-to out of the girl!"

Sparkle cut a hard right, then a sharp left. I grabbed hold of my hat as the vehicle skidded and fishtailed, then finally came to a jerky halt on the sandy shoulder of the base's main road. In spite of my seat belt the thrust sent me sliding across the leather seat, slamming my right shoulder painfully against the passenger door.

Uh-oh, I said the G-word!

"Hold up, dammit." Sparkle's eyes glinted with anger, and her golden head wagged from side to side. "I don't know who you think you are, but you don't know your ass from your elbow about me or New York!" Although she was buckled securely into her seat belt, sistah-girl managed to put her hand on her hip and let her backbone slip! "Now," she continued, "we can do this here military shit all professional-like and refrain from making any personal comments, or we can get right funky and play the dozens—and you can get your little ass told off real quick!"

Aw sukkey-sukkey now!

"Look, Sparkle—"

"No, Sergeant Whatever-the-hell-your-name-is," she leaned into my air space and rolled her two-pairs-for-forty-nine-dollars fake green eyes, "you can address me as Staff Sergeant Henderson—since I *do* outrank you! And if you have a problem with that, I can be sure to let the First Sergeant assign you a new escort before things get ugly around here!"

Well, dayum! I pushed a strand of loose hair underneath my cap. What kind of Army base was this? These folks sure knew how to treat a newbie! First it was that cocky Sergeant Caesar, and now this surly sistah from the 'hood! My feelings were beginning to get bruised.

I held up my hand. "Okay, okay! Calm down, homegirl . . . I was just kidding! Just feeling you out." I lapsed into my own Brooklynese. "You know how us natives can be . . . all touchy and things. I thought you were gonna jerk me clear through the windshield back there!"

"You're from New York?"

"Yep." I poured on the accent. "I, too, hail from Bruwk-lin, New Yawk!"

Sparkle visibly relaxed, then grinned and shook her head.

"Girl, you almost got *told*! I hate it when people automatically assume because I'm from New York I'm either an asshole or a violent maniac."

"Well, the way you pushed up on me a minute ago, I could have sworn my ass was kicked!"

"It almost"—Sparkle looked deeply into my eyes without a trace of a smile—*"was."*

5

KEEPER OF THE CASTLE

I watched closely as Daddy stacked the small black-and-white rectangles upward on their ends. He stood them one directly behind the other until they formed a perfect black line. Then he set his guitar in its metal stand and ran his fingers through the thick wooly mass of hair on my ten-year-old head.

I wore my hair styled exactly the same as his, except Daddy's 'fro had an Ungowah! clench-fisted Afro pick peeking out from the top. I abandoned my tambourine and checked my back pocket. My own cool tool, a smaller and less-threatening version with folding red and green handles, was exactly where I'd left it. I smiled up at my daddy. We wore matching blue-and-gold dashikis, and my handsome daddy looked just like Isaac Hayes's Black Moses and Richard Roundtree's John Shaft all rolled into one!

"Check this out, King Romulus." Daddy pointed to the first rectangle in the line. "Do you know what this one is called?"

"Yes, sir. It's a domino."

"Yeah, little man, it's a domino, but what kind of domino?"

"A black domino?" I asked quizzically.

"It's the number *one* domino," Daddy explained, holding one thick finger up in the air. "The number one domino—and it's symbolic of *you*."

I didn't know what a set of black bones had to do with me, but I waited patiently for him to continue, certain that there was some hidden meaning in his words. My daddy was in his groove. New Birth, red lights, and a few rolled-up sticks of Jamaican Gold usually got him to talking in riddles, and I knew better than to rush him before he had a chance to roll full circle with his thoughts.

"Watch carefully, son. Look at what happens when the number one domino falls."

Daddy took his big finger and pushed over the first domino, and right on cue, all the others fell dutifully behind it.

"In the African-American family, the man—the *father*—is the number one domino. The head of the family. On his merit alone lies the success or the demise of the entire household. If he stands firm, the family will survive and prosper. But if he falls . . . not only will the family crumble, the entire community will go down with him."

Daddy waited for my wide-eyed nod of understanding and then continued, "Whatever succeeds in knocking the number one domino out of position threatens each and every domino in its wake. But the greatest threat is to the number *two* domino: the woman, the heart of the family. Without the strength and protection of her mate, she is forced to step up to the plate and become both dominoes number one," he tapped the first domino, "and two," he held up the second domino. Coconut-scented incense burned in a wooden holder on the low end table, and the first few notes of "Ain't Understanding Mellow" floated in from the hi-fi downstairs.

Daddy stared at that second domino and fingered it thoughtfully. "Although she may be courageous and strong, when such a task is designed for two, it simply cannot be done well by one."

His voice boiled and rumbled in his chest. "Only a *number one* domino can successfully groom a *number one* domino! Remember that!"

Then Daddy put his hands on my shoulders and brought his face down level with mine. His eyes bored into me. "Romulus Caesar," he said, "you must be the keeper of your castle! The number one domino in your home! That is your duty as a black man—your legacy as a king. Not only to your family but to the African-American community as well. Although your mother named you Romulus, it was *I*," he jerked his thumb at his barrel chest, "*Solomon Caesar*, who made you a king!"

What a load of *bull*shit!

Hot bitter tears sprang to my eyes in remembrance of that long-ago day. I stood in the dimly lit bedroom holding a piece of chocolate cake from the farewell party held in my honor.

The Brown Round still rested upon my head.

I gazed down on my sleeping sons and bit into my knuckles to numb the phantom pain. After all of the lip service Daddy had dispensed, it was barely two years later when he jumped down off his soapbox and dropped my sisters and me so hard we bounced. It was pitiful.

Keeper of the castle!

When he left us, I wanted to die. I almost died. But I didn't. Because Daddy was wrong. He'd left me alone with five capable females, hearts of the family. Number two dominoes who knew *exactly* how to groom a number one domino.

And groom me they did.

Between Mama, my oldest sister, Cleopatra, and Big Daddy Jenkins—I think I turned out okay. On the strength of a Bible and a belt, they demanded I live up to my legacy, and they never once let me forget that I was a king.

The basketball-shaped night-light gently illuminated my only two reasons for living. I pulled the sheets over Hannibal and gently stroked Mansa's face. My life was about to change, but not for the better. Come tomorrow I'd be back to regular duty with regular hours. No longer would I be able to use my job as a means of escape. I'd have to come home every day at five like a regular Joe Sergeant.

And I'd have to come home to Lou.

I shuddered. I was miserable living this semi-existence, and I wasn't sure how much longer I could take it. I was ready to find a woman worthy of my love and receive that same love in return. But could I do to my boys what my daddy had done to me?

Hell no!

I wouldn't be able to live with myself! Daddy was a disgrace to his family, to his community. If he ever came back, I swore I'd spit in his path and whip his jive ass! I despised him. He'd left the number two domino to pick up his slack. And he'd left *me*. How could he call himself a king? I looked at my sons and then at my own reflection in the dusky mirror.

I'm a way better man than my father was!

Way better.

The question is, am I good enough?

I'd been assigned to the 515th Headquarters Platoon as the Non-commissioned Officer in Charge of the Movements section. Better known as the NCOIC. As a squad leader I was directly responsible for a group of ten soldiers, all junior in rank, and all male.

Less than a week after my arrival, I received a triple whammy. My application to Officer Candidate School was approved, I earned a promotion to staff sergeant, and my platoon sergeant went to jail. Sergeant First Class Meyers had been under military investigation for smuggling confiscated Iraqi weapons into the United States after Operation Desert Storm and had finally been court-martialed and sentenced to seven years of hard labor.

Suddenly I was the highest-ranking member of the platoon—the HNIC, Head Niggress in Charge—and I became not only the group's leader, but also the only female platoon sergeant in the 515th.

Sparkle, who worked in the company's supply shop, was genuinely happy for me. She approached me in the female latrine after the morning's formation, where the good news had been announced. I stood at the sink rubbing coarse soap over my hands when she touched my back and laughed. "So, I see congratulations are in order!" Her Tommy Girl perfume overpowered the scent of the government-issued no-frills Pine Sol filling the air. "It's always good to see a sistah moving up through the ranks—as long as you don't move ahead of me!"

I grinned and held my hands under the trickle of warm water.

"Well, you better buy yourself some skates or catch the bus, girl-friend, because I'm likely to catch up and pass you!"

"Oh, yeah?" Sparkle laughed and straightened the lines of her perfectly pressed uniform. She passed me a folded brown paper towel. "How about celebrating your pay raise? There's a Kappa step show at the Officers Club tomorrow night, and you can use your extra funds to buy me a few drinks."

A step show? At the Officers Club? I was basically a homebody and hadn't been to a club in ages. For the last few years I'd stayed at home and tended my children and left the nightlife and partying to my sister Ladelle. That girl was party freak to her heart! We'd lived together for five years, and although Ladelle had come with me to Virginia, she'd slept in our hotel room for only two of the five nights we'd been on base.

But what did I expect? Grass couldn't grow on a busy street, and Ladelle's fast pace and party-girl lifestyle were way too busy for me. Ladelle had four children of her own that she'd left for Mama Ceal to raise, but to look at her, you could never tell she'd ever had any. Blessed with the seductiveness of a succubus, men of all ages clung to her like Saran Wrap. They couldn't help it. The sistah sashayed like a fashion model, and her slim, curvaceous body, complete with a tiny waist and proud breasts, could have easily graced the runways of Paris.

Although at thirty-four Ladelle was five years my senior, it was usually me who played the big-sister role and did the looking out for her. "Sandie's the oldest," Mama would say, "but Ladelle was born first." Although Mama's explanation seemed harsh, it was oftentimes true. In a way I resented my sister's freedom and the ease with which she laid down her burdens on Mama Ceal's lap, but like a lot of worldly women, she just wasn't capable of handling adult responsibilities un-less they had something to do with a man.

True to form, Ladelle had slithered up on a visiting Master Sergeant the same day we arrived and, like a city rat, had been holed up in his room ever since. As a result I was alone and bored in the evenings, and since I was temporarily without a set of wheels, I was also stranded.

I dried my hands and tossed the used towel into a plastic-lined can. Sparkle waited for my answer.

Despite my initial impression of my homegirl, she had turned out to be pretty cool. Besides, I hadn't been to a step show since my college days almost a thousand years ago, and Ladelle sure as hell wouldn't miss me.

"Okay," I answered finally. I held the door open for her as we stepped into the brightly lit hall. We avoided the center path of the tiles and walked as closely to the walls as possible so as not to enrage the sergeant in charge of waxing and buffing the glossy tiled floors. "Sure, I'd love to check out the step show. We'll have to finalize things later though, because right now I'm about to receive an in-briefing from the company commander, and from what I hear, she's not the sweetest grape on the vine!"

Sparkle's dimpled smile disappeared. She studied me thoughtfully. "Look, sis. Don't fight the powers, okay? Keep an open mind about her. Personally I don't have any beef with the woman, but I wouldn't get caught standing downrange of her flaky ass either."

"That's what I've been told." I frowned and glanced down the hall toward the commander's office. My stomach clenched and folded in anticipation of our meeting. "Just the sound of her name seems to make the soldiers uptight."

"You'll be okay." Sparkle slung two map supply carriers over her shoulders and headed toward the supply shop. "Just do your job, and she'll stay off your back. I have to run down to Fort Lee to drop off these supplies and pick up some new chemical protective masks," she called over her shoulder. "I'll hit ya later."

I sat in the commander's small waiting area and tried to calm my nerves as I studied the impressive array of framed certificates and diplomas displayed on nearly every wall. Captain Silberman may not have had an ounce of people skills, but she had a wall full of diplomas. Enough degrees to heat a mansion. Or at least to staff a small university.

The butterflies in my stomach had come with a reliable recommendation. During my enlisted in-briefing the First Sergeant had let on that the company commander had been born into a wealthy orthodox Jewish family, where she was taught she and her kind were superior and exceptional.

According to the company rumor mill, while Captain Silberman looked down her nose at most gentiles, she reserved a passionate hatred for blacks and Hispanics. Due to the Army's official position on racism and discrimination, she'd been forced to harbor these feelings in secret, but unfortunately her passion was too strong to hide for long. According to the enlisted soldiers, blatant prejudice seeped from her pores and dripped from her body like perspiration, manifesting itself in her tone, attitudes, and actions.

I warmed a hard bench for nearly twenty minutes before being summoned into her office. Once inside I squashed my misgivings and took a deep breath. Then I smiled brightly and offered my hand.

"Hello, ma'am, I'm Staff Sergeant Coffee. It's my pleasure to be a member of your company, and I'm certain that I'll be an asset to this command. I've enjoyed an exemplary career with quantitative successes. I'm ready to put my skills to work for this unit."

Captain Silberman stared at my outstretched hand and wrinkled her nose as if she would rather eat a ham and cheese sandwich sprinkled with bacon bits! She left my hand floating awkwardly in midair and began speaking sharply in a clipped West Point manner.

"I assume the First Sergeant has briefed you on our policies and the way I like things done. I do not tolerate slackers, or slouchers, or malingerers, or any variations from the orders and directives I set forth. I don't know how business was conducted in your previous unit, and I really don't care, but *here* I run a tight ship. It's my way or the highway. I have a strict duty standard, and I believe in giving the Army the best hours of my day. There will be no bullshitting or lollygagging. *Schedule your personal appointments during your personal time.* Our company motto is 'The Biggest and the Best,' and that's because we don't just desire to be the best transporters in the brigade, we make it happen."

I chanced a peek around her office and was amazed to find that there wasn't the slightest trace of disarray. Not a single scrap of paper was out of place; not a manual or a regulation lay crooked or even slightly askew. *There is a place for everything, and everything has a place.*

A nervous giggle tried to escape me. I was willing to bet my last dollar that her camouflage uniform had a Garanimals tag sewn at the collar and a matching tag sewn into the pants! I remained silent. Captain Silberman's eyes had yet to meet mine, and I watched in amazement as she shuffled a few papers in front of her, brushed away some imaginary dust from her shoulders, and then busied her hands sorting multicolored paper clips and lining them up row by row along the side of her desk.

"You will," she finally continued, "report any and all training anomalies directly to me. I shall repeat that for you:

"All anomalies will be reported directly to me!"

For the first time Captain Silberman graced me with a glance. "You do know what *anomaly* means, don't you?" Her gray eyes were cold, flat pools of smoke.

Yeah, wench. I even know how to spell it!

"Yes, ma'am," I answered. "I certainly do."

"Well good." She lined all of her perfectly sharpened pencils along the windowsill so that the erasers were perfectly flush with the edge of the sill. "First Sergeant tells me you've asked to move into the barracks. Your personnel file tells me you're divorced with three children. I don't know what Army billets you're accustomed to living in, but our barracks are not designed to accommodate children."

"Yes, ma'am." I gave a short nervous laugh. "It's just that I've applied for Officer Candidate School, and my kids are in New York with—"

"Officer Candidate School?"

"Yes, ma'am. I applied just before leaving my last unit in Germany. I still need to take a photo and—"

"What on *earth* prompted you to do that?" She peered over her glasses and down her nose as though I'd insulted her. "*You?* Aspiring to earn an officer's commission?"

The room was suddenly so quiet you could have heard a gnat blink. I shook my head. What was she driving at?

"Ma'am?"

"You heard me. What are your qualifications? What makes you think you have what it takes to be an officer? To become a leader of troops?"

"I've enjoyed an exemplary career with quantitative successes," I repeated. "My records and awards speak for themselves. Besides, I'm already a leader of troops. A damn good one. And have been since the day I earned my stripes."

Her eyes were cold and her face devoid of expression. She stared at me as though I were a blubbering idiot. "Well, why don't you just leave your kids," she waved her hand breezily, "*wherever* they are and complete the tour you've been assigned to pull here?"

I bit down hard on my tongue. There was a five-by-seven color photo on her desk of her, a long-faced man with dark hair, and two towheaded little girls. By their facial features they obviously belonged to her. How dare she!

"We have," she continued, oblivious to the heat rising within me, "more than enough butterball officers in this brigade. What we need in the 515th is a solid noncommissioned officer who can whip our training section back into shape. Prove yourself there, then maybe you can entertain those lofty notions of commanding."

Now that she'd figured out exactly what I needed to do about my kids and the next few years of my life, she treated me to a small but pleased smile.

It was my turn to stare at the blubbering idiot.

"With all due respect, ma'am," I began as my hand inched its way toward my hip and my foot turned outward in a typical Brooklyn battle stance, "I'm more than qualified to become an officer. I've put my time in as an enlisted soldier. That means I've already done all the crappy details and pulled all the hard duty that officers know nothing about. Not only have I gotten my hands dirty up to the elbows, I've led from the front and by example. Enlisted soldiers get the job done because we actually *work*. That makes me *overqualified* to become an officer. And as far as leaving my kids," I waved my hand in an exaggerated imitation of her gesture, "*wherever* they

are . . . thanks, but no thanks. Walking on water in your training section does not take precedence over my career progression, and it certainly doesn't make me feel so warm and needed that I'd leave my
kids"—I did that wave thingy again—"*wherever* they are." I fought to
bring my emotions under control. "I'll always be a mother. I may not
always be a soldier."

"Is that right?" I heard her mental file cabinet creak open as she
filed my last statement under A for ammunition.

"Yes, it is."

"Well, I'll be sure to remember that it was you who said it."

I nodded. "You do that."

Our relationship had been established. We'd sized each other up,
now we stared each other down. Maintaining eye contact, she spoke
with a self-assured authority that told me exactly what she thought of
my skills and qualifications. "Listen, Sergeant. Contrary to popular
belief, officers are born, not transformed out of rogue bands of enlisted personnel with silly dreams of climbing the pay scale. The majority of enlisted soldiers who do manage to complete officer training
usually don't make it past the level of first lieutenant. Besides, you
have to hold a degree in order to earn a promotion to major."

Hah! I thought with smug satisfaction. I had her butt there! I'd
worked damn hard in my night classes at City College. I'd even
graduated with high honors.

"I have a degree," I informed her proudly.

"I'm referring to a graduate degree." She glanced down at my personnel folder. "It says here that you've earned an associate's degree in
liberal arts from City College." She shut my folder with a definite
snap. "I don't think that actually qualifies."

I was silent. I recalled the diplomas and certificates posted on the
walls of her outer office. Defeat crept up on me and tried to put a
slump in my shoulders.

"Okay," she continued calmly. My concession to her victory was
clear and obvious, and instead of twisting the ice pick in my guts she
was ready to move on. "Sergeant Henderson has maintained the unit
training functions during the interim between your predecessor's

departure and your arrival. I expect you to immediately assume all functions of training management and movement control and be prepared to brief me each Monday and Friday at sixteen hundred hours. You are dismissed."

She gave me a crisp salute and went back to ridding her shoulders of the microscopic dust mites that had probably fallen from her dirty hair. Insulted, dismissed, and now totally ignored, I shot her back a limp-noodle salute, executed an abrupt about-face, and stomped out of her office.

First Sergeant was right. Girlfriend was a nut, and that comment about my kids had not earned her any cool points with me. As I emerged from her office, Specialist Burns, the young male soldier who doubled as a heavy-equipment operator and the command secretary, looked up from his desk.

"So you survived 'Mount Saint Rachel,' huh, Sarge?" he asked with a knowing grin.

"Yeah, did she steal Christmas or what?"

He laughed and shook his head. "Oh, she can be a Grinch all right. Just remember," he wagged his finger for emphasis, "if she ever asks to see you again, it means your ass is sweet Kentucky bluegrass and she's the lawn mower!"

I waved my hand. "I'm not worried." I smiled with false confidence. "It'll take that crazy cow a solid week to chew up all of this tough Brooklyn tail."

6

FREE

I took a long swig from my daddy's brass tumbler and winced at the acrid taste of the icy vodka. I wasn't a solo drinker by any means, but since this tarnished tumbler and my bad attitude were all my father had left me, I put them both to good use.

I was feeling funky. A black heat stirred in my soul. And for good reason. I'd stumbled to the john at three A.M., and on the way back to bed my eyes took in the tangled mass of empty sheets and my nose was kissed by a sweet trace of Ashanti that lingered gently in the air.

Lou was gone.

She must have tipped out while the boys and I were asleep, and no doubt she planned to tip back in before we awakened. The stark emptiness of the bedroom brought me fully awake. I pulled a T-shirt over my head and decided to slip into some alcohol and relax to some tunes.

I found a half bottle of knotty-head vodka hanging around under the kitchen sink and filled Daddy's tumbler with ice, then stood barefoot at the counter and poured my own troubles. The sight of last night's dishes congealing in the sink was a huge turnoff, so I flipped on the lights in the living room and kicked at an empty box of crayons in my path. With the tumbler on the floor beside me, I sifted through the mess in the coat closet and dragged out a milk crate crammed with 33s and 45s. I ran my fingers over the smooth circular grooves on the black vinyl surface. I was a seventies kind of guy; rap music didn't do a damn thing for me. All of that kill-your-brother, rape-your-neighbor shit just didn't sit well with me. A brother like me needed to hear the words, to feel the emotions, to understand the groove. Right now I needed me some Isley Brothers, some Bobby Womack, some Blue Magic, and some Persuaders. I flipped through stacks of Four Tops, Mighty Dells, Stevie, Harold, and Marvin, until I found what I was looking for.

Didn't I blow your mind this time? The Delfonics!

Sprawled across our lumpy plaid sofa, I filled and refilled my daddy's old tumbler until the bottle was dry. With a nice buzz crowding my head, I plugged in my keyboard and jammed along with those old-school tunes for what seemed like forever. Zooted, I soothed my soul with the most beautiful lyrics. Tears blurred my eyes as I poured my pain through my fingertips and composed my own masterpiece using the titles of those oldies but goodies that knew exactly how to make a grown man cry: Damn, baby, WHY YOU TREAT ME SO BAD? I'm tired of all of this BREAK UP TO MAKE UP. I treated you just like a NATURAL WOMAN, but you just had to go out there and SHAKE YOUR BOOTY! Friends keep asking me, WHO'S MAKING LOVE TO YOUR OLE LADY? while I was sitting at home PLAYING YOUR GAME, BABY. Mama says I should SAY A LITTLE PRAYER FOR YOU because EVERYBODY PLAYS THE FOOL. But all of that is over now and I'm about to go WHERE PEACEFUL WATERS FLOW. I'll just take to the sky on a NATURAL HIGH because I JUST DON'T WANNA BE LONELY when everyone knows that you were LIVING FOR THE WEEKEND. I'm gonna find myself a woman who'll say, Rom, YOU DON'T HAVE TO CRY because A HEART IS A HOUSE FOR LOVE, she'll say, baby, HOLD ON, my love is ALWAYS AND FOREVER because LOVE MAKES THINGS HAPPEN and SOMEDAY WE'LL BE TOGETHER. So you see, Lou, it's time for THE PAY-BACK. No more TEARS, no more STOP TO START, no more

KISSING AND HUGGING. Just face it, girl, YOU'RE GONNA MISS MY LOVING. No need to tell any LIES, because I'm about to WALK ON BY. No baby, I DON'T LOVE YOU ANYMORE because you refused to STAY IN MY CORNER, so go ahead, girl, catch that MIDNIGHT TRAIN TO GEORGIA. You had a sho'nuff WHATTA MAN who gave you the COMFORT OF A MAN but you treated me like HARRY HIPPIE, and any fool knows that IF IT DON'T FIT DON'T FORCE IT, just find a way to set yourself FREE.

Free. That's what I wanna be. Free.

7

GOING TO A GO-GO!

I, Romulus Caesar, am a king. Dammit!

A king who has lost control of his kingdom, of his very life. A king who longs for a strong and loving queen. Who longs to learn her sensuous secrets and drown in the liquid passion of her love. I laughed out loud. Who was I jiving? I'd killed that fantasy the day I married Lou. Yet a man still has his dreams. And his needs.

"Where the hell are you going?"

I was busy scrubbing the ring around the collar from my favorite red-and-white shirt.

"I told you yesterday, Louise. My Frats are stepping tonight. I invited you to come with me, remember?"

"And what about these boys?" She pointed to my twin sons, who played just beyond us in the living room. "Who's gonna baby-sit — or did you invite them, too?"

I fingered my small mustache and frowned. "Nah, baby," I answered calmly, "kids ain't allowed at post functions where alcohol is being served. You know that."

She gave me a piercing look. "Then your children shouldn't be allowed in your fucking house!" Lou stormed into the living room and turned on the stereo, blasting the volume temper-high.

Instead of rinsing the dirt and grime from my shirt, I wished like hell I could rinse it from my life. Such was the state of my marriage, of my entire world. I'd only been around the house for a few days and already she was on my case. Too bad I no longer had an office to sleep in, because my home life was a twenty-four-hour nightmare. Ever since I'd left the drill trail, Lou had happily cracked her whip twenty-four/seven, constantly riding my ass like a goddamn overseer. But who could I blame? I'd made myself a helluva bed, and now I had to lie in it. As lumpy as it was.

I sprayed a little starch on my wet shirt and smoothed out the wrinkles. I needed to get away for a little while. Felt like running, just hitting the track and shaking it off. Or maybe smoothing it out on the keyboard, letting it fly from my fingers. But the Frats were waiting, and I was already late. And I was also very lonely. Although there was absolutely no love, peace, or tranquillity to be found in my home, I resisted stepping outside of my world to find a little harmony, a little companionship.

A little loving.

I'd tried it once. Some sensual chick I'd met at an explosive ordnance conference. We'd flown in together from Fort Ord, California, and during the entire flight we'd plotted and schemed and planned our secret rendezvous. For three hours straight we talked up a helluva good fuck, and by the time I stepped off that airplane Mr. Bobo was poking me so hard I had a headache.

Huh! Mr. Bobo nearly got me killed!

Now there are two things I know I can do: one is blow lyrics and the other is run, but I must have set a world record going out of that white girl's side door as her husband broke in through the front. Man, I'd been so busy trying to get up on the downstroke that I didn't even hear his car as he pulled into the driveway.

Carl Lewis didn't have *nothing* on me.

I streaked across her yard like a crazed Olympic track star, Mr. Bobo slapping my thighs, my nuts hiding somewhere deep in my chest cavity. If it wasn't for my hat, I'd have been as naked as a jaybird.

That was my first and last attempt at outside sex. When my hands finally stopped shaking and I quit looking over my shoulder like a runaway slave, I promised myself that shit would *never* happen again! Especially with a white woman. I swore I'd keep Mr. Bobo safely at home in my well-oiled right hand, and that's exactly why I couldn't figure me out as I stood outside the Officers Club late Friday night hiding my ring finger and asking this sexy Amazon of a sister if I could drive her girlfriend over to the Z-Club.

I stared down at myself in horror.

Oh *hell* no! I wiggled like a worm until the skintight black Lycra dress lay at my feet. Standing in front of the full-length bathroom mirror, I sighed. The skimpy black number hadn't left a thing to the imagination; instead, it had intensified the spread of my hips and emphasized my ferocious beasts. I held it up by two fingers and peered at the faded label in the neck of the dress. No wonder! A daggone size three-four! I sucked my teeth. Those Twiggy days were long over, and I could stand to lose a few pounds if I planned on becoming an officer.

I was so hyped about the step show that I could hardly wait for Sparkle to swing by. The *Officers* Club! If the good Lord was willing and the creek didn't rise, one day soon sistah Sandie would be a bona fide card-toting member!

I looked around at the mess I'd made. Ladelle and I had been in the small hotel room for only a week, and as usual her side was spotless and my side was littered with clothing and suitcases. I'd promised myself I would clean my area over the weekend, but right now I was facing a clothing dilemma.

I'd tried on five different outfits, and so far I'd been dissatisfied with them all. I threw the black dress on top of a growing pile of castaways on the floor. Wait! I dug into an overstuffed garment bag and pulled out a homemade red skirt suit and a pair of black stockings. Yes! This was it. The length and the color perfectly suited my mood because tonight, I was going to a go-go!

I smoothed the skirt over my rear and examined myself with a critical eye. Oh *yeah*! Plenty of mamas wished *they* could have three babies and still look this good! The saucy little outfit had been made by one of my dearest friends in Germany. Lillie Mae Murphy's tailoring skills were legendary, and as a parting gift and a token of her love, she'd crafted the hot little red number especially for me.

And hot was right. The material was an exquisite silk blend that hugged just the right parts of my anatomy and highlighted my best feature: my legs. The skirt was long enough so it didn't look trashy, but short enough that it sparked male creative juices. The top was a gentle, long-sleeved, Chinese-style crew neck with a zippered back. The bodice gently pinched my waist and flared slightly on its way down to my hips. The effect made it appear to rest lightly on my buttocks as it covered just the jutting crowns and left my hips in full view. Satisfied, I grinned like a fool with bad braces, then clicked my heels and pranced around the small room like a hoochie with a head cold!

But then Sparkle arrived and I damn near lost my natural high.

Girlfriend breezed into my room like a giant black Zulu queen; her regal head held high, curls piled on top of shimmering curls. Her perky breasts thrust forward defiantly, nearly bursting through her skimpy top.

"Sistah, you know those shorts look good on you!" I said with just a drop of jealousy, but inside I was thinking, *You're gonna freeze your ass off and your coochie's gonna be sneezing, hee-choo, hee-choo!*

Sparkle's long shapely legs took all day to rise up into her one-piece black short set with the low-cut back nearly exposing the crack of her ethnically shaped ass.

Bertha, Betty, Bella, and Basheeba!

Homegirl was one of those Butt sisters! Her back and shoulders were completely bare, as were her muscle-toned arms and slender neck. I eyed her skeptically. "Are you sure you didn't leave the rest of that getup in the car?"

"Uh-huh, but my ninnies are falling out!"

I shook my head and watched as Sparkle adjusted her halter straps to cover the sides of her plump breasts.

The décor and ambiance of the Officers Club were stunning. Elegant oil paintings and lush leather sofas set off crystal chandeliers and tasteful carpet. I glanced up as we entered and saw a huge crowd of men gathered at the top of the winding stairs.

"C'mon, girl." Sparkle grabbed my arm as I hung back. "We have to pay for the tickets upstairs."

The catcalls and appreciative stares of the ogling brothers embarrassed me to no end, but Sparkle was clearly in her element and loving every second of it. I followed my new friend as she swished over to a front-row table, then cringed when a bearded old man reached for my hand and cried out in excitement, "Lawd ha' mercy—*fishnet* black panty hose!" I tugged at my skirt. Suddenly it felt far too short. And way too revealing.

I turned my high-backed chair around to give me a better view of the dance floor, then sat down and crossed my legs. With my purse on my lap I watched as a handsome brother decked out in a red-and-white-striped shirt and red leather KAPsi hat—obviously a Kappa—walked over and stood at the table next to ours.

Tall and well built, he had skin the color of burnt mahogany wood, and his shiny bald head looked just as smooth. Through the dimness of the room I watched his mouth say, "Phi Nupe," to an older man seated at the table, but his familiar eyes seemed to crawl all over me. I ignored him and turned my attention to the dance floor. The night was young, folks were just beginning to groove, and I was grateful we'd arrived early enough to get a good table.

As the brother in the red-and-white stripes said a hearty good-bye to his friends, he took a giant step backward and nearly fell into my lap. Then like a total idiot he spun around and jerked forward, and before I could move, his clear plastic cup slipped from his hand and a cold syrupy liquid splattered my lower legs and drenched my feet.

Clumsy ass!

"Damn! Pardon me, sister!" He grabbed a handful of embroidered napkins and dropped to his knees. "I'm sorry." He wiped at my wet feet, his eyes boring into mine. "I apologize for not watching my step."

I sucked my teeth in annoyance. "I can do that." I extracted my foot from his large hands and accepted his wad of napkins. I slipped out of my seventy-five-dollar pumps and mopped up as best I could, wiping them from the inside out. Damn! Now my poor toes were going to be stuck together for the rest of the night!

"I'm sorry," he repeated. His eyes were sincere. "My bad. I hope you'll accept my apologies."

I nodded my head to indicate my acceptance, all the time wishing he'd go away before I got clocked with something else.

"By the way, sister"—he retrieved his empty cup and stood—"I don't know if anybody has told you, but you're looking real good in that beautiful red dress."

I nodded again and took a sip of the straight Hennessey Sparkle had ordered for me.

"Can I buy you another one of those?"

I peered closely at this persistent brother, who obviously couldn't take a hint, and I'll be damned if this time I didn't almost throw my drink on him! I'd thought he looked familiar! This was the arrogant-ass drill sergeant I'd met on Sunday! The same loudmouthed Sergeant First Class Caesar who had called me out of my name!

"Thanks, but no thanks, Sergeant Caesar," I said icily, "but I'm sure *Gloria* would appreciate a Pepsi pedicure!" I gave him a cheesy smile. "So why don't you just run along and find her?"

Recognition spread like a warm puddle over his even features. His smile was broad and blinding.

Damn! Were his dimples that deep last week?

"Well, hello, Miss Puddin' Tame!" He crinkled his plastic cup and set it on the table, then shoved his hands in his pockets. "Now I remember you!" He flashed his dimples again and my knees quivered. "Oh yeah . . . now I do!"

His perfect Kool-Aid smile completely unnerved me. I lifted my chin. "Well, I remember you, too, and since the show is about to start and you're blocking my view, I'd appreciate it if you'd move."

Just then the ballroom was plunged into total darkness and the bright cone of a single spotlight shone on the dance floor. One by one, the light illuminated a solitary stepper posing stock-still with his head down and his hands behind his back. Each time the cone of light touched upon a stepper, he was introduced by his line name as he performed a few choreographed moves. The group at the next table went berserk when the last brother on line was introduced as Magic Hands. He spun around and did a quick Temptations-style one-two swing-around rock-bounce move before coming to rest posed to perfection and perched on one knee.

I whistled and laughed as I clapped along with the rest of the crowd. When the excitement died down, I peered through the darkness for a glimpse of Sergeant Caesar, but he must have taken his cue to leave because he was gone. Good riddance, I thought as I shifted in my seat and waited for the real action to begin. I wiggled my toes. They'd already begun to congeal inside of my damp stockings.

The Kappas stepped like professional linemen. They lifted their red-and-white canes high in the air, twisted their bodies in strong, precise movements, and stomped their feet in syncopated rhythm. Quite a few times I thought I recognized that clumsy Mister Caesar as one of the steppers, but I couldn't be sure. Anyway, I doubted it. He didn't look like he could be that sure on his feet. Especially after the way he'd tripped over those big dogs and spilled his drink all over me!

Hoards of men surrounded Sparkle and me the entire evening. Like flies on cotton candy, they were sticky and persistent. Sparkle clung to a tall brother in a pinstriped suit whose eyes were glazed over and glued to her ass the entire night, but I played the field and refused to become involved in small talk or idle conversation. To ensure this, I made it a point never to dance with the same guy twice.

By the time the blockbuster step show and dancing gala were over, I'd put away four cognacs, and at my last count Sparkle had slammed down at least seven. I hadn't consumed this much alcohol in more than a year, and I was more than a bit tipsy; my heart thumped to its own funky groove, my ingrown toenails were singing a cappella, and I had a merry, gleeful Hennessey head.

I peered across the table. My homegirl was at least two sheets to the wind. Sparkle's hair, now a sweaty mass of feathery curls, rose from her head like a silky halo. She'd cut the rug harder than Janet Jackson, and like the Energizer bunny she was ready to keep going and going!

"Gurl, les' go hit the Z-Club!" Sparkle slurred as we filed out of the Officers Club at the mandatory two A.M. closing time. All traces of her articulate speech were long gone. Her diction, like her hair, had reverted back to its natural state.

I was concerned. "Are you okay to drive? I mean . . . you didn't have too much to drink, did you?"

"Fugg no! I'm a drivin' mulldoon! Hell, I'm drive mama! Hey . . ." Sparkle threw her arms in the air as she popped her fingers, wiggled her butt, and sang, "I'm every wo-man . . . it's all over meeee. . . ." Just then her right foot slid all the way through the open toe of her high-heeled hoe hopper and came down hard on the ground. Flailing her arms, Sparkle stumbled backward and slapped the stew out of a freckle-faced sister who stood behind her all decked out in an orange-and-white polka-dot party dress and clutching a matching orange patent-leather purse.

"Oops!" Sparkle grinned. "Sorry!"

The sister picked her nose up off the floor and hissed, "Drunk bitch! The devil is busy!"

Sparkle threw her head back and screeched like the wicked witch. Then she covered her mouth with one hand and giggled. "Somebody should have slapped her! Stepping up in here in that Pollyanna-ass Sunday-go-to-meeting dress! Call the goddamn fashion police!"

I stared at her. Girlfriend wasn't feeling a bit of pain!

"Damn!" She laughed again and pulled me out the door. "I knocked the shit outta her!"

I tugged down the hem of my skirt as we stepped into the night air. Sparkle batted her eyes and tried to focus, hugging herself against the chill. "Damn! It's cold out here!"

Eyeing her tiny shorts, I smirked. "Nooo, Chief Hoochtress to the third degree . . . you ain't cold . . . you foine!"

"Would you like my jacket?"

We whirled around to face the suited brother Sparkle had danced into the ground. He stood there meekly with his sports coat held out as an offering. Sparkle gushed, "No thanks." She batted her eyes and smiled her best "lil'lady" smile, and that stupid white-girl-from-Harvard act crept back into her voice. "We're going over to the Z-Club. I need to get finished off right. . . . I've still got some excess energy I need to"—she sighed deeply almost moaning—"*burn.*"

"Get over here!" I snatched her by the arm and yanked her toward the car. "Quit sending off those 'hot hoochie' vibes!"

Sparkle staggered along behind me, fumbling for her keys. "Tell that foine-behind sugah daddy to quit catching 'em!"

As we giggled and settled into her small red sports car, there was a tap on the driver's-side window. Instead of rolling the window down, Sparkle opened her door. We were face-to-face with the red-and-white candy cane who'd bumped into my chair, pissed me off, and drenched my feet! Sergeant First Class Caesar himself! Sparkle and I looked at him with our best what-the-hell-do-you-want expressions on our greasy, inebriated faces.

"Excuse me, ladies." He blew into his hands, then rubbed them together in the chilly night air. "I don't mean to intrude, but," he addressed Sparkle, "my partner over there," he angled his head toward the guy who had offered Sparkle his jacket, "would really like to get to know you and thangs and he thought, you know . . . maybe you could ride with him and I could drive her," he nodded toward me, "on over to the Z-Club."

I crossed my arms and smirked. What? Did we look like a pair of new fools?

"Okay, cool!" Sparkle piped. "Where's your car?"

I stared at her like she had two heads.

Cool? Ain't feeling no pain? Girlfriend was tore up!

"Well . . . see"—he gave a short, embarrassed laugh—"I rode with my friend, but I could drive your car. I'll follow right behind you. I've only had one beer and I'm a pretty decent driver. And I swear I don't bite." He turned to me and added with a dimpled, lopsided grin, "At least not too hard."

I looked at Sparkle and waited for Brooklyn's best bashing to gush forth from her parted lips.

Pearls of laughter fell from her mouth.

"You are so funny—and cute, too!" In less than two seconds Sparkle was standing outside of the car pulling her short-shorts down over her butterscotch booty. "Where's your friend parked?"

Shit!

"Sparkle! Hey, Sparkle!" I rolled down my window and called out to my new friend, "Girl, hold up. Wait just a damn minute! I don't know this guy. . . ."

"It's all good, Sandie." She skipped across the parking lot and climbed into a white Jeep Grand Cherokee where her polite dance partner waited at the door. "He's cool, I know his friend. . . . I'll meet you at the club!"

Humph! I folded my arms across my breasts and glared at the long-legged brother climbing in next to me. I may have been a bit tipsy, but that ole Sparkle heffah was pissy drunk!

I cut my eyes left.

And neither of us knew this grinning kneegrow from the man in the moon!

8

THE LADY IN RED

I hope you don't mind." I stole a glance at her as I maneuvered through the maze of parked cars and found the exit. I gripped the steering wheel to stop my hands from trembling and prayed my breath wasn't too bad.

I'd noticed her almost as soon as she hit the door.

The Lady in Red!

She and her friend had made one hell of an entrance as they glided up the stairs like a pair of 747s. One in deep ebony, the other in sexy scarlet; one towering, the other petite; one bronzed honeycomb, the other black coffee; yet both of them equally sexy and appealing. As they maneuvered through the crowd, scores of awestruck Frats parted in their path the way Moses had parted the Red Sea.

Damn! My only thought had been *poetry in motion* as she sashayed over to her table with that little red skirt flapping against the tops of her thighs and hugging her sexy curves. I'd spilled my drink on her on purpose and then hoped like hell her man wasn't around to mop up the floor with me.

I checked her out in the semidarkness as she sat down at a small table. There was something about her eyes that stirred me, but by the time I recognized her, she had already recognized me! Man, Sarge was fine as hell without that cigarette stuck in her mouth, and I must say that uniform hadn't done a damn thing for her! I'd hoped to borrow a few minutes of her time so I could tell her so, but then the show started and I had to duck out on her without saying good-bye.

I made it to the dance floor just as the spotlight shone on my position. Impulsively, I did a slick little Motown dip-bop-dip that made the crowd go wild, and when I looked toward her table, I thought I saw her smiling and clapping. After the show I hung in the background, unsure about how to approach her. Brothers were waiting three deep to get in her face, and I sat across the room and watched as each of them stepped up for their turn at bat, then staggered away, punch-drunk.

And now, by some divine stroke of luck, she sat next to me with her arms folded across her chest and one leg thrown casually over the other. I tried not to glance at her too often because she seemed upset. She wagged that crossed leg like she wanted to break it off at the knee and popped on her strawberry bubble gum like it was going out of style.

Now, I consider myself a conversationalist, a charming intellectual, a gentleman, and a scholar; but try as I might I couldn't think of a damned thing to say! I was nervous like Mervous and my palms began to sweat. I took a deep breath.

"How'd you like the show tonight?"

"What?"

"The step show. Did you like it?"

"Yeah, it was okay. It could have been better."

Oh, okay, she was one of *those* types. Never satisfied.

"My name is Romulus, but my friends call me Rom, and so can you. So, what's your name? I already know it's not Gloria and please don't tell me it's Puddin' Tame!"

She laughed and showed just a hint of her tongue through the sexy little gap in her front teeth. "My name is Sanderella, but my friends call me Sandie. You can call me Sanderella."

Smart mouth. I liked that kind of mouth—not vicious, just sharp. It showed she could think on her feet. "Well, Sanderella, I can respect that. It's my pleasure to make your acquaintance."

"Likewise," she said, and treated me to a grin. I actually felt my heart flutter, and that damned Mr. Bobo smiled.

"Do you live on post or in Newport News?" Since I'd already seen her in a uniform, I knew she wasn't one of those local yokels who were looking to marry a soldier and see the world for free.

"I'm new here. I've just been assigned to the 515th and I'm moving into the barracks."

YES! She was gonna live in the barracks. That meant she was single! Now ain't that some shit?

"Is that right? We're in the same battalion. The 515th is one of my sister units. I'm in the 391st Explosive Ordnance Detachment."

"I've always loved the ordnance field," she said, smiling.

"Well," I told her proudly, "I just came off the drill trail, and I'm ready to blow up a few holes. I've been stationed here for more than three years, so maybe I could show you around, you know . . . maybe we could do the lunch thang sometimes." I tried to sound casual and nonchalant, but I wanted to pant from her perfume as I stole sideways glances at her thighs.

"Maybe" was her simple response. She still had her arms folded stiffly across her chest, and I knew that unless I turned on the charm she'd think I was just another hard leg on a bowwow mission.

"You wanna hear something that happened to me today?"

"No, not really."

"Well, I'll tell you anyway since I gotta tell somebody."

I swallowed hard and began.

"This afternoon me and a few of the fellas were on the basketball court, and there was an accident." I glanced in her direction. Whew! I had her attention, so she wasn't rock-solid ice. "While we were out there hoopin' and ballin', there was this old guy, a contractor or something, and he was riding on a lawn mower cutting grass, right?"

She nodded slightly, all cat eyes and shapely thighs.

"So, I was killing the brothers—faking left and cutting right—and all of a sudden out of nowhere we hear this guy screaming like he was running through a fire wearing gasoline drawers!" I licked my lips, pausing for effect.

"And? What happened?" she asked impatiently. "Did the old man run somebody over or what?"

"Nah, it was worse than that. He must've hit a large rock or something because the lawn mower flipped over and threw him to the ground."

"So? Was he hurt?"

"Yeah, he was pretty fuck—I mean messed up. Blood was all over his face and neck. By the time we got over there, he was on his back hollering, 'Find my ear! Find my son-of-a-bitchin' ear!' We tried to calm the old dude down, but he was carrying on so bad we thought he'd have a heart attack out there in that hot sun! No matter what we said, he kept on insisting that we look for his ear."

Sanderella listened closely, captivated by the emotion I poured into the story. She digested my words, then asked in a huff, "He was worried about his ear? What about his ass? Nobody needs an ear! Did y'all get him to the hospital?"

The ice was melting! She had a heart behind her tough exterior, and already I wanted it to be mine.

"Baby, that old man wanted what he wanted and he wanted his ear! His head did look bad though—like he'd pissed in Mike Tyson's cornflakes and made the big guy relapse. Anyway, we split up and began to search for his ear. We combed through that freshly cut grass searching for a mangled stub of white flesh, and all the while the old guy is crying and moaning and going on and on about finding his damned ear."

I followed Guy around a hairpin curve; my headlights flickered and danced off the narrow tree-lined road. By this time Sanderella had shifted left in her seat; her arms were uncrossed and her hands were where I longed to rest my head. She stared into my eyes and caught my words while they were still unformed thoughts on my tongue.

"Then what?"

"Well, we searched and he screamed, then we searched some more and he screamed some more, and finally Guy stood up and yelled, 'I got it! I found it!' We ran over and held that piece of ear up for the old man to see, and he looked up and hollered, 'Hey! That's not my blasted ear! *My* ear had a pencil behind it!'"

Thunderous laughter ricocheted around the interior of the small car, and I smiled. Watching her laugh felt like Sunday dinner at Grandma's house—I just couldn't get enough, and I never wanted it to end.

"Okay . . . okay dammit. You got me . . . you're a bug-out . . . that was funny! I didn't even realize you were pulling my leg. Here I was feeling sorry for the old man—and for you, too, for having to witness it—and you were bullshitting! That's one for you, Rammie, but I'll get you back."

My balls tingled, and the hair stood up on the back of my neck. Hopeful anticipation! She was gonna get me back! That meant she planned to see me again, at least long enough to jerk my chain. That was enough to send me swinging into fantasies of sugar and spice and everything nice.

We were still laughing as I followed Guy's Jeep into the parking lot adjacent to the Z-Club. Cars were jammed in bumper to bumper, and he led me to the far end of the lot next to an open field. I had no choice but to park on the low-cut grass. I turned off the ignition, and before Sanderella could pop her gum, I was out of my door and opening hers.

The way she unfolded her compact physique from the car told me I had a real lady on my hands. I watched as she pivoted her hips to the right then easily swung first one leg and then the other out of the car. Next, she adjusted her purse strap on her shoulder, placed both hands on her thighs, and stood up in one fluid, graceful motion.

Damn! The sister had a pair of legs on her!

Not like the table legs I've seen on a lot of women. My eyes had already inventoried the rest of her, and that hot red dress fit her snugly in all the places that counted.

I held her arm as she tiptoed through the soft grass in her high-heeled shoes and led her over to Guy's parked Jeep. "It looks like they're busy." I peered through the window. The occupants were locked in a passionate embrace, kissing like it was a contest. I was jealous. Sanderella's girl was all over my Frat. She'd already warmed him up on the dance floor, and now she looked ready to finish him off.

Sanderella banged on the glass and shouted, "Sparkle! Hey, Sparkle! Come up for air, girl! You're fogging up the brother's windows!"

I wouldn't have objected to taking up residence in Guy's backseat and following their example, but I knew that if I so much as touched Sanderella she'd slap my ass to the *moon*, Alice.

To the *moon*.

Guy opened the Jeep's door, and I handed the keys to her girlfriend, whose name I figured was Sparkle, then said in my best Barry White baritone, "Thanks for letting me use your car. I really dug your girlfriend's company."

Sparkle giggled and Sanderella did, too. I hoped they were laughing with a brother and not at one. Because I wasn't trying to be no joke.

I was trying to be her man.

The club was jumping, the music was blaring, and the sister was stealing my heart. Our conversation was smooth and easy. Sanderella had just the right blend of intellect and down-to-earth sister-girl savvy, and my nose was opened so wide you could have driven an eighteen-wheeler straight to my brain!

We found a small corner, and I stood behind her as we watched the crowd grooving on the dance floor. She was the perfect height, no more than five-two, and I could see clear over her head. She swayed to the thunderous beat of the house music, and I caught the scent of her hair, the scent of a woman.

"Sooo," I bent down and yelled into her ear, "is this your first time here?" *Stupid question!* I wanted to bite my tongue off as soon as those idiotic words were out of my mouth. How could she have been here before when she'd just arrived on base?

"Yes, it's my first time, but not my last!" She pulled me onto the brimming dance floor, and we moved alongside the other sardines.

I really dug that red on her. It made her look like a Keebler fudge cookie. Uncommonly good. I usually went for lighter-skinned sisters. I guess at one time you could have called me color-struck, but right now I was ready to testify in open court that this untouched black-berry contained the sweetest of sweet juice.

I tried to keep up with Sanderella as she did what looked like the funky chicken, the funky Broadway, the funky cold medina, *and* the funky boogaloo! When the music finally ended, we squeezed in together on a small bench seat. She'd shaken the hell out of her groove thang, and beads of sweat glistened on her brow. I draped my arm around the back of the bench and asked cautiously, "Do you have a man, Sanderella?"

"Why do you want to know?"

"I'm just curious. Do you?"

"No, but I have three children, so if you don't enjoy kids, you can step off now."

"Hey!" I was offended. "I love kids. I have two sons myself."

She seemed pleased. "Really? How old are they?"

"My boys just turned eight. Their names are Hannibal and Mansa."

"And they're both eight?" She twisted her lips. "Oh—I get it, two different mamas, huh? I knew it! You're a piece of work!"

"Nah, not at all. My sons are the same age, but they share a mother. They're twins."

"Sorry." She smiled and sent electric impulses screaming down to my feet.

"No need to be," I assured her. "How old are your children?" She was popping her fingers and shaking her shimmy like she wanted to dance again.

"They're ten, five, and four. Jamillah, Hanif, and Kharim."

I was impressed with their names. They sounded as if they had meaning. I'd fought Lou hard and long for the right to name my sons after great men. Like my mother, I believed everyone's name should have a meaning, a legacy to live up to. For once, I'd won. My son Hannibal was named after Hannibal the Great, a North African general who conquered major portions of Spain and Italy. Hannibal's overpowering armies had marched African war elephants through the treacherous Alps to surprise and conquer northern Italy, and to this day he's regarded as one of the greatest generals of all time.

Mansa got his name from Mansa Musa, King of Mali, who led more than seventy-two thousand followers on the Haj, or Islamic holy pilgrimage. His caravan crossed the Sahara Desert from Timbuktu to Mecca, traveling a distance of more than six thousand miles and gaining international prestige for Mali as one of the world's largest and wealthiest empires.

"How'd you choose their names?" I asked Sanderella after sharing the origin of my sons' names with her. I wanted to see just how deep this beautiful young sister could be.

"All of their names are Arabic," she answered proudly. "Muslim names. Jamillah means 'beautiful one,' Hanif means 'true' and 'upright,' and Kharim means 'noble' and 'generous.'"

I whistled. "They're all meaningful names and very well chosen. They'll have a lot to live up to later in life."

"Thanks." Her smile was sad. "I hate it when we're separated. I really miss my kids something terrible."

"When will they be here? Have you put your name on the waiting list for housing?"

Sanderella shook her head. "No, I submitted an application packet for Officer Candidate School, and, thank God, I was selected. Since I'll be reporting to Fort Benning in a few months, my dependent movement orders have been frozen. Right now my kids are with my folks in New York City."

Officer Candidate School? I was sinking deeper by the minute. A woman with ambitions, goals, and aspirations to match my own! At one time I'd considered OCS, but after hearing all the horror stories associated with it, I decided to apply for Warrant Officer School instead. I'd been accepted, too, but had turned down the offer after injuring my back in a football scrimmage. I proudly informed Ms. Sanderella of this, and she had the good grace to make impressed little noises.

"So," I continued, not wanting our conversation to end, "where'd you get your name, Sanderella?"

"From my mama—where'd you get yours?"

"From my mother. She named me after a king."

"A *king*?" she peered at me skeptically, boring into me with those do-you-wanna-get-funky-with-me brown eyes. "King Rammie *who*?"

"King *Romulus*," I gently corrected her. It wasn't unusual for black people to mess up my name. "King Romulus was the founder of Rome. He was the mythical first ruler of the Roman empire. He and his twin brother, Remus, were the sons of the Greek god Mars. Romulus and Remus shared Rome, and Romulus built a wall around his portion of the city and vowed to kill anyone who vaulted it. To mock his twin, Remus jumped the wall. Romulus had his brother killed and became known as a fierce ruler. Remus died, and Romulus survived. Mama named me after Romulus because I'm a survivor. Romulus Caesar. 'Caesar' means supreme ruler of an empire. So I'm a king any way you slice it."

It was her turn now. I wanted to know everything she had to tell. "How'd your mother come up with your name?"

She didn't miss a beat.

"My great-grandmother's name was Queen Sandra, and her mother's name was Queen Ella. They ruled over a small African-American queendom in Denmark, South Carolina. When Queen Sandra gave birth to her first female child, she honored herself and her mother by naming the child Princess Sanderella. Time passed and the young princess became Queen Sanderella. She gave birth to a beautiful daughter and named her Princess LuCeal—after her younger sister.

"When Princess LuCeal was seventeen, there was a huge fire. The heavy rains were late that year, and uncontrollable brushfires were destroying the entire countryside. Well, one night after fighting a particularly stubborn fire, Uncle Butchie, the Prime Minister of Safety, declared the castle and its surrounding areas unsafe. The queendom stood right in the path of the hungry blaze, which was just about to engulf everything in its massive inferno. Folks had to get *out*.

"But everyone didn't move fast enough. In the midst of the heat and confusion, Princess LuCeal was left behind. Confused by the thick smoke and the darkness, she'd gotten lost and turned around in the labyrinthlike layout of the castle.

"Now, when Queen Sanderella realized her precious child was still inside of the burning castle, she damn near lost her mind. Shitloads of brave peasants and subjects tried to rescue her daughter, but they were all driven back by the heat and smoke. Not nary a one of them was able to locate poor Princess LuCeal!

"As a last resort the queen's sister made a bold play. She recommended that Franklin, Earl of Buscobel, be commissioned to rescue the pretty princess. Well known for his strength and courage, Franklin had been imprisoned due to a long-standing debt incurred by his granddaddy. Now, like most brothers, the earl didn't work for free, so he was promised his freedom and a share of the queendom for his efforts.

"Franklin was their only hope. He was a sharp dude, and his warrior spirit enabled him to not only locate the princess, but also to save her from a certain death as she lay trapped beneath a heavy wooden beam. As the story goes, young Princess LuCeal immediately fell for the earl—who wouldn't? Bruh-man looked *good*! He was rumored to be as black as midnight and fine as sunshine! So the wise Queen Sanderella allowed them to marry. Out of gratitude and respect the newlyweds named their youngest child in honor of the great queen. So that's how I received not only my name, but my beauty, my intelligence, and my legacy as a queen."

I was impressed.

The sister was not only gorgeous, she was also quick, smart, and could spin a wicked tale! She obviously believed herself to be nobility, a queen—which to me was utterly perfect.

Because I, Romulus Caesar, am a king!

9

THE COMFORT OF A MAN

Making a good impression on my commander was proving to be quite a challenge, and all work and no play had made this sistah a very lonely girl. After hanging out a few times with Sparkle, I began to rediscover my interest in the opposite sex, but I absolutely refused to date any of the men in my unit. Instead, I consistently turned the brothers down like two sheets and a heavy blanket. Just yesterday I overheard one eager sergeant exclaim, "Man, that ass even looks good in a uniform!"

"Bro," his friend had replied, shaking his head sadly, "that evil-assed wench ain't gonna give you the time of day. She acts like her shit don't stink—like she poots Fruity Pebbles or sumpthin' with her stuck-up self!"

Good, I'd thought as I strolled past with my head in the air. They'd finally gotten the message. But it was sho'nuff lonely at the top. Or as close to the top as I could get right then.

My sister had finally bailed out on me. A week ago she'd decided to catch the first thing smoking to North Carolina to visit her pregnant daughter and her husband. For the first time in a long time, I was away from home and all alone.

"It's time for me to move on, Sandie," Ladelle told me. "Time for me to find a place and get settled in so I can handle my business. Besides, you don't really need me anymore. Your kids are with Mama, and before you know it you'll be going off to officer school."

My eyes searched hers. "But what are you gonna do? Go back and live with Mama, too?"

She gave me a strange look. "I dunno. I'll stay in North Carolina for a while, then maybe I'll meet up with you later on in Georgia or Virginia."

Despite our many differences and in spite of both of our many faults, Ladelle and I were tight and I loved her. She was my sister, my pizo, and our blood ran thicker than mud. When I decided to divorce Maurice it was Ladelle who showed up in Germany to help me with my kids. My sister had been there when I needed her, and for that I would always be grateful. And things had worked out well for both of us.

I nodded and dropped my eyes to hide my tears. I was used to having her around, and it was hard for me to let her go. But I respected her decision, and in a way she was right. It was sink-or-swim time for Ladelle, and I prayed she would show the world her swimmingest tail.

I moved out of the base guest quarters and spent a solitary Friday evening in my new barracks room. With the torn pieces of a brown paper bag securing my curls and a mudpack covering my cheeks, I screwed a gallon of Breyers chocolate ice cream and murdered theme songs while watching old Shaft reruns. I'd had my fill of blaxploitation by the end of the second movie, so I decided to call my best friend, Charmel Dawson.

Tall and leggy, with a face the color of hot sunshine, Charmel was a street-smart, book-smart sister-friend, with the tiniest waistline you've ever seen. We'd grown up together in the Marcus Garvey projects in the Brownsville section of Brooklyn. Mama Ceal lived on five and Charmel's family lived on two, and believe me when I tell you we'd worn a permanent groove in the stairwell from running back and forth between our apartments. It was Charmel's younger sister Charmaine who had stolen Kevin from under my nose, and the last I'd heard she was pregnant with their fifth child. I found a prepaid phone card with five minutes remaining, and as I dialed Mel's number, I tried to remember if I'd ever had a chance to properly thank her sister.

Charmel picked up on the first ring, and after barely saying hello she launched into a vivid description of her latest groove thang.

Mister Big Stuff.

"Hunny-*chiiile*, the boy is huge! I mean big everywhere! Big hands, big feet, big legs, big eyes . . . gurrrl, big teeth, big tongue—and dick for days!"

Charmel had been estranged from her husband on and off during the past two years, and playing the field-by-alphabet had become her favorite pastime. "Damn, Red," I said, laughing. "Does Mr. Bigum have a name?"

"Oooh yeah, hunny. Can you believe I'm working on my N's? His name is Nickolae, sounds to me like Nick-Oh-Lay, but I calls him Nick . . . ," Charmel moaned ecstatically, ". . . with the big black dick!"

Despite her raunchiness, I giggled at Mel's excitement.

"And I bet he's madly in love with you, right?"

"Damn right! He can't get enough of this funky stuff!"

"So what alley did you drag him out of?"

Mel laughed. "Hunny, I met him at the Club, and I just had to have him! You know I needed something hard and strong to lay on—"

"You should've laid on your husband."

"Hunny, please! That long, tall drink of water? Laying on his narrow ass is like laying on the floor!"

"Ohhh . . . ," I drawled, a little bit jealous, "so you just had to go out and find a ruffneck to pop that poontang, huh?"

"Hunny, yeah! And he tears it up, too! Pow! Pow! *Pow!* I've been getting my head slammed every night and in the mornings, too! Big Daddy's been eating me up for breakfast *and* dinner. Humph . . . I stand up on the bed butt-nekked—"

"What?" I shrieked. "Stand on the bed? Naked? You?" I screwed up my face at the mental picture I envisioned—pancake stomach, but hips and thighs wider than all outdoors!

"Hunny, yesss! I put one leg up on the wall—"

"Up on the wall? You? Naked? Standing on the bed with a daggone tree trunk propped against the wall? Just where the hell do you tuck that nasty butt? And those thighs—they're huge!"

"Shut up!" Mel giggled. "Those are the good parts. He likes them like that—you don't know? The brothah says I'm soooo beautiful—"

"He *means* you're soooo booty-full!"

"You don't know nothing about this . . . you probably ain't had no good lovin' since that married sucker broke your heart in Germany! Humph, you probably still have Saudi sand up in that stale-ass cootie of yours! I'ma have to hook your dry ass up. Lemme see . . . have you tried any B's?"

I groaned. "Mel, please! The last time you recommended a B I went out with that bigheaded, bucktoothed Bartholomew Baines! By the time I got rid of him, all I had left was a bus pass, a black eye, and a bunch of bad credit!"

"Well, maybe things will be better for you in Virginia. They say it's the state for lovers."

"Ain't no loving happening around here," I snapped. "I can't even pay a man to put up with me. They're three and four deep for every female, and even the ugly ones think they have it going on! There's one guy from my job who's been hounding me, but . . . nah."

"Why not, San? You need somebody. What's his name? Is he single? Did he ask you out?"

"Yeah, he did. . . ."

"So?"

"So, I told him no!"

"Why, dummy?"

"Because I don't shit where I eat! Plus, his bites are shot. Dude looks like he's got a mouth full of oatmeal!"

"Yuck. And there's nobody else?"

I twirled the phone cord around my finger. "Well, I met this other guy at a step show and I gave him my number, but he hasn't called yet . . . good thing, too, because he might be married and like you said, I ain't had two words for another woman's husband ever since—"

The thirty-second buzzer sounded.

I frowned. "Damn! My card's expired! Hit me back later!"

"Okay, hunny!" Mel yelled over the mechanical voice of the operator threatening to disconnect us. "Love, peace, and hair grease, my sistah! I'm out!"

I hung up and stared at the phone. Charmel was right. I did need something. The comfort of a man. Maybe I should call the newspaper and take out an ad.

Wanted: Young man, single, and free! Experience in mature love preferred, but willing to accept a young trainee!

On more than one occasion I'd thought about calling up a few of my exes. Kevin was busy pimping the hell out of Charmaine; Maurice called me on the regular crying for one more chance, begging to come back home; and the last I'd heard from Antoine, he was going to court in Alabama, accused of breaking into a lingerie shop and stealing edible undies. Maybe it was best to just let sleeping dogs lie.

For some reason my thoughts turned to Rom.

Strong, humorous, and sincere, he seemed to be the kind of man who could actually measure up to my father. To my daddy's standards. And the fact that he was fine as hell didn't hurt either. I smelled his cologne as I shook him from my mind. Dude could have been the East River Strangler for all I knew. It didn't matter how nice he seemed. My record at the track was pitiful.

No, I told myself as I stared at the phone and wondered what to do next. Forget about King Romulus. This time not only was I playing it solo, I was playing it safe. Besides, although I was lonely, I wasn't quite that desperate.

Yet.

10

WHY CAN'T WE BE FRIENDS?

Once again I was in the shit house, but this time there was good reason. I hadn't touched Lou in more than four months, and she swore up and down that I was drilling some freak. That's exactly what she said, "You're probably ten inches deep-drilling some freak!" She was wrong though. I didn't wanna freak anyone, especially her. I wanted to make love. Mentally first, emotionally second, and finally, physically.

I wanted Sanderella.

I'd only seen her once since the night of the step show, and wouldn't you know it, everything got all fucked up. I bumped into her at the personnel records office where I'd gone to check on my promotion status. Sanderella was there reviewing her personnel file for Officer Candidate School, so I made myself comfortable in the chair beside her and chatted nervously, cracking corny jokes and praying to God she still thought I was funny. Her smile and easy laughter told me that she did.

Then I told a real stupid joke, and I couldn't help but join her as she laughed at what I'd said. Like a fool I covered my mouth with my hand in midlaugh, and that's when Sanderella froze. Her slanted eyes shot daggers and arrows as she grabbed my left hand and stared at my thin gold wedding band.

My stomach flipped.

I know I read disappointment in her eyes because I felt it ripping straight through my heart.

"You know what, Sergeant First Class Caesar?" She dropped my hand like it was a rotten onion. No longer was I Rom; our relationship had plummeted down to a strictly professional level. "I don't do *husbands*," she spat. "The only thing a married man can do for me is show me which way a single man went!"

"Sanderella, let me explain—"

"You don't owe me no explanations! Explain to your wife why the hell you're sitting here trying to push up on me!"

"I ain't pushing up on you!" I lied.

"Then step off," she said without batting an eye.

"Sanderella—" I began, but then changed my mind. It was useless to sit there and dig myself a deeper grave, so I got up and walked over to the door. "I'm sorry, Sanderella. This isn't what it looks like. I know you've probably heard it all a thousand times before, but this is different. I swear to you. This is different."

"You weren't wearing a wedding ring before. You told me about your children, but I assumed you were divorced. Divorced men aren't wearing wedding bands these days, are they?"

I shook my head. "I just wanted be your friend," I said weakly. I sounded just like a million other no-good husbands on a get-some mission.

"Well, this ain't friendship, baby. It's hen shit!"

And with that, she turned around in her seat and buried her head in her records, cutting off my air supply without even knowing it.

That was several weeks ago, and since then I've spent almost all of my free time on the track trying to forget her words and swallow my shame. I called her room for almost a week straight, but no one ever answered her telephone, and if she had an answering machine, that shit was never turned on.

As I approached the one-mile gravel track, I mentally psyched myself up for my run. I felt like a cheetah, ready to tear the road up and send clouds of dust and pebbles flying at least a mile in my wake.

I ran the first lap blind. During the second lap I noticed about five other runners, none as good as I. On the third lap I really began to loosen up and look around. As I turned onto a zigzag stretch of the road bordering a man-made pond, I noticed a womanly figure just ahead of me. Struggling.

She looked like baby two-step as she shuffled along at a snail's pace. She had a cute little twist to her run; women usually do. I watched as her arms wagged back and forth across her body, side to side in direct opposition to her wiggling round hips, wasting all kinds of energy.

That was the problem with female runners. They ran from the shoulders down, misusing their arm swings and leading with their hips instead of their quads. This girl was pitiful; she would do better in a wheelchair.

As I lapped past I glanced at her out of the corner of my eye. Sanderella?

I sped up quickly and nearly tripped over my own feet. I sprinted another quick lap until I was behind her again.

Sure as shit, it was her!

As I jogged toward her, I gradually let my pace fall to match hers. I could have walked faster than she was running. "Hi," I said as I approached her from behind. I wasn't even sure she would speak to me.

She flashed me a tired grin. "Well, it's about time you stopped! You zoomed past me three times! I wanted to stick my foot out and trip you, but I just didn't have enough energy."

My face broke open, happy as hell. If she had merely graced me with a glance, I'd have thrown myself down on the hard track and groveled at her feet, but she had actually smiled!

"How have you been, Sanderella? I've been trying to reach you, but you're never in your room."

"I've been around," she answered. "Keeping a low profile."

I smiled. "That's great. So . . . getting in shape, huh? Not that you're fat or anything," I stammered stupidly. "I mean, you're getting in shape for OCS, right?"

"Yeah, I was recently notified that I'll be attending the January class, so I need to shave about five minutes off my run."

It was more like fifteen minutes, but I wasn't going to be the one to tell her. What I told her was, "I run for the post track team, and I used to coach the junior varsity track club—I love to run. I'd be more than happy to train you. I could help you get ready for those ass-smoking monster runs I hear officer candidates have to pass. I'll even help you give up those cigarettes. They slow you down, you know."

Sanderella stopped shuffling and stared at me. The wind lifted her hair, then resettled it gently around her head.

She looked beautiful.

"Just what do you want in return for all of this help?"

I held my hands out, palms up. "Nothing, Sanderella, I swear. I just want to help you and maybe one day we can become friends. Why can't we be friends?"

She looked at me for a long moment, her eyes darkly suspicious, as if she were searching for signs of larceny in my heart. Finally she answered, "I've got enough friends. Just get me in shape for school, okay?"

"Okay. However you want it. I'll teach you to run. I'll get you in shape."

She placed one hand on her hip and used the other to wipe the sweat from her cinnamon brow. Studying my eyes intently as if searching to see the real me, she said with a grin, "One more thing, Mr. Caesar."

"What's that?"

"You can call me Sandie."

Hot-diggity-dawg! I wanted to leap like a frog!

11

WHEN A MAN LOVES A WOMAN

Once again I sported my lucky red-and-white shirt, but this time instead of washing it out by hand I'd had it dry-cleaned. Pressed. Starched. I wanted to look sharp this evening.

I tucked the shirt into my black linen pants and slipped into my shiny new Stacy Adams shoes. I flashed myself a smile. Damn, the brothah looked *good*! As an afterthought I splashed on some cologne, then got fancy and rubbed a few drops on my freshly shaved head. My scalp tingled and shined like freshly minted money. I grabbed my car keys from a hook near the dresser and my black leather jacket from the closet, then slipped out of the empty apartment.

Lou and the boys had gone to visit who I considered to be her main squeeze: some white chick in her writers club who spent more time with my wife than I did. Not a problem. Things had been decidedly cool between us for the past few months. The sex was nonexistent, and the conversations weren't much better. I'd been sleeping on our worn-out sofa bed and having liquid dreams of the sweetest nature.

And they all involved Sandie.

I didn't bother to tell Lou that I was going out tonight, not that she would have cared anyway. She had her girlfriends to occupy her time, and for all I knew, they were both occupying her time and beating mine.

But it really didn't matter anymore.

I had Sanderella in my life. Or at least in my dreams. Believe it or not, I spent my entire day thinking about her and dreaming up different ways to impress her. Wondering what it was I could do for her that no other man could.

Man, Sandie was *fine*. I mean *fine*. Not in the way that some men might think. I mean she wasn't high yellow with hair like Pocahontas or anything, but the girl had something about her that made most men take a second look. Something that was ethnically pleasing. Straight from the motherland. Like Anita Baker, she had style. An inner sense of beauty that made her femininity a burning mystery. An aura. Not high-siddity like, but rather a comfortable, down-to-earth, dignified black womanliness about herself that made a brothah want to crawl up inside of her and die a happy man!

But unfortunately I wasn't the only hardhead who noticed it. Lemuel Ricks, one of my longtime fraternity brothers, was pushing up on Sandie harder than a mutter. Lem had wined and dined her, bought her presents, sent her roses, and even did a funky slow grind with my baby at the Z-Club! I just couldn't compete. Hell, Lem was a divorced Master Sergeant with a nice ride and, from what I'd heard, a laid-out crib.

Here I was a broke-dick Sergeant First Class! And married to boot! One or two other Frats who hung in our general circle had put the moves on her, too. Guy found out from Sparkle that Sandie had not only gone to the movies with Jackson Price, but Vickers Anderson had cooked dinner for her in his cozy little GQ fuck palace.

That long-headed so-and-so!

I got mad as hell when I heard about that one. I wanted to kick Guy's ass for telling me, but for what? Sandie was a much-right woman. I had just as much right to her as the next guy did.

None.

But when a man loves a woman, a lot of things seem right.

Still, I felt helpless. I was in a no-win situation. Especially when you stacked me up against brothers like Lem and Vic. Those dudes were single. They could offer her their undivided time and attention. Shit, after a long evening of running with her, I had to rush back to the crib and fix dinner for my boys. If I didn't cook, Lou would feed them KFC seven days a week.

Besides, Sandie had already told me how she felt about married men. Even in our casual conversations she was guarded and reserved, suspicious of my intentions. At first I tried to be nonthreatening and harmless in my attitude. Like running with her was all I had on my mind. But for the first time in years it was the furthest thing from my mind.

After a few weeks I got bold and went for broke. Since I was searching for that good stuff I had to tighten up on my backstroke! So like a lovesick bloodhound, I stayed on her trail, writing her dumb lyrics of friendship and singing her corny lines of encouragement. I called her three and four times a day from work and then again at night when she was safely in the barracks.

Every evening I put my boys to bed and waited until Lou climbed into the shower, then I'd steal a few precious minutes feeling the sweet sound of Sandie's voice as it caressed me through the telephone lines. I'd stand at my keyboard and let my heart fly through my hands, and, cloaked by the background sound of fingers coupling with columns of black and white, I'd stand accused, pouring my heart out on the witness stand.

It was a one-sided love affair.

Sandie would at times be polite, other times barely cordial, and a few times she got right pissed and reminded me that she didn't "do" married men.

I told her I didn't plan to remain married too much longer.

She told me to call her back when I got my divorce.

She refused my offers of dinner—even Red Lobster, which she had confessed was her favorite restaurant. Lunch dates were also out of the question. The only things she allowed me were my secret phone calls and the honor of being her track coach.

So I made myself happy watching her as she struggled on the track, swinging her arms like a lady and mesmerizing me with the rhythm of her rump. Quite a few evenings she stood me up, and like a fool I'd wait around for hours. I'd stand there too mad to run, fuming like a motherfucker as if I had a *right*. On those nights I went home like a hungry 'gator. Lou, seeing her funeral reflected in my eyes, would stay the hell out of my way.

I was trapped between two worlds.

The only reason I didn't go crazy was because of my sons. Those boys were the music that tamed the savage beast within me. The glue that bonded my fractured soul.

It was going to be hard leaving them.

I merged onto the crowded freeway and drove to Norfolk with the windows down; the warm air rushed my face and cleansed the cobwebs of doubt and desire from my mind. I was on my way to the Third Annual Kappa Alpha Psi Hard-Hard Boat Ride, and I wanted to arrive early. This was an annual event that my Frats and I sponsored, and it was always a crowd pleaser.

For the last three years we'd leased a triple-decker cruise boat and partied hearty. We'd hired two DJs, opened three bars, and posted three roving photographers. Tonight the active Frats would be wearing our trademark red-and-white shirts, and this year we also sported red-and-white leather caps.

I pulled into the port parking area and popped a breath mint into my mouth. Tonight was my night. I had to either make it or break it with Sandie. Here I was deeply in love with the girl, and she treated me like a forgotten piece of furniture. I checked my face in the mirror. Good. No boogers in my nose or green shit stuck between my teeth.

Good.

I grabbed my jacket from the backseat, slipped on my shades, slapped on my hat, stepped out of my ride, and stepped into my future.

12

ROCK THE BOAT

Sparkle and I sat on the metal bench outside the cabin door and watched the snaking line of bodies as they boarded the party boat. The brothers looked cool and relaxed in their linen shorts and designer shirts, while the sistahs, supertrim, were screaming to be noticed in half yards of skimpy material.

As we waited in the heat for Guy to arrive with our free tickets, I sucked in my gut and wished that my 139 pounds of prime rib would magically turn into 125 pounds of ground turkey. Although I didn't look big, my hips and legs felt thick, and after comparing myself to the dozens of chef-salads-with-no-dressings who kept sauntering past, it was no wonder the sistah's self-image was shrinking!

Sparkle sat beside me as cool as the ocean as she sipped from a berry-flavored wine cooler. Girlfriend shined. Her hair was bumped into tiny spiral waves, and her golden complexion went well with her skimpy, stark white sailor dress. Men strolled past her with a grin and a wink, while the sistahs threw their lips out and rolled their eyes.

"Bitches are jealous!" she exclaimed happily and stood up to flirt with the next man in line. I laughed aloud and watched in amusement as Guy ran up the wooden plank and grabbed her around the waist, spun her around like a disco hustler, and thrust his tongue down her throat.

"Hold up, Daddy!" Sparkle laughed and pushed him away. "You paid for the tickets, not for me!"

We followed Guy onto the vessel, and he led us to our reserved booth. A rowdy group of sailors from the Norfolk Naval Base sat nearby, dressed in their Navy whites and drunker than Cuda Browne. They were harmless; most of them were barely over twenty-one and determined to get their drink on. This wasn't a BYOB affair, but their table was littered with several bottles of Mad Dog 20/20 and Wild Irish Rose.

Watching the young brothers guzzle the cheap wine made me thirsty. The cabin air was dry, and my throat felt parched. As if by magic or mental telepathy, Romulus appeared by my side.

"Hello, Sanderella. You look really nice this evening."

I glanced at him, and my eyes bucked open wide.

Dayum! Dude was cleaner than the Board of Health and didn't look half bad himself!

"Hi, Rom baby. How you feeling?"

The warmth of my greeting surprised the both of us, and an unexpected heat spread through my groin.

I shook it off.

"I'm feeling good, pretty lady. I'm feeling good." He smiled and held out his hand. "You wanna dance?"

I shook my head. Partying with Rom was definitely not what I had in mind for a funky good time. He was a persistent and patient man who made no bones about his feelings for me, but he was married. Although he was fine and I dug the way he carried himself, I was resolute in my stance.

"Then how about a drink?"

He looked at me with puppy-dog eyes.

Damn, he smelled good!

What the hell, I thought, and shrugged my shoulders. I was thirsty and he was harmless. Besides, the way he rolled my name around on his tongue made me shiver. No one else had ever managed to make the name Sanderella sound like anything other than what it was: homemade; but with his deep, sexy voice and his unusual pattern of speech, Rom made my name sound exotic and mysterious.

I looked at him again. Although he was a pest he was also a gentle-man, which was a refreshing change from a few of his Frats. I took great pleasure in disappointing that bunch. I figured they had a bet going on as to which one of them would hit the jackpot and get to "do" me first.

Rom waited.

That drink sure sounded good. I was so used to holding him at arm's distance that giving him the cold shoulder was almost second nature. But for some strange reason I didn't want to repel him to-night. He was a decent brother, and when I looked into his eyes, all I saw was adoration and sincerity. His nightly phone calls had turned into hilarious joke sessions, and I loved his sense of humor. Plus, it felt nice to know that some men appreciated a little rump roast every now and then, unlike some of the fine dudes who were out here parading around with their undernourished Olive Oyls.

"Well, actually, I'm dying of thirst. A Coke would be nice." I gig-gled like a nervous little girl and instantly clamped my lips tight.

Did that come out of me?

I allowed him to take my hand as he maneuvered through the crowd of dancers. He purchased my Coke, and we stood against a rail and watched the crowd as they grooved to the beat.

"The last time I stood this close to you and a Coke you wore it home in your shoe."

I turned toward him and laughed. "Yeah, I wanted to tell you about yourself that night!"

"I know. But I'm glad you didn't."

He gazed deeply into my eyes and smiled.

I shifted my glance and tried to take a sip from my glass. The frothy beverage sloshed over my trembling hand, and if he noticed he didn't comment.

The DJ pumped up the volume with a popular tune, and I began to rock a bit. Instead of asking me to dance again, Rom held my free hand and we sorta grooved in place as we moved our bodies slightly and enjoyed the beat.

"You look really nice, Sanderella."

"You already told me that."

He smiled again. "For a lady so nice, I had to say it twice."

I laughed. "Aaiight now, don't go M.C. Rommie-Rom on me!"

"Nah, baby. I meant that. I mean everything I tell you."

I extracted my hand from his grasp. Static pulses crackled where our fingers had meshed, and I felt an undeniable rush of desire. I was uncomfortable. This was getting way too deep for the sistah. He was a married man, and I wasn't about to rock the boat. But the brother was looking better by the minute. And smelling good, too.

It was time to *go*.

"Thanks for the Coke, Rom." I backed away from him quickly. "I'ma go and find Sparkle . . . ain't no telling what kind of trouble she's stirring up!" I excused myself and stepped off lively. I could feel him watching me as I left. His eyes were caressing my body, but somehow his gaze didn't feel vulgar. Actually, it felt damn good. Manly and appreciative.

I found Sparkle and pulled her out of some young dude's lap. The music rolled over us in thick waves as we stood along the edge of the dance floor and watched brothers copping copious feels as their partners contorted their bodies into complex pretzel shapes.

"Girl," I shouted, "that damn Romulus is playing me close enough to count my cavities!"

"He's nice, San—cute, too!"

"Forget that!" I waved my hand and sucked hard on my teeth. "Monkeys are cute. The man's married with children, and I ain't nobody's home wrecker!"

Sparkle's bright grin disappeared. "Home wrecker? What damn home? If his wife wanted him at home, she shoulda kept his foine ass there!" She tossed her curls. "How can you wreck something that's already broken?"

"No, Sparkle. I think *he* steps out on *her*. I hope he doesn't think he's gonna get with me, because if so, he's got about twenty more thinks coming! And as much as I miss my own, I'm not about to ruin the lives of anybody's innocent children."

"Girlfriend," Sparkle drawled with a bitchy twist to her lips, "I'm sorry to have to tell you this, but you ain't got shit to do with that.

Your pussy *ain't that good*! If he leaves his wife, it's because he wants to leave. Anytime a good man walks away from his marriage, it's because he went out and bought himself some walking shoes and had enough balls to put 'em on and step!"

"Well, whatever." I shook my head. "I'm not down with O-P-P. I'm having too much fun playing games with his Phi Nupes! Besides," I tried to make her laugh, "did you see his head? It's *big*! Looks like a damn bowling ball! Nah—a tater. Yeah, that boy looks just like Mr. Potater Head!"

"Okay, Sandie." Sparkle's tone was dry. "You ain't fooling nobody but *you*. Rom's either forever calling you or he's up in your face wanting to hand-feed you Red Lobster. You know a decent brother when you smell one, so stop playing games with the man. If you don't like him, then quit showing him your teeth and show him your ass! Humph, you need to go on and give up a little bit of that trim. I know I would."

"Then you give him some."

"Nah, baby." She danced away from me. "Rom's not my type. Too nice. Bad enough I have to put up with Guy's little tiny pee-pee! Poking me like I'm a piñata and he's desperate for sweets!"

Sparkle was a tactless mess, but I was growing to love her. And she was right. Rom stayed on me constantly. I had to give bruh-man his propers; he was determined. And *fine*. I made my way to the ladies' room and rinsed the syrupy cola from my left hand.

The hand that Rom had held? Well, I left that one dry.

"So, which one do you like best?" I came up behind her as she studied the Bold Black Art display. Crowds of people milled around the foyer of the second-level dance area as they examined the vast display of artwork, jewelry, and other African-American artifacts.

Sandie looked scrumptious. The sexy red short set she wore revealed the puff of her cleavage and the funk in her thighs.

"I like this one," she said finally. "Yeah, this one right here."

She'd chosen a print of two young boys, the older giving the younger a piggyback ride. The boys were perched under a bright blue sky in a field of blossoming wheat. Both of their young faces smiled broadly at the camera. The smaller child had the skin of a Hershey's bar, smooth and rich dark chocolate. The older boy's complexion reminded me of the inside of a Reese's Peanut Butter Cup. The caption on the bottom read, *He's My Brother.*

I watched Sandie as she gazed at the print with a sad little smile on her face. "They remind me of my sons. And of my brother." She turned away.

I promptly pulled out my wallet and purchased it. I rolled the print up and handed it to her, then I took her arm and led her inside to the dance area. I found an empty table right next to the dance floor. Sandie smoked and I joked while we watched Sparkle out on the floor doing the rump-shaker with her spacious moneymaker.

Whenever I looked at Sandie, she looked away. I felt a new tension between us. Something that hadn't been there the last time we'd been together a week ago on our two-mile run. Something sexual. Instead of being nonchalant and cool, Sandie seemed a little nervous. Coy maybe. The way women act when they're around a man they wouldn't mind getting with. My mojo was working. I was getting closer.

"How'd your photo come out?" I asked. I'd hooked her up with an official photograph that she needed for her OCS packet. She'd told me her final board was convening in two weeks, and I offered to help her tie up some loose ends. A good friend of mine ran the Training and Audiovisual Service Center, and he did me a solid by expediting her request.

"The photo came out great! Thanks a lot, Rom. I really appreciate you looking out for me. Now, do you know anyone who sits on the structured interview board?"

Although she'd already been selected for a class date, each officer candidate had to pass a structured interview; an hour-long question-and-answer session where a panel of four officers grilled a prospective candidate and graded her based on the accuracy and timeliness of her responses. These grades were sent up to Headquarters, Department of the Army as part of the candidate's official package. This was a heavily weighted interview because it was the only personal contact the board could use as a measuring tool. Everything else came in the form of a photo or a report. I'd sat through a similar inquisition when I'd applied for Warrant Officer School, and it was tough.

I smiled. "As a matter of fact, I do. Major Jake Mitchell and Captain Buel Royster sit on that board, and they both happen to be running buddies of mine. Don't worry, Sanderella, I'll take good care of you."

Her face lit up like a bonfire.

"Dagg, Rom! You're always coming through for me, I—"

"Wanna dance, baby?"

Dissing my rap, Vickers Anderson scooped Sandie out of her seat and pulled her into his long arms. I felt my hackles rise. Vic the Dick, star of the base hoop team, had me by at least three inches, but I was ready to go to his ass!

"Quit, Vic," Sandie laughed as he bent over and nuzzled her neck. "C'mon, I'll dance with you, teddy bear. I'm sure Rom won't mind." She looked at me and grinned. "You don't mind, do you, Rom?"

I stood up. "Hell yeah, I mind!"

Her eyes narrowed. "Well, you don't have no business minding! If you wanted to dance with somebody, you should have brought your wife out with you!"

Vickers, that waterhead son of a bitch, shot me a Phi Nupe sign and danced off with my baby snuggled in his monkey-ass arms. I was through. Not mad, just through. Her words revealed her true feelings, and the truth really hurt. I could've kicked myself up the ass for even thinking Sandie might want me. I mean, what the hell could I offer her? What made me think a sister like her would be interested in a man like me? I shook my head and headed back outside. Pain filled my chest, and I actually wanted to cry.

I knew I was made to love her, if only she would let me! It wasn't my fault that Lou had gotten pregnant! That she had refused to get an abortion. I had to marry her and I had to stay with her. Didn't I? My name is Romulus *not* Solomon!

I am not my daddy; I am a true fuckin' king!

A king who did what a king had to do!

I felt sick. The mistakes I'd made in my past were haunting my present and denying me a future. Knocking dancers out of my path, I rushed outside and into the cool night air. From my position at the rail the sea looked inviting, all-knowing. For a split second I wanted to either fall out on the floor and cry like a baby or throw myself overboard and let the waves have their way.

But I'm a king.

I zipped my jacket against the cool breeze and took a seat on a wrought-iron bench; then I lay my head back against the railing and closed my eyes. Deep inside, I cried. Invisible tears of love.

It was a good thing Sandie didn't want me. All the love I had bottled up inside of me would've drowned her little ass! I took a deep breath and held it. Then another, and then another. I'd be damned if I was gonna sit out here and steam just because Sandie was inside having a good time with another man, but that's exactly what seemed to be happening. I swallowed a groan and screwed my eyes closed against the salt of my own tears. I took in a huge breath and held it as long as I could.

Hours passed.

My lungs threatened to burst; yet I refused to breathe. Bright dancing yellow lights flashed across the insides of my eyelids, but I denied myself a breath. A weighty fullness settled against my chest. I refused to breathe. It moved down into my lap and seemed to snuggle there. I deprived myself of life-sustaining oxygen. A weight was upon me. Warm and heavy.

Is this what death felt like?

"Hey, Big Daddy!"

My eyes flew open.

I exhaled in a great rush and sucked in an eternity of air. Dizzily, I peered into the face that was two inches from my own. Her legs were thrown across my thighs as she sat side-straddle across my lap. She pressed her forehead to mine and smiled. Instinctively, my arms closed around her warm body. I don't know who moved first, but in the next instant my lips were greedily devouring hers. Her mouth opened to mine.

Goddamn, I was hungry.

I cried.

My tears were of joy, and as the waves lapped gently against the sides of the boat, I kissed Sanderella, the queen of my heart. And wonder of all wonders, believe it or not, she kissed me back!

13

DIDN'T I BLOW YOUR
MIND THIS TIME?

Never say what you'll never do," Mama Ceal had once cautioned me, "because I know this monkey who swore he wouldn't eat nothing but bananas. Don't you know hard times came and that sucker ate some red-hot peppers?"

I wasn't down to eating peppers yet, but I wasn't far from it. For some strange reason I'd felt like crap after screaming on Rom about his wife. I mean, damn! He was a married man; didn't he have any shame? Don't get me wrong: I'd taken a few laps around the wrong block a time or two, but I'd promised myself I'd never go that route again. Still, the expression on his face made me feel terrible. He looked like I'd actually hit him. Straight up knocked his funk sack loose when I danced off wrapped in Vickers's arms.

"You told his ass, baby." Vickers licked my earlobe and laughed as we watched Rom stride out of the cabin. Yeah, I'd told him all right, but as soon as those evil words were out of my mouth—as truthful as they were—I felt just like a pile of doo-doo.

The metallic strobe lights flickered and flashed as they illuminated the hundreds of gyrating bodies swirling on the dance floor. The DJ switched grooves and played the Electric Slide. I squirmed out of his Vic's grasp and left him to fend for himself as the swell of dancers added their own flavor to the black folks' version of a line dance. Adrenaline flowed swiftly through my veins, as I made my way across the crowded dance floor and over to the exit. I searched the open deck for a sign of Rom, as I hugged myself against the chill in the night air.

There were couples galore lounging on the partitioned deck; some kissed in quiet corners, others cuddled closely under the bright moonlight. I found Rom at the far end of the boat where he sat alone on a wrought-iron bench. He looked peaceful and serene, his eyes closed, long lashes nearly touching his cheeks, his sleek head lolled back gently against the boat's railing. He seemed oblivious to the world as I stared down into his handsome face, and I wasn't sure if he was meditating, contemplating, or just plain perpetrating, but a pigeon could have taken refuge on him because he was as still as a statue.

Just when I was about to make my presence known by stomping my foot and hollering "Boo!" I got a much better idea. Quickly, and before I could lose my nerve, I threw both my ham hocks across his strong thighs and snuggled down completely into his lap.

I was a perfect fit!

Rom remained so still that I thought he might be in a coma, so I leaned into him and whispered, "Hey, Big Daddy!" and that's when all hell broke loose. Before I knew it those pretty soup coolers of his were all over mine, and I couldn't help but open my mouth for more. The strength of his tongue played electrifying games with my lips, and in five seconds flat my beasts began to roar and moisture filled the crotch of my Victoria's Secret panties. The stiffness of his erection probed at my eager thigh, and to my dismay he quickly shifted my position, breaking the delightful contact. Hot damn! I was disappointed, because this was the closest I'd been to anything hard, strong, and male in a very long time!

"Sandie," he moaned, and pulled away from me as he ran his strong hands over my back and up my arms. I could still feel the gentle touch of his lips, taste the sweet nectar of his tongue. His eyes met mine. "We need to talk. I need you to understand my situation, to know what's in my heart."

I was all ears.

Rom and I stayed on that little bench for the rest of the night, and when we walked off that boat three hours later, it was hand in hand with a mellow understanding.

Now I stood in the middle of my cluttered barracks room feeling kind of stupid for bending on my principles and bringing a married man home with me. I had no idea what to do next.

"Relax, Sandie. Everything's okay."

He stared down at me with a strange look on his face. A mixture of happiness and wonder. Like he couldn't believe he was actually where he was, and with who he was with.

Didn't I blow your mind this time?

"You can sit on the bed, Rom," I offered awkwardly. The only other place for him to sit was the floor. He put his hat on my dresser and took off his jacket and his shoes. Then he stretched out lengthwise on my bed, his feet crossed at the ankles and his head resting on a mound of fluffy pink pillows. He patted the bed next to him and indicated that I should join him. I kicked off my shoes and sniffed the air for signs of foot odor—his, not mine—and then lay down gingerly next to him.

I barely touched him at all on the twin bed. Instead I waited for him to put his arms around me, or at least kiss me again and make me feel that electricity between my legs, but he simply closed his eyes and breathed deeply. In less than two minutes he was snoring lightly, fast asleep.

Well, I'll be damned! After my long, hard, self-imposed drought, I'd finally lured a choice Mandingo warrior to my bed, and he goes out before the lights do! I turned over on my left side and propped my head up on a pillow, then curled my legs close to my body in the fetal position and tooted out my neglected boomkus in his direction.

Let him see what he's missing when he wakes up!

Two seconds later I joined the king in my dreams.

I opened my eyes slowly so as not to kill the fantasy I'd been floating in, but as soon as I saw the frilly pink curtains and the kindergarten drawings Scotch-taped to the walls, I knew my dream had been for real. I was actually lying in bed with Sandie. Her warm body was snuggled spoon fashion against mine; her thick female scent hung heavy in the air. In a flash old Mr. Bobo was up and at 'em. I moved away from her and cautiously adjusted his position in my briefs. Mr. Bobo could just lay his greedy ass on down because wasn't none of that shit happening in here today!

This was my dream opportunity, and I wasn't about to ruin it with a play for quick-fast sex. Nah, I wanted to chill with this lady. I planned to take it real slow and easy. I looked down at Sandie's sleeping form, and for the first time I was able to study her totally unchallenged. Her back was to me, and she slept balled up like a baby, her rhythmic breathing causing her body to gently swell and fall. I glanced at her feet and smiled. Yes! Not only were they clean and unscarred, she had some pretty red polish on her short lil' toes.

I let my eyes roam freely over the playground of her feminine physique, and damn was I mesmerized. Sandie was a shapely woman; big thighs and calves set off her slim ankles and trim hips. She didn't look as though three babies had come from her tight body, but there was a definite womanish plumpness about her.

All woman.

I wanted to stick out my tongue and pant like a dog.

Instead, I slid from the bed and stood up to stretch my frame. I ran my hand over my face and dug a few goobers from the corners of my eyes. I yawned. My mouth tasted like shit, and my tongue had somehow sprouted a five o'clock shadow.

I didn't want to awaken her yet, so I slipped into my shoes and grabbed my jacket from the foot of the bed. I left my hat on the dresser and quietly slipped from her room, but not before looking down at her sleeping form and whispering, "She's mine, she's mine! Hot damn, the big-leg girl is mine!"

I jogged across the street to the military shopping center with the morning breeze rushing over my smiling face. I felt pumped, ready to take to the sky on a natural high! So what if I had on these hard-ass brogans? I felt like running, sprinting. But today the track would have to wait. I had better things on my agenda.

Ten minutes later I walked back carrying two shopping bags in my hands and a whistle in my heart. Outside of Sandie's door, I hesitated. What if she felt differently now that the sun was up? You know females go through a lot of crazy changes, and maybe after sleeping on things she'd changed her mind about being with me.

Panic snatched at my heart.

Oh well, I thought as I set the heaviest bag on the ground. I pumped myself up with false bravado. I'm just going to have to take that chance! I knocked loudly on the door three times and waited.

And waited.

I knocked again, even harder. I stretched the knock out longer. And longer. Like a drum roll. I stared at the door like a chump and just as my false bravado did a downward slide toward my shiny new shoes, it swung open.

"Hi," Sandie said sleepily. She looked great in yesterday's clothes, even with one side of her hair plastered flat against her head.

"Good morning," I answered and stifled a huge sigh of relief. I handed her the single red rose I'd picked up from the store.

"Thanks." She smiled. "It's beautiful."

And so was she. She stepped back to let me in, and that's when she noticed both the shopping bag on the ground and the one I held in my hand.

"Dagg. What did you do? Go grocery shopping?"

"Nah, baby, I didn't make groceries. I just picked up a little lunch."

I spread the contents of the bags out on the floor of her tiny room and stepped back to survey the items. I'd bought a six-pack of Heineken for me, a six-pack of tropical-flavored wine coolers for her, a pack of smoked turkey slices, a hunk of Swiss cheese, a small jar of deli mustard, a jar of kosher pickles, some seedless green grapes, a bunch of ripe bananas, and a bag of poppy-seeded kaiser rolls. The second shopping bag contained a small bag of ice, a toothbrush, some breath mints, and at the last minute I'd tossed in a pack of olive-drab Army-issue drawers. I was set.

I excused myself and ran outside to my car and pulled a small beer cooler from the trunk. I dumped out a few bottles of spring water and saw that it was just large enough to hold all of our picnic items. I gave my rims a once over with a dry cloth and popped open a new can of solid air freshener. When I reentered her room, Sandie was talking quietly into the telephone receiver, and from the pain etched on her face and the anguished tone of her voice, I could tell it wasn't a social call.

"Please, Maurice," she whimpered. "We can't keep going through this! It could never work. Remember? We've already tried a thousand times." She paced around the room with thick-smelling energy rolling from her in waves. Suddenly she stopped and closed her eyes, her hands clutching her stomach. A low groan escaped her lips. "I can't, Maurice . . . you've said all of this before," she breathed. The tears dripped from her chin. "I just can't."

I had no idea who Maurice was, but as I listened to Sandie's monologue, I felt like a fly on the wall. Privy to their most intimate thoughts and feelings. A witness to their pain. I busied myself by pulling the covers up neatly to the top of her bed, then I turned on the TV and packed up the cooler. A minute later Sandie ended the call by placing the receiver gently in its cradle. When she turned toward me, her eyes searched the floor.

She bit her lip. "I'm sorry, Rom. Sorry you had to hear all that."

In the closeness of the tiny room her emotions took up all the air and her essence was heightened. I did my best to keep my eyes to myself as she turned her back on me and sifted through her underwear drawer, pulling out all kinds of silky-looking panties and hooter holders. Since I hadn't heard the entire conversation, I had no idea what was being demanded of her, other than her love, but whatever he said that caused her eyes to fill with tears ripped at my heart and left it bleeding. I tried to lighten the mood.

"Nice picture." I pointed to an eight-by-ten glossy of Sandie and a small girl. I figured the child to be her daughter, Jamillah. The child's skin was a few shades lighter than Sandie's, but they had the same high forehead and slanted eyes, and a hint of Sandie's humor peeked from her daughter's smile. "Do you have any pictures of your boys?"

"Here." She reached across me and picked up a black-framed photo I hadn't noticed before. It was a close-up of a light-skinned brother with wavy hair and wide green eyes. He wore a white Nike crew shirt, and pressed closely to each of his cheeks was a smiling little boy, each dressed in identical white shirts; one with skin of rich chocolate, the other with the same skin tone and green eyes of the man I presumed to be his father. The man had his arms around the shoulders of both of the boys, and from the way their cheeks smashed his and the looks of glee that burst like sunshine from the three of them, I figured it must have been a real happy time in their lives.

I was jealous.

Sandie watched closely as I studied the photo, then reached out and took it from my hand and placed it back on her nightstand. "Maurice," she said miserably, and blew a sheen of dust from the glass. "My ex. That was him on the phone." She tapped the forehead of the handsome dark boy with eyes like marbles. "Kharim." Then she stroked the face of the other boy, a ring of red, perhaps from Kool-Aid or an Italian ice, surrounded his smile and streaked his chin. "Hanif."

"That must have been a good day. At least your boys look happy," I offered.

A wistful smile curled her lips as she gazed at the image of her children. "Yeah, they were happy. Maurice wasn't good for much, but he was a great father. This picture was taken on the Fourth of July at his mother's house." She sat down next to me and tucked her feet beneath her. "None of my children have the same father," she admitted.

"Really?"

She nodded. "Jamillah was almost three when I married Maurice. And like my father, Maurice doesn't play favorites when it comes down to kids. That's my standard." She looked at me pointedly. "That's probably what attracted me to him. He loved Jamillah enough to claim her as his own, so we changed her last name to Coffee."

My face must have revealed my confusion as my eyes strayed back to the dark-skinned little boy in the photo. She touched my hand.

"Maurice and I had been separated for six months when I got pregnant with Hanif. We got back together shortly afterward and he claimed Hanif as his own. Even though Kharim is his only natural child, he loved them all equally and treated them all the same. Still does, and that's why it breaks my heart each time he calls me begging to be a family again and I have to refuse. Especially when I know how badly my children need a man like him in their lives."

She covered her mouth with her hand, her eyes wide.

"Damn! I'm putting my business out there rather thickly, huh?"

I shook my head vigorously. "Nah, baby, no, no, no." I leaned over and kissed her cheek. "Not at all. I think you're a beautifully strong black woman, and I bet you're a terrific mother." I motioned toward Maurice's smiling face. "And I think my brother here is one hell of a man." I chuckled. "He must have been a Superman, a Superdad, and a Superhusband! So why did you leave him?"

Sandie shifted her position, swung her legs around, and dangled them from the edge of the bed. She ran her fingers through her curls and pursed her lips, and once again a reflective look clouded her eyes. "Maurice was good at a lot of things. My kids definitely benefited from having him in their lives, and for the most part he treated me with love and respect." She sighed and then tried to smile. "But I could never go back to him. The man is a klepto. A straight-up thief. It was never my intention or aim in life to become a single parent and raise my kids alone, but sometimes no matter how good someone is to you, there are certain things a woman just can't tolerate."

Sandie patted the bed around her, searching for the remote control. Her mood had turned pensive once again, and she held her head down in an attempt to hide the pain pouring from her eyes. Using my thumb, I smoothed her tears and dried them gently, and out of nowhere a tune filled my heart and begged to burst from me. I closed my eyes and hummed softly, then opened my mouth and sang:

> Please don't weep . . . Sandie, dry your eyes,
> Rom is here, there's no need to cry.
>
> Baby let me keep you close, wrapped in my arms,
> Where you'll be safe . . . away from harm.
>
> I wanna know all of your fears
> I'll protect you, girl, you're safe right here.
>
> He can't love you right, the way I can,
> Oh sweet Sandie . . . let me be your man.
>
> I hate to see those tears running down your face,
> With my love there'd never be a trace
> Of misery and sadness
> Baby, I can help you stop this madness
>
> I would never make you cry,
> You don't have to put up with his lies,
> When I can heal your pain inside . . .
>
> I'll make you feel so right . . . so right

When I reopened my eyes, Sandie stood staring at me. Her head was tilted to one side, and there was a strange but serene smile on her lips. Her eyes were still wet, but now they shined radiantly. I coughed, embarrassed by the volume of raw emotion I'd just laid upon her, and said, "I'm a musician. I play the electric keyboard and thangs, and sometimes I compose a few lyrics here and there. I hope

I didn't take you anyplace you didn't want to go. I just wanted to share that with you."

Sweet Sandie smiled, then stepped away from me and crossed the room. She bent and took a pair of pink flip-flops from the bottom of her wall locker, then looked over her shoulder and asked, "Share something else with me?"

"Anything." I meant it, too.

"How long do you plan to stay married?"

"Not long, baby," I promised, as I crossed the room in one stride and pulled her into my arms. "Not long."

She rested her head against my chest and allowed me to hold her for a few moments. Then she gave me a small smile, gathered a small bundle, and left the room. The bathroom was a communal barracks-type joint right next door, and it took her damned near forever to get back, but when she did . . . let's just say my baby was well worth the wait.

She stepped inside the room, bringing with her a ray of sunshine and a gentle cloud of delicate perfume. She wore a pair of cutoff blue-jean shorts and a white T-shirt with some type of black body hugger showing underneath it. Those pretty feet of hers were perched in a pair of black leather sandals, and I swear, I could've popped that big toe in my mouth and swallowed it whole!

She showed me to the men's latrine, and I took my toothbrush and new drawers, her borrowed towel, toothpaste, and soap, and went on in there and did the personal hygiene thing.

The sky was sun filled and powder blue as we drove down to peaceful Virginia Beach. We walked along the shore's edge: Sandie, barefoot, with sand tickling her toes as she carried her sandals in her hand; me, jacking up my Stacys, and happy as hell as I carried the cooler and stared at her with wonder and awe.

On a subtle bend near a cove, I found the perfect spot and we lay in the silky-soft sand. As the wind danced tiny circles around us, I broke bread with Sandie, popping bits of grapes and mashed bananas into her mouth as she laughed and smiled and promised me the world with her eyes. As good as I felt, I couldn't help but think about my future. I'd never before stayed out a whole night without calling Lou, and I knew she was probably having a fit. But I didn't care. My days with her were numbered. As I laughed and chased Sandie down the warm, peaceful beach, I hoped and prayed my days with her would be endless.

14

HOT FUN IN THE SUMMERTIME

Girls are fast," Mama used to say. "And hot, too."

Sho' you're right, Mama! I screamed inside.

The sistah was hot all right, and not just from the sun. I sat cross-legged in the sand with Rom's head resting in my lap. I leaned over and dangled both of the beasts in his upturned face, then slowly and deliciously guided my throbbing nipples into his mouth. Damn! He knew just how to lick them. Like they were sweet black plums. Only juicier.

A gentle breeze washed over us, doing very little to cool the sheen of perspiration clinging to my skin. I'd stripped out of my shorts and T-shirt when I decided to stick my feet in and test the water, and now I wore only my black bodysuit with my wicked beasts spilling out over the top.

Rom had found a secluded spot near the edge of the shore and what had started out as a little light kissing had quickly turned into something else. I moaned as his tongue made wet, lazy circles around my nipples. He nibbled and sucked until I thought I would scream and then suddenly . . . he stopped.

What? I wanted to yell. *Get your tongue back over here!*

He sat up.

I lay back with my chest heaving from desire and let him get a real good look at my insatiable beasts. Pushed up over the top of my bodysuit, they looked like floating brown coconuts with sweet blackberry tips.

"Sandie . . ." He covered his erection and avoided my eyes. "I don't want to rush you into anything. I have a lot of respect for you, and I'd never want you to think that I only wanted you for sex."

I stood up and pushed my tetas back inside of my bra.

"I'm willing to wait," he said, his eyes glued to my thighs.

I pulled the bodysuit down and stepped totally out of it. Bruh-man developed a "hundred-yard stare."

"I know I'll have to prove my love to you, and I swear I will. . . ."

My royal purple Victoria's Secret panty and bra set stood out starkly against my ebony skin.

"I want you to know that I feel good just being here with you. Just courting you. I don't even have to touch you, I mean. . . ."

I took off my bra (he'd already seen the goods) and stepped out of my panties.

His eyes were on the prize.

"I mean . . . I mean . . . *goddamn*, baby, I don't know *what* I mean!"

I stood there on the near-deserted beach, naked and reveling in the hot sun that tickled my bare skin and stoked the boiling inferno that blazed between my legs. I felt beautiful. Supersexual. Totally confident in my wanton decision to give myself to this wonderfully kind black man.

Rom licked his lips and crawled toward me on all fours. I parted my thighs, and he buried his head in my treasure. Moaning deeply, I allowed him to brace me with his strong arms as he plunged his lips and tongue deeply into my hollow of love. My knees were like rubber. He palmed the thickness of my ass with both hands. I grabbed hold of that sexy bald head of his and shamelessly pumped away at his slippery face. Lawd ha' mercy, this man was just as good as Antoine. No—uh-uh! He was even better! My body exploded, and I went limp.

My breasts tingled like slow-moving wind chimes, and I cupped them in my hands. It had been far too long since I'd been with a man, and that was just an appetizer. I prayed he wouldn't think I was some sort of sex-crazed slut, but there was no way in hell I was letting him go without getting my head slammed!

Rom lowered me gently down to the soft sand, and it was his turn to stand up and strip. His body was long and lean, a perfect runner's physique. I stared in awe as he unbuttoned his shirt and revealed his hairy chest. Sexy, sexy, *sexy!* My eyes dropped lower, and I glimpsed his erection as it struggled to burst forth through the fabric of his pants. Have mercy! I was afraid of what would happen if he freed it!

"Baby . . . ," Rom said softly, "I have someone I want you to meet." Slowly, he unzipped his pants. "Sandie," he said as he reached inside of his briefs and carefully extracted his family jewels, "this is Mr. Bobo. And he's all yours."

Out jumped a Florida blacksnake, and my first mind told me to get up and run! Bruh-man had put the *J* in Johnson! I wanted to cry! It was *huge*. And *damn*, was it pretty!

Slowly he advanced toward me, barely able to control the beautiful black serpent that leaped and lurched as it struggled to escape his hands. My mouth filled with water, and greedily, I licked my lips. Mr. Bobo looked powerfully strong, and a road map of veins ran haphazardly along its length. But when the eye on that thang winked at me—honey, I knew I was in *deep* trouble. I wasn't sure if my body could accommodate the length and girth of the king's offerings, but I was game to die trying.

Romulus Caesar was a king in every sense of the word.

Mister had skills. *And* stamina!

During the next thirty minutes he gave me three royal orgasms using just his tongue, his hands, and the tip of that winking eye!

Remember when I told you that I'd been around? Well, Rom showed the sistah that you *can* teach an old dog a few new tricks! By the time he actually laid that royal blessing deeply between my quivering thighs, I was already covered in sweat from head to toe and screaming out his name.

15

AIN'T NO WOMAN
LIKE THE ONE I GOT

I told Lou I was leaving her. Said I wanted a divorce. After just one taste of Sandie's loving, I didn't ever want to lay down with another woman. So I went straight home and told her. Just came right out and said it was over.

"I'm leaving, Lou. I'm moving out."

My girl flipped like a pancake.

"What the *fuck*?" Her chest heaved and lurched. The devil-red bodysuit she wore was violent against her tough pale skin. Even in the heat of battle I couldn't help remembering how sexy the color red looked pressed deliciously against Sandie's nutmeg curves.

"Moving where?" she hissed. "With who?"

I reached under the sink and found my daddy's brass tumbler, then moved into the foyer. Lou followed me, her bare feet grazing the back of my shoes.

"Answer me, goddammit! Where the hell are you going? Who the fuck do you think you are?"

I opened the hall closet and yanked a few shirts from their hangers. I told her, "Lou, for the first time in years I know who I am and where I'm going."

She searched my eyes, and I let my determination show. She switched tactics.

"Please, baby, please . . . I know things have been a little rough lately. But, Rom, we've been through worse shit than this before," she said, sobbing.

Two-week-old laundry sat piled on the sofa, pressed into wrinkles and begging to be folded. I sorted through the mound as best I could, grabbed a few of my things, and began shoving them into a bag.

Lou clutched my hands and begged, "I swear I'll change, Rom. I'll make things right between us again!"

I stared at her. Right again? Who was she kidding? Things hadn't been right between us since the day we met! I didn't dare remind her of that minor fact, so I moved into the bedroom and continued throwing my gear into boxes, garbage bags, and anything else I could get my hands on.

"Please, Rom, please!" Lou grabbed me around the waist and held on tight. She squeezed briefly, then dropped to her knees and pressed her tear-streaked face into my trousers before sliding to the floor, where she bear-hugged my right ankle.

"C'mon, Lou," I said quietly. I limp-dragged my leg across the floor with all ninety pounds of her resting atop my foot. "Don't act like this." For someone who didn't want me around, who couldn't stand my touch, my tone, or my 'tude, she was sure as hell hanging on to me like I was the last fucking Mohegan!

"But I *love* you! I *need* you!" She jumped from the floor and rushed over to the closet. She lifted a thirty-gallon Hefty Cinch Sak and dumped out its contents. My underwear and socks spilled out onto the floor. "Don't go nowhere, baby! Don't you go nowhere! I'ma do right. I swear. *I'll do right!*"

I almost chuckled. Lou was singing a song from En Vogue. The one where that fine big-booty sister belts out their hit single, "Baby Don't Go."

Lou's eyes were hopeful as she wiped snot from her nose with the back of her hand. She closed the gap between us, kicking clothes and scattering my belongings across the floor. "Here," she breathed. "Here, honey. I know what you want." She grabbed my ass with both hands and pulled me in, her body pressed tightly to mine. Then she straddled my leg and gyrated her pelvis in short, hard movements, sliding her thin crotch up and down my thigh and humping like a bitch in a brothel. With her tongue stuck between her teeth, she stared at me with glazed eyes and panted, "I know what's wrong. You want your stuff, right? Well here is your *stuff*, baby! How are you gonna go somewhere and leave your stuff?"

I did chuckle then. After floating on top of Sandie's curves of softness, Lou's body felt dry and brittle, all harsh angles and spiny twigs. I swear I felt her pubic bones popping and cracking like the snap of fresh string beans.

I grabbed her upper arms and pushed her away gently. My thigh felt bruised and sore. "Don't do this, Lou. Please. It's not fair to either one of us."

"Baby, no," she whimpered. Her eyes and nose were the exact same shade of red as her shirt.

I'd promised Sandie the world, and I meant to deliver it, but for the life of me I couldn't understand my wife. For more than ten years—eight years of marriage and two years before—she'd cut me up, down, and sideways. Her words were lethal weapons: booby traps and punji sticks, claymore mines and Bouncing Bettys, always posed to flank me with a surprise attack and leave me for dead. I'd lived a pitiful semi-existence for years, and now that I had sunshine in my life, she wanted to act like she'd really loved me all along. But I wasn't going for it. Maybe having me around to rag was better than ragging on herself.

I picked up my shirts and pushed my drawers back inside the Cinch Sak, then I grabbed a large Air Force flight bag I'd brought back from Korea and started toward the door. "I'm leaving, Lou. There's two hundred dollars in my checking account. The bills are paid; use it any way you need to. There'll be more deposited in there on my next payday. If you need me, you can call me at work or page me." I put my hand on the doorknob.

Lou played trump.

"But what about the boys?"

My lungs almost collapsed.

I'd thought things through as carefully as I could, but no matter how I sliced it, my boys still came up losers. "C'mon, Lou. I'll still take care of y'all." There was a tremor in my voice. "I'll see the kids as much as I can; I'll still be a part of their lives. . . . I just can't live here anymore. I'm sorry," I whispered.

"Baby," she wailed pitifully, "don't you love us anymore?"

I set my bags down and took her hands in mine.

"It's not you, Lou. It's me. We've had some good times, but for so long now they've all been in the past." A tear slipped from my eye. I hugged her tightly for a brief moment, then loosened my grip. "I have to leave for *me*, Lou. For *me*."

Her face twisted into a grotesque mask as she picked up a pair of socks and threw them at me. "It's always you, *you*, YOU! When the hell are you gonna think about someone other than your fuckin' self?"

I didn't answer. I picked up my bags and started out the door. I wanted to turn back and scream at her, Thinking about myself? This is the first goddamn thing I've done for myself in over ten years! It had always been her and the kids, her and the twins—her, her, her. *Never* me. That's what happens when you're a giver living too long with a taker. You give until you can give no more, and they take until there's no more to be had.

But this time I was doing something for *self*. Something that made *Romulus Caesar* happy.

I closed the door quietly and left.

I stood at the front desk of the ordnance shop and felt liberated. Like a man who had just been released after a long stint in the county jail. I picked up the telephone with trembling hands. Hands unused to such freedom. "Hey, baby," I spoke softly and cradled the receiver close to my mouth. I didn't want the guys in the shop to overhear me. I'd borrowed the unit's military truck to transport my few things, and the boys were getting curious and suspicious. "I'll be a little late, but I'm coming, baby. Big Daddy is on his way."

"Okay." Sandie's voice was warm and textured like black velvet. "That's cool. I'll be right here, so take your time."

I stared at the receiver, still holding it in my hand.

Ain't no woman like the one I got!

I was amazed. This would take some getting used to. My baby had such pleasantry in her voice. No anger, no suspicion, and not a trace of a funky-cold-medina disposition. That's why I loved this girl! She took everything in stride; she had a sweet personality and an even temperament, not like those damned mood swings Lou suffered from.

I hung up the telephone with a whistle in my heart. I'd be a little late, but I'd still be right on time. For the first time in years I felt nervous butterflies dancing in my groin. I pictured sunny mornings and insatiable midnights, the endless days in between filled with good loving and hearty laughter. I pictured myself smiling, my inner being at peace, my mind finally at ease. I saw myself standing tall and looking good. Planning my future, our future. Our wedding. I pictured my queen sitting beside me on our throne. Our children, all five of them, with skin tones in various shades of ebony, gathered at our feet. I saw myself happy and satisfied. I saw Mr. Bobo smiling.

Grinning like a motherfucker.

'Cause I was moving in with Sanderella!

16

YOU DOWN WIT' O-P-P?

Romulus, Romulus, Romulus!

That man. I just couldn't stop saying his name. Somehow, in a moment of pure wanting, I allowed dude to break through the prison of my doubt and invade my unguarded soul. At first I tried to pretend that we were simply knocking boots. You know—having fun and making soup. But after a while it was painfully obvious that the sistah had gone and gotten herself hooked and reeled, just like a fish.

Rom told me all about Lou. How she performed like Angela Bassett the day he left her. I told him Lou was so close to white he was lucky she didn't faint on him and crack her head open on the floor and fall into a coma. If that mess happened, he'd never be free!

For a while I was ashamed to be seen with Rom in public. My guilty conscious had me thinking folks were staring at us and whispering, "You down wit' O-P-P? Yeah, you know Sandie!" I soon found out that Rom and Lou didn't travel in the same circles. They had very few friends in common. Lou hung around with a bunch of white girls, and I guess since she was dirty yellow, shaped like Barbie, and had hair like Rapunzel, she was the next best thing to being white.

But forget about Lou. It wasn't about her. It was all about me. For once my whole world looked beautiful. Colors were more vivid; laughter more vibrant; touch, taste, and smell were magnified beyond belief. According to Sparkle, I had that glow women get when they're in love and getting their heads slammed good every night!

Shortly after moving into my room, Rom made me a solemn promise. "Sandie, sweet lady, I'm gonna make you fall in love with me," he said, then kissed the palms of my hands and slipped his tongue in and out between my fingers and whispered,

> I promise to do for you
> Whatever it is you want me to
> 'Cause I'm just that deep in love with you
>
> I'll pay the price for you
> If it means I can keep on loving you
> 'Cause I wanna make you love me too
>
> Girl with you I'm inspired
> And I wanna take you higher
> I'm sending love in your direction
> Showing all my affection
>
> Yeah, it's you that I treasure
> Of this I can assure
> I promise to make you love me
> Yes I will! You know I will!

And he was true to his word.

We shared romantic dinners at intimate restaurants. He washed my feet in the tepid waters of Lake Lorraine. We enjoyed late movies and smoky jazz clubs. We took long drives in the country, and Rom basked in the beauty of nature as I nodded off, inebriated from half a bottle of peach wine cooler. And we took long walks along the Chesapeake Bay, where Rom surprised me with my first illegal helicopter ride. With night-vision goggles strapped to our faces, we soared through the starry night in a misappropriated UH-60 Black-hawk helicopter, courtesy of the post commander's personal pilot.

It was hard to believe that, after all the yang I'd talked about married men, I'd fallen deeply in love with one. And to think I hadn't wanted anything to do with him! Wisely, Rom had ignored my cold shoulder and chased me harder than a monkey chasing a weasel. Obviously, he'd caught me, cornered me, convinced me, and claimed me.

And I gave him my love. Body and soul.

Sparkle had been right about his predicament. Rom's marriage was over. Dead and done, it needed a decent burial. Rom swore that he was planning to leave his wife way before he even met me. It just so happened the timing coincided, that's all. Besides, like he said, he didn't have a marriage. He had two sons and a bad situation.

In what seemed like an instant, Rom had moved out of their base apartment and into my barracks room. He'd made it clear to Lou that it was over between them, yet she continued to cling to him like a stubborn shit stain. I knew Rom was doing all he could to get his divorce, but that evil heifer just kept throwing rocks in our plans.

Lou claimed they needed to stay married because she was sick and she didn't have any health insurance. She claimed to need the military benefits. First it was her head, then her toe, then her wisdom teeth. The next time she blinked, her daggone eyeball was gonna fall out! Yeah, the girl was sick all right. Sick in the head if she thought she could mistreat and neglect her man for all those years and he would never get tired of it. She just never missed her water until her well ran dry.

And Lou's dry well was my bubbling pool.

Rom was so loving. So steady and true. So gentle and affectionate. It was hard to imagine any woman dogging him out.

But Lou was one strange sistah.

I'd only seen her twice, but immediately I could tell she wasn't Rom's type. I don't know what he saw in her in the first place. Maybe she'd looked better in high school, but I couldn't even imagine Rom rubbing noses or anything else with her. She seemed arrogant and manipulative—and weighed about seventy-five pounds soaking wet, which is probably why Rom couldn't get enough of these thunder thighs of mine.

"Girlfriend must suck a *mean* dick!" Sparkle commented dryly as we watched hoards of men vying for Lou's attention one Saturday night at the Z-Club. Although I wouldn't have put it quite that way, I had to admit it was possible. Lou was surrounded by goo-gobs of fine brothers, but for the life of me I couldn't see what the big attraction was. Sistah-girl looked like a plucked chicken, highly anemic and borderline anorexic! But I didn't have any bones to pick with Lou. I had absolutely no beef with her. On the other hand, I'm sure I rated somewhere near the top of her shit list.

Right on the heels of her happy husband.

I didn't want to turn into the bitter other woman. One who made a thousand excuses as to why some dude should have his cake right next to his ice cream. Hell no. It wasn't like that with me and Rom.

Our thing was for real.

I'd tried him and tested him a thousand times. I'd shown him my Brooklyn bag, my bitch, and my stretch-marked booty, and he'd held fast. I'd cursed like a sailor, eaten like a pig, and let my hair go nappy around the edges; still, he stood by me like a mighty oak tree.

So I believed in him. We were friends. I trusted him with my heart. He was for real, his loving was real, but his life was complicated. I asked him how long he planned to stay married. "Not long, baby," he promised. "Not long. Just be patient, San," he begged me. "Have faith in me, baby, and I promise you with everything that makes me a man, I'll never hurt you. I'm always going to make you happy."

It was a strong promise, weighty and absolute. At first I had my doubts. Hell, I've been fooled before. Could even the mighty King Romulus stand firm on such a promise? I quickly rebuked the demon that caused me to doubt the strength of my man's love.

If not the mighty Romulus, then who?

So I was holding on to my baby, giving him something he could feel. I guess you could say I was learning my man while I was earning my man, and so far he had remained steadfast. To me and to his sons. Rom was a wonderful father. He had a great relationship with his boys. I couldn't wait until my children were able to benefit from having such a strong man in their lives. Unlike Kharim and Hanif, Rom's sons were two lucky little boys. He visited them at least twice a week and once each weekend; oftentimes he returned to my room depressed and guilt-ridden. During those rough times, I'd simply take my sweet daddy in my arms and hold him close, then I'd rock him to comfort until the sun returned to his smile.

Honey, I was happy.

For the first time in years I had a real live M-A-N. No more Maurices or Kevins for me. Believe it or not, I'd found myself a true king and I was happy.

But my contentment was about to cost me my career. For the love of a man, my OCS dream was slipping through my fingers like dust particles on the wind. For weeks I'd been locked in a bitter battle with a crazed and savage opponent: Captain Rachel Silberman. The woman was a straight-up loon! Obsessed! While I was accustomed to battling sexism and abuse of authority from male soldiers, this was my first time encountering a woman who had it in for me. I just didn't understand it. In my experience, female soldiers, both black and white, stuck together. As sisters united in the struggle, we protected one another. We looked out for one another. We damn sure better had, or else Joe would've slapped those little pillbox hats on our heads and sent us scuttling right back to the Army's Nurse Auxiliary Corps!

For some reason Captain Silberman had it fixed in her mind that I was unworthy of an officer's commission. I figured it was because she was a control freak who needed to have her thumb in every pie, so she misused her rank and position to intimidate soldiers into following her game plan. Well, her game plan for the sistah was for me to grovel and beg. Straight-up kiss her wide ass before she'd recommend me for the Officer Candidate School course. What she didn't know was that I'd already been accepted and would run her over like a cheap shoe if she stood in my path.

Somehow she'd got wind of my relationship with Rom (like fools, we were too in love to hide it) and tried to stockpile enough evidence to bring me up on charges of not only wrongful cohabitation but adultery as well.

It was late Friday afternoon, and while the summer wind whipped leaves from low-hanging branches, storm clouds frowned upon the base as if the very heavens disapproved. I sat at my desk tallying training scores from the annual rifle range, and, as luck would have it, my stomach gave a few telltale cramps. I grabbed my emergency hygiene kit from my third drawer and rushed into the latrine to handle my business.

"Sergeant Coffee?" A female voice intruded on my private moment. From a squatting position I peeked under the door. The tips of a very dull pair of combat boots were positioned outside the stall at the position of attention.

"Yeah?"

"The company commander wants to see you in her office right away."

I drew my breath in sharply. "Can't she wait until I'm out of the latrine?"

"She says for you to report to her immediately."

Bitch.

I took my sweet time in the stall, then lazily soaped, rinsed, and applied scented lotion to my hands before reporting to her office.

"I do not support your bid to become an officer candidate," Captain Silberman informed me as I stood with my heels locked before her desk. I watched as she simultaneously rubbed some imaginary object from the tip of her elephant nose and picked eye boogers from the corners of her dead gray eyes. Talk about neurotic? When I entered her office, she'd been sucking and chewing on several long strands of her dirty-blond hair. Not only did she have one helluva weird oral fixation, the heffah was also nasty!

"Well." I spread my feet and placed my hands easily on my hips. "The board has made its final selections, thank you very much, and your expert input was not required."

We'd long since dropped any and all semblance of military courtesy and protocol. I was two steps away from inviting her to my ass.

And she was two steps away from cutting it like grass.

Girlfriend wanted to *burn* me!

She jumped from her seat. "You just wait! I'll have you prosecuted! I know that Sergeant First Class is living in your room, and I also know he's married! His wife is an editor at Army Garrison Publications, for crying out loud! I'm sure she'll be happy to write a statement testifying to your affair with her husband!"

I leaned forward and sneered, my head bopping from side to side. "Do you have us on film? Did you catch us screwing on *Candid Camera*? Were you there holding the light? No? Then it's your word against ours, and the entire command knows how psychotic you are!" I spoke with more bravado than I felt.

Actually, I was shitting bricks because she was right. Our situation was raggedy, wide open. Everyone knew Rom and I were a couple. Hell, I'd almost forgotten he had a wife! If Captain Silberman made any noise about us, the whole damned base could confirm her story, and Lou could print it! I stormed out of her office and grabbed my hat and keys. I walked back to my barracks room in the rain, my mind churning faster than my stomach. My career was on the line, and I sensed things were about to get real ugly. I was between a rock and a hard spot, and Rom couldn't help me. Losing my only opportunity to become an officer loomed closer every day.

And all because I'd fallen in love with a married man.

But also because I had a big mouth. Captain Silberman would use anything I said as proof of my contempt for command authority and military law. And true to form, I nearly handed her my commission on a platter the next broiling hot Saturday morning during the unit's Annual Command Inspection.

My platoon had been designated to inspect Physical Training, Mobilization, and the Unit Supply. But first thing in the morning Captain Silberman deleted my troops from the inspection roster, citing a mandatory field problem as justification. Instead of donning red inspection caps and heading for the brigade's filing cabinets, my soldiers and I were ordered to get into full field gear, complete with Kevlar helmet, rucksack, two full canteens of water, shelter half, tent poles, and pegs.

"Why the hell are we going to the field, Sarge?" one of my privates asked, but I was as clueless as the rest of them. The most I could get out of the commander was some cockamamie story about the post commander's plans to inspect all active training sites. According to Captain Silberman, each battalion had been tasked to contribute a detail of capable soldiers to assist in the preparation. I knew a load of bullshit when I smelled one, but I had no idea what the demented commander had in store for us.

We started out about eight-thirty in the morning. The First Sergeant drove the Headquarters Platoon in a military "cattle truck" troop carrier, while the company commander rode shotgun with a mysterious smirk on her dingy face. My soldiers and I sat butt to toe on the dirty floor, loaded down with heavy gear as the inside temperature crept up near ninety degrees. I was highly disappointed that we wouldn't be working inside with the benefit of blessed air-conditioning, and all I wanted to do was reach the destination, perform my mission, and get the hell back to headquarters and out of my hot equipment.

A steady buzz of dissatisfaction swirled in the air.

"Let's just do our best and get it over with," I soothed my troops, who were plotting a mutiny against the commander. I hated her just as much as they did, but I couldn't show it. I was a Noncommissioned Officer, their leader, trained to remain professional and obey all orders, no matter how ludicrous or absurd they seemed.

The heavy truck lurched and spun as it left the hardball road and bumped along a dirt path. We traveled for nearly an hour before finally rolling to a shaky stop. The front compartment door opened, then slammed. Seconds later, Captain Silberman slid back the troop door. A twisted grin played along her lips, and her normally flat eyes were now dancing a merry little jig.

"Have your troops exit the ve-hi-cle, Sergeant Coffee," she demanded in a funny voice, almost as if she were attempting to remain composed, attempting to contain her glee. I grabbed my equipment and struggled up from the floor. It was just as hot outside as it had been in the truck, and as I wiped the sweat from my face, Captain

Silberman let loose with a thin giggle. I didn't see a damn thing funny, but before I could fully understand the joke, my platoon members were standing beside me muttering and swearing in disbelief.

I held up my hand and demanded silence.

I surveyed the situation. We were standing in the middle of what had once been a parking lot. A huge parking lot. One that had not been used in roughly ten years. The concrete had settled and collapsed in most places, and tough bits of weed and crabgrass poked out defiantly from the thousands of hairline cracks in the sunken surface. There was nothing else out there as far as I could see. Just us, the cracked and disintegrating concrete, and a few lonely trees off in the dusty distance.

"This used to be a National Guard training site," Captain Silberman explained, "but as you can see, it's no longer in use. All of the structures were torn down a few years ago, yet according to brigade policy, it still qualifies as an inspectable area."

I swatted at a starving honeybee. "Ma'am," I began slowly, "I thought this was a field problem. Where is the Tactical Operating Center? Where are the rest of the units? Who is the NCO in charge?"

Captain Silberman grinned like a widemouthed frog. "You are, Sergeant, all of that and more! Brigade needed a team they could depend on, one that could get the job done. I assured the brigade commander he could depend on the 515th to prep this site just as if it were the most active site on the base." Her smile stretched wider than her hips. "Of course, I had you in mind, Sergeant Coffee. As a future officer candidate, this type of detail should be a great exercise in leadership training."

I threw up my hands. "What detail?" I demanded. "Just what the hell are we supposed to do?" I peered into her face. The jig was over. Her eyes had ceased to dance, and bright yellow sparks seemed to fly from their centers.

Captain Silberman scrunched her lips and hissed through her teeth, "Your detail is to unwrap your bedrolls, extract your tent pegs, and dig up every goddamn blade of grass in this parking lot! By the time the colonel's Jeep rolls onto this flattop tomorrow morning, there better not be a single sliver of green left to mar the surface of this lot! And that's an order!"

Shouts of protest cut through the still air as the soldiers exploded over her asinine, moronic order. My first instinct was to join them, but I didn't.

The old bat was testing me.

My body sought to sabotage me. My foot jerked spastically as it begged to plant itself in her behind. My throat constricted and heaved as I fought to swallow the words *crazy bitch!* before they rolled off my wayward tongue. We stared each other down for what seemed like forever. Her eyes bored into mine, daring me to defy her. My eyes were filled with contempt, simultaneously acknowledging her power while showing her just what I thought of her.

I took a bite of humble pie and slammed my teeth down on the little oral membrane that was about to get me thrown into jail.

"Yes, ma'am." I cleared my throat. "At what time will the truck return to pick us up?" Captain Silberman glanced at her watch and then peered at me suspiciously. Clearly, she'd expected me to put up more of a fight. To give her a much better run for her money.

"At the end of the duty day!" she said, and thrust out her chin, ready to rumble.

"Yes, ma'am." I turned my lips down slightly at the corners, then sniffed the air and wiggled my nose as though I smelled something rank. "Y'all smell that?" I turned toward my troops, who now eyed the commander with the same scornful disdain as I. They followed my lead and sniffed the air, staring at the commander as if the odor came from her direction.

"It smells like," I said, and spat on the ground before her, "somebody's standing in a fresh pile of bullshit." Then I turned my back on the captain and dismissed her psychotic ass without another glance.

"Okay, Headquarters Platoon!" I snapped to the position of attention and barked in a sharp command voice. "Let's rock and roll!

Equipment check! Grab your canteens, drop your bedrolls, and hold your tent pegs up in the air. We've got a job to do!"

As the First Sergeant drove the troop carrier out of the parking lot, the soldiers went back to grumbling and complaining. They cursed the commander something fierce. They damned that rotten bitch to hell and called her everything except a child of God. Ordinarily I would have stopped them. Put a quick halt to any form of disrespect for authority. But this time I let them vent. Let them blow off steam. Every now and then I'd even put in my two cents' worth and mutter, "Yep, right!" But the entire time we fussed and cussed, we were also digging and yanking blade after blade of tough crabgrass out of those tiny little cracks in the hot concrete.

Captain Silberman turned out to be tougher than she looked. Girl-friend knew more than one way to skin a cat, and at the last minute she cautioned the battalion commander against signing my move-ment orders. Specialist Burns overheard her discussing me and asked me to come upstairs during lunch so he could to drop a bug in my ear.

"I told you your ass would be grass," he reminded me. His teeth were ivory against his chocolate skin, his dark eyes laughed out loud. "When Mount Saint Rachel decides to erupt, you can just bend over and kiss your black ass good-bye!"

While I appreciated Burns's warning, there was no way in hell I shared his vision. Captain Silberman had picked on the wrong sistah this time. I refused to sit idly and allow her to mess up my plans. I just had to figure out a way to stop her. Well, thank God for home-girls, because that's where Sparkle stepped in and helped set Little Miss Neurotic straight!

"Sandie, listen," Sparkle whispered a few days later. I stood at the oversized paper shredder, destroying reams of classified telex mes-sages. Sparkle grabbed me by the arm and yanked me into the fe-male latrine, then pressed a large folder into my hands and said in a conspiratorial tone, "If it was anybody else but you, I'd turn my head like I didn't see shit, but there ain't no way in hell I'm gonna let that cracker ruin your career! You know that fat hussy can't run worth a damn, right?"

I nodded. Captain Silberman made me look like the prodigious child of Michael Johnson and Marion Jones.

"Well, for the past two years I've been fudging her physical training test scores! Straight hookin' that dirty bitch up, just so she could stay in the Army and feed her nasty little brats! In here"—Sparkle tapped the manila folder and leaned closer to me—"is all the evidence you need. Before you came to this company I was in charge of training functions, and I kept two sets of PT cards: the real ones and the *fudged* ones. Now, you take a photocopy of the card that shows her failing scores with my signature on it and slap it on her desk. But first," Sparkle narrowed her green eyes and cautioned me, "first pin a transmittal slip addressed to the battalion commander to it so the heffah knows *exactly* who's gonna see it next! If the old man asks me anything about it, I'll lie like a motherfucka and tell him she's had her failing scores the whole time. Just watch"—Sparkle grinned like a Cheshire cat and her eyes literally sparkled—"that dizzy bitch is gonna back off of you like a trailer! I *guar-an-tee* it!"

I stared at my friend in openmouthed amazement. I was impressed! Falsifying government records! My girl had *skills*!

"Gimme some, gurrrl," Sparkle drawled and dapped me a high five. "I'm from Bruwk-lin!"

That afternoon I made the copies as I'd been instructed and typed up the transmittal sheet. Although I detested Captain Silberman, my nerves weren't up for the confrontation. My mouth was stale, and my palms were clammy as I made my way down the hall toward her office. A tiny thread of fear wound around my heart and caused it to thud dully in my chest. Stalling for time, I paused at the command conference room where Captain Silberman had concluded a quarterly training briefing a few minutes earlier. As the headquarters platoon sergeant, part of my responsibilities were to retrieve the platoon's briefing slides from the large stack kept near the overhead projector and return them to the battalion files.

I twisted the doorknob.

Returning the slides would give me a little more time to prepare for the battle I was sure to wage with the commander.

I stepped inside.

The spacious room held a huge polished mahogany table surrounded by twelve chairs spaced equal distances apart: a plush black leather armchair for the head honcho and eleven burgundy velvet high-backs. Perched neatly on the table in front of each chair were wooden nameplates arranged in descending-rank order, from the battalion commander all the way down to Specialist Burns. Framed photos of famous generals and their illustrious battles decorated the glossy cream-colored walls. The rosy carpet was freshly shampooed and gave the room a pleasant floral aroma.

I moved toward the back of the cool and shaded room and observed a familiar figure cloaked in a soft shadow near the window, her silhouette distinctly in view as she stood there picking her nose and calmly wiping her treasures on the tinted-glass panes.

Uh-huh, you guessed it!

I ducked behind a wooden panel and watched her nasty little ritual, gagging back bile the whole while. Digging two knuckles deep, Captain Silberman made squiggly pictures with swirls and designs along the bottom edges of the glass. *Watch out, girl!* I wanted to holler. *If you dig any farther, you'll poke a hole in China!* When she was finally done, the trifling heifer walked over and—get this—she *sniffed* the seat of the battalion commander's chair!

No shit!

The company commander went around the room smelling seats from the rankingest to the peon, pressing her nasty nozzle deeply into each chair and savoring the aroma as if it were a meal! She was two chairs away from the panel I stood behind and zooming in for direct contact when I slipped out of my hiding place and stepped into her path.

Busted!

My shadow fell across her upturned face.

Her gray eyes grew wide and round.

I sneered into her beet-red face with my lip curled in undisguised disgust, then slammed down the manila folder on the table and said, "Well look a' *here*, look a' *here*! When you get done sampling that *eau de asshole*, you might want to take a peek in this folder. It's what your boss will have on his desk first thing tomorrow morning. That is, if you keep messing with me!" Then I narrowed my eyes and nodded toward the chairs. "And then we'll see just whose ass stinks the most!"

I smiled at that flat-ass floozy and walked away with my head held high—shaking what she didn't have and feeling damned good about it! The next morning when I arrived at work, I found a set of OCS assignment orders on my desk. They were enclosed in that same manila folder I'd given to booty-blowing Silberman!

It was a good thing Rom was working on his divorce and we'd be married soon. The Army was going to hell in a howitzer. Uncle Sam had tightened the reins and issued new policies that cracked down hard on unmarried sex as well as adultery.

17

BABY, HOLD ON TO ME

Like sand in an hourglass, my precious moments with Rom slid by. All too soon it was time for me to leave Virginia. My dream of becoming an officer loomed closer to reality, while my love for Rom grew ever stronger. Somehow I'd rationalized loving a married man until it looked right, felt right, and damn near smelled right.

But deep within my heart, I knew better.

I wasn't raised to play second fiddle or to settle for second best. Uh-uh, I was top shelf, and I wanted Rom to put things in perspective with Lou and legitimize our love. I kept reminding him that I couldn't have a long-term thing with anybody's husband other than my own. He knew how terrible I felt about his situation, and he promised me that it wouldn't last long. He whispered, "Baby, hold on to me . . . see I'm a special kind. . . ." And I held on for all I was worth. I held on while he took me on the most ethereal journey of my life.

The day I was scheduled to leave was cloudy and damp. Sparkle had come to my room to say good-bye, her green contact lenses floating in a sea of tears. "I don't usually like heffahs this much," she told me as, enveloped in her signature Tommy Girl cologne, we hugged each other tightly. "But girlfriend, I done learned to love me some *you*! Now get your titties off of me 'cause you're wrinkling up my dress. C'mon, turn me loose, heffah, before you mess up my hair!"

My farewell visit with Rom had been even more painful. Our eyes were filled with sorrow; tearstains stood out on both of our hearts. "Don't worry, baby"—Rom stroked my hair as emotion clouded his smooth voice—"it's not time for us right now. But one day, one day soon, I'm gonna come to you *proper*. I'm gonna approach you with all that you deserve, in the way that you deserve it, baby. You'd make any man a fine wife, Sandie."

A sob snagged in his throat.

"A damned fine wife. I just hope that one day soon I'll be worthy enough to get down on my knees and ask for your hand in marriage." I nearly lost it then as I wailed like a banshee and cried hard, powerful tears. Over the months I had really missed my family, but right then and there, I would have given almost anything to stay with my man.

I'd always known that no matter what happened in my life, whatever perils that befell us, my children and I had a home. My parents were my biggest fans. Mama Ceal was my ace in the hole and Daddy my trump card. The two of them had always had my back, and I knew they always would. The flight to New York City had been short and uneventful, and aside from the ache in my heart from missing Rom, I was excited about seeing my children and spending time with my family.

"I just called your daddy"—Mama told me as I gulped an icy glass of red Kool-Aid and kicked off my mules—"and I let him know you made it home safely. He took your rug rats off my hands for the day, but he's getting them together right now, and they should be here soon."

My folks hadn't lived together in close to fifteen years, but they were best friends, allies, lovers, and soul mates—as long as they didn't have to live under a single roof. My father lived in the East New York section of Brooklyn, which was only a fifteen-minute drive away from Mama's apartment in Brownsville, so I grew up with the benefit of having the physical and emotional presence of both parents.

My daddy, Franklin Brown, loved me unconditionally. He was my bridge over troubled waters, my only constant in a world of change. Daddy was my *rock*, and I've often heard Ladelle and Bunchie describe him in similar terms.

I was Daddy's only natural child, although you wouldn't know it unless you'd been told. When I was born, Daddy insisted every child in the household bear a common last name. Instead of dividing our siblinghood by giving me a name different than Ladelle and Bailey's, I carried the surname of Vann, Mama's first husband, until I married Maurice.

Years later I asked Mama about that. Knowing how deeply my father loved me, how could he allow his only child to carry another man's last name? Mama Ceal looked at me and said in a strong voice filled with pride, "Honey, *everybody* ain't Franklin! It takes a helluva special man to sacrifice his own pride so his child doesn't stick out like an elephant in a chicken coop!"

Daddy hadn't wanted me to feel different from anyone else in our home, and he didn't want anyone else to feel different from me. When I was a child, he would frequently remind me, "Pook—my love is with you wherever you are. I'm always just a telephone call away." And he was ever true to his word. Every time I had ever needed him, he was there, and even times when I didn't think I needed him, he was still there.

And I looked just like him. Like he spit me out. After one look at me the neighborhood old-timers immediately knew whose child I was. I was simply a female version of Franklin, and his manhood was the measuring stick upon which I judged every other man in my life.

When Daddy arrived with my kids, I spent more than an hour hugging and kissing them and catching up on the details of the past few months. I examined their teeth, ran Q-Tips around the insides of their ears, inspected their haircuts, and clipped their toenails. This was part of the process we went through after each long absence. Not because they weren't taken care of while I was away, but because they needed to know I was always concerned for their welfare when we were apart. All of them seemed to have grown like wild weeds, and, of course, they all clamored for my attention at once.

"I was talkin' first!" pouted Kharim. I looked at him with a prideful smile. My kids were all so different. Where Hanif was dark, Kharim was light, and Jamillah was caught somewhere in the middle. I loved them so much it made me weepy. I lifted my baby to my lap and planted kisses all over his smooth face. Hanif clambered on my back while I gathered Jamillah in my arms.

"You all have to take turns," I said gently. "There's enough of me to go around for everyone." The long months living apart from my children had taken a toll on all of us. It took time for us to actually reacquaint ourselves. Refamiliarize the patterns of our lives like dear but distant cousins you visit only during the summer. Their emotional resilience was one of the main things I worried about, leaving them as often as I did because of the Army. Secretly, I envied those women who were military wives and got to keep their kids with them all the time. Wished like hell I had an Army husband and lived in their shoes. They enjoyed all the benefits of military life without ever stepping into a pair of boots or onto a C130 aircraft. I got pissed when I overheard them in the Post Exchange or the Commissary talking about how they were actually *in* the Army, albeit vicariously through their husbands. Always complaining about how much they had to sacrifice in order to travel with their men and keep their families together.

It was sometimes hard for me to feel their pain. No field duty, no deployments, no long separations from their kids. They were involved by choice, not because they had to be. On any given morning, when it was o'dark-thirty and ten below zero, their perfectly plucked, teased, fried, and dyed tresses were at home tucked safely in bed, tearing up their sheets in the middle of their third dream, while I stood cursing the fading moon on a cold training field. Huddled right next to their husbands. Freezing. Pissed off because I'd had to drag my kids out of their warm beds and shuttle them before dawn to a cold child-care center.

What aggravated me even more was the disparate medical treatment provided for pregnant soldiers and pregnant wives. I'd given birth to two children while in the Army, and while the military doctors had coddled and supported my civilian counterparts throughout their pregnancies, expectant soldiers were seldom given any kind of break. We worked full-time until we felt our first contraction, and God help you if it was false labor. You'd be given a vaginal exam, a pat on the ass, and sent straight back to work.

Even our convalescent periods were inequitable. Army wives who worked outside of the home were given six months' maternity leave. When my kids were born, I was required to return to duty two weeks before my six-week checkup.

Dripping titties and all.

Although I had many civilian friends and loved them all dearly, they simply couldn't relate to what it was like for me to constantly have to leave my children.

Like the year I spent in Saudi Arabia.

During Operation Desert Storm I was assigned to a sister unit of the 515th at Fort Eustis; the 509th Transportation Company, which provided logistical support to Port Operations at Dammam, Saudi Arabia.

As the contracting officer's representative, part of my job had been to counsel units on the measures they could take to reduce accidents and cut material distribution costs. This type of position was normally filled by a high-ranking civilian, but I'd been handpicked by the Commanding General to be part of a special contract administrative and quality control team deployed to Southwest Asia.

Due to the nature of my job and the seriousness it required, I found it hard to make friends and gain acceptance from my military peers. Of course I stood apart from the crowd; I was a lowly black female buck sergeant E-5 who was required to make a lot of tough and unpopular decisions.

Most soldiers were unable to understand the entire scope of operations and considered my attitude and determination unnecessary. They made me out to be a brownnosing bootlicker, which, of course, was a goddamned lie. I was constantly pressured to kick back, lighten up, and relax my standards.

Until a life was lost.

Or until an expensive piece of equipment was damaged due to negligence. I hated avoidable accidents, especially if they were caused by clear violations of the military's safety codes. When they inevitably occurred, I turned into eighty percent taskmaster and twenty percent bitch.

Sexist and chauvinistic, many of my male soldiers were threatened by my position of authority. They'd stick their dicks up in the air and whine and bitch about doing the right thing just because the order came from a woman.

Any woman.

They'd rather lose a limb than submit to female command.

During the air war, I investigated an accident where a group of old-timer soldiers neglected their common sense and training while attempting to move an Army potable water trailer. The trailer, called a water buffalo because of its size and extreme weight, was a real bitch on wheels to move.

After deliberately ignoring my instructions to move the trailer by using a tow bar, the jock-headed GI Joes tried to manually attach the trailer's heavy tongue to the bumper of a small Jeep. The ensuing cluster fuck led to an accident that cost a young private his right index finger.

They mashed it! They mashed it! was what the young soldier cried before collapsing in a crumpled heap in the soft desert sand. I was hard, but I was fair. I slammed their asses like a tennis ball— including the injured soldier. They were all charged with, and punished for, disobeying a direct order and the willful destruction of government property.

That finger belonged to the *Army!*

Needless to say, my actions gave me a reputation as a hard-nosed bitch out to tear the skin off as many necks as possible.

Surprisingly, though, I had a few good memories of my days spent in the Arabian desert. My first impression of Saudi Arabia—after the thick wet heat slapped me in the face and wrapped itself around my body—was the sheer multitude of African-American men in the military theater of operations.

It looked as though every swinging-black-Richard in America had been sent to hold down the desert fort!

Dayum! A sistah could have it going on up in this joint! As it turned out, the sisters did have it going on, because the brothers sure as hell weren't particular. I saw some of the raggediest heads I have ever seen in my life!

Tore *up.*

It was mid-September when I arrived, and some of the initial transportation, infantry, and quartermaster units had been on the ground as early as the first week in August. After the unaccustomed heat and the drenching humidity, the sistahs' wigs were totally out of whack.

I wanted to throw the mother of all perm parties.

I'd relaxed my own thick tresses before leaving the States, but after seeing the sorry condition of the other sistahs' heads, I wrote Bunchie an urgent message: Help! Attack of the Killer Naps! Send twenty-five heavy-duty black straightening combs, ten jars of Dixie Peach Pressing Oil, fifty Ultra Sheen Blowout Kits, and twenty jars of superstrength permanent hair relaxer with extra-extra lye! Also, send thirty-five jars of Vaseline, one hundred large bottles of Listerine, two cases of extra-protection Right Guard, and enough Wet Ones to wipe down an army!

It actually made my eyeballs blister to see some of those kinky kitchens sticking out from under the floppy Army-issue desert caps! I could just visualize the near blue smoke emanating from a steaming-hot straightening comb; I could truly hear the sizzling *pop!* the hot comb would deliver upon its first contact with the heavy pressing oil. I could even smell the blessed odor of fried hair, heady and heavenly. Now don't get me wrong, I don't have anything against the natural texture of black hair. My own is wonderfully thick and kinky. Straight out of Africa, coarse and strong. It's just that in the desert inferno, virgin black hair, including my own, seemed to turn ashy and dusty, curl into tight balls, and scream at approaching combs and brushes, *Get the hell 'way from here!* Yeah, a few of the sisters over there were hurting, but the dudes didn't even seem to notice.

Their coochie-cats were doing just fine.

After the initial fear and uncertainty during the short war, the Saudi Arabian mission became pretty routine. Life was tolerable.

Except for the bathrooms.

I didn't get it. In a country where the average citizen is filthy rich and manual labor is hired out cheaply to peasant immigrants, why couldn't they build a decent toilet?

Almost every toilet in the country was a urine- and feces-splashed, fly-infested hole in the ground. It was impossible for anyone to accurately aim their water into the narrow holes, not that most people bothered to try. Most folks simply squatted over the holes and did their business, letting things fall where they would.

Well, the sistah has an intense aversion to toilets, so you know I was just appalled! I'd hold my water until my eyeballs floated before I'd break down and use one of those holes. A bunch of soldiers got together and bitched and complained until finally the Department of Engineering and Housing came in and ordered a ceramic toilet bowl be placed over the hole. Well, the geniuses forgot to put in the plumbing so there was no water in the bowl! Now we had a dry toilet bowl full of cah-cah and no way to flush it.

At least the millions of green flies had someplace to sit!

I chuckled thinking back over the absurdity of it all as I allowed Hanif and Kharim to switch spots on my lap while Jamillah scratched my scalp with a snaggletoothed comb. Scud missiles be damned. For me, the bathroom conditions were the worst part of the war.

18

SHINE, SHINE

K eep livin'," my granny used to say. "Just keep livin', chile, because life is funny. Just when you think you know yourself, you done
stated your rules and chose your path—the road bends. The road
bends, and somehow you get caught up in somethin' you swore you
never would. Swore you *never* would!"

The bright lights of New York City danced over an ivory winter
wonderland as I stood at the window and watched the thick
snowflakes drift slowly to their frigid resting places. Already, four cottony inches blanketed the ground, and at least three more were expected. Shivering, I opened the oven and turned it all the way up to
broil and huddled near its mouth for warmth. I hated the projects,
but still, I was glad to be home.

Although I was officially on five weeks of home leave, I still
needed to stay in shape. I'd called JC Penney's and ordered an expensive treadmill and had it delivered to Mama's house, and each
morning I faithfully climbed my 128 pounds of Sizzlean on it and
ran my obligatory three miles. I'd put a lot of effort into my training,
and as a payoff I'd been able to shave nearly twelve minutes from my
run. It was a good thing, too, because OCS would be an ass kicker,
and I didn't want my hard training with Rom to be in vain.

Two days ago, on Christmas Eve, Rom had phoned and spread his love over me like a protective cloak. He'd missed me so much that, after only a few weeks of our being apart, he booked himself a flight to spend a snowy, white Christmas vacation in New York.

With me.

We were going to be reunited, and it felt so good! It felt so good to have a man like him and a near-perfect love. At seven P.M. sharp Daddy and I set out to LaGuardia Airport to meet Rom's flight. I was superparanoid. Thought somebody would try to pick my empty pockets or snatch my empty purse. I don't know why I was so worried; they'd have to cut off one of my legendary beasts to get to my stash, but believe me when I say I felt like a frightened tourist in my old stomping grounds!

Daddy looked serene and relaxed. He was accustomed to the hustle and bustle of New York. I was a little concerned though. Every few minutes we had to stop so he could rest and catch his breath. He'd worked in the tunnels and electrical subway systems for New York's Transit Authority for more than thirty-five years, and during most of that time he'd been a heavy smoker and exposed to asbestos. Daddy had quit smoking seven years ago. Cold turkey. After nearly forty-two years of puffing Marlboros, he was free. I was so proud of him. Not many people could kick a long-term habit just like that. Hell, I was a witness; Rom had taken me to a hypnotist so I could finally shake my monkey!

I'd told my family all about Rom, and they agreed he seemed like quite a catch. I managed to leave out the part about Lou. About him being married. I was too ashamed to admit that part. I knew my people would judge us long before they gave him a chance to turn on his charm and capture their hearts.

Bailey's absence was devastating, which was a pity because Rom would have loved my brother. Ladelle was still absent, too. She'd said to hell with New York City and had made herself comfortable at Fort Bragg, North Carolina, with her daughter Tenea and her new granddaughter, Kharyse.

As it turned out, Rom's flight had landed a few minutes early, and he stood waiting for us in the baggage claim area. I melted into his arms and gave him a conservative peck on the lips, then glanced at Daddy to see his expression. He stood smiling at us with love in his eyes.

As the car rolled to a stop outside of Mama's apartment building, I looked up at the towering concrete structure and my eyes were immediately drawn to a second-floor window. Ever since I could remember, Miss Mary Mack had been perched in that window looking out over the projects, and I always drew comfort from her watchful presence. When I was a kid growing up, we'd marveled over the fact that Miss Mary Mack had played stork and home-delivered almost every child on our school bus, including me and Ladelle, and the fact that she was a midwife and had taken a peek at all of our mothers' private parts made her almost like a god. We'd stand underneath her window and jump rope or sing and clap until she threw us handfuls of peppermints and shooed us on our way. Today the curtains were closed, the window empty. There would be no more peppermints and no more home deliveries. Miss Mary Mack had been gone for a year now, and the sadness of her passing still put a small damper on my spirits whenever I saw that empty window.

As Daddy and I led Rom down the passageway to Mama's apartment, I cringed inwardly. Rom couldn't possibly see what I saw here. The joy, the love, the steaming pots of neck bones and rice, the Spam sandwiches, the Italian ices and penny candies, the tight-knit closeness of a poor black community trying to raise its young to a station higher than the one it claimed.

To Rom's eyes, I was sure, the project building looked bleak and depressing. Thick graffiti nearly obscured the original paint, and KIESHA WUZ HERE; BURN IN HELL, TUPAC; and R.I.P. BIGGIE had become as aesthetic as wallpaper or wood paneling. I took his hand in mine, and as we exited the elevator on Mama's floor and rounded the corner a thick, gravelly voice met our ears.

"Shine turned 'round and saw dat whale—he showed dat fish his *swimmingest* tail! The whale said, 'Shine, Shine, you swim jes' fine—but you miss *one stroke* and yo' black ass is mine!' Shine say,

'You may be king of the ocean and you may be king of the sea, but you'll hafta be—'"

"One *swimming mutherfucker* to outswim me!" I screamed.

"*And Shine swam on!*" We yelled the last line in unison as I leaped into my old uncle Boot's massive arms.

"Girl, you betta watch your mouf"—he laughed and nodded at Daddy—"afore Franklin turns around and cuts your ass!"

I gave Daddy an apologetic look and gestured. "Uncle Boot, this is Romulus Caesar. Rom, my uncle Boot."

My "uncle" Boot and his wife, Bessie, had lived next door to Mama since before I was born. North Carolina natives, they'd tragically lost all three of their young children two months after arriving in New York City when a faulty space heater burned their tiny flat to the ground. Years later they moved into the projects (with walls made of *concrete*, Aunt Bessie liked to boast) and set about helping Mama and Daddy by becoming surrogate uncle and aunt to Ladelle and me, as well as to my now-deceased brother, Bailey.

A few years after they arrived, Uncle Boot's young sister Gloria and her husband, David, were arrested and given two twenty-five-year sentences for allegedly killing a cop during an Oakland, California, raid while they were visiting a Black Panther Party headquarters late one autumn night. The cops had burned the Panthers' home and headquarters to the ground, leaving three people dead and Uncle Boot and Aunt Bessie to adopt their niece, Bunchie, who was a year younger than Ladelle. Although Bunchie wasn't really our blood, she spent the majority of her years at our house being raised by Mama Ceal, and since we loved her as a sister, we also referred to her as such.

I grinned at my uncle. He was too old to do much more than sit on his stool and entertain the young bloods with his wide expanse of jive, and as a youngster I, too, loved to sit at his knee and soak up every minute of his animated rap. Today he was dazzling the guys with his Dolemite renditions of "The Signifying Monkey" and "The Legends of Shine."

I smiled at Rom nervously and took his hand. He gave my fingers a reassuring squeeze, and I knocked on the door whose nameplate read L. VANN. As a teenager, whenever I got grown and began to smell my own pee, LuCeal would pull herself up to her full five feet two inches, put her hand on her take-no-shit hips, and ask, "Did you see the name on the door as you came in? It was L. VANN. And that's *me*! Now, if you don't like the way I sling hash in my house, then get your *own* dungeon, baby—'cause I've got mine!"

I had that speech as well as several others memorized. At sixteen it pissed me off whenever Mama Ceal went to preaching, but later on I realized that those impromptu speeches had served as the motivating forces in my life. God blessed the child who had her own, and my Mama had raised us kids to stand on our own two feet. I closed my eyes and inhaled the tantalizing scents that wafted from the house. The delicious aroma of roasted chicken and cornbread dressing seasoned with sage sausages drifted from the small apartment and made my stomach rumble in anticipation. As we entered the kitchen, Mama dried her hands on a dishcloth and pulled up a chair, then proceeded to chat with Rom like he was the most important person in the house. Like Daddy, Mama Ceal had a special way of making people feel warm and welcome, and I was happy that she extended her loving hospitality to my honey. It took the edge off things and made them less awkward.

"Jamillah!" I called. "Come into the kitchen and bring Kharim and Hanif!"

I introduced Rom to my children and although Jamillah seemed to take to him right away, Hanif and Kharim were slower to warm to him, and they hung together back in the shadows. I'd been very careful never to entertain any casual dates in front of my children, and after having me all to themselves for practically their whole lives, I guess it was hard for them to see their mommy relating to a strange man. One who wouldn't be a stranger for long, I hoped.

As Mama was boring Rom with a faded photo album full of my naked baby pictures, Bunchie swept through the front door like a March wind. A dynamic bundle of energy, she raced through everything she did, and, as usual, she was dressed to the nines with every hair in place. Bunchie was a major broker for Morgan Stanley in Manhattan, and although you'd never know it to see her in her cream and aqua Chanel suit and matching sling-back pumps, she was also an abused woman. Her roguish husband, Vernon, had a habit of getting up in her face whenever his pockets told him he was a boy but his whiskey convinced him he was a man.

"Sorry it took me so long." She stared at Rom and me as we sat with Kharim and Hanif between us, and Jamillah at our feet. "Uh-oh, a Kodak moment." She paused with her hand on her hips, her professional-length nails sporting a European manicure. "Let me find a camera!" She breezed over and kissed my cheek and ruffled Hanif's hair before I could say hello. Without a word Jamillah deserted me and hugged Bunchie's waist then rummaged for sweets in the leather Coach bag hanging from her aunt's shoulder.

Bunchie passed Jamillah her purse, then turned and held out her hand to Rom and grinned. "Hi. I'm Beulah, but if you love your life, you'll call me Bunchie. You must be King Romulus." She looked at me and winked. "Sandie said you were fine, but dayamn!" She turned toward Mama and asked, "Where's Aunt Bessie? I thought this was a family affair."

I gazed at my sister-friend and smiled. According to Mama, Bunchie had moved back in with Aunt Bessie after being emotionally battered one too many times, but like I said, you couldn't prove it by looking at her. She looked remarkably calm and well put together. I stood up and hugged her tight. The mere thought of a man threatening my sweet sister pained me, and I made a mental note to curse her out for putting up with Vernon's crap as soon as we had a minute alone.

"How've you been, Bunchie? Really, how are you doing?" My eyes searched hers.

Her dimples flashed. "I'm fine, San. Finer than I got any right to be!" She flicked a few tufts of my wilted hair. "You look like you could use a perm. I'll put one in for you tonight. Okay?"

An hour later dinner was piping hot and ready to be served. Mama had prepared two beef roasts, a large roasted capon with dressing, baked macaroni and cheese, yellow rice, turnips mixed with collards, and a huge pan of brown sugar–glazed candied yams.

Bunchie, who was pissed because Vernon showed up to take advantage of the free meal, helped me get the children situated at a foldout table I'd set up in the living room before rounding up the adults. The food looked delicious, and sitting around a table with my family again was wonderful. My older brother, Bailey, had been gone for almost a year, but his absence was still keen and painful. There were small pauses in our conversations where his name had once been, and although he was surely in our hearts, the loss was still too raw for us to mention him out loud.

Daddy sat at the head of the table, and Mama was at the end; Aunt Bessie and Uncle Boot sat to her right. Bunchie and I were on Daddy's left, while Rom and Vernon squeezed in on two small barstools. Aunt Bessie sat perched with her hands folded neatly and her "'bacca" can on the table right next to her false teeth. Every few seconds Vernon would steal a glance at the can, then at me, and then look back at the can. It looked like he was trying to tell me something.

"Quit, Vernon!" I whispered as I tried hard not to laugh. I didn't want to be humored by him. I wanted to punch his lights out.

"Just watch," my brother-in-law promised with a knowing nod. "That bald-headed old hag is gonna hock-spit in your plate!"

"Go on, Uncle Boot," said Daddy, waiving his duties, "you can bless the table." Uncle Boot had turned seventy-two a few weeks earlier, and the only thing he seemed to love more than talking trash was having a good meal. The mere sight of Ceal's home-cooked vittles made his hands tremble and his lips quiver.

And Mama's food did look scrumptious. Not at all like that canned stuff Aunt Bessie was forever feeding him. My uncle Boot may have been deaf, but he sure as hell wasn't blind. Every meal Aunt Bessie cooked looked like cat shit mixed with hockey stew, because as sweet as she was, my dear aunt Bessie couldn't cook worth a damn. But Lord ha' mercy—the old gal could *bake*! Bake her tail off! Today she'd baked pumpkin pies, lemon pound cakes, fudge brownies, and seven-layer jelly cakes. I could hardly wait to taste those jelly cakes!

"Can I have every head bowed and every eye closed?"

We obediently bowed our heads.

Uncle Boot began, "Jesus wept, Peter slept, and John fell down the backdoor step—Amen! Now pass the meat and let's eat!"

"Like hell you will, Boot!" Aunt Bessie jumped up from the table and hollered. Her bottom lip trembled, and her lopsided wig was broke down and partially covering her right eye. "You betta not touch one speck of that there food until it's been blessed proper! How dare you blaspheme at this here table with all a' these chirren settin' round here?"

"They asses grown, Bessie—and hungry, too! Now pass the peas and let's eat, old woman!"

"Shut up, fool."

"I ain't gotta shut shit."

"All right now," Daddy spoke up. "Quit flapping all those lips! Y'all are making the food get cold!"

Everyone ate with gusto, especially Uncle Boot. Oblivious to all conversations, he was locked into his own happy little world where he stuffed himself like a fat, happy pig.

"LuCeal," Aunt Bessie said in her high-pitched voice as she scratched her toothless gums with a piece of smoked neck bone, "you shole stuck your toe in that pot a' greens, baby."

"Her toe?" Uncle Boot slurped. "She put her whole damned foot in dat pot!"

After dinner Uncle Boot was first to grab the pretty pound cake for his dessert. He sliced a huge chunk, nearly a quarter of the cake, and slapped it on his plate. He held it down with one enormous paw and lowered his face to the table, then took a massive bite and began chewing noisily, his eyes closed, apparently in hog heaven.

Suddenly Uncle Boot quit chewing and began to moan.

Then he began to cough.

His cough grew steadily worse as we sat mesmerized, helplessly watching as he struggled for air. Just as Daddy jumped up and grabbed him around his middle to do that Heimlich maneuver thingy, Uncle Boot opened wide his glistening maw and spat out a huge runny hunk of partially chewed pound cake.

Bunchie retched.

Vernon snickered.

Rom laughed.

Uncle Boot farted. Then he cussed.

"Goddammit, Bessie! What th' hell you tryna do? *Kill* me? What the hell kinda cake is dat? Ain't no sugar in there, woman—you put *salt!*" He was fired up. "Bessie," he warned, and pointed his finger at my embarrassed aunt who sat there with her toothless mouth caved in on her gums, "you either hang up dat goddamn apron or pass it on down to one of these here gals, 'cause from now on your Betty Crockin' days are *over!*" And with that, Uncle Boot dismissed himself from the table and retreated into the living room muttering, ". . . needs her ass cut . . ." and ". . . up an' married a damn fool . . ." all the way.

"That's what he gets for being so damned greedy," Vernon said, laughing when Uncle Boot was out of earshot. Mama shushed him and popped him on the back of the head with a potholder, but everyone had to agree. Uncle Boot *was* greedy!

With engorged bellies and clean dishes, the inevitable game of bid whist began. Daddy and I were partners, and Mama and Rom paired up.

"Scared money ain't no money."

"Come on, baby. Study long, study wrong."

"Bid high or stay the hell home!"

Everyone in Mama's house was a shit-talking whistologist.

Although we enjoyed other card games like coon-can, tunk, poker, and spades, as a family we held a Ph.D. in whistology. I knew I was good. I was my daddy's child and could be an analytical, cutthroat somebody when I played cards. Besides, like my mother I was creative. Mama Ceal had a way of making something out of nothing, and I followed her example.

Mama dealt the first hand, and it was up to me to tell the first lie. Unfortunately, I held three cards from each suit in my hand.

"All right!" I bluffed. "Five low whist."

"Five? Five?" Mama stared at Rom. "I know you ain't letting no five special go by, partner!"

"Dagg!" I complained. "Stop talking across the board . . . you might as well go ahead and tell him to take the bid out!"

"Watch your mouth, Sanderella," Mama warned. "Who the hell are you dagging? I'll knock you into the middle of next week. . . . I ain't one of your friends. . . ."

Rom grinned. "No trump."

We played seven games before finally calling it quits. My game was off, but Daddy didn't seem to mind. Rom and Mama kicked our butts and shut us out, seven–zip.

"Vernon and I have next," Bunchie called, and for once I gave up my seat without a fight.

That night I made a pallet, and Rom and I slept on the living room floor cushioned by mounds of thick, soft patchwork quilts sewn by my grandmother. Although I knew I was wrong for bringing a married man into Mama Ceal's house, it felt so good having him there! I quickly pushed my guilt aside. Although I missed Ladelle and my grief over Bailey was still intense, somehow my life felt complete. Right now I was surrounded by my close-knit and loving family, and life felt good.

It felt safe.

It felt warm.

Like the calm before a storm.

Sometime during the night I awoke as Rom took me in his arms and held me. We didn't move, nor did we speak. There was no need. Slowly he began touching me. Squeezing and rubbing, just the way I liked it. I felt kind of funny "doing it" in Mama's house. Rom kissed me deeply and plunged his head lower. I arched my back as he began smelling me, tasting me, loving me. I was totally absorbed—mesmerized.

For more than a year this man had made my body and soul come alive with his gentle yet strong and sensuous approach to lovemaking. My future husband was the perfect lover for me, and as I felt my body responding to his loving attention I whispered, "Thank you, Lord," then held on for the ride, my arms dragging his strong back as he guided me down an exciting path of ecstasy and harmony until

my body became a kaleidoscope of brilliant colors and patterns and
I collapsed as one with the man I loved.

Sandie had a happening family, but every time I turned around they
were engaged in a goddamn group hug. I mean, damn! This crew
was worse than the lily-white Waltons! Sandie was the baby, and as
such, they spoiled her rotten. Her kids were nice though, very well
mannered and respectful. They ate at the table like little grown-ups.
Hell, they even used their knives and forks. I was impressed because
my boys were good if they even made it to the table before tearing
into whatever fast-food bag Lou had bought them and plopping
down on the floor in front of the television. But not Sandie's kids.
They put their napkins on their laps and cut their meat into neat little chunks and said shit like, "Please pass the Kool-Aid." For project
folk they sure were proper.

Her parents were good people, too. Especially her mama. Like
most people, I could tell when I was loved, and dammit, LuCeal
Vann *loved* me!

And I loved her right back.

She was some lady. I could see where Sandie got her spirit and
backbone, her style and her grace. Mama Ceal's strong and gentle
nature made me wanna pour my heart out and tell her all of my secrets.

Well, not all of them.

I wasn't about to tell her I was married. But I did tell her that I'd
be honored to become a member of her family someday. I couldn't
help it. I felt so warm and welcome until I started hinting around
that I wanted to one day marry Sandie.

And I did.

I had promised my baby the world, and now I had the burden of
delivery sitting on my shoulders.

The day after I hit New York, I called Lou and the kids. Lou
sounded dry. Pissed, but controlled. The boys were bubbling with
excitement. They couldn't believe I was actually in New York City!
Already I missed my sons, and I was glad I'd spent Christmas Day

with them before coming up to visit Sandie. That way I didn't feel so guilty. At least the boys were happy.

With Sandie gone from Virginia I'd been forced to move back in with Lou and the boys. Sandie had been hurt when I told her, but she understood there was no other way. I couldn't keep living in her barracks room, and I sure as hell couldn't afford an apartment of my own. Even the stray tens and twenties I'd chipped in while Sandie and I lived together had nearly thrown Lou and the boys in the poor-house.

Six months earlier Army Garrison Publications had downsized, and Lou was part of the layoff. I was back to paying all of the bills. I had no choice—I'm a king, right? But as broke as I was, Sandie still loved me and wanted me around. I hated that I couldn't do more for her financially, so I made it my business to do whatever needed doing in other areas. Like being her chauffeur and brushing her hair. Like ironing her clothes and massaging her feet, cooking her break-fast and running her bath. Like singing her love songs and serenad-ing her in the moonlight. Like visiting with her family for the holidays and driving her down to Georgia for school.

I was so proud of her, going to OCS and all. I bragged about her to anybody who would listen because I knew what a big accomplish-ment it was just to be selected for that damn school. But Sandie was stressing hard. Every sock had to be folded just right, and she went over her packing list a hundred times, checking and rechecking every little detail. I knew one thing. She was going to be prepared when it came down to that run. My baby had made miraculous im-provements on her two-mile run time.

I'd watched her take her final physical training test the week be-fore she left Virginia. As I stood at the finish line in the bitter cold, several runners were visible as they rounded the final stretch of the course. My heart pounded. Fourteen minutes into the two miles, and no Sandie in sight. Then out of nowhere she sprinted up from be-hind, her short legs pumping and her arms stroking—*up and down*, none of that side-to-side stuff for my baby anymore!

"Goddamn, that bitch kin run!" her First Sergeant whispered, and

looked at his stopwatch in admiration. If it hadn't been so cold out, I'd have put my foot in his ass for calling my baby out of her name. But he was right. She *could* run. I was positive that she was ready for the course. All that remained was for me to get her there.

I looked forward to the drive down to Georgia. We planned to stop in North Carolina, where her sister Ladelle lived. Her entire family obviously missed brother Bailey, and I saw deep pain in Mama Ceal's eyes when she asked Sandie to stop and check on her sister.

"I don't have a problem with that," I said when Sandie asked me if I'd mind the delay. I'd make a pit stop in west hell if it would please my baby. I was just happy to be allowed in Sanderella's presence. I liked the way she rode in a car—not like some of those evil-ass women you see riding around with their lips poked out, staring out the window like they'd rather be walking! Sandie rode like she loved you. She liked to massage my neck with her left hand and pop her fingers with her right, all the while singing, laughing, and smiling in my face. I loved driving Miss Sandie. Shit, I'd sold my daddy's electric guitar just to finance this trip!

And I couldn't wait for her to meet my family.

I came from a loving bunch of folks, too, and my sisters would really like her. They'd hated Lou since high school. Called her stuck-up and vain. Lou just never fit in with my family, especially after she threw that spaghetti in my baby sister's face at a Parents' Day luncheon. Athena, who was a year younger than me, tried to kill Lou, and I jumped in the middle to break up the fight.

Dumb move.

Those women nearly shredded me like confetti! They scratched like cats and hissed like snakes! And all because of a stupid sweater they'd both worn. Actually, the sweater looked a lot better on Athena since she had something to put in it, but I couldn't tell that to Lou because hers was the one I was trying to get up under. Things cooled down a little after we had the twins, but there was never any love lost between our families.

As Sandie and I lay on a pile of soft old blankets in her mother's living room, I couldn't help but grin while I feasted on her warmth.

I couldn't believe I was actually in New York with her. In her mother's house. Couldn't believe I'd been privileged enough to sit at the same table and eat with her folks. I waited until her breathing was soft and even, then I folded my arms and legs around her and gathered her against me. I awakened her with my tongue as I licked and rubbed her slick spots until she purred like a fat, happy kitten. When she opened herself to me, I reached deep inside and gave her all I had, plus a little bit more. I couldn't wait to share her with my people. They'd love her. I just knew it. I didn't know how I planned to tell them about her, but I was certain they'd approve.

19

EVERY GOOD-BYE AIN'T GONE

The day of my departure arrived all too soon and with it came a profound sadness that leaked from my heart and nestled in the core of my bones. After packing my clothing I gathered my children to prepare them for my impending absence. "You guys know Mommy has to leave again," I told them as I hugged them close and kissed the tops of three small heads.

Hanif and Kharim clung to my legs, their tiny bodies trembling, their eyes larger than saucers. The tears they shed nearly drowned me. Jamillah was more reserved, more accustomed to my frequent comings and goings. She kept her chin up and promised to help Mama Ceal out with the boys, but I could tell my firstborn really wanted to break down and cry like a baby, too. I took her in my arms and held her close as I smelled her sweet fresh-from-the-bath scent and rubbed her bony little back.

"Now Sweet Pea," I soothed my baby girl and rocked her gently back and forth, "you know every time I leave you I leave a part of me with you, right?"

"Yes."

"Which part?"

"The best part, Mommy."

"The part that has to yell and holler and tell you to make up your bed and pick up your toys?"

"No!" Jamillah giggled.

"The part that fixes you lumpy grits and mashed potato salad with big hunks of red onion?"

"No!" She pinched my cheeks, clearly enjoying our familiar charade.

"The part that makes you eat raisins and prunes, while I chow down on Milk Duds and Jordan Almonds?"

"Nooo, Mommy! Not that yucky part!"

"Then what part, baby? Tell Mommy what part stays with you whenever I'm gone?"

"Only the good parts, Mommy. The warm bubble baths"—Jamillah counted on her slender nail-bitten fingers—"the parts that make fish and grits with gravy." She wrinkled her nose. "Instant grits," she said with a giggle. "The bear hugs, alligator kisses, and Eskimo nose rubs, the bedtime stories, and the good-night prayers, and the I-love-you-till-the-cows-come-home—"

"And even if they don't!" we finished in unison.

"That's right, sweetness," I told my precious daughter. "And remember. No matter how often I have to leave, I'll always come back for you."

This was part of the pep talk I gave my children each time I was forced to leave them behind. Especially when I left for long deployments like those to Antarctica, Honduras, and Saudi Arabia. I realized how blessed I was to have a loving family to count on whenever my soldierly duties conflicted with my parental responsibilities. I knew lots of soldiers who didn't have a family, or at least not one they could rely on, and I constantly thanked God for my ultrasupportive clan. They made the long absences tolerable.

I gave each of my kids a warm bath, then rubbed their dimpled bodies with baby oil and tucked them under the fluffy covers of Mama Ceal's king-size bed. I found my old copy of *The Norton Anthology of African-American Literature* and read them a little James Baldwin, then lay down with them until they fell asleep.

As the sandman sprinkled his magic into my babies' eyes, I kissed each of their lips and buried my nose in their delicate necks, inhaling their distinctive scents and searing an imprint of their essence on my heart for future recall. Fighting tears, I turned off the light and closed the door before going to the kitchen to give Mama a few last-minute instructions.

"Mama, remember, Hanif doesn't eat eggs and Kharim can't have anything to drink after six o'clock—or you'll wake up floating in his river."

"Sandie, please." Mama paused with a jumbo pink hair roller in her hand. Half of her sandy-brown hair was tightly rolled; the other half fell past her shoulders. She reached out and hugged me. "I know what to do with these children. I've had them here for months. You go on, baby. Do what you have to do. They'll be fine, and as soon as you find a place to live, you can have your babies back. Just hurry, because I don't want Jamillah to stay here too long. This school district is pitiful—that's why I had you bused out to Bensonhurst."

I nodded. There was really no need to tell Mama anything. It was my own conscience that needed soothing. My parents were always right on time.

The next morning Rom and I slipped from our warm pallet just before sunrise poked a hole in the sky. With a heavy heart I folded our comforters as Rom stacked our bags near the door. I figured if we left early enough we'd be south of Virginia by early evening. Rom hoisted my duffel bag onto his back and gave me a small overnight bag to carry. I held on to Mama Ceal's hand as we made our way downstairs and through the thick mounds of snow. As we stuffed the heavy duffel into the Protégé's trunk, a burgundy Toyota Camry pulled up alongside of us.

"Daddy? What are you doing here? I thought we said our good-byes last night?" I leaned into the open window and hugged my daddy's thick neck, drawing comfort from his familiar West Indian old-man aroma.

"Hi, Pook. I wanted to see you off. Have you ever left home without me coming to see you off?"

I didn't answer. I simply gave him another hug. Snowflakes fell between us, and Daddy pulled back slightly and slipped an envelope into my hands. "Here's a little something for your pockets. Take care of yourself, baby. And be careful. Do the best you can, and call me if you need me."

I hugged my parents again and climbed into my car. I held my head down low so that my tears would not be seen. As deplorable as New York was, my *mama* was here.

And so was my devoted father.

I raised my eyes to his. My daddy felt my pain. It was no less intense than his own.

"Pook," my father said quietly, "as much as Ceal and I love you, you can't stay here—there's nothing here for you. Go on, baby. Live your life. Call us while you're on the road."

"Go ahead, Sandie," Mama backed Daddy's play. "It'll only be a little while, baby. Every good-bye ain't gone."

I waved my hand as Rom pulled away from the curb. Tears streamed unchecked from my eyes while I struggled to stifle the heartache in my chest. Saying good-bye was so very hard to do. Especially when my children remained behind. For the one millionth time I asked myself if this Army mess was really worth it. Most of the time it seemed like just too much of a sacrifice.

It snowed horses and mules the day we left for Georgia. Sandie's Dads looked me dead in the eye and shook my hand until it hurt as he cautioned me to take care of his baby girl. "Be careful with her," he said, and I knew he wasn't talking about the car. He squeezed my hand again and nodded toward Sandie. "That's my baby over there."

"Mine, too, sir," I said respectfully. "Mine, too."

On the drive down Sandie slept fitfully, whimpering occasionally while curled up like a cat beside me in the passenger seat. Leaving had been hard on her, especially when she'd said good-bye to her kids. As I drove slowly on the snow- and ice-glazed roads, I thought about my life. I felt good. I had a woman who deserved the world, and I desperately wanted to give it to her. She was still cautious about our relationship, though. My moving back in with Lou had really messed up her head. I watched her struggling to understand as she tried hard to keep the faith, and I was proud of her. But I knew she still had doubts about loving me. Who wouldn't? I was a married man; married with children, and all kinds of crap seemed to come up whenever I tried to talk to Lou about getting a divorce.

I needed to prove to Sandie that I was married in name only. That there was no funny stuff happening between Lou and me. She slept upstairs and I slept down. Yeah, we still looked like a couple on the outside, but on the inside Lou could get no rap, no rhapsody, and definitely no rhythm!

Sandie shifted in her seat, and I smiled inside. No matter what she thought, I was hers. Her mama loved me and her daddy trusted me. The way I saw it, Little Miss Sandie was just going to have to come on line, because when it came down to her family—I was in like Flynn!

20

TROUBLED WATERS

I was stiff from exhaustion by the time we hit the North Carolina state line, but at least the weather was a lot better than it had been in New York. Officer Candidate School was only a few hours away, and already nervous butterflies were beating their wings in my stomach. I gazed out the window. Small cold-water flats and whitewashed shacks preserved from an era gone by sprinkled the scant landscape approaching Fayetteville, and the gray cast of the sky added to my depression. My plan was to hit Fort Bragg, check on Ladelle, and get the hell out of Dodge, so after settling in at the EconoLodge on Jackson Street, I gave Rom directions to Tenea's house.

Reggae music blared from Tenea's two-bedroom apartment. A deaf man would have winced at the volume, and I could actually see the door moving like a tuning fork as it vibrated to the thunderous beat. I banged on the metal door with my fist several times, then gave up, turned around, and back-kicked powerfully with my feet. A straight-up project move.

"What are you doing?" Rom gawked, as I rolled my eyes and raised my foot again.

The door swung open just as I stood poised to kick it in.

"Hi, Aunt Sandie!" My niece grinned happily, her heart-shaped yellow face still slightly bloated from her pregnancy. "What are you doing here?" She hugged me briefly, then stepped away and searched my face for signs of bad news.

I smiled. "I just stopped by to check y'all out!" I introduced her to Rom, who looked damn delicious in his burgundy slacks and white crew-collar shirt. I allowed myself a brief fantasy about us back at the hotel, taking a shower together and then a long roll between the sheets.

I looked around. "Where's your mama?"

"Next door at Miss Ernestine's house. Let me run over and tell her you're here." Tenea grinned again. "She'll be so happy to see you!"

As the door slammed behind my niece, her young husband emerged from a back bedroom, looking like death warmed over. Wearing a pair of cutoff shorts and a gray ARMY sweatshirt, Gary shuffled into the living room cradling their wailing four-week-old daughter in his stout arms.

"Hey, big head!"

He came over and kissed my cheek, then held out one big paw to Rom. "Gary, man."

Rom dapped him. "Rom, bro."

I squealed in delight at the sight of my newborn niece, although at first look all I could see were tears and tonsils. Sleep deprivation had invaded their home, I could tell. Gary's eyes were red and bloodshot, and he looked relieved to see an extra pair of arms.

"Come here, Auntie's baby!" I held my arms out to accept little Kharyse, and Gary dropped her like napalm, then quickly plopped down on the plaid sofa across from Rom. The two of them started talking Army talk, and I turned down the volume on the stereo and shushed the baby until Tenea returned.

She walked through the door and immediately went over to the stereo and pumped up the volume and shouted, "She's on her way. She's a little tipsy, too."

Tipsy hell, I thought. Ladelle was more than likely *high*.

I held the whimpering baby over my shoulder and bounced to the reggae rhythm as I studied the framed photographs on the pale yellow wall. There were color photos of nearly everyone in my immediate family, and my heart clenched as I studied a few smiling snapshots of my kids. Delicious smells floated in from the kitchen, and my stomach grumbled.

"Are you hungry?" I cooed, repositioning baby Kharyse and hoping to soothe her cries. "Or maybe Auntie's baby is wet." I slid her pink-and-white onesie aside and poked my finger into her Pamper, testing the absorbent cotton for signs of wetness. My finger sank into moisture, and I thanked God there had been nothing solid. It had been eons since I'd last changed a baby's diaper, and just as I psyched myself up to give it a try, the front door swung open and I stopped breathing. My heart thudded twice, then came to a standstill.

I didn't know whether to scream, cry, faint, or run.

I stood frozen.

Eyes bulging, mouth opened wide, air snagged wildly in my lungs. My arms locked and turned to useless jelly.

Tenea rushed to catch her child as she slid from my grasp.

I was breathless. Suffocating. I reached out blindly and steadied myself on my niece's shoulder.

"Hi, Sandie." My sister stood before me. Nonchalantly, she popped her fingers and swayed her hips to Yellow Man's beat. "What brings you here?"

I closed my mouth and swallowed a whimper.

"N-nothing," I mumbled. "Just stopping through. . . . I'm on my way to Georgia . . . to school. Mama Ceal asked me to check on you." I stared hard at Ladelle, and when the shock my eyes absorbed registered in my soul, I looked away.

In the year since I'd seen my sister, she'd undergone a miraculous transformation. Her light brown skin seemed dusted with cocoa powder and smoother than a baby's ass. Her hair was thin, like a forest devoid of trees, and I could see straight through to her scalp. Even the color was wrong. The front was a strange reddish-brown hue like Mama's, but fine and silky-smooth, with glossy ringlets and deep cowlicks framing her face. The back of Ladelle's hair was jet black and covered in a bone-straight weave.

Her thick and luscious, straight-out-of-Africa crowning glory was completely gone.

I found my voice. "Ladelle, what happened to your hair?"

"Oh—you see this shit?" she waved her hand. "Tenea put this damn weave in my hair, and I can't get it out! It's glued to my scalp. I told that girl to take this mess outta my hair!"

"But Ladelle," I pleaded, "when did you get 'good' hair?"

"I *know!*" Tenea bubbled. "Doesn't she look just like Uncle Bailey?"

That was exactly what I was afraid of, and Tenea seemed clueless as to what it implied. Ladelle's clothes, once worn tighter than snakeskin, now hung listlessly from her gaunt body. She weighed no more than eighty-five pounds, and her large eyes dominated the landscape of her face.

This had happened in little more than a year.

"Come in the back," Ladelle commanded, and led me toward the bathroom. As usual, I followed her lead. But my feet were heavy, weighted by fear. Ladelle paused at the bathroom door, then turned around and looked straight into my eyes. Waiting.

I whispered. "What's wrong? What's happened to you?"

"You know, Sandie."

My face dropped like a bomb. Those three words pulverized my heart. I didn't *want* to know. The truth was as clear as day, but *I didn't want to know!*

I couldn't bear to know.

"Check this out." She opened her mouth and pulled back her lips to expose cherry red gums stained with raised white splotches.

I jumped back.

"I brush my teeth constantly," she wailed. "I rinse my mouth with Listerine three times a day, even though it burns like hell, but this shit just won't go away!"

I wiped at my eyes. "Ladelle, it's thrush," I soothed her. "You can't brush it away or rinse it away with Listerine. You need medication. Remember how Jamillah used to get it when she was a baby? It's the same thing." I took a deep breath and was thankful when she closed her mouth. "Have you seen a doctor? Are you on any medicine?"

Ladelle backed away from me, shaking her head vigorously. "I ain't going to no damn doctors!" she shrieked. "They're gonna think I'm *filthy!*"

"*Ladelle!*"

She held up one hand. "No, Sandie . . . there's no help for me. I'm just gonna live until . . . until I die." Her words hung between us, loaded with fear, pain, and sorrow.

My head grew light, and my vision blurred. I'd never fainted in my life, but if I ever deserved to, now was the time. Of course I stood there firmly. On my feet and conscious. That pass-out shit only worked for white folks on TV. Black women *never* simply fainted. We were made of tougher stuff. We faced our trouble standing upright.

We bore it on our feet.

But I was physically sick with grief and pain. This couldn't happen to her. Not Ladelle! Not my big, beautiful, take-no-bullshit *sister-friend*. I had never, ever seen her weakened. She was like Mama to me, invincible and stalwart.

I pushed her hand away and put my arms around her. "Ladelle, how can you say that? There *is* help for you; there are all kinds of social programs. Remember how much support Bailey had; he was into ninety-nine different support groups—"

"*Yeah*, and he still died!"

"Yes," I admitted, "he did, but he died at peace with God *and* with himself." Although my thoughts were reeling, I did my best to comfort and reassure her. "Ladelle, you have to see a doctor. You can get help for your mouth. There's no need for you to suffer like this."

She gave me a strange look and promised to think about seeing a doctor later. When she asked to borrow twenty dollars, I reached into my purse and handed her a fifty-dollar bill. I was totally numb as my sister hugged me tightly, and before I knew it the door slammed shut behind her and she was gone. I knew she was going out to get high, but I didn't care. What was the use in telling her not to go? The damage had already been done.

I stumbled into the living room.

"Rom . . . I'm ready to go." I couldn't help it. Tears rolled freely down my face, and I was powerless to stop them. Tenea also began to cry.

"What? *What?*" she demanded and searched my face for a clue.

"Your mother," I croaked. My mouth was full of cotton. The cotton called grief. "She's *sick*," I whispered.

Realization was suddenly all over her like white on rice. I guess she'd been in denial. She was only nineteen, just a baby, not equipped to handle this type of trauma.

Neither was I.

Rom helped me to the car, and I trembled and sobbed all the way to the hotel. As soon as he opened my car door, I ran into the room and dialed Mama Ceal's number.

"Mama," I cried, almost choking on her name, "Mama, please get Bunchie. Tell her to pick up the other phone. I need to talk to both of you at the same time." I waited until I heard the click of the second phone extension, then I took a deep breath. "Ladelle is sick."

Mama asked sharply, "Sick? What do you mean, sick?"

"Just sick," I sobbed.

No one spoke. Rom held my hand in his. We were all numb. Finally Bunchie said, "I knew it was possible, but I never thought it would happen again. Not twice."

She'd spoken for all of us. Although crack was Ladelle's current drug of choice, during her earlier years she'd experimented with powdered cocaine and heroin. Ladelle's friends, as well as many of our cousins, had shot up and nodded out until they were either too sick to cop the drugs or too weak to hold the needle. None of them had lived to see their thirty-fifth birthdays.

Except Ladelle.

Now it looked as if life had caught up with her.

Bunchie was right. We'd all known another bout with HIV was a possibility, but we'd never imagined it would become a reality. After all, we'd paid our dues, hadn't we? We'd lost Bailey, our only man-child. Wasn't that enough?

Mama Ceal asked, "How does she look, Sandie?"

Did she really want to know?

"Not so good," I said carefully. "She's very thin and has a horrible case of oral thrush."

"Well, she can't look all that bad! She was just here a few months ago. . . ." Mama's voice trailed off hopefully.

"Yes, Mama. She's that bad. Hell, she's worse than bad."

Throughout my conversation Rom had listened quietly, and now I watched as a lone tear slipped from the corner of his eye, then hit the pillow and disappeared.

Later that night while lying in his arms on the cold hotel sheets, I cried and cried and cried. When I couldn't cry anymore, I cursed and cursed. I was furious!

Hadn't I asked God to bless and protect my family on a daily basis? No, I didn't go to church much, but I was certainly no heathen. I did my best to live decently. I didn't steal or rob or deliberately hurt people.

How could God bring this wrath down on my family again?

I'd read somewhere that every family in America was affected by HIV. The article reported that each American had at least one relative who was infected with the virus.

Well, we had two!

Two out of four children. This would just kill my parents. I felt their pain as well as my own. Above all, I felt my sister's fear and hopelessness. I knew she was afraid to die because she wasn't living right. I wanted her to find peace of mind and spiritual relief. I wanted her to get proper medical attention. Someone once said that into each life a little rain must fall.

My poor family was drowning in troubled waters.

I jumped out of bed and tore off my nightgown. I coaxed my beasts back into their cages and slipped into a pair of red sweatpants and a wrinkled plaid shirt. Rom turned over and looked at me as I pulled a black knit skullcap down over my hair.

"Sandie, it's almost two o'clock in the morning. Where are you going, baby?"

"I have to go and see about my sister," I said shortly and grabbed my jacket from a chair. "I can't just leave her like that, just waiting to die!"

I paused at the door. "And in *North Carolina*? Who the hell is going to come to her funeral way down here in Cacka-lacky? I've got to go and get my sister, Rom. I've got to get her to a hospital before that crack steals the last two pounds of meat off her ass!"

Rom offered to drive me back to Tenea's, and as tired as I knew he was, I accepted the offer. He dressed quickly and grabbed a thick heavy sweater, and we left the hotel room and ventured back out into the windy night. I banged on Tenea's door again, this time to wake her up.

"Hey."

She stood in the doorway fully clothed, with a blanket around her shoulders. I could tell she had cried herself to sleep.

I said, "Your mother needs to go to the emergency room, Tenea. Where is she?"

She sniffed. "At Miss Ernestine's."

There was no doubt in my mind that Ladelle was next door sending my fifty spot up in a cloud of smoke. Rom stretched out on the sofa to catch a quick nap, and Tenea and I went over to the next apartment.

Tenea tapped on the door lightly at first and, when no one answered, much harder. Eternal moments sailed by, then someone finally yelled, "Who the hell is it?"

"It's me, Miss Ernestine. It's Tenea. Is my mother in there?"

To my surprise, Ladelle opened the door. She was no bigger than a hastily drawn stick figure. A cigarette dangled from her lips and hell shot from her eyes. Her sparse hair stood up wildly on her oval head, and she looked *pissed*.

"What are you doing here, Sanderella? I thought you left a long time ago!" She was clearly not happy to see me. I'd interrupted her while she was trying to get her high on.

"Ladelle," I began slowly, "you have to see a doctor. You can't sur-vive like this. You need medical attention."

My sister put her hand on her imagination and gave me a dirty look. "Don't tell me what the fuck I *need*, Sandie! I'll *kick* your little ass all the way back to Brooklyn!"

"Yeah," I said sadly, "maybe last month you might have, but I doubt if you could tonight." I held my arms out to her and prayed she would just step into them. "Come on, Ladelle. Just come outside and talk to me."

"No, goddammit! Now mind your fucking business!" She slammed the door in my face.

"You *are* my fucking business!" I screamed from the bottom of my heart as I banged futilely on the unyielding metal.

Tenea sprang into action. "Come on, Aunt Sandie. We'll go around and knock on the windows!"

We ran around to a side window that was at ground level. The night was dark, and we could just barely see through the blinds and into the dim bedroom inside. "Ma! Ma! Come outside, dammit!" Tenea screamed over and over as she pounded on the glass. The shadowy occupants ignored us. The air was crisp and chilly. I hud-dled down in my jacket against the biting wind.

"Forget this!" Tenea pushed upward on the window. It gave a lit-tle, then stuck fast. She tried again. Pushed harder. This time it slid up all the way. Before I knew it, girlfriend had pulled the Venetian blinds clear down from their mounts and hoisted herself up and through the open window.

Like a fool, I followed her.

I found myself standing in the messy bedroom of a musty old man who, by the looks of him, had old Methuselah beat by quite a few years. His gaunt body lay prone among the grimy, disheveled sheets, and as Tenea and I entered through the window, a shadowy figure rushed out through the door. The smell of age and dried piss perme-ated the air, and I nearly gagged as another, more toxic odor nearly overwhelmed me.

The shrunken form in the bed struggled to assume an upright po-sition. "Y'all cain't jes' come up in here like dat!" His eyes were nearly shut, and he waved a smoking crack pipe in one dark, trembling hand. "Dis my goddamn house!"

Tenea balled up her fist and shook it in his direction. "Just shut up and lay down, old man," she threatened, "or I'll give your wrinkled crack-smoking old ass something to puff on besides that pipe!"

I shook my head. She was definitely her mother's child!

"Ma! Ma!" Tenea screamed as we moved through the apartment. "Ma, where the hell are you?" She tried the knob on a door to our right. She pushed against it and someone on the other side pushed back.

The voice on the other side of the door screamed loudly, "Ladelle, Ladelle! Get the hell outta my house and take your crazy-ass child with you!"

Tenea shrieked, "You're damned right I'm crazy! Now send my mother out before I go crazy on your raggedy house! And when I'm finished I'll start on your *ass!*" To prove her point, she began kicking over end tables and pulling cheap pictures down from the walls.

I was too shocked to say anything. I just stood there stupidly, my jaw unhinged, my mouth hanging wide open. I wasn't too shocked not to be scared though. I didn't believe in going into other people's houses and starting fights. They knew where all the knives were! I preferred to start my trouble outside where the odds were a little more even.

"Ladelle!" I yelled. "Come on now. You know better than this. Bring your ass out here! Tenea—quit tearing up their stuff. These people aren't holding your mother hostage!"

Suddenly Ladelle stepped out of what I saw was a bathroom and said simply, "Okay, I'm ready to go." Just like that we walked out of the trashed apartment and left the terrified residents behind to clean up the mess.

Outside the wind was spitting mad. We huddled in Tenea's vestibule to talk. "Ladelle," I said firmly, "I'm taking you to the hospital. We'll get some medicine for your mouth and then we can take it from there, okay?" To my surprise, she agreed without a fuss or a cuss. I guess her battery had run down.

Tenea went into her apartment to get Rom, then we drove Ladelle to Parkside Hospital's emergency room, which to my surprise was nearly empty. It took me about two minutes to figure out why.

As we approached the desk, a thin white woman with a ready smile asked if she could be of assistance. Her blond hair stood up in wiry spikes, giving her a punk-rock appearance, but her eyes were warm and pleasant.

"Uh, yes," I began. I didn't know what to say. Did I just come out and say Ladelle was HIV positive? Nah, that didn't seem right.

"Well, um . . . my sister needs to see a doctor. She has a mouth infection that needs treatment, and we'd like to discuss the details with a doctor, if you don't mind."

"Certainly." She smiled. "If you'll just fill out these forms and give me your insurance information, I'll have the triage nurse screen you right away."

Insurance? That's why the place was so empty! This wasn't a city or a county hospital! It was *private*! The décor itself should have told me that!

"Look," I said to Miss Pleasant Face, "she doesn't have any insurance. Does that mean you can refuse her treatment?"

She leaned close to me and said, in a conspiratorial tone, "No. We're not allowed to refuse treatment if she declares this to be a true emergency. She simply has to sign these forms and promise to either provide her insurance information or pay for her treatment within fourteen days."

"Where does she sign?"

We completed the paperwork and answered a bunch of questions, then sat down to wait on one of the soft, comfortable couches. We didn't wait long. The triage nurse took Ladelle's vital signs and weight, and I wasn't far off on my guess.

My big sister weighed eighty-seven pounds.

Her little butt was just a pimple in her sweatpants, and her shoulder bones looked sharp enough to poke someone. I felt so bad for her. It was killing me to even look at her, but for her sake I tried to act naturally.

And I tried not to stare.

When the doctor called her in, Ladelle looked over at me expectantly. Like she was afraid and didn't want to go in alone. I stood up and followed her.

"Hello, ladies," the young doctor greeted us at the door. "My name is Dr. Cornell, and I'll be taking care of you tonight." He was cordial but direct. "Open wide," he instructed Ladelle and shone a penlight in her mouth. After wiping a swab around Ladelle's mouth, Dr. Cornell confirmed my layman's diagnosis of oral candida, or just plain old thrush. It was an opportunistic infection, he explained. A result of her HIV infection.

"I'll be frank," Dr. Cornell warned. "A lot of your problems, including your drastic weight loss, seem to be a result of your lifestyle rather than the HIV in your blood system." Dr. Cornell handed Ladelle a hospital robe and instructed her to undress, then he stepped quietly out of the room. My sister shed her clothing and stood before me. Naked. Stripped of her pride.

Ladelle had always enjoyed a damn near perfect physique: high, rounded booty; sweet hips; flat, muscular stomach. Curvy but lean. The kind of body most women pray for and most husbands leave home for. Now she was almost as small as Bailey had been. Her normally full, perky breasts were just dark nipples attached to loose, pendulous skin.

When the doctor reentered the room, she climbed on the examining table and turned onto her side as he palpated her kidneys. The tails of her cloth gown slid open, and I caught a glimpse of her ass.

It was gone.

In its place lay a large puddle of wrinkled skin, fanned out on the examining table like a harlot's hair. I felt sick. My upper arms were thicker than her thighs.

Dr. Cornell had a technician draw her blood to get a T-cell count and an official confirmation of her HIV status. Then he checked her lungs and her stomach, as well as her limbs.

"Aside from the infection in your mouth, you seem to be in pretty good shape. Tell me, are you using illegal drugs?"

Ladelle nodded. "Crack cocaine."

"Well"—Dr. Cornell shook his head sadly—"in your condition, crack will kill you quicker than AIDS. There are four major stages of HIV infection," he explained, "and judging by your physical examination you seem to be entering the second stage. Many people with AIDS live very healthy and productive lives during this stage of the disease, and with the proper diet and medical treatment, there's no reason why you should be an exception." He took both of Ladelle's hands in his and bent down until his eyes were level with hers. "That is, unless you refuse to help yourself and continue to abuse illegal drugs."

I was amazed at the great compassion and respect he showed for Ladelle. Dr. Cornell treated my sister like an important person who deserved to live, and I prayed she'd take his good advice to heart.

We found Rom and Tenea fast asleep in the waiting room. I rubbed Rom's head, and when he sat up a thin trickle of saliva escaped his parted lips. Poor baby. His eyes were fire red. I knew he had to be exhausted, all of that driving and then trying to be there for both Ladelle and me. I insisted on driving home, and we dropped Tenea and Ladelle off at Tenea's apartment. There was no way Rom could get up at five A.M. and make the drive to Georgia, so we decided to sleep late and spend the day with Ladelle before heading further south.

The next morning I awoke in the strange bed with sunlight filtering through the thin curtains and Rom's arm across my back. My stomach clenched with nervous cramps as my emotions surged inside of me like a deadly tide. All my life I'd been my sister's keeper, but there was nothing I could do for her now.

Lord, I just can't take it, I silently begged. Here Daddy was sick, Bailey was dead, and the monster had bitten Ladelle. Stuff like this didn't usually happen all at once. Why was this happening to my family? And how could we withstand it? Pain enveloped my heart, and I put my face into the pillow and cried. Normally, I was the last person in the world to have crying jags, but lately I seemed to weep every day. It was a good thing tears were free and plentiful, because before it was all said and done I would cry me a river.

—

That afternoon Ladelle and Tenea arrived by taxi at our hotel. I called out for Chinese food, and Rom watched the game while Ladelle and I talked. Tenea sat quietly next to Ladelle, gripping her fingers tightly, her face pale with shock and confusion.

"I don't know exactly what my purpose is here on this blue and green earth, Sandie," my sister said, sounding much stronger than I felt. "But I do know that I have a lot of catching up to do with my children and my grandchild. I'm staying here with Tenea so I can start right away."

"You're not going home to Mama Ceal?"

"No," she said firmly. "I'm not. Mama Ceal doesn't need me — except to hear me apologize for all the pain I've caused her and Daddy. But Tenea and that baby need me. Things aren't so good between her and Gary, and any amount of relief I can bring them will help."

I had my doubts about that. "And just how are you gonna help them?" Tenea lived in an environment surrounded by drugs and easy money, and I doubted if Ladelle had the willpower to resist the lifestyle she'd always been so drawn to.

She grinned and patted my hand. "I know what you're thinking, Sandie. But this time you've got another think coming. It's not like that anymore. I ain't going out like that. This is my wake-up call, 'cause ain't no telling how much longer I'm gonna be here with you all. It's no secret what kind of mother I've been . . . everybody raised my kids but me. I've been irresponsible and I know I'm gonna answer for every dirty thing I ever did. But maybe I can do better by my grandbaby. Maybe if I do right by Kharyse and Tenea, that'll count for something when I have my final day in court."

Although I knew it was useless trying to figure out where Ladelle had picked up the virus, I wanted to know if she had any ideas. "Ladelle, do you think this thing came from Sharita?" Sharita was one of Ladelle's longtime friends who had died from AIDS two years earlier.

Ladelle shrugged. "I don't know, Sandie. To tell the truth, it could have been Frieda—she's been gone about a year—or it could have been Cousin Nate. Or anybody else I shared a needle with." She continued, "I can't even begin to say who it came from. I just know all of my partners have died from it, so I guess it doesn't really matter, huh?"

She was right. It didn't really matter. Bailey had felt the same way, refusing to say who had infected him. All he would say was that he'd had unprotected sex and that his fate should serve as a lesson to all of us. AIDS was a terrible disease.

It had destroyed my family.

Some people reasoned that AIDS was developed in a laboratory and purposely introduced to black Africans. From there it supposedly spread to other countries, finally invading gay and straight, black and white America. I had no theory myself; I just knew that I hated it. Bailey had tried to ease my anguish; he told me that throughout history there had always been a disease or scourge that killed millions of people. Polio, bubonic plague, leprosy, scarlet fever, tuberculosis—there were incurable diseases for all seasons. Eventually a cure had been found for other diseases, and so he reasoned that a cure would one day be found for AIDS. Bailey called it nature's way of ridding the earth of an unsustainable populace.

I called it a damn shame.

"Ladelle, did you have any idea that you were sick?" I asked gently.

"Yeah, I knew," she said poignantly. "Right before Bailey died last year I kept getting yeast infections, and this same shit kept popping up in my mouth. Then I passed out cold in the street one night. My friend took me to a little clinic on Avenue of the Americas, and I took a free test. When the results came back, they just said I was positive—they didn't tell me what to do about it or anything. I was scared, and I didn't want to face it—especially after I saw what it had done to Bailey. So I forgot all about it and didn't claim it."

She had been in denial. I could certainly understand it. I reached over and hugged her. What else could I do?

We left North Carolina early the next morning. Although Rom

seemed rested and refreshed, my head hung low and my thoughts were chock-full of Ladelle. My sister. My friend. This was some heavy stuff to swallow. Ladelle was so full of life I just couldn't imagine her dead and gone. In the back of my mind I thought of something Mama had once said: "Don't ever go around burying folks before their time, 'cause honey, the sickest man doesn't always die first."

21

FEET DON'T FAIL ME NOW!

Rom made good on his promise and delivered me safely to Georgia, and it was now up to me to do the rest. Although I'd trained hard and was confident in my mental and physical abilities, Officer Candidate School was proving to be every horror story I had ever heard.

And then some.

There were 287 candidates enrolled, and during our initial orientation there were representatives on hand from each Army directorate waiting to brief us regarding the multitude of services they provided. We sat through speeches and presentations from Army Community Services, the Army Chaplain Corps, Army Emergency Relief Society, and a host of other support commands.

Then the brigade commander spoke into the microphone and puffed out our chests by telling us how honored he was to have each of us under his command. "You candidates are the cream of the crop! The best the Army has to offer! The future leaders of this great country!"

The brigade commander was followed by the battalion commander, who quickly assured us that the hellish rumors pertaining to Officer Candidate School training were just that.

Rumors.

"Today's Army is a kinder, gentler Army," he insisted. "The mission of this command is the quality training of officer candidates, and the officer candidates' mission is to focus on training!" By the time the head honchos were done buttering us up, calming our hearts, soothing our nerves, and doing everything except giving us a warm bottle, burping us, and putting us down for a midday nap, all 287 of us had visibly relaxed. The gray knot of tension sailed out of the room in a great big whoosh and was replaced by a feeling of camaraderie born of a shared anxiety.

I glanced around at my peers. Instead of the stiff, awkward posture of discipline and attention we'd started out displaying, the candidates were now lounging; some were slunk down low in their seats, others had their camouflaged legs crossed at the knee and were laughing and grinning among their new compatriots. A few were brazen enough to break out the chewing gum and tobacco, the fear on their breaths and brows now replaced by a we-can-do-this-shit air of bravado.

Suddenly the company First Sergeant was on the podium screeching into the microphone, "All right, candidates!" His shocking red hair stood out prominently against the sea of army green. He yanked at his belt loops and hitched up his battle britches like Steve Urkel, and hissed, "You's have gotten all the warm and fuzzies you's are gonna get for the next four months! *The battalion commander has departed the building*, and alla you Joe's and Joe-Etta's—you's asses belong to *me*!

Honey, it was on.

"No pain, no gain, candidates! Don't cheat your body!"

It was my fourth trip down, and I was seriously beginning to wonder if OCS was really worth it. The First Sergeant ran us like herds of confused cattle. Up and down the double-flighted stairs of the four-story building we trekked, with our duffel bags strapped on our backs, our rucksacks clutched to our fronts.

"All right, goddammit!" he bellowed. His hair was so red it looked like an open flame. "Ah'm not feelin' a sense of urgency round here! You's better move like you's got a purpose in life! You's candidates are slower than pond water! Git yo' knees up! Let go'a that thar handrail, you's are s'pposed to *run* up, not pull you-selfs up!"

I sucked in hot wind. My breath strained through my chest, and my heart felt ready to burst at the seams. Each time I made it to the bottom landing I thought it would surely be my last trip. The only thing I heard above the noise of my own ragged breathing was the thunderous sound of boot leather slapping against hard concrete; the smashing cadence of nearly three hundred pairs of combat boots as they pounded the seemingly endless flights of stairs.

"Hey, you!" the First Sergeant barked and yanked a chunky blond female out of ranks. She was clearly approaching her limits and looked ready to faint at any moment. The girl stumbled drunkenly, then staggered to a standstill, causing an accordion effect behind her and a wide gap in the long line of double-timing candidates in front of her.

"Get on down and beat your face!"

Dutifully, she fell to the ground and began struggling through a wobbly set of push-ups.

Talk about muscle failure!

Each time we reached either the top or bottom landing, we were ordered to drop down (with our duffel bags still hoisted on our weary backs) into the front-leaning-rest position and pump out push-up after push-up after push-up. We remained in this position, arms trembling and lungs gasping for breath, until the First Sergeant's command of "On your feet!" Then we'd jump up, don our heavy rucksacks, and begin the manic trek all over again.

"I thought hazing was illegal," I heard someone mutter, but I kept moving, concentrating on putting one throbbing foot in front of the other. Finally the First Sergeant blew his whistle and signaled the command to cease running. Scores of sweaty soldiers dropped their gear and sprawled along the stairs, desperate to catch their breath, steamy perspiration trickling from their chins and noses. I just stood there dumbly, shaking and depleted. If I sat down, I'd never manage to get back up.

We were ordered to report to our assigned rooms and set up our wall lockers, dressers, and bunk displays in accordance with the diagrams prominently displayed in each room. I was assigned to room 213 along with a slender dark-haired white girl whose name was Courtney Fitzpatrick. Our room was approximately twelve feet by fifteen feet with a set of bunk beds, two wall lockers, two dressers, and two desks. There was one large window that sported a pair of dull beige drapes, and the white-tiled floor held enough wax to shine both of our boots for a year.

Courtney and I did the duffel-bag drag into the sparse room, and I immediately began unpacking my things and assembling them on the stripped, unmade bed. Thank God, I was ahead of the game. I'd taken care to roll each of my socks regulation style and fold my T-shirts in twelve-by-twelve squares with my name stenciled faceup and centered on their fronts. Cold-weather hats, leather Class-A gloves, awards and decorations, field-glove inserts, neck tabs, hand-kerchiefs, panties, bras—you name it; there was a prescribed place for everything and a prescribed manner in which everything was to be displayed.

When I was done meticulously arranging my displays, I was ready to make my bunk. Each bed had a stockade-style pile of sheets and blankets at the foot, and I chose the lower bunk out of a dislike of heights. For fifteen minutes I pulled, and tugged, and tucked, and shoved, until the sheets and blankets fit smooth and tight.

It had been a challenge, but I'd carefully followed the instructions on the display cards and measured every item and placed it in its proper place. I looked over at Courtney. Her cheeks were flushed, and her black bangs flopped against her forehead. Her shirts were still unfolded, her socks were paired the way her mommy had taught her, and all of her little odds and ends were scattered in complete disarray.

Damn! I thought miserably. I'd hoped to get a sharp, squared-away room dog who had her stuff together and would be an asset to me.

There was no way in hell this girl could pull her act together long enough to complement anyone else.

I felt sorry for her.

"Here." I reached into her drawer and pulled out her wrinkled, misshapen shirts. "Don't faint on me now! Let me help. You work on your wall locker display while I fold your shirts." When we were finished making her bunk, Courtney and I scrambled outside of our room and stood as we'd been instructed: feet apart at a 45-degree angle, arms rigid at our sides, fingers curled and touching the seams of our pants, head and eyes straight ahead. A classic example of a soldier at the position of attention.

"Good," said a roving training officer as he thoroughly inspected every inch of our room. With deft hands he measured the dimensions of our clothing, ran a white-gloved finger under the soles of our spare combat boots, and bounced a shiny quarter off the taut surfaces of the olive-drab military blankets hugging our beds.

He smiled. "Supersoldiers! Excellent work!"

His grin went south.

"Now break it all down and pack it all up again. You two are moving up to room 420."

I could have kicked him!

Room 420 turned into room 325 and then into room 412. By the time we were finished unpacking, setting up, repacking, moving, and setting up for the fourth time, we were pissed off, exhausted, and weak from exertion.

Forty-seven candidates had quit.

Our platoon was ordered to stand outside again, and as luck would have it, the earlier drizzle had been replaced by a steady downpour. The sun had surrendered to a watery moon, and almost instantly the fabric of my battle fatigues became saturated and I was soaked to the skin. There was a deep chill in the Georgia night air, and I hunched my shoulders and tugged down my cap, but rivulets of icy rainwater ran down my neck and trickled down my back nevertheless.

The wind blew with the howl of a hungry wolf. We stood in close-interval formation, rigid and still at the position of attention, battered by the cold rain and heavy winds until we were nearly hypothermic. Suddenly, the soldier huddling against my left side began to violently shiver. As if we were one, I joined him in concert. As did the soldier on my right, and the one next to him, and the one next to him, and so on, and so on, until, huddled together for comfort and warmth, we were one big shivering, jiggling, soggy mass of Army-green Jell-O.

"Right, *face*! Forward, *march*!"
Thank God we were on the move. I ran to keep up with the long-legged Louies positioned at the head of the formation, and after a few quick paces my body temperature began to rise. Briskly, we trudged through the wet grass leaving sucking holes of mud in our wake as we headed toward the wooded tree line. We marched right through the thick forest, our boots squishing in mire and our feet tangled in prickly shrubs and wait-a-minute vines until we reached a small clearing.

The First Sergeant held up his bullhorn. "Okay, candidates!" he screamed in a voice that I had already begun to hate. "You's will now extract from your rucksacks one entrenching tool, type fo'teen and three. You's will then break down into five-man squads and construct defensive fighting positions a-long Phase Line Charlie. Remember, you's bunkers must provide cover and concealment! Be sure t'dig them foxholes armpit deep to the tallest man!"

I peered at my watch. It was going to be a long night.

Hours later we'd dug our foxhole to an acceptable depth and found enough foliage and natural materials to construct a fighting position that concealed us from aerial view. It would have been a perfect time to sit back and rest, but instead of the rain slowing, it had built up to a crescendo. Sheet after gushing sheet poured from the heavens, as if there were an entire tribe of ancestral Cherokee upstairs hosting one helluva big rain dance.

In a matter of minutes our hole was flooded.

A training officer sauntered by and tossed down a few empty coffee cans and sneered, "Stay alert, stay alive!"

We jumped up and began bailing out the muddy water, but it was a futile effort. The more we bailed, the heavier the downpour, the quicker the hole filled, the more sucking mud that settled in, the deeper we dug, the more we bailed.

Finally the First Sergeant, who was going around personally inspecting each and every position, happened upon my squad. "Dabnabbit, candidates! Why's that hole so durned deep? It ain't s'pposed to be any deeper'n the armpits of the leet'lest man!"

Through the darkness and the rain, my squad members and I stared at one another. We'd dug our hole until it was armpit deep to the *tallest* man: a soldier by the name of Bose Fredricks, a six-foot-three strapping country boy from West Virginia. The leet'lest man? Hell, that was *me*!

"*You!*" the First Sergeant barked, and pointed one long, crooked finger down at me.

My teeth chattered visibly as I peered up at him through the pellets of rain stabbing at my eyes. His hairless white finger looked like a fat slug in the darkness. The water level was rising; the thick clay mud had quickly swirled above my shoulders and was now creeping up around my neck. I shivered. "Y-y-y-es, First Sergeant?"

"What's your name, candidate?" he demanded.

"M-my n-n-name B-b-b-asic Officer Candidate Coffee, First Sergeant."

"Well," he mimicked me, "B-b-basic Officer Candidate Coffee, you's better climb you's tiny ass outta that thar hole before you's nose fills with mud and you's eyes turn black and you's tiny ass takes off floatin' downriver!"

With the help of my squad members, I climbed out of that sucking hole of mud, all the while cursing that ignorant country-bumpkin First Sergeant out. I told him just how stupid he was. How he needed to take command of the King's English before he tried to take command of me or any other college graduate he happened to meet. I told that redheaded, rednecked First Sergeant just how jealous he was, just mad as hell because in four short months we would all outrank him, and not only would we give him our asses to kiss, we'd also give him our boots to shine. I told that stupid First Sergeant some of everything! I mean, I told him some things I'll bet he never knew!

I *told* him!

But of course I told him quietly.

And safely, under my breath.

22

LOVE HURTS

Sandie's Moms had a heart attack.

Her surgeons were changing a valve in her heart, and she went into cardiac arrest right there on the operating table. Good thing for her she was where she was and the attack was pretty mild; now she was recovering in the intensive care unit of a New York hospital.

Sandie's Dads had taken sick again a week later, right before he was scheduled to break out of New York City and head for a simple country life in South Carolina. Unfortunately, all of this shit hit the fan while Sandie was in Officer Candidate School and unable to do a damned thing about it.

"Don't worry about anything," I'd told her. "Just get through school. I'll take care of everything else." Sandie's biggest worry had been that her sister's condition might get worse before she completed the course, but Ladelle was doing better than they'd expected. She was still living with her daughter at Fort Bragg, so that left me and Sandie's Dads to pick up all the slack.

I'd kept in touch with my baby through letters, telephone calls, and even an occasional visit, assuring her that I was helping her family out the best I could. Her OCS graduation was only two days away, and today her Dads and I were driving down to Georgia to witness her journey across the stage. My baby had made it. She'd hung like a trooper and completed the course. I had every reason to be happy, but instead my dick was dragging in the dirt.

I glanced over at Dads. We'd covered quite a few miles of road together over the last two months, and Dads was one sick man if I'd ever seen one. I hated it that the responsibility for Sandie's kids had fallen into his lap, but I'd just been reassigned to Missouri and alternating weekends were the best I could do. Out of love for Sandie and concern for his health, I took a week's leave and helped Dads move down south. I'd purchased a ticket, flown to New York, loaded a Ryder truck with his few possessions, and driven him and Sandie's kids straight to his new home.

But by the time we arrived in South Carolina, Dads was in bad shape. He was so sick I rushed him to the nearest emergency room. Not enough oxygen in his blood is what the doctors said, and he's been sucking on an oxygen tank ever since. Right now he's hooked up to one of them little green oxygen canisters, but he has a big electric breathing machine in the trunk that truly scares the shit out of me. I was afraid he'd stop breathing while I was driving, and then what the hell would I do? All of that military combat lifesaver practice was done on dummies. I didn't know if I could handle the real thing.

Sandie's kids were great though. During most of the ride they'd been quiet and low-key, which was good because I wasn't up for any stuff out of them. I was stressing hard enough over my own children. Just the thought of my sons made me feel like ten brands of dog shit. I'd chosen to be stationed in Missouri because it was where Sandie would complete the second phase of her officer training. She'd been rebranched into the Engineer Corps, and I wanted us to be together. She seemed happy when I told her we'd be on the same base, and she reminded me that her best friend, Charmel, was also stationed there.

But in order to be with Sandie, I had to give up something equally as important. A transfer to Missouri meant I had to leave my boys behind. Lou had bitched a little, but she'd just landed a good job writing for a major directorate, so she decided to keep the boys in Virginia and continue to live in our old apartment. Her only other option would have been to move back to Philly and live with her sister.

A little over three weeks ago I moved into a nice little room in the barracks and went about dedicating a shrine to my sons. I hung their pictures, cards, and letters everywhere, and most days I just sat at my desk staring at their faces and crying for hours. Guilt and loneliness were eating my black ass up.

And it showed.

I was down to 179 pounds soaking wet, and when I looked in the mirror I saw death riding a horse backward.

I was too depressed to eat. Or to blow cadence. Forget about my music.

I *never* ran.

I didn't have the strength or the desire. If I wasn't working, I either slept or wrote long lyrical letters to Sandie.

My baby.

The next time I rolled into Fort Leonard Wood she'd be by my side, and that was the only thought that kept me going. Sandie had become my everything. I'd placed my baby up on a high pedestal, and if not for the promise of her presence in my life I'd have probably drunk myself to death—or done something else equally as stupid. Sandie had been awarded a few weekend passes during the last two months, and each time she called I'd hauled ass down to Georgia and tightened that ass up.

My baby was smart as hell! Her grades were near the top of her class, and she'd done well on her runs—but she was skinny. Sandie had lost far too much weight. She almost didn't have any dip left in her hip, and she was nowhere near as plump as when I met her. Shit, I'd had enough of puny women to last me a lifetime, and I kinda missed those sister-girl curves.

But Sandie was happy as hell. She loved the way her jeans fit and the way her ass had ceased to jiggle in those sexy little dresses she wore. Not me. I wanted more meat in my rice, and I didn't pull any punches when I told her so! I'd rented a Lexus and gone down to visit her early last month, and we'd had some of the best sex ever. Skinny or no. I'd told her to go off the Pill when she started OCS— no need in pumping all those drugs into her body when she wouldn't be having sex for months—so I stopped in Atlanta and bought a big box of latex designer rubbers.

I never even opened one.

I'd needed to actually feel her satin, and I did. Her sex was soooo good! Sandie was bottomless. Strong and steady. When we made love I shot my grief, fear, and doubts—along with my life—into the endless well of her womanhood, and she was able to absorb it all.

Every drop.

Everything about her turned me on. Her smell, her taste, her touch, her laugh. Sheeiit, I swear. I could've drunk more than just her bathwater. I could've eaten her drawers! As it was, I licked every inch of her from her forehead to her feet, and nothing in this world had ever tasted so sweet. I was in tears. I swear.

I could barely wait to see Sandie march across that stage tomorrow. Across that stage and into my future. She was the oxygen tank from which I drew my breath. I needed her. I needed her to assuage the guilt and anger I felt at myself for leaving my boys alone with their crazy excuse for a mother.

Fatherless is how I kept thinking of my sons.

Another number one domino gone from the life of a black child, and, therefore, another black child left alone to live the struggle.

Hannibal and Mansa. Two lost little black boys.

Just like my daddy, I'd failed to be the keeper of my castle. Instead, I'd forced the number two domino to step up to the plate and fill my shoes.

What kind of king am I?

Deeply ashamed, I struggled with my conscience day and night. It was a struggle I was steadily losing. If the sun was shining, I wanted it to rain. If the heavens released liquid, then I prayed to drown quickly.

Damn, love *hurts*.

As I glanced at Sandie's children in the rearview mirror, I couldn't help but wish the faces reflected there were a combination of mine and Lou's. I wanted my boys so much that it was making me crazy. I needed my children. I needed them *bad.*

And no other man's kids would do.

"Second Lieutenant Sanderella D. Coffee, United States Army, Engineer Corps."

That would be me! I stepped up proudly and snatched the mock diploma with my left hand and shook hands with the Commandant with my right. Then I half stepped past him and pumped the company commander's rough, dry hand, and then squeezed the sweaty palm of the post chaplain.

And then I was free!

I held my shoulders proud and erect as I stepped across the highly polished wood floor and marched off that stage like a lean, green killing machine. Bright snatches of light flashed on my left, and I heard my babies yelling, "Way to go, Mommy!" Rom and Daddy clapped furiously.

It was over.

I'd completed Army Officer Candidate School. I was a graduate. A Second Louie. I could barely believe it! I glanced down at the rank insignia on my lapels to confirm it. Fourteen weeks of running like a dog, cussing like a cretin, living in the woods, and peeing behind bushes was finally over! I was fifteen pounds lighter and four shades darker, but I felt good. Damn good.

When my entire class had crossed the stage, the drill officers marched us outside to a large parade field. It was our last time in formation as Officer Candidate School trainees. We were now bona fide officers, the cream of the crop. OCS graduates. My dream had come true! The rest of my career would be gravy.

I scanned the crowd under the warm April sun, searching for a sign of my family. Hanif spotted me first. "Mommy!" he yelled, and then took off running. His short legs pumped furiously, and he hurled his body toward me like a loose cannon. I caught my son in my arms and planted loud, wet kisses all over his smiling chocolate-snap face. It was good to see my children, and even better to see my daddy. He looked trim and handsome in a starched white shirt, his initials embroidered on the chest pocket, tucked into navy blue dress slacks. He wore a light and dark blue tie I'd given him one Father's Day, along with his trademark Kangol, this one in ivory.

I buried my face in his neck. Daddy patted my back and told me how proud he was of me. Rom stood off to the side with a slight smile as he allowed me to bask in the pleasure of my family. I'd make it up to him later.

Daddy tired easily, so we decided to get on the road right away. We were taking him and the boys back to South Carolina where they'd stay until I was settled in at Fort Leonard Wood. Jamillah would come with me, and once I found a house, I would return south and pick up Kharim and Hanif.

"I hope they won't be too much on you, Daddy," I said, with a question in my voice.

"Nonsense, Pook. I can handle it. My boys will be fine. You just go and get yourself settled. Don't worry about us."

Daddy managed to ease my mind well enough for us to take off two days later. As we pulled away from Daddy's new red-brick home, Kharim and Hanif waved sadly from a large bay window. I felt terrible about leaving them again, and I cried for a long time before falling asleep next to Jamillah in the backseat. Rom drove the entire eighteen hours to Missouri, stopping only for food and gas, and twice to use the rest room. He was unusually quiet. Polite but reserved, and although I could tell something was bothering him, I had too much on my mind to labor over it.

Mama was still in the intensive care unit and hooked up to a respirator. Daddy couldn't breathe worth a damn, even though he was tethered to an oxygen pump twenty-four/seven. Ladelle was sick, yet trying her best to make a difference to her child, and the look in my little girl's eyes told me she was unhappy even though her mouth would not.

Rom's problems would just have to wait.

I had bigger fish to fry.

—

We arrived at Fort Leonard Wood's temporary housing unit late Thursday night. Since Rom and I were both in the combat arms field, I ended up being assigned to a small engineer unit in his brigade. At seven o'clock Friday morning I met my company commander, a freckle-faced man of about thirty who blushed quickly and grinned even faster. Captain Perry seemed to be the perfect antidote to Captain Silberman, and I thanked my lucky stars for getting a commander whom I could stomach.

I asked, "How many female officers are assigned to this battalion?"

Captain Perry shook his head. "Just one. You."

"How about the brigade?"

He smiled. "You're it, L.T.! Don't worry. I'm sure you can hold your own."

I stared at him. "How many minorities?"

A red flush crept up his neck and darkened his cheeks. "Sorry. Just you."

"Wow," I whispered. I had been one of few in the past, but never had I been the lone raisin in such a vast bowl of oatmeal.

Captain Perry brightened. "Why don't you take the day off, Lieutenant Coffee," he said touching my arm. "I'll see you Monday morning at six. We'll schedule your in-brief with both the brigade and battalion commanders, and after that you can in-process the installation at your leisure."

Yes! In-process at my leisure! Only spot in the pot or not, I liked this officer stuff already!

Later that evening Rom and I made sweet love in the shower. He lifted me easily, his strong hands gripping my hips as he raised and lowered me faster and faster, our bodies slippery and coated with scented bubbles beneath the drizzle of warm water until we both exploded like a truckload of artillery. Afterward, we dropped Jamillah off at Charmel's and headed out for dinner at the home of Kharel Rogers, one of Rom's long-time fraternity brothers.

Kharel was tall, fine, bowlegged, and single. He was an explosive ordnance expert the same as Rom, except Kharel was an officer and

held the rank of major. I'd met him through Rom while we were stationed in Virginia, and I was forever trying to hook him up with one
of my friends. Kharel was a known player, and he just *knew* he had it
going on! I thought he needed a steady woman in his life. A strong
sister to anchor his fickle ass. I had to give it to him though—his stuff
was tight. He was fine, funny, educated, articulate, progressive, and
pro-black. Everything a black woman was looking for, and certainly
what most of us deserved!

To celebrate my graduation, Kharel had invited Rom and me over
to his bachelor condominium for dinner and some funky jazz. He
also invited his latest diversion: a tall, leggy sister he introduced as
Tami Woodson.

A Vanessa Williams clone, Miss Tami (with one *m* and an *i*, she
pointed out) looked like she could faint at the drop of a hat. She sat
on the buttery leather sofa with her knees pressed so tight I was sure
a pat of pure butter wouldn't melt in her mouth. It surprised me that
an Afrocentric brother like Kharel could be attracted to her. At first
glance I'd taken her for a cousin instead of a sistah, because Tami
was as far from black as you could possibly get and still claim a drop
of African blood. Hers was the kind of fair face and frail wisp of a
body displayed on the covers of leading magazines, the typical token
Negro—not black enough to be threatening, but not white enough
to actually pass.

If you bought into the dominant ideology standard of European
beauty that society insisted on holding up as a measuring stick for
African beauty, then Tami would be considered attractive. But her
priggish attitude worked on my last nerve. Every time I asked her a
question, she glanced at Kharel for permission to speak. I knew she
was a flipping Oreo when she admitted that she had never played
spades.

"You've never played spades?" I bucked my eyes at her and
gasped. Now what kneegrow in these United States of America had
never before played spades? I was through with her Barbie-doll ass
after that. Miss Tami must have noticed my cold attitude, because
she tried to make small talk.

"I hear you've recently completed officer training. I just landed a job as a senior financial analyst with Merrill Lynch." She said this without boasting, as a mere statement of fact.

"That's great," I replied. "How'd you manage to land a position like that at your age? You can't be more than, what? Twenty-three?"

She grinned. "Actually, I'm twenty-seven. I graduated summa cum laude from Harvard University. I worked my way through college while enrolled in a financial program. I also have a three-year-old son."

I was impressed with her educational and professional achievements, and I told her so. We chatted for a few more minutes, and to my surprise I found myself beginning to like her. After a few more minutes of conversation it was plain to see that Tami was a real sistah, of that there was no doubt, and because of that she faced some of the same hardships I faced, fair-skinned or not. I admonished myself for making such a hasty judgment of her based on her outward appearance, then excused myself and rummaged through a stack of CDs. While Kharel and Rom fixed our plates, I let Michael Franks serenade me with the lazy tunes of *Crayon Sun*.

I stuffed myself on porterhouse steak, salad, and home fries, then stretched out on the shaggy white carpet in Kharel's den and closed my eyes. I left Rom and Kharel up talking smack about Mike Tyson, while Miss Tami sat on the sofa making goo-goo eyes at Kharel.

I dozed lightly, then felt my stomach lurch and opened my eyes. Either my period was coming or Kharel had fed me some bad meat. Whatever the origin of my ailment, I felt like crap, and I wanted to go home. I walked to the bathroom with the feathery carpet tickling my toes. As I squatted over the toilet, the odor of fresh urine assaulted my nostrils. Wow! My water sure smelled funny. I must be coming down with something. I flushed the toilet and washed my hands. I glanced in the mirror and saw the beginnings of what looked like acne fanning my cheeks and forehead. I frowned. My complexion was usually smooth and clear; I thought those days of puberty-induced acne were long gone.

I wandered into the living room and found Rom. I gave him the signal that I was ready to leave, and he responded promptly. He knew when I was ready to go, I was ready to *go*.

I was thankful when we reached our driveway. Jamillah was spending the night at Charmel's, so I fell into bed with my clothes on, whispered my prayers, and drifted off. At some point during the night I felt Rom unbutton my pants and slide them down past my hips. He pulled the covers gently up to my chin. I wanted to thank him, but I was too tired to speak. Sometimes he could be the most gentle, loving, considerate man in the world.

This was one of those times.

A few weeks later I stood at the bathroom sink brushing my teeth and my eyes rested on an unused pack of birth control pills sticking out of my cosmetic bag. They'd been in my bag for so long they'd become part of the décor. I hadn't really noticed them. Until now. A cold panic slid through my bones.

Right before my OCS graduation I'd been waiting for the Sunday after my period in order to begin my new pack of pills. But that Sunday had never come. My period had never come.

Frantically, I backtracked in my mind. I remembered having a menstrual cycle during the last field exercise of OCS. It had been a bitch being out in the field and on the rag, but Rom had made it up to me when I returned to garrison to find him waiting for me in a rented Lexus. I'd rocked his world that weekend. I swear. My stuff was so good I made the boy *cry*.

My memory whirled on rewind. I'd expected another period a week or so before graduation, over three weeks ago. Could that be right? I thought and thought and finally had to conclude that yes, indeed, that field period had been my last period. I was late.

Could I be pregnant?

Hell no! My God wouldn't do that to me. He knew I couldn't take it. I'd be foaming at the mouth and pulling my hair out if I had another baby! Maybe I had an infection, something wrong inside my pocketbook. Or maybe it was stress. With all of the worrying about Mama, Ladelle, and Daddy—and still grieving for Bailey—I'd been more than stressed-out lately. I'd heard that stress could sometimes hold up a period. Besides, I remembered feeling crampy a few weeks earlier, proof that it had been trying to come down. I stepped out of my bathrobe and took off my panties and bra.

"Ouch!" I caught my right nipple on my bra strap. It stood throbbing and erect, as if it had been chewed on. I gently extracted the left beast. It hurt, too! Maybe my breasts were sore because I was getting my period, right? That sometimes happened to me. Not always, but every now and then they'd get a little tender around that time of the month. Yeah, I reasoned. That must be it!

I tried to think back to when I was pregnant with Kharim, how did it feel? Hell, it was so traumatic I'd blocked the entire nine months from my memory bank!

I stepped into the shower and turned the water on hot. Slowly, I added cold water until it was just as I liked it. I soaped up and enjoyed the silky feel of the scented bubbles. I attempted to wash the beasts, then winced with pain. They throbbed ferociously. Instead of rubbing them with the washcloth I was forced to squeeze warm soapy water over my great balls of fire.

This was strange. I'd have to see a doctor. Maybe I needed a breast exam. I was very slack about doing them myself every month. Yeah, I needed to get my tetas checked. I made a mental note to call my family practice doctor and make an appointment. I dried off and wrapped a towel around my torso. Then I washed my face thoroughly with plain Ivory soap and hoped it would clear up some of those damned pimples that seemed to be invading my mug.

It was Saturday, and Jamillah was at the beauty parlor with Charmel and her daughter, Aminah. Rom and I planned to spend a little quality time together, making love while listening to our favorite old jams. I walked into the bedroom and began slathering my skin with Halston body creme. As the fragrance filled the air, I covered my mouth and wrinkled my nose. Halston didn't smell nearly as good as it used to. Maybe I'd had it too long. Nah, lotion didn't go bad, did it? Rom walked in as I massaged the smooth creme into my arms, legs, and belly.

"Damn, San! Look at those hooters!"

"Leave me alone!" I giggled. "I've always been busty. You like big breasts, remember?"

"I know, baby, but they look even bigger than usual."

I turned and looked in the mirror. He was right. They were huge, with blue-green veins running along the sides. My nipples were hard and thick. And at least an inch long. Rom came up behind me and cupped one breast in each hand.

"They're heavy, too."

I felt his nature rising against me as his fingers wandered over to squeeze my nipples. "Don't!" I hollered. I moved out of reach and left his hands empty and still up in the air.

"What's wrong? They can't be sore. I haven't tasted them in almost a week."

I winced. "You won't taste them any time soon either. I'm making an appointment with Dr. Musgrave next week. I think I need a breast exam. They feel like live wires. Like I should put warm compresses on them or something."

"I know what you need," he grabbed my hand and placed it on his swollen crotch, "and it sure as *hell* ain't no warm compress!" With my hand pressed to his groin, he made an obscene movement to be sure I got his drift.

Suddenly my wild beasts began to throb with a different rhythm. Now *this* was a beat I could boogie to! I stepped into Rom's arms and inhaled his musky masculine scent, which never failed to turn me on. He rubbed my slippery body, and we began a slow, sensuous *nasty dance*. We slid down to the floor and began showing each other wordlessly what there was no need to say. He slipped his fingers inside me, then brought them up to his lips and sucked my juices from their tips. I couldn't wait a moment longer. I grabbed his thickness with both hands and guided him toward that ache in my center. I gasped as he pushed himself into me and covered my breasts with kisses. We rocked together in long slow movements until I thought I would die. I saw glistening stars and heard a symphony of glee as my man hovered above me and gave me all he had, then slid down my hungry body to taste my joy. Through the haze of my climax I realized that this was one of those *real* good times, and much later I would cherish the memory of that sweet afternoon. In the height of his passion, my king licked and kissed and made love to me as though I was the sexiest, most beautiful woman alive.

It's a shame the good times can't last forever.

23

FIGHT OR LEAVE

I sat up so fast I got dizzy. The room spun around like one of those crazy teacup rides, and I gripped the damp sheets, hoping their solidity would give me a reality check. I wasn't one for dreams, and if I had them I sure as hell didn't remember them, but this one was different. Garbled scenes of my sons. Of me as a kid. The dream held me in its clutches, and I fought like crazy as I dragged it with me into the wakeful world, leaving my body drenched in sweat and my pillow soaked with guilty tears.

I glanced at Sandie, surprised she'd not been disturbed by my thrashing. My mouth was dry, and the odor of my stale sweat was in the air. The need for my sons ached and ricocheted within me like the pulse of a rotten tooth. Festering and overrun with pus, my wounds were self-inflicted, and while that alone dashed any hopes for sympathy, the fact that I'd done this to myself is what made it even harder to bear.

I eased from the damp bed and tiptoed into the bathroom. There I stood beneath the spigot, the angry spray of water biting my skin as I turned the cold tap left, increasing the water temperature and inflicting a physical punishment upon my body that I hoped would obliterate the haunted torture in my soul.

Back in the bedroom I dressed quietly, then kissed Sandie on her cheek. It was Sunday and the over-thirty league at the gym was scheduled to play a few games of ball. Since it was still early I jogged the half mile to my barracks room and turned on the jazz station while I sorted through a week's worth of mail. I threw the circulars and other junk items in the trash and stacked the bills atop my desk. I'd just rubbed some odorless Ben-Gay into my shoulders and was sliding a knee brace onto my right leg when the heavy banging on my door startled me.

I stood up, then quickly sat back down. There were six rooms on my wing, and most of the guys were lower-enlisted members. Whoever was out there knocking had to have the wrong room.

"'Sup?" I called gruffly. I wasn't in the mood for any half-blind, hungover privates pissing on the carpet and searching for a spot to lay their heads. "Yo," I said loudly. "Keep on stepping down the hall. You got the wrong room, bro."

The pounding grew louder. More insistent.

"Step on down the fuckin' hall!"

The door rattled in its frame.

I stood up and crossed the room in two strides. I wasn't in the mood to mess around with these bonehead soldiers, and I had to remind myself to maintain a little military bearing. I snatched the door open. "Damn! Can't you hear? Didn't I say—"

"Yes," he said, "I can hear. I heard you just fine."

We locked eyes and I stared, afraid to believe what I was seeing, yet hopeful at the same time. I'd waited a lot of years for this day. Had practiced for hours in front of the mirror at karate class, and I was ready.

He stood there like we'd seen each other just yesterday. Calm and composed, a slight grin on his face, his hands clasped easily in front of him. His goatee and beard were now salt-and-pepper but still neatly trimmed, and his chin was square and set in the manner of a man at peace with himself. His eyes were the same as I remembered, and he was heavier and more muscular, but it was him.

He was quiet even as he broke the silence. "I know you've got the proper manners 'cause I taught them to you myself. Now are you going to invite your old man in, or are you going to make me stand outside in the hall?"

I felt like ice inside. Like a huge iceberg, a solid block with no soul. The last time we'd stood this close I'd had to bend my head back to look up into his face. Today we stood toe to toe. I was finally eye to eye with my mirror image fast-forwarded twenty years, and I glared at him like he was some stray nigger in the street who had crossed me. I took a slow step backward and swirled my tongue around the inside of my cheeks until I gathered a thick glob of spit in my mouth. I watched him like a hawk as I spat forcefully at his feet, then I raised my fists and went into a crouch, because no man spit on Solomon Caesar and lived to talk about it.

His jaw went tight. "You can put your hands down, son. I didn't come here to fight."

I thumbed my nose and sniffed like a boxer. My shoulders alternately bobbed up and down.

"Fight or leave, motherfucker."

"Not fighting, not leaving." He stood rooted. Planted in place.

"Then bring your ass, Solly." I was up on my toes, motioning him forward. "Bring your ass."

"I didn't come to fight," he repeated. He took a white cloth from his pocket and bent over and carefully wiped my spit off his shoe. "I came to talk, Romulus. To set things right between us."

I laughed bitterly. "There's nothing happening between us. How did you find me?" I kept my hands up. A punk like him was not beyond a sucker punch. He'd suckered me for years, but that was then and this was now.

"I called Athena. She told me where you were stationed. The rest was easy."

As much as I wanted to open up a can of whup-ass on him, I was curious. After all these years, what had compelled my father to come all the way to bum-fuck Missouri just to see me? What the hell had he told my sister to make her give up the goods on my whereabouts? I was more than curious. My inquiring mind wanted to *know*.

"State your business," I barked. "You've got five minutes."

"That's plenty of time."

I stepped back, and he stepped in.

"I've got cancer. Prostate cancer."

"And? So what? I'm supposed to feel sorry for you? I had the mumps when I was thirteen. Where were you?"

I'd pulled a chair into the center of the room and motioned for him to sit. I was perched on the edge of my bed. Ready to rush him. Clip him at the knees and take him out at the slightest sign of static. Solomon's gaze was steady. His eyes strong. He didn't look sick at all to me. He looked like he could put his fist through my chest and break my backbone.

He sighed and hitched up his pants legs at the knees. "One, I'm not telling you this to make you feel sorry for me. Two, I know you had the mumps. I paid for your hospital care. Three, I didn't come here expecting your sympathy or your forgiveness." He spread his hands apart, palms up. "Look, son—"

"My father's name is Eddie Jenkins," I growled, "so you can chill with all that bullshit. Just call me Rom, and let that 'son' shit roll."

"Okay. Look, Rom. I came here to apologize. To explain. Your mother and I were finished. Through. But I was wrong to leave you the way I did. Wrong to leave your sisters that way, too. At the time I thought I was doing what was best in the long run. I mean, you heard all of the arguments. All the fights. I didn't want you kids growing up with that kind of trauma, with those kind of memories—"

"So you did the bird and left us no memories at all?"

He sighed again. For the first time I saw the age in his face, and even a hint of his sickness.

"I went about things the wrong way. I know that now, but by the time I realized my mistakes, you were a teenager and I told myself I'd already lost you. I was a coward. Ashamed and afraid to come back into your life. Afraid you'd react this same way. I didn't want to face your rejection."

I leaped from the bed and circled him like a vulture. "*Fuck* you!" I raged. "My rejection? Your abandonment! Keeper of the castle . . .

you disgust me. We almost starved! You left Mama alone to scratch out a living with five mouths to feed!" I towered above him shaking with rage, my fists clenched harder than two steel girders. Daddy raised his eyes slowly to mine and as clear as day I saw his regret. His remorse. His pain . . . and yes, even his love. It pissed me off even further.

"Okay. I've earned your wrath. But I came to tell you that I'm sorry, Rom. Yeah, I left. I felt like I had to leave. But not like that. I could have asked for joint custody or something, but in those days a white judge would have looked at me, a black man, and laughed. Still, I have no excuse for those wasted years. Years when I sent money when I should have sent letters. When I should have called you. Should have been at your games. At your wedding. There for the birth of my grandkids. I fucked up and made a mess of everything, but having this cancer has taught me something. Taught me that as long as I'm still breathing I can make amends, atone for my sins. I can forgive myself, correct my errors, apologize, and continue to live. So go ahead and hate me if it makes you feel better. But while you're hating me, do something else, too. Be a better father than I was. You have what it takes to be a real Caesar. To be a true king."

I exhaled fire down at him and prayed he could feel the heat of my hell. My voice was so quiet I scared myself. "You fraud-ass mother-fucker," I whispered. "Of course I'm the better man! I picked up your slack, didn't I?"

"What?"

"You left me there to fill your shoes, remember? To be the number one domino! The man you didn't have the balls to be. Know what, Solly? I hope that cancer eats you alive. I hope it grows tiny little feet in your nuts and makes your dick fall off before tramping up to roost in your chicken-shit guts. I hope it blinds you. Takes your sight and terrifies you during the night. I hope it makes you piss your bed. Makes you scared to go to sleep. I hope that cancer lurks in your closet like a big black boogeyman who wears my face. Our face. I hope it tears out your worthless heart. The same way you tore out mine."

He stood up and stared at me for a long time. His lower lip

quivered, and his broad chest quaked. A tear slipped from his eye, the moisture shone on his skin like oil. "I love you, son."

"Fuck you. Get out."

My daddy moved toward the door and paused with his hand on the knob. Then he threw me the sucker punch of my natural life.

"Tell me something." Daddy's face was unreadable as he crossed over the threshold. His face was stone as he questioned me. "What's your story? Where are your sons? And why aren't you there with them?"

24

WHATCHOO TALKIN' 'BOUT, WILLIS?

We were having Sunday dinner with Charmel and Troy, and it felt damned good to have a homegirl around. Rom had faked a headache and wanted to stay at home in bed, but I threw a huge hissy fit that quickly made him see things my way. He was working my *last* nerve. He'd come home from the gym this morning in a funky sullen mood, and now he expected me to cater to it. Picture that!

Charmel lived five minutes away from us on the other side of the base, and we saw each other almost every day. Today she'd prepared a large dinner for us, and while Jamillah and Aminah went outside to play, Rom sat like a zombie in the den with Mel's husband, Troy.

As soon as the men were settled in front of the large-screen television, Mel grabbed my arm and dragged me upstairs to her bedroom. She shoved a pile of clothes off the bed and motioned for me to sit. "Hun-nee, I am *pissed!*" She stood over me with her hands on her wide hips. "That muthafucka!"

"*Who?*"

"That no-good pussy-chasin' two-timing stank-breath son of a bitch!"

I was lost. Beads of sweat stood out on Mel's nose, and her breasts quivered beneath her shirt. She *was* pissed!

"Look." I grabbed her hand and urged her to sit beside me on the bed. "Slow down and talk to me. Now what's wrong?"

"That damned Nick!"

"With the big black dick?"

"Yeah! That Shaba-Ranks-Shaka-Zulu-*Seal*-looking muthafucka!"

I shook my head dumbly. "Hold up . . . I thought your N's were working? So now he's an S?"

She screwed up her pretty face. "No, he's a goddamn M! He . . . he's married!"

My eyeballs bugged out of my head. "Whatchoo talkin' 'bout, Willis?"

"You heard me! He has a wife and seven goddamn kids!"

Whoa! So I wasn't the only fool with my fingers in the wrong pie! "Dayum." I made a low whistling noise. "How'd you find out? Did he tell you?"

Mel snorted. "Naw, hunny, he wasn't man enough for that, but he didn't have to *tell* me anything, because I ran into him in the commissary with his worn-out wife and seven rug rats trailing behind him like ducks in a row! And they had the nerve to be pushing *two* shopping carts, each one filled to the top with milk, diapers, and enough generic Cheerios to choke a fucking herd of cattle!"

"I bet you cussed his ass out!"

She grinned. "Uh-huh, sho' did, but that's not all I did. . . . I called that liar's house about a trillion times—till he got smart and took the phone off the hook! Then I beeped him like a motherfucka. Hunny-chile, I put in all kinds of numbers! I blew that pager up to the stratis-fuckin-phere! I put in the numbers to the Pulaski County Animal Shelter, the Hair Replacement Center for Men, the judge's chambers in Family Court, the Missouri Battered Women's Shelter—I even sent that asshole some dehydrated sea horses and a foot fungus kit!"

I let Mel rant and rave, but I really didn't understand her beef. She could have saved herself a lot of energy by calling 1-800-Rent-a-Dog. She was just as married as Mr. Big Stuff, or Shaka, or Seal, or whoever he was to her today. Unlike Rom and me, both Mel and Nick were scandalous, so what was the problem? Mel had lost it. Gone off the deep end over some smooth criminal who had played her just as hard as she'd played Troy!

But Mel wasn't the only one who seemed to have gone fishing. Rom had turned into a weeping willow. Every time I turned around, he looked as if somebody had just killed his pet rock! He never wanted to do anything fun anymore. He was short in his speech and manner with me, he snapped at Jamillah for the littlest thing, and he slept like a pregnant woman. He even had the nerve to admit, "I'm depressed."

Like I was supposed to feel sorry for him!

Who the hell had time to get depressed? In my family one got depressed before lunch, and that mess was over with by dinner! Or you got depressed before going to bed at night and snapped out of it by morning. We seldom admitted it, we never wallowed in it, and we sure as hell weren't proud of it!

Although he was still sweet on occasion, Rom's attitude and personality had changed drastically. He seemed distant and sad most of the time, sleepy and cranky at others.

He'd turned into Lou.

For the entire day he'd walked around like his lips were glued together. He even stayed quiet during Charmel's dinner, and on the way home he never said a single word. Inside, he marched up the stairs and went straight to bed. Whatever was eating at him was tearing him up, but I had a hard time feeling for the brother when his statements were so abstract. The most I could get out of him was that he missed his boys, and while I could understand that and certainly relate to his pain, I couldn't believe it had dragged him to these depths.

I took a quick shower and sat on my side of the bed. I stared at Rom's broad back. His shoulders rose and fell rhythmically. I told myself his sleeping binges were better than him starting another argument, or worse, shuffling around like a zombie who was already dead.

To hell with it, I thought as I turned down the heavy spread and climbed into bed. I felt under my pillow, found my scarf, tied it around my hair, then slid between the sheets with my fists balled up—just in case while I was sleeping old raggedy King Romulus tried to start some shit!

That I'd become my father's son, there was little doubt, but even as I plotted my departure, I knew I had to make love to her one last time. To feel her. Once more I had to taste her love. To spread her thighs and drown in her wetness. To dive into the well of her womanhood and surrender my sanity to the peaceful waters of her love.

Solomon Caesar had really struck me this time. Daddy's latest sucker punch had caught me high in the chest and felled me like a tree. But his brutal blow was just what it took to restore sight to my love-blinded eyes. He'd ripped off my love-colored lenses and slammed my face into a full-length mirror until I finally saw myself—straight, no chaser. Like him, I'd placed my own happiness ahead of the welfare of my boys. I'd taken away their stability, their family structure, and I'd made them a statistic. Here I thought I was being my own man and making my own decisions, when in reality I'd been traveling along the roads my daddy had already paved. Walking in his foolish footsteps. And all in the name of love.

I knew what I had to do. That much, at least, was very clear. My manhood demanded it. My obligations as a father mandated it. It was going to be rough and painful, but I deserved it. The trouble was, Sandie didn't. My going back to Lou would devastate Sandie, but I had to figure out a way to tell her. To let her down gently without destroying all the goodness our love had built. My need for her clogged my throat like a million bubbles, suffocating me and threatening to choke all the life from me. I'd spent the whole day with her and her friend, yet I couldn't speak in her presence. Couldn't bring myself to look her in the eye. Somehow I thought she'd read the betrayal in my heart. She'd be able to hear the guilt in my voice and see it in my face. That's why I needed to touch her. There'd be nothing but tenderness in my arms, and that's how I wanted her to remember me.

After putting Solomon out, I'd sat in my room crying until I threw up. I walked around touching the walls and caressing all the cards and pictures of my sons, and then I reread every single letter Sandie had ever written to me and cried even more. I felt absolutely no love for Lou. In fact, I detested her. But was my love for Sandie worth losing my boys? Was loving any woman enough of an excuse to leave my kids? I had to be one worthless nigger to do what I'd done. A chip off the old block is what I was, and just like Solomon I was a sorry-ass excuse for a man and for a father. My boys were gonna hate me twice as hard as I had hated him. But they could never hate me as much as I hated myself. As I hated my daddy. Hated my wife. And a certain part of me also hated Sandie. For loving me so perfectly. For allowing me to love her, to hope for a future with her.

During dinner at Charmel's house I made my decision. I would call Lou and ask her to give up her apartment and come to Missouri. I would put my name on the housing list and get a set of government quarters for my wife and my sons. Right here on the same post with the woman I loved. I would sacrifice my happiness for the sake of my kids, and I'd live an empty life and die a slow, agonizing death. By degrees. A little bit more each time I thought of Sandie.

I suffered in silence the entire day. Sandie got pissed when I refused to talk to her and shoot the shit with Charmel's man, but it took all of my energy to hold back the storm raging inside of me until I could feel her one last time. When we got home, I jumped right in the bed. All desire for tenderness had left me. I'd wanted to tear her clothes off in the car and make love to her until we both cried, but I managed to control the fury brewing in my gut. To momentarily suppress my self-loathing.

She took her time climbing in beside me. I felt her eyes roaming over me, burning me with her reservations, but I remained still. Like a panther. Stalking that ass.

I pounced on her as soon as she wrapped that ugly red scarf around her head.

I pulled her into me and ground my rock-hard dick into her stomach. Moaning, I squeezed her full breasts, kneading them with both hands. I snatched her shirt off and buried my face in their warmth, suckling from her nipples like an infant, forcing them together and pulling both dark knobs into my mouth at once, rolling them around like sweet raisins on my tongue. I felt her breath deepening and I pulled her panties aside at the crotch and thrust my fingers into her wetness. She tried to back away, to run from my wrath, but I held her fast and dug my fingers around in her slickness until I could feel every bit of the surface inside her. "Rom, wait," she protested, but I covered her mouth with mine and completely ripped off her panties.

With my knees thrust between her legs, I entered her roughly. Grabbing her ass with both my hands, I bit into her neck as I pulled her up, making her climb the length of my dick before slamming my pelvis into hers. Over and over I rode her like a tidal wave. Bucking and thrusting like an animal, I chewed her nipples and screamed into her breasts as the tears fell from my eyes. I forced my tongue down her throat until she gasped and choked. Her nails raked skin from my back. I turned her over and hammered her ass from behind. Then I flipped her onto her back again and thrust myself into her sweetness once more. I felt my orgasm rushing through me, pounding upon my head like a sledgehammer, and I prepared to meet my death. Sandie was helpless as I nailed her to the bed. My dick acted on its own accord, impaling her through the stomach and forcing its way out of her throat. Cries for mercy scraped my senses as they burst from the back of her throat, spurring me on to glory.

And at the moment of my death, her name fell from my lips.

25

WHOSE TITTIES ARE THOSE?

The moment I touched the sheets, Rom rolled over and jumped my bones. He was like a demon possessed; never before had he touched me with so much fury and naked desire. I was helpless beneath him as he pulled me into his arms and proceeded to make a violent, almost desperate love to me that left me sore and crying, until my hair, wet with our sweat, lay plastered against my scalp and my scarf sailed to the floor. It was a full fifteen minutes after his orgasm before I could convince him to release me from his death grip. When he finally let me up, I staggered into the bathroom, and to my horror, found drying streaks of blood coating my thighs.

With my insides throbbing, I took a quick shower and slipped into a pair of cotton underwear. My private parts ached down to the core, and I slipped into a yellow cotton duster, then stormed back to our bedroom and slapped Rom's bare back so hard, a cracking sound like white lightning filled the air.

"What the hell was that all about?"

He mumbled something but did not move.

I slapped him again. "Turn your ass over and look at me! Answer me! Why would you try to hurt me that way?"

Slowly, he rolled over, his body tangled in the bright sheets, the yellow splash of daisies threaded through his strong dark legs and wrapped around his tapered waist. Tears glistened in his eyes and lit up the room with immeasurable amounts of sadness and pain.

"Sorry, baby. I'm sorry I hurt you. That's something I never intended to do."

"I don't understand, Rom. Something is very wrong here, and I just don't understand it."

"It won't happen again," he whispered, reaching for me through the darkness, his eyes mute and begging my forgiveness. "I'm sorry. It won't happen again."

I knelt on the bed and let myself be pulled into arms that were once again strong with tenderness, bewildered by this sudden change in my man. Whimpering his apologies and begging my forgiveness, Rom massaged my arms and shoulders and kissed my hair until I finally relaxed and drifted into slumber.

It seemed like minutes later when my eyelids fluttered as the ringing telephone dragged me from the depths of a troubled sleep. My arm snaked out blindly as I reached for the handset and nearly knocked over a half-finished glass of Welch's grape juice.

"Sandie, it's Mama. Baby, are you awake?"

Although Mama Ceal was still hospitalized, she'd been transferred to a cardiac step-down unit a week ago, and, thankfully, she seemed to be doing much better.

"Mama? Is everything okay?" I peered at my digital clock. Eleven-twenty P.M. I'd been asleep for only an hour.

"Baby, we need to talk. I'm at the nurse's station, and I'm going to connect Bunchie on the three-way, so hold on. Don't hang up," she warned.

Uh-oh. A conference call. That couldn't be good, especially at this time of night. Mama Ceal clicked over and connected Bunchie.

"Hi, San."

"Hey, Bunchie, what's going on? Is Ladelle okay?"

"Ladelle is the same. This is about your daddy."

My stomach clenched. "What about Daddy?" I demanded in a voice filled with fear.

"Well, you know he hasn't been feeling well lately. His neighbor, Fat Lady Fields, called Mama and told her your daddy's breathing is really, really bad."

"Has he seen his doctor?"

"Of course he has." Gently, with no annoyance.

"*And?*" With attitude and an impatience born of fear.

"And, the same thing—he's on an oxygen tank around the clock, but he needs to be in a hospital."

"Why didn't anyone tell me?"

"Calm down, Sandie. We didn't want you to worry. We're telling you now."

That was Mama. Ever since I'd joined the Army I was always the last to know everything. Although I spoke to someone in my family on the telephone nearly every day, they persisted in hiding bad news from me. That really pissed me off. I wanted to know what was happening in "real time" as it happened, not after it was all over.

"Where is he? I spoke to him two days ago, and he didn't mention anything to me."

"Like Mama said, we didn't want you to worry. But now, we have a problem."

I was silent. I think I was holding my breath.

"Your daddy won't go to the hospital; he can't stay alone any longer, and he can't take care of your boys. He's too weak, and he needs help fixing his food and stuff—he just shouldn't be alone."

This was serious. I didn't know what to say. Daddy was not a sickly person. Mama Ceal had had three heart attacks before she was forty-five, but even though he'd smoked, Daddy had always been healthy and robust.

"Well, what are we going to do?"

"We have to find someone who can take care of him," Bunchie answered. "Mama Ceal's not healthy herself, or I'm sure she'd do it. Right, Mama?"

"Of course I would, baby. Shucks, Franklin is my heart, but I have no idea when I'll be out of the hospital and able to take care of myself."

I didn't hesitate one second. I never missed a single beat.

"I'll take care of him. I'll go pick him up and bring him here with me."

Mama asked, "Sandie, can you handle that type of responsibility?"

"Mama, I'll do whatever it takes. Daddy has always been there for me." My voice cracked. "Now it's my turn to take care of him."

"What about Rom?" Bunchie asked cautiously.

"What about him?" This was my *father* we were talking about! "Sorry, Bunchie, but Rom ain't Vernon, and I'm not you! I don't need anybody's permission to do right by my daddy!" My mind was made up. I didn't know how we would manage, but somehow I knew we'd make it. Rom knew how I felt about Daddy. He wouldn't object. He'd probably insist on it himself.

I half listened to the rest of their conversation. I was engrossed in making plans to get to South Carolina and back. I knew I might have to do it alone; Rom might not get the time off to take me. No matter. Franklin Brown was *my* father, and I was going.

I decided not to call Daddy. He'd give me a million reasons why I shouldn't come. He'd try to convince me that he was just fine, had a full head of hair, and had been out just last night doing the Electric Slide! No, I'd catch him by surprise and take him prisoner, if necessary.

I hung up the telephone and turned over to Rom. He lay sound asleep; a trickle of clear liquid slipped from the corner of his mouth and stained the fabric of his pillow. I slapped his shoulder, and he opened his eyes.

"Rom, my daddy is sick. He's still on oxygen around the clock, but he can't stay alone any longer."

I didn't pull nary a punch.

"I'm going to get him, baby. I want him here with us."

Rom sat up. For a moment I thought I saw torment on his face. Uncertainty, as though a million conflicting thoughts were surging through his heart. But then it was gone. "Damn, baby," he said. "I'm sorry it's gotten so bad for him." He reached out and tenderly smoothed my hair. "I tell you what. I'll put in an application for ordinary leave, and if it's approved, I'll drive you. If we can get Dads's condition verified by the Red Cross, then I can get at least a week off work." He leaned over and gently kissed his favorite spot on my forehead, then pulled me into his strong arms. "Don't worry, San. I'll help you."

That was just what I needed to hear. All thoughts of that wicked love-whipping he'd just given me were forgotten as I snuggled into the safe haven between his chin and his chest and overlooked all his funky mood swings. As he rubbed my back and kneaded my taut shoulders, I thanked God for making Rom the understanding man that he was and for sending him my way.

Now if I could only stop worrying about my daddy.

It was impossible. I loved Daddy so much I couldn't express it. Although Daddy wasn't a large man in physical stature, he was the strength that I relied on, thus Herculean in my eyes. This was probably because Daddy carried himself like a giant and commanded respect in all he did.

I tossed and turned the rest of the night.

The next morning I called my new commander and gave him a heads up about my emergency leave request. Captain Perry was sympathetic and supportive and promised to put in a good word with Rom's commander, too. When that was done, I sat on the bed and stared at the wall, unsure of what to do next.

"Sandie." Rom poked his head into the bedroom. "Go ahead and pack a few clothes. I'll go to brigade and pick up our leave forms, and then we'll hit the road, okay?"

I nodded. It was a good thing Rom knew how I felt about my daddy. There wasn't a thing I needed to say. I heard the door slam behind him, and I continued to sit, glued to the bed. I wasn't ready to move yet. I felt like I was underwater, my body heavy and leaden.

After a while I dragged myself into the kitchen and dialed Mel's number. I spoke briefly with Jamillah and explained our situation as best I could, then packed a few things for Rom and me to travel with. Suddenly I felt heavy. Weak. Tired. After all, I hadn't slept all night. I slipped into a baby blue duster and sprawled across my unmade bed, intending to catch about twenty winks. What seemed like seconds later, the front door slammed, and I bolted into an upright position. Rom!

Damn. Dizzy.

I staggered into the bathroom to splash cool water on my face, and just as I leaned over the sink a huge wave of nausea engulfed me. I spun around to the toilet and dry-heaved my ass off, which was actually much worse than vomiting. Choking, I brought up a yellow, salty liquid that seared my throat and tongue.

Snot ran freely from my left nostril.

Panting like a heat-struck yard dog, I lay there and hugged the shit can with my cheek pressed mercifully to the cool porcelain. I'd forgotten all about my aversion to toilets; I couldn't have moved if my life depended on it.

"Sandie!" Rom ran over to me. "What's wrong, baby? Did you fall? What happened?"

I shook my head to his barrage of silly questions. Couldn't he see I was dying in the toilet bowl? Just then a fresh wave engulfed me, and this time I simply pointed my nose toward the Ty-D-Bol–tinged water and allowed the egg-colored gook to flow.

"Okay, baby . . . let it out. It's okay." Rom held me around the waist and murmured sweet endearments. Rocking me from behind, he mopped my brow, rubbed my back, and held me tightly each time I heaved.

I realized I was dying. The lining of my stomach was no doubt forcing its way up through my throat. Surely my esophagus was raw and bleeding. No human could possibly retch so horribly without requiring throat surgery. Just when I was convinced that the next heave would send me hurling into the depths of the sewer system, my stomach relaxed and I was finished.

"Here, baby." Rom handed me a toothbrush and blotted my face with a cool cloth.

"Uh-uh!" I managed to grunt. I shoved the toothbrush out of sight. If I stuck one inch of it into my mouth, it would be just like sticking the whole thing down my throat. The heaves would start all over again.

Rom carried me into the bedroom and gently slid me between the covers. My eyes fluttered as I looked up at him.

He studied me as if he'd never seen me before.

"You okay, Sanderella?"

He was getting heavy on me. Not baby, or San, or even Sandie. It was Sanderella. That meant he was serious. Well, two could play that game.

"I'm fine, Romulus." Actually, I did feel a lot better, but he continued to look at me like there was something else he needed to say and couldn't quite put his finger on it.

I smiled and sat up. "See? I'm really okay. Maybe it was just a stress reaction from worrying about Daddy."

Rom shook his head and stormed out of the room. Hell, I was worried, too. I hated to throw up! It was for weaklings, and it was nasty. Besides, it brought your face too close to the toilet. All of the creepy crawlies you thought you'd hit with the bowl brush were brought into zoom view!

I swung my legs over and sat on the edge of the bed. Then I took off my duster and panties and walked naked into the bathroom. Rom stood there shaving, facing the mirror. He spun around and almost cut his own throat when he glimpsed my reflection.

"All right, goddammit, Sanderella!" he roared. "Whose titties are those?"

I cupped my chunky breasts, crossed my legs, pulled in my stomach, smiled, and said demurely, "Yours, King Romulus! All yours!"

Boyfriend was not amused!

"C'mon, San. Those aren't your *real* titties." A beard of foam covered his cheeks, and he hunched his shoulders and held out his hands. "What's up?"

I looked at him and then down at the beasts. Could this be? My breasts felt like they had ten-pound weights hanging from each nipple, I was tired all the time, and I kept a foul taste in my mouth that made it water constantly. And to top it all off, I'd thrown up egg yolk without eating any eggs!

"Are you pregnant, Sanderella?"

"No!"

My heart slid down to my stomach, and suddenly I was scared.

"Oh my God . . . are you sure?"

"No," I said, even more afraid. But why? If I *was* pregnant, it was Rom's fault, too! It's not like I'd been out humping the milkman or freaking the iceman! I mean, he had been there, too, right along with me, or should I say on top of me. Right?

I covered my milk jugs with both hands and stepped past him into the shower stall. Rom's eyes scorched my bare ass as I went by. It was a terrible feeling, and I jumped into the stall and slammed the clear plastic door. The force of the water cascaded across my body and pelted my neck and back. I adjusted the temperature as hot as I could stand it and stood stock-still within the moist white clouds. I hoped the scalding water would generate enough steam to smother the hell out of Rom and literally force him from the bathroom.

A sweet kiss of Sunflowers filled the bathroom as I soaped my body in slow, lazy circles. The fluffy washcloth slid over my skin and invigorated my senses as I scrubbed myself from neck to toes, taking care to avoid contact with my pulsating breasts.

I rinsed the creamy suds from my dark skin and watched the tiny bubbles swirl around my ankles and slip into the drain. I wiggled my toes and wished I could stay in the shower forever. I'd be an old, wrinkled-looking prune by the time somebody pulled me out, and I wouldn't have to worry about Daddy or Rom or my period or *anything*. I turned off the water, opened the stall door, and was greeted by a cool gush of reality.

Rom was right where I'd left him. Fixing me in his strange glare, he sat down on the closed toilet seat and rested his elbows on his knees, then he cupped his chin in both palms and stared. All he needed was a bowl of Doritos and a brew, and I would have sworn he was watching the game!

I cut my eyes at him. His face seemed set in stone, except for a little spot on his right jaw that twitched like a dying cockroach. I grabbed a towel and hurriedly wrapped it around my damp body. As I turned toward the door, Rom snatched at the towel until it was around my knees and then on the floor.

For the life of me I couldn't read his eyes.

Suddenly I was self-conscious. I looked down at the rug. It needed washing something terrible. Rom moved and took my chin gently in his hands and lifted my head. His ebony eyes forced me to step into them. He lowered his face as if to kiss me, then with his lips millimeters away from mine he whispered, "Sandie . . . I'm scared. I don't know what exactly all of this means, but I'm scared. And you should be, too."

I froze for a moment, then jerked away and stomped out of the bathroom. Rom was crazy! He had some damn nerve being scared! There was no way I could be pregnant, so if anybody deserved to be scared, it was me!

I sucked my teeth in annoyance. Now that I had to go and get Daddy I wouldn't have a chance to make a doctor's appointment. It would just have to wait until after I came back. After the doctor checked me out and diagnosed me with a rare sickness that caused my period to come late and my breasts to swell, Rom would be sorry instead of scared!

I slipped into a hot pink sweat suit and pulled my hair back before choking down a slice of dry toast. I sat reading the newspaper and sipping from a cup of milky tea when Rom breezed into the kitchen.

"Suit up, Sandie. Our Red Cross requests were approved and I'm ready to roll."

I poured the tea down the drain and placed a quick call to the hospital to let Mama know we were about to get on the road, then I ran and jumped in the car before Speedy Gonzales could take off without me.

Rom spoke quietly. "Since it's already late, I'll drive until it gets dark and then we'll get a hotel room for the night."

I was silent.

"Okay?" he asked in a conciliatory tone.

"Okay," I answered, my voice silky-soft. I wasn't sure about this new level of tension between us, or how we would handle our looming situation, but I loved Rom with all my heart, and I was more than willing to call a truce.

As usual, I slept for a good portion of the trip. I was the opposite of Mama Ceal, who couldn't close her eyes in anything that moved. With me, if you rocked my chair, I'd pass out. Rom stopped for the night in a small town on the edge of North Carolina. Woozy and weak, I climbed gratefully out of the car.

"I'll be right back." He deposited my luggage in the spacious air-conditioned room, watching me closely. "You need anything?" His eyes were hooded and shadowed and revealed little about his mood. Not that it mattered. After sitting in the car for so long, my legs were like marshmallows and I couldn't care less about what Rom felt. I shook my head and watched the muscles move in his back as he strode from the room.

I sniffed. There was a faint antiseptic odor that made me queasy. I looked around. The room held a double bed and a small oak dinette table with four matching chairs. There was a miniature refrigerator pushed up against the wall next to a long dresser, which held a large gold lamp and a color television. The bedspread was an inviting hunter paisley print with matching wall borders, and the carpet was gold with erratic specks of the same soothing shade of green.

I yawned. Standing upright made me feel woozy, so I stretched out on the paisley bedspread and tried to stop the room from spinning. It didn't work. I turned over onto my stomach and swung my leg over the bed until my bare foot touched the carpet. Good. Now I felt grounded and secure and the room came to a gentle halt.

I must have dozed off again because I gradually became aware of someone in the room. I turned over quickly and busted Rom staring at me. Quiet fury brewed in his dark eyes and burned a crater into my back.

"Hey!" The intensity of his gaze puzzled and frightened me. I sat up. "Why'd you sneak up on me? You're giving me the flippin' creeps!"

"Sanderella," he said quietly, "go in the bathroom and pee on this little thang." He extracted a thin box from a small brown paper bag.

Now, what was this? A home pregnancy test.

Well, kiss my ass! I threw my head back and cackled like a witch.

Giggles and chuckles spilled out of my mouth and littered the cool air.

Rom never cracked a smile.

His gaze traveled to the bathroom and then back to me.

The brothah ain't bullshitting! I thought as the last traces of my hysterical laughter faded and echoed hollowly in the sterile hotel room. I snatched the box from his outstretched hand and read the outside. The label claimed the test could detect pregnancy hormones in your urine when your period was only one day late. I opened the box and pulled out a thin sheet of paper that contained instructions in ninety-nine languages. It took me a full minute to locate the English version. The instructions directed me to urinate on the thin indicator stick, and promised that in five minutes it would show either a positive plus or a negative minus sign.

"No, Rom," I sighed. "It says here that I'm supposed to use my first morning urine. I'll do it tomorrow." I tossed the box and its contents on the bed and slipped out of my jeans.

I was ready to hit the pillow.

His hand snaked out with lightning speed. He grabbed my upper arm and squeezed hard. Hard enough for me to wince and bite down on my lower lip.

"Don't play with me," he growled. "If you're as pregnant as I think you are"—he steered me toward the toilet—"you can use your piss *all day long* and it will still come out positive! Now get in there and pee!"

Dude came in with me, too.

I couldn't believe his tone of voice. Or the feel of his fingers as they dug into my flesh. This was one of the few times he'd ever shown any real anger toward me, and the intensity of it was astounding. And so was my reaction. I'd never before played the subservient role with Rom. From the time I met him I was my own woman, handling my own business and doing my own thing. I'd never felt the need to be submissive to him; however, the man looked right deadly tonight and something told me it would be truly dangerous to cross him or to defy him.

I wasn't a total fool.

I squatted over the porcelain and dutifully directed my stream all over the stick, saturating it. My urine was sharp. It had a funny *off* smell. "Whew." I wrinkled my face at the offensive odor of my own fluid. Rom ignored me as I handed him the detector and wiped myself thoroughly.

I washed my hands and flounced into the room, then rushed over to the bed and picked up the phone to call Mama Ceal. Rom's hand covered mine and slammed the receiver back down in its cradle.

"Not yet, Sandie. I want your full attention right now."

I rolled my eyes and turned toward the television.

After a few minutes he touched my arm and said, "San, look! You see that shit?"

I glanced over without really looking and said, "I see a piss-covered stick."

"No, really—look. It's a plus sign. A *fuckin' plus sign!* Sandie, you're *pregnant!*"

I looked closely at the stick. There was a faint pink plus sign that was gradually beginning to darken. I took the indicator from him and held it up close to my eyes. The scent of urine assaulted me. I rotated it slightly to the left.

That was better.

"See Rom, look at it this way. It's not a plus sign, it's an X!" He sucked in a huge amount of air like he was preparing to blow up a balloon. Or his top.

For the second time that day I'd made a funny, and boyfriend was not amused. "Okay, okay." I held up my hands to ward off his anger. "No more bullshit, I'm being straight." I tried hard to compose myself, but my head was full and I just couldn't seem to handle any more. I forced myself to look him squarely in his eyes. As my eyes met his, I saw the hint of a twinkle as a faint smile played along his lips.

I slapped him on the arm. Here I was thinking my man was plotting to do me in, and now he was trying to grin! I didn't find a damned thing humorous. "What's so damn funny, Rom?"

His eyebrows shot up a full inch. "What's so funny? Funny? Sandie, I'm not laughing. I'm terrified!" He buried his face in both hands. "Who did I piss off? I just can't believe this shit would happen to me right now!"

I cocked my head sistah-girl style. To him? Last time I checked men couldn't get pregnant!

"I mean—you know how I feel about my sons, how rough it is for me having to deal with life without them. This is the wrong time for something like this. As soon as I decide one thing, I get hit with something else. Shit, I feel like I just up and abandoned my own kids and now this happens?"

Well, I didn't have an egg in that omelet!

He went on. "There's just no way I can deal with this. Not now. We really need to talk about what you're going to do. I don't know how this happened." His dark eyes pierced mine and the look on his face made no bones about his sincerity. "But it was a mistake. A big mistake."

Now if that wasn't a mouthful! The brother must've *bumped* his head! Surely this was part of the Pregnancy Revelation Stress Syndrome some men experienced when they found out they had a baby on the way. I'd heard about brothers who tripped harder than hell when they found out their woman was pregnant. After a while they usually digested it, and accepted it, and as soon as the sistah began to show they walked around with their chests poked out with pride.

"So what are you gonna do, Sandie?" Rom towered over me.

The air left the room.

His eyes bored into mine and dared me to oppose him. He wanted me to state my position, to make my decision immediately.

He'd already made his.

"Back off!" I snapped. I scooted away from him and rolled my eyes. "Don't ask me any questions! I don't even believe I'm really pregnant, and you're already planning my moves. Why don't you just grab a daggone coat hanger?"

"Sandie!" he yelled, counting off on his fingers. "Be for real, baby! You haven't had a period, your titties are bigger than Miss Etta-Mae's, you're around here calling Ralph, and the pregnancy test is positive! Stop burying your head in the sand and for once face the facts!"

He snatched the bright pink detector and waved it like a flag. "*You are pregnant!*"

The force of his fury pounded me like a sledgehammer. I staggered under the weight of his words. He'd screamed the last sentence the same way he'd have yelled, "You are revolting!" or "You have AIDS!" His voice and his eyes held nothing but tons of rage, contempt, and disgust for me. There wasn't an ounce of love to be found, and believe me, I *searched*.

Trembling in disbelief, I waited for him to crack a smile. To laugh. To slap me on the ass and tell me how gullible I was to fall for his crazy charade. I waited for Rom to chuckle and pull me close, to kiss me on that favorite spot of his, my forehead, and begin his search for a meaningful name for our new prince or princess. I waited for a production crew to jump out of the closet and yell, "Smile! You're on *Candid Camera!*"

I just kept waiting for my king to pull those daggers out of my heart and tell me this was all a silly joke.

I just kept waiting.

And Rom just kept fuming.

He swore and spit, and howled and roared, and when he was finally drained and devoid of words, he stepped up in my face with his chest heaving and his lips quivering. My man was much more than angry. He was ready to beat the living hell out of me.

"You're pregnant," he said again. This time his voice was quieter, but no less deadly. He slapped his thigh and stomped his foot. "Go ahead! Give me another goddamn baby to worry about leaving! Fucking pregnant!"

I snapped. The sistah rolled straight out of her funky Brooklyn B-A-G!

"Now how did that happen?" I asked him, rage narrowing my eyes to mere slits. I balled up my fists and pushed up on him like I stood six-five. "Did I lay down and *fuck myself* and get a baby? Or am I *Mary* and was this an Immaculate Conception? Dammit, you were *there!*"

My fist crashed against his broad chest. "I didn't see you complaining when you were jamming like Rambo and loving it! You're the one who told me to stop taking the Pill, and now you want to act like a fool and make me act like a bitch? That's not a problem, I can handle that—"

"Yeah," Rom stepped back and cut me off with a stiff arm, "because a *bitch* is what you really are!"

Did this kneegrow just call me a bitch?

Aw, *hell* no!

Okay, Sandie. Get ready to climb this motherfucker like a tree and chop his ass into chunks! I flicked out my fingernails like I was a female version of Freddy Krueger and prepared to slice him up like Edward Scissorhands, but before I could get close to him, Rom hurled the indicator against the wall and slammed out the door.

Well, I will be *damned*! Rom had gone out of his rabbit-ass mind! Surely he was crazy. Talk to me that way? Curse at me like I'm some kind of up-the-street, around-the-corner, back-alley hoe? I'd always thought his ass was too tight to cuss and swear that way!

Calling me a *bitch*?

He'd *never* done that before! My head spun in amazement. I didn't even know Rom's lips could form those words when it came down to me!

This was some brand-new stuff.

Some stuff I never thought could happen.

I slid down the smooth wall and collapsed on the carpeted floor. Never in a million years would I have thought something like this could happen! Never!

That's what you get for thinking!

Little did I know it but my sweet lover man—my righteous and noble king, the one who had just pulled a drive-by on my heart—was about to do a *Felix* on me and show me his entire bag of tricks.

26

WELCOME TO BURGER KING

Women are all the same! Every time I close my eyes one of them is trying to run a goddamn game on a brothah! I was so mad I wanted to put my foot up in Sanderella's ass. Here she sees me suffering like hell and she pops up *pregnant*. And says she wants to get married before the baby is born!

Now what kind of shit is that?

I already have a wife! Doesn't she know I already gave at the bone marrow bank? Hell, I married Lou because she was pregnant and look what the fuck happened. I did damn near ten years for that mistake, and here I was just about ready to walk *back* inside that lion's den! Ain't no way I'm doing hard time again just because some girl doesn't have sense enough to take the Pill!

Can't she see I already flunked Fatherhood 101?

Do I look like the keeper of anybody's goddamn castle?

Doesn't she know *whose son I am*?

I stormed across the street to the 7-Eleven and slapped a ten-dollar bill on the counter and walked out with two forty-ounces of Old Gold without waiting for my change. I plopped down on the curb right outside the store and guzzled the cold brew like it was a fifth of something good.

Man, the king done messed around and got trapped by that thing called love. Just when I decided to go back to Lou and salvage my sham of a marriage for the sake of my sons, I'm about to become a father again? With Sandie? What am I supposed to do now, walk away and leave another child behind? Whose children should I save first? Lou's? Sandie's?

Fuck that. The brothah has got to save himself!

Save my sons!

Pregnant. Damn!

I've never in my life called a woman out of her name. Never even thought to call one a bitch. Not even the time Lou came home with a bad case of crabs and a nasty dose of the clap. But I can't take this shit sitting down. I need my sons, my boys. My children who are already *here*. I already feel like a failure as a father, and here Sandie's getting ready to pick up her boys, and just because she's pregnant I won't be able to be with mine? Sheeiit, I'm really going to stay in my barracks room now! Although my billets are only a few blocks away from her house, Sandie wants me with her all the damn time—like we're already married or something. Why is it that women are all the time trying to fence a brother in?

That's probably why my daddy left!

She planned this whole thing. The baby—everything. That goddamn girl is choking me! Does all of my laundry and then puts it away in her dresser drawers. Like I live there for real! She even has my telephone calls forwarded to her house. Don't call my room and I'm not at home because you'll get some fucked-up message saying, "You've reached 555-4121 *and* 555-6432. Rom and Sandie are unable to take your call, but leave your number and we'll get back to you."

That's how Lou found out about her ass! I'd had my wife thinking I left her for myself, not for some other woman. When she found out I was living with Sandie, she promised to make it as hard as possible for me to see my kids! What kind of stunt is Lou gonna pull if Sandie has a goddamn baby?

She'd better *not*!

And what about our careers? I've worked hard to build a solid reputation. Did damn near everything strictly by the books until I met her little ass! Hell, it's not like we work for fucking Kmart! Uncle Sam *does not play* when it comes to adultery and cohabitation. Sandie knows as well as I do what can happen to us—what almost happened to us in Virginia when that stupid commander of hers got hot on our trail. Well, what's gonna happen now that she's got the evidence growing in her belly?

Welcome to Burger King. Can I take your order?

That's what!

Just because Lou got pregnant I didn't get to finish college. Now I'm going to be out there flipping fuckin' horsemeat burgers trying to feed six kids!

And three of them ain't even mine!

I can't believe my history is repeating itself. I don't know how the hell I keep getting myself jammed up like this, but it's got to stop. This shit is gonna stop right here and right now. I know I hurt Sandie and I'm sorry, but there's just no way I can let another woman dictate my future. My life. Lou will never come back to me now. Solomon was right!

Dammit, I'm supposed to be a king!

I'm not putting my dreams on hold again for *nobody*! I'm not forsaking my sons again for *nobody*! And I ain't taking care of nobody else's kids but *mine*!

I've got news for Miss Sandie. I ain't about to lay down for the old one-two. This time—instead of going along with the program—the king is coming out fighting!

My hands trembled, and my breath came in short, irregular heaves. I felt dizzy and my throat was a burning oasis. Get it together, dammit! I reprimanded myself. This was no time to faint.

I sat on the bed and tried to calm myself and digest the situation. If I was pregnant, I had to decide what to do about it. Whether I was pregnant or not, I had to decide what to do about Romulus. I longed for a cigarette. Anything to stop my heart from galloping around inside my chest like a frightened Clydesdale.

My man had never called me out of my name. Never acted such a fool or behaved so irrationally. Even during our worst throw-downs he had always remained respectful. Sometimes an argument could take you to a place that was past the point of no return, and we had vowed never to go there.

I just couldn't believe he'd wigged out on me like that!

He was crazy! Like most women, I thought I knew my man well enough to read him like a book, but I could *never* have predicted he would go this ballistic. Rom had sworn he'd never hurt me. Sheeiit, that was a lie and a half because he just did! He'd promised to always be there for me, no matter what. Through thick and thin.

Damn, baby. Are you gonna break your promise?

My feelings were hurt, and I was flustered and confused. If I was pregnant, there was no question about what I would do. Lord knows I'm the last woman on earth who wants or needs a baby! Jamillah's birth had not only kicked my behind, I'd truly hated getting up at night to feed her. I also hated colic and teething and diarrhea and formula and spit up and cradle cap and heat rash and thrush and any damned thing else that had to do with a baby!

Especially crying.

Whenever I heard a baby cry in public, I gave the mama a look that said, Why don't you shesh that baby up? I felt people who allowed their children to cry in public and disturb the rest of us normal adults were low class. Nobody sane wanted to hear all that noise! And let someone bring a screaming brat to work.

Oh that shit was unpardonable!

After all, a military unit was a place of government business, not *Romper Room*! I even detested baby showers. If one of my close friends invited me to a shower, I usually sent an expensive but practical gift. For someone who had a house full of kids, I just couldn't get with that ga-ga, goo-goo crap, swooning over miniature undershirts and tiny booties that got devoured by the washing machine during the very first wash!

Nah, babies weren't my thing. Never had been. My kids were lucky to have had loving grandparents and aunts to help raise them. My aversion for babies was worse than the one I had for toilets.

Much worse. That's why I doubted if God would allow some crazy mess like this to happen to me!

I reached down and picked up the test indicator from the floor. The positive sign was now a bright, proud pink. I stood up and faced the mirror and pulled my shirt and bra up over my breasts in one motion. The beasts bounded free. My nipples hardened at the kiss of cool air. I scrutinized them carefully and finally said out loud, "I'm pregnant."

There.

I'd admitted it. I didn't have my head buried in the sand as Rom had claimed. Even if I did, my head wasn't as deep in the sand as his was up his ass! I felt soiled, grimy, like I needed a shower. Call it escapism or whatever else you want, but showers helped me relax and put things in their proper perspective. I removed my shirt and bra and gathered my hygiene items. Slowly, I slathered my body with my Sunflower shower gel, using enough to make the whole room smell of sunshine and happy days. As I stood under the sheet of warm water, the salt of my tears stung my skin.

That's a kneegrow for you!

Ladelle's favorite admonishment clamored in my head, and at this point it seemed she was right. I didn't dare ponder what would happen next. I figured Rom would eventually come around and act like he had a little sense, but right now I could do without the added stress and aggravation. I was about to go get my children and my sick daddy, and I needed things to be peaceful in my home.

Shame on Rom. He knew that.

Still sniffling, I dried off and put on one of Rom's T-shirts and a pair of cotton panties. I smelled myself down there. It was a strange odor, not unclean but unpleasant. It smelled the same as my urine. Maybe it had something to do with my hormones. Damn, this baby was inconveniencing me already! I squeezed Shower to Shower deodorant powder into my panties and fanned them until puffs of white clouds dusted my thighs like powdered doughnuts. There. That was better.

I picked up the telephone to call my mother, then quickly put it down again. I was still too angry and hurt to talk about Rom. Mama had told me years ago, "If you ever get mad at your husband, if he ever does something to hurt you, work it out— don't tell me. Why? Because *you* might forgive him, but I never will!" Well, Rom wasn't my husband, but if Mama Ceal could hear how he'd spoken to me, sick or no, she'd be waiting for his black ass in the bushes!

I pulled back the heavy spread and climbed in between the crisp hotel sheets. With all the questioning pain that reverberated in my head and pressed into my heart, I didn't think I'd be able to rest, but I was wrong. I slept soundly, like a pregnant woman. I never even heard Rom when he came in. The ringing telephone signaled our wake-up call at five A.M., and I rolled over carefully so as not to trap the beasts beneath me. I looked over at Rom.

His eyes were open wider than Uncle Fester's, and his brown skin looked just as ghastly. "I apologize for what I said last night, Sandie," he stated mechanically. "For speaking to you the way I did. I was angry and I was wrong and I hope you can accept my apology."

I didn't bother to comment. Instead, I cut my eyes at him and turned away. He'd have to come a lot better than that to make up for all he'd said to me! Besides, he didn't even sound remorseful. He sounded like the playground bully who apologized only because his parents forced him. No, Rom wasn't sorry. It was simple home train-ing that forced his words, but his heart remained unchanged. He'd shown me his true colors last night, revealed a part of his inner self. A part that I never knew existed. King Romulus Caesar had allowed me to peep his hold card, and at that instant a part of me was forever sealed off to him. Like the heavy door of a steel vault, something in-side of me slammed shut, never to be reopened.

The bathroom door closed and the rushing sound of water ca-ressed my ears. I ignored the hypnotic pull of the liquid sounds as I dressed quickly and combed my hair. "I left the shower running for you," he said, stepping out of the bathroom. Beads of water glistened on his strong shoulders and chased each other around his muscular chest. "But since you're already dressed I guess you don't need it."

I pushed past him, turned off the shower, and plopped down on the toilet. My urine came out in a rush, and I felt pressure as well as relief on the top of my bladder. I washed my hands and face and brushed my teeth, and that was it. I was rett' to go.

Rom loaded our bags into the car and paid the bill. I sat in the front seat looking straight ahead as if he didn't exist. As we pulled onto the expressway, I yawned. Damn, I couldn't be tired! I'd been sleeping almost nonstop for over a day. I guess I was what the old folks called "drunk-sleep." That's what happened when your body got too much sleep—you felt lethargic. Made you seem lazy. It was a vicious cycle.

I tried to stay awake, but it was impossible. The mighty zzzz-monster had his arms wrapped around my eyes and his legs clamped around my neck. I didn't even bother to ask Rom if he wanted my help with the driving. In my narcoleptic condition I'd have driven us straight into a ditch. I placed my seat in the recline position and turned onto my side facing away from him. Not only was I resting, I was also giving Rom my ass to kiss.

I hoped he could dig my drift.

27

HURRY, MAN, HURRY!

Daddy was caught completely by surprise when Rom and I strolled through his front door. He listened quietly as I explained why I felt it was best he come to live with the kids and me. His mood was reflective, but he agreed to my plans. He trusted me.

"Pook, I want to talk to you." Daddy summoned us to his bedroom late the next night. We were driving back to Missouri the next morning, and I was busy ironing our traveling clothes. The children were already in bed.

"Baby," he began in a haggard voice, "there is something I need you to hear." I looked at Rom, and he looked at me. Daddy looked so serious that I knew whatever he had to say wouldn't be good. "Look," he began slowly, as he tried to take in the oxygen and speak at the same time. "I know things are pretty bad for me, and I appreciate everything you two are doing. I don't object to staying a spell with you all, because I realize that I can't surround myself with canned food and sit around this house waiting to die."

On the word *die* my eyes widened, and I saw Rom raise his right eyebrow. Daddy continued, "Some people can sit and look out the window and watch life pass by, perfectly happy to just be alive. But that's not enough for me. I want to plant some pretty flowers in my own garden and maybe have a little birdbath built out front. I want to enjoy the breeze, play chess with my partners, toss a football to Kharim and Hanif, and do whatever else pleases me. *Whenever* it pleases me."

Fire crept into his eyes as he spoke.

"Don't you all be upset if I decide to go somewhere else. I am not afraid. I've had a good life, and I love you, but I wasn't born to sit around and watch the grass grow."

My head whipped toward Rom. What was Daddy saying? My eyes were question marks. "Daddy, I don't understand. What do you mean? What do you want to do?"

"I want to *live*, Sandie!"

The fire in his eyes was suddenly extinguished as if a cold spirit had spit on its fingers and pinched out the flame. I closed myself off. I'd heard Daddy, but I refused to listen. I didn't want to hear such talk from him. It was as though he was making plans to die. I wasn't ready for that. Hell, Daddy wasn't that sick. Mama was the one in the hospital with a bad heart. I jumped up from the bed and began to throw underwear and socks into his small suitcase.

"Daddy, there's no need for that kind of talk. Let's just get you to Missouri and everything will be fine."

Later I wanted to kick my own ass for not listening. I jumped up when I should have remained seated. I blocked him out when I should have tuned him in. I didn't ask any questions; I just pushed the unpleasantness to the back of my mind and tried to pretend things weren't as bad as he made them seem. I guess I was burying my head in the sand, which is exactly what Rom had accused me of.

It was easier than burying my daddy.

For the trip home we loaded Daddy and his oxygen apparatus into the backseat of Rom's car. The boys were squished, but they were excited about the move. Rom put all but two portable canisters in the trunk, and we used pillows and blankets to make Daddy comfortable. Every thirty minutes or so I checked the tank's dial to make sure the canister hadn't run low.

Cramped in the backseat, Daddy kept shifting his position. After a while he accidentally brushed his leg against the rotating lever that regulated his oxygen flow. Unfortunately, I didn't notice it right away. As usual, I'd drifted off to sleep. Sixty miles past Spartanburg I got the scare of my life. I came awake with a start and turned around to check on Daddy, and to my horror his eyes were rolled back inside of his head, his mouth was slack, and his face ashen.

"Daddy!" I screamed and reached back to shake him. He moaned but didn't respond. "Help me, Rom! Pull over!" I nearly climbed into the backseat on top of Daddy as I desperately pulled at the oxygen tank.

"The lever is stuck!" I reached under Daddy's leg and struggled to yank it free.

"Hold on, baby, hold on, baby, hold on . . . ," Rom chanted over and over as he swerved onto the shoulder and leaped from the car. Scrambling over to Daddy's side, Rom flung the door open with such force I thought it would be hurled into oncoming traffic. Our frantic hands flailed every which way as we battled to free the lever. Rom's grappling grip finally won out, and he disentangled the canister, which had gotten trapped between Daddy's legs, and succeeded in turning the free-floating dial up to its maximum.

"It's okay, it's okay, it's okay," had become Rom's chant, and I couldn't tell whose breathing was more desperate and ragged—his, Daddy's, or mine. Alarmed, the boys started crying in the backseat, and without intending to, I joined them. I had no idea how long Daddy had been back there without oxygen. I felt terrible for sleeping while his body was slowly being deprived of what it needed.

"Daddy?" I sobbed as I rubbed his hands and stroked his forehead. I prayed that he was okay and begged the Lord not to hold my trifling need for sleep against my precious father.

Daddy moaned softly, and I heard him whisper, "Dizzy, Sandie."

"Yeah, Daddy," I said sadly. "I know I'm dizzy. I should have been paying attention. I'm sorry."

"Not *you're* dizzy, San," Rom snapped. "*He's* dizzy. It must be from lack of oxygen. Let's just give him a few minutes to catch his breath, and he'll be all right."

After a while Daddy began to look around, and soon he was able to speak, although with great difficulty.

"I got dizzy . . . very nauseous. I felt myself drifting away . . . just leaving. I didn't have enough strength to reach out my hand and tap you on the shoulder."

I continued to cry as I thanked God that my daddy was okay, but an hour later we had another problem.

"Pook," Daddy joked, "I think it's time to pay my water bill." Daddy's lung condition caused him to retain large amounts of fluids, so his doctor had placed him on a very high dosage diuretic.

Those damned pills picked the wrong time to kick in.

"Pull over, Rom," I demanded. "Pull over right here! Daddy, you can go on the side of the road, right by the car."

"Oh no, my darling." Daddy spoke with quiet dignity. "We don't relieve ourselves in public. I can wait until we find a rest room." He motioned forward. "Keep going," he commanded Rom, who had begun to slow down. "Just keep moving until we come to a rest area."

Rom drove on like a bat out of hell. I searched desperately for a rest area, but mile after agonizing mile passed without a single blue and white sign in sight. Twenty miles later we finally saw a sign, but by then it was almost too late.

Talk about conflicting needs?

Daddy's need to relieve himself was so great that he forgot all about his need for oxygen. As Rom extracted him from the car, I heard Daddy mutter, "Hurry, man, *hurry!*" It was agonizing as well as humiliating to see my daddy totally dependent on another person for his most basic needs. I winced as Rom half carried my father toward the rest room. Daddy wanted to hurry, but he needed to breathe, and even though Rom held him firmly under his arm and bore most of his weight, it was still very slow going.

They stayed in the rest room forever. Each time the doors swung open I watched anxiously, hoping it would be Rom helping a smiling Daddy outside. But each time it was the face of a stranger that appeared. Just as I was about to go over and knock on the door, they emerged.

Somehow, Daddy looked much worse than when he'd gone inside. Due to the severe swelling in his feet Daddy walked with a half limp, half shuffle, which was further exacerbated by his body's demand for oxygen. Rom's face was also grim and ashen, and they moved so slowly that I wanted to jump out and help.

Finally we settled a trembling Daddy into the backseat and I checked his condition. He was in bad shape. His skin was damp and gray, and beads of sweat stood out on his nose and upper lip. I kissed his forehead and checked the oxygen canister again. And again. I was careful to check it every thirty minutes. My fear of losing my father transcended my need for sleep and managed to keep me awake for the rest of the trip.

We pulled into our driveway just as the sun tucked itself away for the night. I was stiff and tired and would have slapped Rom's grandma for a hot soapy shower. Daddy looked pooped, his eyes showing the misery his weakened body endured. One glance at him made my own discomfort seem trivial and insignificant and caused me to swallow hard. My heart hurt for him.

"Rom," I called as he unloaded the car, "after you put the boys to bed, could you please set up the oxygen unit in the guest room?"

I helped Daddy from the car and into the house. He gratefully accepted the condensed oxygen while I propped his swollen feet upon a stack of oversized pillows and spread a hand-knitted blanket over his legs. "Thanks, Pook," he whispered. "I don't know what I'd do without you . . . don't know what I'd do."

I looked into the weary eyes of the man who had always been my lifeline and replied softly, "Daddy, there have been many, many days when I've said the same thing about you."

28

MOUNT EVEREST

Rom situated our luggage while I fixed grilled-cheese sand-wiches using pathetic slices of week-old Wonder bread. After our meager supper I unpacked Daddy's suitcase and gave him his medi-cine, then I fluffed his pillows and pulled the comforter around him before kissing him good night. His lips were stretched in a tight line, and his cheeks sagged back against the pillow. He was so exhausted he could barely nod his head.

Rom made the obligatory call to Mama Ceal, then offered to pick up Jamillah from Charmel's house. Kharim and Hanif begged to wait up for her, but I sent them straight to bed.

Finally, I was able to take a long hot shower. I spread a generous amount of Sunflower shower gel on my washcloth and began soap-ing my tired body in big lazy circles. As the sweet familiar scent permeated my senses, my stomach jumped and a sudden wave of nausea buckled my knees. I sat down in the shower stall Indian-style, then gripped my thighs and fought the urge to hurl.

"Deep breaths, Sandie," I told myself over and over until the ten-sion in my stomach unfurled and settled into a calm serene noth-ingness. This throw-up stuff was getting old. I stood and turned off the water. Forget about washing tonight! Stepping out of the stall, I grabbed the offending shower gel and tossed it into the trash can. While *I* might like sunflowers, this baby sure as hell didn't!

Rom returned with Jamillah, and although she was anxious to see her brothers and her beloved Pa-Pa, I told her to wait until morning. I put her to bed and gratefully slipped between my own clean and familiar sheets.

I was almost asleep by the time Rom finished showering. Peeking through one sleepy eye, I watched him as he dried his lean brown body and rubbed deodorant under his arms. His sex hung loose and dejected, like a long inner tube with a slow leak. His eyes were tired and pensive.

Rom lay down next to me and pulled the covers this way and that. He used his long feet to disengage the bottom ends of the sheets from their resting places, sandwiched between the mattress and box spring. When that was accomplished he punched his pillows and pulled the covers over his head. Apparently he hadn't found the right spot, so he tossed left and right, flopping and floundering about madly. Then he heaved so violently I actually bounced up and down on the bed, my helpless body hydroplaning on the smooth sheets.

The room whirled like a cyclone before my eyes.

Finally, Rom turned away from me and with one great heave and a mighty lurching roll—pulled the sheets, blankets, and bedspread clear off my body. His weight sighed, then settled down into the mattress. There. He was comfortable now.

Oh hell no, I thought. Chill bumps rose like Braille lettering on my exposed skin. Using both hands, I yanked the covers back over to my side of the bed and left him with his ass hanging out. Rom rolled over and looked at me, his eyes bright and menacing in the semidarkness. "Do you have a problem, Sandie?" His voice was hard. Tough.

"Do you?" I came right back, just as hard.

With Daddy and the boys safe and sound, the truce was apparently off. Rom sat up and leaned back against the headboard. He sighed deeply, then I heard him suck air through his teeth. I stayed put. "We need to talk, Sanderella."

I smirked into the darkness. Fish ain't biting! *He* could talk—I wasn't about to say a mumbling word!

"Look, I know you're tired and you have a lot going on in your head right about now but—" He paused and cleared his throat.

Mama always said anything after "but" was bullshit.

"I really think we need to lay this out on the table. We're making a mistake," Rom declared. "I don't think you realize the repercussions that having this baby will bring. It's just not a good time for us, and I want you to know that."

Well, he was right on one count. I did have a lot going on in my head, but after all the emotions I'd sucked up during the last week, the sistah was too full to hold water!

"Are you telling me to get an abortion?" I demanded.

Rom was silent. He knew my history, my position on abortion. My thoughts went to Mama Ceal. I'd finally broken down and called her at the hospital. I'd spilled my guts. Told my mother everything, including how Rom had spoken to me at the hotel. Mama was instantly pissed, as I knew she would be.

"Uh-uh, Sandie," she said, disgusted. "I don't like that mess one bit! He ought to be supporting you at a time like this! He knows how you feel about babies, and he knows your father is sick. It's not fair for your man to lean on you when he knows you're already down."

I sniffed. "Mama, you should have heard him! He was *mad!*"

"Well, you should've told him to scratch his black ass and get glad!" Mama paused for a second, still simmering, then continued, "So, when are you due?"

Yes! It felt good to have a mother who understood. Mama Ceal had known full well that I couldn't get an abortion. Remember those "whosits" I told you about? Well, years ago, after I'd had Jamillah and before I'd left Kevin, I'd popped up pregnant again. Jamillah was only three months old at the time, and Kevin was getting heavily into P-funk. He'd already lost his broom-pushing piece of a job at Harlem Hospital, and we were barely making it.

I wasn't ready for another baby. Hell, I was still a baby myself, so after discussing it with Mama I made a decision. At my request Mama not only took me to get an abortion, she paid for it to boot.

I remembered the day as if it were yesterday. Mama and I took the subway uptown to the Harlem Women's Center, where a pleasant white-cloaked nurse greeted us at the door. I filled out a lot of forms and waited with a lot of other women, surprised to find that most of the other patients were white.

I was so frightened that my knees knocked together and my teeth chattered audibly. I kept wishing the whole situation were just a bad dream, but my missing period and the morning sickness were proof that it was all real. Mama stayed with me and tried to comfort me with her presence, and she never once questioned my judgment, nor did she attempt to sway my decision either way. She simply said it was my life and I would be the only one who had to live with the consequences of my actions.

The procedure room was stark and sterile. A sympathetic nurse gave me a paper hospital gown to wear and held my trembling hand as I tried to climb atop the cold, formidable metal table. Over and over I silently recited the Lord's Prayer, like it was a special mantra that would somehow keep me from harm. My guilty conscience had me convinced that I would somehow die laid out on that cold table, half naked in a state of supreme sin and with a vacuum hose jammed up my stuff!

That was no way to meet your Maker.

It took me forever to scale that table. Although it couldn't have been more than two feet off the ground, to me it was like climbing Mount Everest. I was put to sleep for the procedure, and afterward I awoke, lying on my stomach and crying like a baby.

I had made a mistake.

I knew it as soon as I opened my eyes. I'd made a mistake that I couldn't fix, and the good Lord Himself was going to deal with me. In that instant I understood my purpose in life and where I fit in with God's plan for the universe. I wasn't put on this earth to kill babies. I was put here to bring God's children forth into the world.

I was His vessel. Made to carry, not to kill.

Through my tears I made a vow. However many times the Lord saw fit to allow a fetus into my unworthy womb, that was the number of children I would bear. I would never get another abortion. Never kill another baby. It was going to be hard enough to atone for killing this one. They let me get dressed, and when I stepped into the waiting area and saw my mother, I cried even harder.

I was so ashamed of myself.

Here she stood, the mother of three, who had survived much worse than I would ever encounter, and she'd never had an abortion. When I explained how I felt and why I was so ashamed, Mama smiled at me and said, "Stop crying, funny face. You did what you had to do, and you've paid a price for it. Besides, they didn't have legal abortions when I was your age or *you* wouldn't be here!" We laughed, and when Mama Ceal hugged me and kissed my cheek, I felt a little better.

I held Mama's hand all the way home on the subway, nearly fainting through my killer menstrual-like cramps. When we reached her house, Mama made me lie in her great big soft bed and told me to sleep. Mama never mentioned my procedure again, and neither did I. I also never mentioned the fact that ten months later I'd broken my vow. I'd shamefacedly made the trek back to Harlem and dutifully scaled Mount Everest.

And climbed up on that table again.

I never did tell Mama about that.

Yet Mama had known without me telling her that I *had* to keep this baby. I had no choice. I'd made a vow to the Lord, slipped and broken my word, and landed right back in a pile of shit.

That'll learn you, durn you!

I didn't intend to renege on my word again.

Not for love, not for security, not for Romulus.

Not for *nothing*.

I'd been careless, and now I had to bear it. It was a terrifying prospect, but I was certain it was the right thing to do. Not the smart thing, but certainly the right thing. Besides, if this was God's way of testing me, it was one test I didn't plan to fail.

I told Mama I must have gotten pregnant during one of Rom's visits at OCS, but I had not yet seen a doctor.

"Well," Mama told me firmly, "he won't give you more than you can bear. If you can feed three, you can feed four."

I was grateful to her for her support and advice, and would have given anything to have a man who was even half as supportive. Instead, his lip was twisted in a funky pout and there was hot steam rising off his big, bald head.

"Are you asking me to get an abortion?" I repeated.

His voice was even. "Yes, Sandie. I think it would be best."

"Best for who?" I sat up. "Damn sure not best for me! Best for your selfish ass!" My temper crept up on me like a fever. Brooklyn was definitely in the house!

Rom shook his head and touched my arm. "No, baby. Not just for me." He pleaded. "For *us*. Can you live with the repercussions? Because I can't! This just isn't the right time. I've had to make a lot of tough decisions . . . about my family and all. This is just . . . hard on me."

I forgot all about Daddy sleeping in the next room.

"What repercussions?" I shrieked in falsetto. My eyes were wild in the darkness, my voice bounced off the walls and crashed to the floor. "We fucked and made a baby! *So what?* People do it every day! No, we didn't intentionally lay down with making a baby in mind, but it happened. Now be a big boy and just deal with it!"

Rom pressed his index finger to his lips. "Sshhh! Your father might hear you!"

"So? Are you ashamed to let him hear what you're saying? You love him more than you love me?"

He took my hand. "Sandie, you act like it's just a baby we're dealing with! It's not! It's everything else, too—me, you. My wife! Your having a baby will affect my relationship with my kids! I just don't want any more burdens right now!"

A switch went off in my brain and I ripped a hole coming out of that Brooklyn bag. "Wife? Oh so suddenly you're the thoughtful husband thinking about your wife? What burdens do you have?" I demanded. "Huh? You wouldn't know a burden if it landed on your neck! I'm the one who's knocked up with a sick father, a sick sister, a sick mama, and a sick-assed man! You don't have any *real* problems! Your spineless ass is just trying to create some! You know what, Rom-u-fuckin'-lus? You ain't nobody's *king*. At the first sign of a crisis, instead of squaring off like a man, you tuck your tail between your legs and run away like the turncoat you really are! And you say your daddy ain't shit? Well he sure as hell taught you how to be a good black man, now didn't he?"

I was on a roll. Mama always said it would be my mouth that got me in trouble. I continued to scream obscenities at him, digging deep into my imagination and repertoire of cuss words and desperately trying to make him feel the same pain that was tearing my soul apart.

Throughout my rampage Rom listened quietly, his eyes never leaving mine, his face expressionless. Finally I was finished. Out of words. Depleted and exhausted. I'd managed to completely sterilize the gutter.

Rom spoke calmly and evenly.

"You know something? Whenever I try to talk to you, you go *nigger* on me. But that's okay, Sanderella. I see how you're living. We're just gonna do what we should've done a long time ago."

He faced away from me and pulled the covers over his head. He was talking about splitting up, something he'd been hinting around at a lot these days.

Like that was supposed to hold me.

I was so mad I felt like slapping the hell out of him. I stared a hole in his back as the tears streamed silently down my cheeks. How could he treat me like this after all I'd been through? Rom had picked the wrong time to get brand-new on me. He knew my daddy was in the next room, sick and depending on me! He knew I was stressing about my sister, my mama—he knew this pregnancy had me as sick as a dog! And not to mention my new job! I was an officer now. I was under a lot of pressure. How could he dump this bullshit on me at a time like this? How could he think of deserting me when I needed him most?

Aside from the health of my family, this was a time in my life when I should have been happy and ecstatic; I was having a baby by the man I loved, and who supposedly loved me. It wasn't like we were sixteen-year-olds, broke and destitute. We were grown and employed! Why should I get an abortion? Forget him!

But Rom had really messed my head up. I'd expected him to have some reservations—hell, I had a whole bunch of them myself—but I also expected him to be comforting and supportive. I thought he'd say something like, "Well, baby, our timing sure is bad, and there are a lot of details to work out, but I love you and I'm gonna take care of you and mine." Then he was supposed to smile, kiss that special spot on my forehead, and take me in his arms and carefully make love to me.

Not even close! I continued to cry silently, not wanting him to hear me and get the satisfaction of knowing he'd hurt me. And he did hurt me. I was also confused like a mother. It wasn't as if we couldn't afford this baby. We both worked and drove our own cars. We had a little money stashed away, and we paid our bills on time. As much as I hated the idea of being pregnant, it was already in my belly. It was mine.

Get an abortion?

Me? Climb up on another table? Scale that mountain again? Was he crazy? How could he even ask me to consider doing that to myself *or* to our child?

These were the unanswered questions on my lips as I drifted into an exhausted sleep filled with horrible dreams of a laughing Rom, tearing the tiny limbs off of my unborn baby. In my dreams I fought him and clawed at his face, desperately trying to snatch the dismembered fetus away from him. Blood was everywhere as I screamed and screamed and cried out, begging him to stop killing our child.

The next morning I awakened with the nightmare a fuzzy cloud on the horizon of my consciousness. I felt sick from betrayal. Rom was climbing out of the shower when I entered the bathroom. I sat on the toilet wordlessly. He looked at me as he dried his glistening body, and I stared right back at him. I prayed he could read my eyes just as well as I read his.

He stomped out of the bathroom and slammed the door.

I took off my gown and turned the hot water on before stepping into the wet stall. Slowly I added cold water until the cascade felt perfect. I grabbed a bar of plain Ivory soap that I kept there for Jamillah and soaped my body under the jolting stream until the water ran cold.

I looked at my profile in the mirror. Damn! I looked thicker around the middle already. Was that possible? As I studied my stomach and ass, Jamillah walked in and plopped on the toilet.

"Good morning, Sweet Pea," I said pleasantly and wrapped myself in a fluffy pink towel.

"Morning, Mommy. I had a dream about you last night."

I smiled. Jamillah used to tell me that she loved me so much that, when she slept, she dreamed about me. "What did you dream, baby?"

"I dreamed that you and Rommie were fighting and you called him a bad word. The one that starts with M and ends with R."

She pronounced the letter R "Are-er." I assumed she was referring to the string of "motherfuckers" I'd called Rom during our fight the night before. She must have overheard us.

"Well, it was only a dream baby, so don't worry about it."

"Sometimes you do say a lot of bad words, Mommy. I bet God doesn't like that."

Out of the mouth of a baby! I really needed to work harder on my language. My mouth was a sewer, and my baby had noticed. Hell, she even knew how to spell the words. I needed to get my act together. My life was falling apart.

Fast.

"You're right, honey. God doesn't like it when I say bad words and mean things. I promise to try and do better, okay?"

She yawned, nodded, and flushed the toilet. Kharim and Hanif were still asleep, so I got dressed and went into Daddy's room, where I found him awake and watching the morning news.

"Good morning, Pook," he said cheerfully.

I stared at him. His voice sounded normal, strong and full of bass. Just like his old self. He looked bright and alert, nothing like the sick old man of yesterday. Hardly like a sick person at all.

"Hi, Daddy." I hugged him tightly and planted a big kiss on his rough cheek. "You sound good this morning, are you feeling good, too?"

He smiled. "Yeah, baby, I feel about as good as I can feel on a good day. Right now I feel rested and refreshed, but it won't last long. As the day goes on, my energy wanes. So," he said brightly, "I take advantage of the times I feel good, and try to sleep when I feel bad."

I sat down next to him on the bed, and he grabbed my hand. "Pook." Daddy looked at me sadly and rubbed the back of my hand. "Baby, when you hurt, I hurt. I don't even have to know why you're hurting, and I hurt." Daddy paused and breathed deeply. "Sanderella, in our family we keep our babies. Other families may do things differently, but whatever God gives us, we keep. Anything else is not an option for you. And don't worry, you'll do fine. Your back is strong, and your shoulders are broad. That's part of your heritage. It runs in your blood."

I smiled at my daddy. This was exactly where I got my resilience and ability to make the best of a bad situation. I wished Rom could rub up against Daddy and steal some of his backbone, but like Mama had said, "Honey, *everybody* ain't Franklin!"

29

GOOD LUCK, SISTER

I waited three weeks for the appointment, and I could hardly breathe when the big day finally arrived. I sat in the waiting room with a few other women and leafed through an old issue of *Time* magazine. Occasionally, I looked around as a name was called or someone entered, but for the most part I was so embarrassed about being there I kept my head down and my nose buried deeply between the glossy pages before me.

"Sanderella Coffee?" a pretty receptionist behind the partitioned desk called my name. She was a slender brown-skinned sister with a feathery haircut so precise it looked like it had been styled only minutes before. She smiled and handed me an orange chart. "You can take this down the hall to room 4 and slip it in the tray outside the door." Her dimples flashed and she lowered her tone. "Good luck, sister."

"Thanks," I said, and tried to smile in return, but all I managed was a small grimace. I walked down a short corridor and found room 4. There was a row of seats along the wall opposite the examining offices, and I plopped myself down in one and waited.

"Ms. Coffee?"

I stood up.

"Hi, I'm Marilyn, and I'll be the technician handling your procedure. Here's an examination gown. The dressing room is two doors down on your left. When you're done, just step through the blue door and I'll take care of you."

I accepted the gown like it was a noose and followed her instructions. As I lay on the cold table, slimy blue-tinged gel slid across my lower abdomen and was smeared around like finger paint by the small white hand holding the ultrasound probe.

"You may feel a bit of pressure here," the chatty technician warned me, her thigh pressed against my arm, her hand moving intimately along my pubic bone, "but I'll finish as quickly as I can."

I had no desire to watch. I turned my head toward the wall, uninterested in what was happening both in my womb and on the small black-and-white video screen.

"It seems your doctor was right." She clicked a few buttons, then plopped a fresh glob of gel on my stomach. "The size of your uterus and the dates you gave for your last menstrual cycle don't match. That could be a problem." The probe continued its journey. More pressure from on top, then a sudden urge to empty my full bladder.

"Okay. Turn toward me, dear. I need to find the baby's head and measure it to determine an accurate fetal age."

Reluctantly, I turned in her direction, but I swear I wanted to squeeze my eyes shut tight.

"Just a minute . . . should be right above your bladder . . . wow . . . this is the baby's head and this is . . . ." Her voice trailed off into nothingness, and I felt her body stiffen.

I stared at the screen, and my jaw dropped.

"What the hell is that?" I demanded. "Is that . . . is that . . . ?"

Marilyn giggled. "It sure is! Congratulations, Ms. Coffee!"

As black as I was, I fainted dead away.

I'd been tasked as the visual aide slide flipper for the battalion's weekly officer development meeting. Captain Perry and I walked upstairs to the battalion area together, chatting lightly and discussing operational phases for the new demolition range being constructed.

We were getting along just fine. We had a similar work ethic, his demeanor was always pleasant and respectful, and I felt pretty lucky to call him my boss.

Inside of the command conference room I was as conspicuous as a black peppercorn on a field of white rice. I rested my growing bulk on a small podium next to the slide projector and watched as two dozen or so young camouflaged officers hovered around the battalion commander like green flies on shit.

Colonel Burton was a seasoned infantry officer who'd been involuntarily detailed into commanding an engineering battalion, something he never let anyone forget. A muscular dwarflike man with a prematurely balding dome, he suffered from a bad case of short man's syndrome and seemed determined to bully anyone taller than him, or anyone he deemed unworthy.

Although the Army's official policy prohibited us from drinking alcoholic beverages while on duty, a rear table was stacked high with cases of Budweiser purchased with unit funds, and the pale-faced cheese eaters surrounding the colonel were scoring their mandatory brownie points by listening to his war stories, dutifully sucking down his beer, and hanging on his every word.

I hated the colonel's eyes. They were flat and crafty like Captain Silberman's, and whenever they touched my flesh, not only did my skin crawl, he made my teeth itch. Although I did my best to stay out of Colonel Burton's way, whenever our paths did happen to cross, I refused to kiss his ass. Instead, I spoke to him with confidence and maintained direct eye contact while keeping our conversations brief and professional. I prayed today's meeting would be short and sweet. I wanted to get out of the battalion area and back down to my company before he even noticed I was there.

Fat chance.

"Say, Lieutenant Coffee," he yodeled through the crowd of soldiers who were jostling for a piece of his jock strap. "Take a load off! Come on over here and suck down a cold one!"

The eyes of the pack were upon me, their noses in the air, their faces canine thin. My skin grew flushed. If I sauntered over and popped the ring on a beer, I stood a slight chance of being included in his inner circle of flunkies. If I didn't, I'd have hell to pay for rebuking an offer from a senior officer. I looked at my fellow officers.

They circled for the kill.

I smiled an apologetic little smile and busied myself adjusting the neck on the projector. "Sorry, sir. I don't drink."

"Well, I don't drink either," Colonel Burton sang out in a thick Georgia twang, "at least not since swallowing came into style!"

Guffaws and hee-haws rang out loudly, and I even dropped a chuckle or two in the collection plate myself.

"Come on, Lieutenant. You know it's bad protocol to refuse when the old man offers you a drink! Here—" He tilted his can in my direction. "You don't have to drink the whole thing. Just take a sip of this cold one and join in the fun!"

I pursed my lips and looked around the room. Hard eyes stared at me from blotchy, bitter faces, daring me to defy the battalion commander's wishes. I felt like the lone darkie at a Klan rally. Like they were waiting for me to make a wrong move so they could whip out the white hoods and string me up from the flagpole.

"Sorry, sir. I'm not drinking today, but I'd be happy to be the designated driver for those who are drinking."

Captain Perry piped up, "Sir, I think this has something to do with that five-mile run tomorrow morning!" He looked at me and winked. "I bet the lieutenant plans to lead the battalion formation and run us 'wussies' into the ground. She probably doesn't want any alcohol in her system to slow her down!"

Good try, Captain P, I thought, but at this point I knew it would take more balls than there were in the entire room to keep Colonel Burton off of me.

"Is that what you think, Perry?" Colonel Burton rose to his full five feet and rocked back on his heels. In turn, his flunkies fell back and took up fighting positions to his rear, leaving me standing alone without cover in the heart of the kill zone.

"Well, I think you're wrong," the colonel said, his eyes dark and fierce, his brows rigid as quills, nearly sitting atop his nose. "Lieutenant

Coffee ain't gonna lead nobody's run tomorrow morning. In fact, she won't even be in running formation, now will you, L.T.?"

The silence was deafening.

"And," he continued, deadpan, "I'd bet my shorts she ain't sour on beer any more than she's sour on milk. No, I think all this has something to do with that profile report I received from the Troop Medical Clinic last week. The one where it shows Missy Lieutenant here is on a temporary profile list. A profile that doesn't expire for, say, roughly six months." The colonel passed me the ball and waited for me to bounce it.

I swallowed hard but said nothing.

Captain Perry shot me a questioning glance, then asked, "Uh—could you explain that, sir? What profile? I haven't heard anything about my lieutenant being on any restrictive profile."

Colonel Burton nodded toward me. "Tell him," he ordered. "Tell your company commander why you've been coded red on a physical profile."

Suddenly my stomach felt like it had swollen to near-basketball size in less than two minutes. I was sure every one of the rednecked rascals in the room could see the bulge poking through my uniform. I laced my fingers across my middle and ground my teeth. There wasn't a thing I could do about my situation at this point, but I'd be damned if I'd let the colonel or any of his cronies see me sweat. I wasn't the first female officer to have a baby, and I wouldn't be the last.

"Well?" He gestured at me roughly. "Tell him!"

I raised my chin and spoke. "I'm having a baby."

Captain Perry balked. "What?"

"I'm pregnant."

Cruel snickers filled the air, and some asshole in the back of the room chirped, "By who?"

The pack howled.

I searched the maze of faces and located my attacker, some Mr. Snuffleupagus-looking white boy with a king-size case of acne and bad bites.

Captain Perry held up his hand, silencing the officers. "That—gentlemen—was unnecessary. And it was also in poor taste. Now whoever said it needs to apologize."

"Now, now . . ." Colonel Burton walked toward us with his head lowered like a charging bull. He stopped in front of Captain Perry and thrust his hands into his pockets. "Don't be so hasty! I'm not so sure if apologies are in order here. After all, the lieutenant *is* single. In fact, I think it's a pretty valid question." A cigar appeared in his right hand and he pinned me with his glare as he bit off its tip. Before the colonel could blink he was surrounded by four Bic-flicking first lieutenants bucking for captain.

Colonel Burton accepted a light, then grinned. "Sayyy there, Lieutenant Coffee. *Miss* Coffee. Pregnant and without a husband." He snorted twice, curled his lip, and snarled, "Just when is that ordnance sergeant going to make an honest woman of you, anyway?"

I swallowed a dust ball and stared down at my feet. My stomach felt bigger than a Mississippi watermelon.

The colonel took a few short tokes from his stinking cigar. Its tip burned an angry orange. "You're no longer in the enlisted ranks, you know. You're a member of the Officer Corps now, and we don't take our core values lightly. If the Army wanted you to have a family, we would have issued you one. You've already got more children than you can handle, and I'm warning you," he sneered, "you'd better get married real quick or find yourself another place of employment, because a soldier in your condition won't last long around here!" He took another puff from his cigar.

His grin was wider than all of Texas.

"At least not if I can help it!"

I felt small enough to fit into a thimble. I was so ashamed, so embarrassed, so humiliated! How could Rom have done this to me? He'd promised to marry me even before I became pregnant. Where was his promise when I needed it most?

I rushed from the room with tears spilling down my cheeks and the echo of male laughter assaulting my ears. I paused in the main foyer near the fountain and splashed cool water on my face. My back itched like crazy as sweat rolled from my hair and dampened my collar and undershirt. I'd run out of the room so fast I'd forgotten my purse, but there was no way in hell I could go back in there.

"You forgot something."

Captain Perry. His face was red, his eyes sympathetic.

I took my purse. "Thanks."

"Don't worry about those guys in there." He tried to smile. "The Officer Corps is well known for eating its young."

"Yeah. I guess."

"So." His eyes searched the polished tiles of the floor. The tips of his ears stood out like red-hot chili peppers against his white skin. "It seems congratulations are in order, huh?"

"I guess."

"Why didn't you tell me about the profile, Sanderella? What's so bad about having a baby? We can work with that."

"Without a husband?"

"Oh."

Silence.

"Well, don't worry about going back in there. I'll flip the slides for you if we ever get around to conducting the meeting. In fact," he said as he touched my arm, "take the rest of the day off, Lieutenant. Get some rest. It's not the end of the world just because you're single and having a baby."

I did my best to return his smile, then nodded and fled down the stairs. Just wait, I thought miserably. Just wait until he found out that his little lieutenant was having not one baby, but two.

30

DOGHOUSE OR CAT BOX

glanced at the face of my field watch and slammed my fist on my desk in frustration. The minutes were moving slower than cold molasses! Work was almost intolerable. These days it was something I did simply because to do otherwise would have landed me in the stockade.

It had been nearly three weeks since our argument. Or rather, since the night I asked Sandie to get an abortion. Every time I thought about her being pregnant, I wanted to run back to my barracks room and bury myself under a rock, but I didn't.

I stayed put.

Right there next to her. Or at least in the same house with her. Even though I'd been mean enough to ask her to go through with an abortion, things would get much worse if I just upped and left. At least that's what I told myself.

Everybody at her place was acting funny. Jamillah refused to speak to me, and the boys ran when they saw me coming, but at least Sandie's Dads was still cool. He still treated me well and smiled when I came into his room for our evening game of checkers, although more and more often I felt like shit even breathing the same air as him when I knew how lousy I was treating his daughter.

I couldn't help it, though. I'd been on the verge of going back to Lou, and the mere thought of telling my boys I'd been loving another woman, let alone another family, sent lightning-sharp bolts of pain lancing through my skull. My body would tremble, and I'd retch each time I even considered facing the thought of what I'd done. Of what Sandie was trying to make me do.

I called my sons constantly. I wrote letters and mailed packages so often I knew every clerk in the post office if not by name, certainly by sight. But nothing helped. Nothing. I had absolutely no feelings for Lou, but deep in my heart I was just like Solomon, doomed to a life without my sons, and for me, that kind of life was simply unacceptable.

I glanced at my watch again, then said to hell with it. I was leaving early. All who didn't like it could go straight to hell. I grabbed my jacket from a hook and slipped it on, then picked up my hat and keys.

"Sergeant Caesar?"

I whirled around.

"What's up?" I stood facing two strange white boys dressed in civilian clothing. Immediately I sniffed them out and my back stiffened.

"Would you mind coming into your First Sergeant's office for a moment, please?"

I stepped past them slowly; the combination of their little-white-boy-gone-big-Johnny-Law clothes made me swell with anger. I hadn't committed any crimes that I knew of, but my nuts still went tight with anticipation.

My First Sergeant stood at his window and turned to face me when I entered the room. The sharp buzz of his high and tight made his thin blond hair stand on end like the bristles in a brush, clearing a visible path to his blotchy pink scalp that was now beet red with agitation. I stood at the position of parade rest in front of his desk.

"Sergeant Caesar."

"Top."

"Stand at ease, soldier. Have a seat. This is Special Agent Boyton

and Special Agent Carr. They've come to ask you a few questions
about your personal life."

Agent Boyton looked like Moose in the old Archie comics, and his
amicable-looking sidekick could have passed for a young Michael
Douglas.

Top held up his hand. "Let me warn you. You're not obligated to
answer anything you feel uncomfortable with, but if you fail to co-
operate, they do have the authority to take you down to Central Intelligence Division and conduct a polygraph exam."

"What for?" I stammered. "I haven't done anything."

"Well, it seems your girlfriend, what's her name?" He glanced at a
sheet of paper on his desk. "Lieutenant Coffee's government quarters are in the officer housing area, and we got a call from her battalion commander who suspects some wrongful cohabitation is going
on over there. The BC claims his young officer has an enlisted man
living with her, and he gave us your name."

"What?" I recoiled like an innocent man. The Army was a goddamn trip! All the time digging into soldiers' private lives! "I don't
live with her," I lied hotly. "Top, you know I have a room in the barracks!"

"I know you've been *assigned* a room in the barracks, but I don't
know shit about where you sleep at night."

That damned Sandie! We'd known how wrong we were from
jump street. We should've learned something when that white chick
tried to hem us up back in Virginia, but *nooooo*. We not only had to
keep the shit going, but on top of that, we go and make a baby!

Agent Carr pushed a piece of paper at me. "Here's a copy of the
Army's regulation on cohabitation." He chuckled. "Hell, if she were
living off base, no one would even care about who she had in her
house, and just between us I think the regs are outdated and sense-
less, but when you're living on base and CID gets a call from a full
bird colonel . . . well, we gotta go through the motions."

I skimmed the page of tiny print and legal jargon.

"Basically," Carr explained, "it says that you're in violation of the
regulation if you live with a woman other than your wife. Perhaps

you two should consider moving off base, because it's usually only pushed if either of you live in government quarters. The charge falls under Conduct Unbecoming of a Noncommissioned Officer and is punishable under the Uniform Code of Military Justice."

Top pushed another sheet of paper in my face. "Read this and sign it when you're done. It's a general counseling statement. A warning. Although I like you and I know you have a good track record in the Army, the regulation says you have to be counseled in writing when facing this type of offense."

He fingered his small mustache and gave me a hard look.

"I don't know what you're doing, Caesar, but I'm putting your ass on notice. I don't need to have Lieutenant Coffee's commander call her on the carpet, do I?"

I shook my head quickly. "No, First Sergeant. That won't be necessary. I'll take care of everything."

He nodded. "Good. Do that. Be a man and protect your woman, Sergeant. Because if you so much as sleep in her doghouse or roll around in her cat box, both of your asses are going up the river for wrongful cohabitation."

He didn't have to tell me twice!

I pretended to read the counseling statement, but secretly I was overjoyed. I wanted to live in my own room anyway. I was sick and tired of Sandie always trying to sandwich me in with her family. "Rom, what do you want for dinner, baby? Rom, where are we taking the kids this weekend, honey? Rom, could you take the boys to get a haircut, please?"

I got two fuckin' boys, too! Who the fuck was taking them to get their heads cut? Her boys weren't my responsibility! My responsibilities were right where I'd dropped them.

In Virginia.

With the number two domino.

While it would probably embarrass the hell out of Sandie, moving out was going to be right up my alley. I'd pack my toothbrush and two pairs of drawers and book out of there quick-fast and in a sho'nuff hurry! I was going to *run* my ass out of there because walking would be much too slow.

I darkened the "concur" box and scribbled my signature across the bottom of page. Then I handed the document back to Top.

"Can I go?"

Top's face blinked like a big fat caution sign. I moved toward the door. "One more thing, Sergeant . . ."

I paused, one foot already on the other side of his threshold.

"I noticed you have two dependants listed on your personnel form. I assume they're your children." He stared a piercing hole straight through my eyes and out the back of my head.

"You wouldn't happen to be married, now would you?"

I felt the air swoosh from my left lung and my knees tried to betray me. Instinctively, I pressed my thumb to my ring finger to make sure it was still bare.

"No, First Sergeant." The voice of sincerity emitting from my mouth was not my own. "Why would you think that?"

Top nodded his head knowingly. "Well, if these gentlemen ever call for proof, I'm sure you can cough up some documentation. You're dismissed."

31

TOAST TO THE FOOL

I slammed down another shot of gin and glanced at the barmaid as she swished hurriedly by. There was absolutely no reason for me to be ass watching, because ever since Mr. Bobo had died, sex was the last thing on my mind. Besides, this chick's behind looked too much like Lou's. Nonexistent.

Signaling the barmaid, I ordered another round. This time a double. I'd already had about four stiff ones, and I planned to put away at least two more before Sandie showed up. She'd called me at work and asked me to meet her at the NCO Club for happy hour. I didn't know what she wanted to talk about, but I needed to be drunk just to look at her.

I sat on the barstool hunched over my drink and wallowing in my troubles. Suddenly the hair on the back of my neck stood up. I spun around sharply and nearly fell off the warped-leg stool.

She was a sight for sore eyes.

I began at her feet and let my gaze travel the length of her thickening body. Instead of her camouflage Army pickle suit, she was wrapped up in that sexy red number she'd worn the night I fell in love with her. Damn! Sandie still looked damned good, but I wasn't about to tell her.

"Hi, Rom."

"Whassup."

I turned away from her and made the double all gone. The straight liquor rolled down my throat and burned like a forest fire before settling in the pit of my stomach to percolate. Sandie took a seat on the stool beside me, but I didn't even ask if she wanted a drink. I needed every dime in my pockets to pay for the rest of the firewater *I* planned to put away.

"So, have you heard anything else from your First Sergeant?"

Did she have to bring that shit up?

Everyone we knew was giving me dirty looks like I'd done Sandie wrong, and my First Sergeant was no exception. These days Top looked at me with a mixture of suspicion and disgust, but nobody could make me feel any worse than I already felt.

"Is that what you wanted to talk to me about?"

"Well, yeah. No. I mean, yeah—that, too."

I glanced at her and nearly saw double. Good. The gin was doing its job. "Well, I don't wanna talk about it."

Ever since that come-to-Jesus session in my First Sergeant's office, I'd stayed far away from Sandie's house. Good thing, too, because my attitude toward her and her kids was totally messed up. I saw tons of pain and hurt in her eyes whenever I opened my mouth and let my guilt fly out. Once I told her, "You and me don't need no baby! I should've never fucked with you in the first place!" You should've seen the look on her face.

It was pitiful.

I hated myself for everything I said, but I just couldn't help it. For some crazy reason it made me feel better to see her cry, so I hurled insults at her left and right. Sandie's tough exterior made me want to hurt her even more, and I said things to her that I'm ashamed to remember—let alone repeat.

But Sandie was no slouch. She could give it just as good as I could. My girl had a fight in her. She was strong and full of pride, and her mouth was a dump! I mean, the girl could get downright uncouth! Whenever I leaned on her too hard and said something truly foul, she'd go off like a damned firecracker. If I'da known she could cuss like that when I met her, I'd have walked right on by. I could've drunk my Coke! It was obvious that Sandie had more style and class than I would ever have, but just to hurt her feelings I called her "ghetto" and asked her if she wanted to shoot some joints.

She probably wanted to shoot my nuts.

I probably deserved it.

I studied her eyes. They were ringed with dark circles. She looked tired as hell, and she'd already gained back every pound she'd lost during OCS. Plus more. The way I counted she was only about four months pregnant, but already she had a tight little belly in front of her. I sighed and turned away. I still loved Sandie, but I was too tired and too mad to feel it. I signaled the barmaid and ordered another drink.

"You're sure putting them away, huh?"

"I'm paying for them, ain't I?"

"Yeah. We're both paying for all kinds of things."

I let that one fly right over my head. She kept hollering about how I was making her pay for my decision to leave Lou and my sons. Bullshit! I was the one paying for that mistake—in blood, sweat, and tears! And to add bear shit to the bullshit, I found out Lou and the boys wouldn't be moving to Missouri with me after all. My sons were gone for good. Lost to me forever, because their mother had gone and found herself a permanent man. If I'm lying, I'm flying. Guy wrote and said dude was some technical captain in the Air Force and the bastard had the nerve to be Frat! I guess Lou was ready to move on with her life, to quit all of that tipping and settle down, because she served me up a dish of quick-fast divorce papers and I signed them and expressed them back to her the *same* day!

So much for repairing my damage and reclaiming my family.

"Look, Lou—I mean, Sandie. You asked me to meet you here. I'm here. So whassup?"

"I went to see the doctor," she said softly.

"Oh, yeah? That's nice."

"He says I'm due right around Christmas."

I tossed back another shot. "Well, whooptie-fuckin'-doo and a Merry Christmas to you, too!"

That was my liquor talking. My head was spinning like a clothes dryer, and when the barmaid answered my call this time I ordered a beer. A boilermaker. I looked over at Sandie and frowned. She was staring at me like I was crazy.

Or drunk. Or both.

"Plus I had an ultrasound."

"And?"

"There were two heads, and they heard two heartbeats."

"Who hears two whats?" I shook my head to clear it.

"The doctor heard two heartbeats, Rom. They gave me an ultra-sound. We're having—I'm pregnant with twins."

She smiled at me and tried to look happy.

Jesus wept, and so did I.

"So," she said, like life was peachy. "What do you think we should name them?"

My tongue felt enormous in my mouth, and there was something seriously wrong with my hearing. Sandie's voice was distorted and distant. Suddenly I realized I was *tight*. If I stood up, I'd probably fall over.

But I was still mad.

And that gin was still talking.

"Name 'em?" I slurred. "Name 'em?" I waved my hand breezily in the air. "Shit, you can name 'em Here and There, This and That, Do and Don't, Will and Won't. . . . Name 'em any goddamn thing you wanna name 'em. Except Romulus and Sanderella." I looked over at her and shook my head. "Those two names don't go together at all!"

My girl slid off her barstool and took a few steps backward. I knew she couldn't just walk away without cussing me out. She wasn't built that way.

I braced myself for the nuclear explosion.

The heat rose off her, and it warmed me and made me feel good. I glanced in the mirror behind the bar, and her candy-apple red shirt stood out like the bloodstains on my heart. She stood there silently, fighting for control. Her head held high, her back straight. Her chin proud.

She looked beautiful.

Regal. Dignified.

Like a pot of strong black coffee. No sugar, no cream.

Just like an African-American queen.

"You know what, Romulus?" Sandie asked softly.

I didn't answer. I knew a lot of things, none of which meant shit.

"You ain't *blank* enough for me, and I'm too *blank* for you. You can fill in the blanks!"

I turned and watched her as she walked proudly away. What a back view my baby had. A hot tear rolled down my cheek, and I stuck my tongue out to taste it. I'd finally hurt her as bad as she had hurt me. So what if I didn't know exactly what it was she'd done wrong!

She pushed through the door.

She's gone, she's gone! Oh Lawd, the big-leg girl is gone! I turned back around and gazed into the mirror, then lifted my brew and gave a toast to the fool who let her go.

I was hotter than fish grease, but I refused to let him see me sizzle! When Rom dissed me at the bar, I'd wanted to shout, scream, and piss a Brownsville bitch—but I didn't. If I reached into my Brooklyn bag today, he would *never* recover! I marched out of the NCO Club and climbed into my car, splitting the back of my hot, red skirt suit in the process. I'd squeezed my big booty in it with the hopes that it would help bring back good memories, but all of my good memories with Rom were really just his good lies.

Like the importance of a name.

I looked down at my hands. They were trembling. I didn't know if it was from fear, rage, or what, but my entire body felt feverish. Rom had really hurt me this time. That man had promised me everlasting love, and like a fool I'd fallen for the razzle-dazzle. I'd been lied to, misled, hoodwinked, *and* bamboozled! Rom had shoved me across the thin line between love and hate. I hated him. And I never wanted to see him again.

Before I met him my stuff had been *straight*!

Yeah, it got lonely sometimes, but I'd been handling my business and doing my thing. He should've left me alone and kept his ass at home with his wife. Nobody made him step out on her. He was probably swinging his dick long before I met him!

Romulus Caesar was no king.

He was a piddling-ass pauper!

And just look at what he'd done to me. This wasn't the kind of life I had planned for myself. I used to have high hopes and dreams for my future. And now I was worse off than when I started. Instead of being a single parent with three kids I was about to become the single parent of five.

Unwed.

And an officer, too. Now how would that look?

I was filled with shame and self-disgust. My entire life was going to be one tough row to hoe. My commander, the First Sergeant, and every other white cracker in the brigade would have a mouthful of tobacco to chew on this one! I could just imagine the spiteful stares and slanderous comments I was in for. Not to mention the shitty treatment. But who could blame them? In a few short months I'd look like just another stupid nigger bitch who couldn't keep her legs closed.

I placed my hands on my hardening stomach.

I was about to turn into the little old lady who lived in a shoe.

She had so much heartache she didn't know what to do.

32

ONE MORE NIGHT

gazed out my window at the stars dotting the sky like a spattering of silver freckles. It was a still night, and the moon hung low like my heart, heavy and filled with anguish. Jamillah had gotten up to use the bathroom, and, seeing the glow of my lamp, she stumbled into my room and dove under the covers. I sat quietly rubbing her back with the flat of my hand as my eyes searched the darkness. How had I gotten to this point? Where exactly had my life taken such a drastic turn, where had my train jumped its track?

Even with Jamillah sprawled across it, the bed seemed vast and empty without Rom. Hell, after his treatment of me today during happy hour, life felt empty without him. I'd never seen him so roaring drunk. So belligerent and angry. I was mad, too, but even through my anger I just wasn't ready to let things end this way between us. We had promised to love and respect each other, and I just didn't understand why we couldn't seem to communicate about our relationship without fighting. I knew I was being stupid, and I had no reason to make up to him, but I loved him and I needed him to know it.

The digital clock read twelve-ten. There was still time. I threw back the covers and slipped into a pink jogging suit. The kids would be fine here with Daddy. This could be a pivotal night for Rom and me. A night that might dictate the rest of our relationship. The rest of our lives.

I drove the few blocks to his barracks room and parked in the lot right out front. I couldn't care less if someone saw my car and reported us; the damage had already been done to our reputations and if Central Intelligence Division was watching us that closely, then they'd be able to gather a full report tonight.

Rom's room was on the ground floor, and even from the parking lot I could see a light reflecting from his window. Good. That meant he was awake, too. Probably up drinking himself further into a coma. I hurried across the street and, ignoring the stone-edged footpath, trekked through the grass on the side of the building. The twinkling sounds of a Spanish hacienda melody drifted through the air like secret wind chimes, and even before I reached the entrance, I heard the faint cry of his words riding above the melodies of his piano.

Baby . . . so much has happened in so little time
Thoughts of you keep me troubled, running through my mind

I'm sorry . . .

I filled your heart with pain and I know I'm wrong
Sandie, let me change my song

I've never loved the way I've been loving you
The air I breathe is heavy with my need for you

My heart will forever be true
This song I sing for you . . .

I pushed through the doors and entered the building, moving slowly down the semidark corridor. I clutched my hands to my mouth, the raw pain falling from Rom's lips the only sound in the universe. The beauty of it astounded me, and I staggered under the weight of his words with my body pressed close to the wall and hot tears burning my eyes.

> Sandie, give me one more night
> Sweet baby, let me make this right

> I'll hold you in my arms so you can feel
> All pain my love can heal

> So sorry . . .

A slice of light fell from his open doorway and cut across the dark carpet. As I eased toward it, his fingers massaged and caressed and coaxed haunting notes of love from his electric keyboard and sent them hurling straight into the core of my soul. I peered into the room then snapped shut my eyes, blinded by his shine.

> If I had another chance I'd show you how
> How I can love you with a heart you'd never doubt

> My soul belongs to you
> I need you and there's not much else I can do
> Except ease the pain you feel
> Your heart please let me heal

> Sandie, I need one more night
> Baby, I can make things right

> Take your time, make up your mind
> My heart is yours, and yours is mine
> Dry your eyes, no need to cry
> Rom can heal your pain inside . . .

Rom had become one with his machine. His fingers melding and merging with the keys, his lashes rested on his cheeks and he stood as naked as the day he entered this world. Behind him, a gentle breeze danced along the open window, twirling and bending the white lace curtains with the soft caress of an invisible hand. His skin held the sheen of black gold. The muscles along his arms and belly shifted just beneath the skin's surface moving in time to an inner rhythm. Sweat seeped from his pores and trickled from his eyes. His glow gathered strength and speed and swelled and bulged until it finally encompassed my soul and sent me crashing to my knees.

> Sandie, give me
> One
> More
> Night . . .
> Baby, let me
> Make
> Things
> Right . . .
>
> Step into my arms
> So I can show you
> All the hurt my
> Love
> Can
> Heal . . .

I crawled toward him on all fours. He sank to his knees and met me halfway. I was enveloped in his arms, drowning in his love, the air in our lungs inadequate to sustain the both of us. Rom covered my mouth with his, and I fed from him. Swelling and rising and gasping, I absorbed the beauty of his soul until the only reality of which I was certain was his love.

> Sandie, give me
> One
> More
> Night . . .

I won't rush you
Just take your time
Let's take it slow . . .
We have all night
Stay right here and never go
Dry your eyes
No need to cry
Let me heal your hurt inside . . .

33

PEOPLE OF ACTION

I awoke to the sound of cadence. The troops were on their morning physical fitness run, and the rhythmic boom of their voices penetrated my slumber as the bright sunlight streaming through the windows illuminated the room. Sandie lay on her back, her face turned away from me. One arm was flung over her head while the other rested lightly on my thigh. It was weird having her in my room. In my bed and among my stuff. I was much more accustomed to being on her turf, in her element, and I felt emboldened by this change of locales.

We lay naked from the night before. She'd shown up while I was in some kind of half-drunk emotional trance, and good thing she did, because my liquor had me thinking about leaving here. Doing myself in and ending all of this nonsense. I'd run a tub of hot water and taken out an old straight razor. I figured I could record Sandie a farewell song, then get naked, cut my wrists, and sit in the tub and enjoy my final lyrics until my pain subsided.

Like a sign from above, Sandie arrived as I was recording the song, and the very sight of her sent all thoughts of suicide rushing from my mind. I kissed her lips and held her in my arms, and the moment I entered her I knew for sure that I wanted to live. I needed to live.

But I was still unsure about our relationship.

Her chest rose and fell as she snored lightly. I allowed one finger to touch the skin of her stomach as I traced the darkening line running from her navel over the thickening mound of her belly and down into her soft pubic hair. My babies were cocooned just beneath my hands, yet I felt no connection to them as beings. Her breasts were fuller than ever and stood straight up, her nipples soft and relaxed. Soon, they'd be ready for the suckling of tiny mouths. Filled with a perfect source of nourishment without any participation required on my part.

There was no doubt that I loved this girl. No doubt that my heart belonged to her. But I just wasn't ready for what she offered. I was unworthy. In my present condition I couldn't see myself being a decent father to anybody's kids. Not mine. Not hers. Not ours.

Although I was grateful Sandie had been there for me during the night, I cursed myself for needing her. For making love to her. I'd meant every word I said about her and those babies. There was no room in my life to hurt anyone else. To cause any more pain. Sandie had to go.

I shook her awake.

"Hey." She smiled slowly and ran her soft hand up my leg.

I shifted my position and steeled my heart. "Hey. It's time to get up. Time for you to go home."

"C'mon, baby." She closed her eyes and stretched lazily. Her stomach went flat on the left side as the babies huddled together on the right. "It's still early. Daddy is there with the kids. Let's lay back down for a little while and cuddle." Her hand inched toward Mr. Bobo, and he jumped up to meet her halfway.

It took everything I had in me, but I got up from the bed and slipped into my briefs. "You don't understand, Sandie." I forced the steel into my voice. "Last night was a mistake. In more ways than one. Nothing has changed between us."

I saw the old pain reenter her eyes, and it almost killed me.

She sat up and pulled the sheet up to her neck. "What are you talking about, Rom? Yes, things have changed between us. Last night

proved that." She narrowed her eyes and stared at me, totally confused.

"See, that's how wrong you are. Women always mistake sex for
something else."

"So, I'm mistaken?"

"Yeah. I guess you can say that."

She stood and let the sheet fall back to the bed. Her skin glowed
in the morning light, and her stomach stuck out as a reminder of all
of my faults. "We need to talk, Rom. Please. Let's try and communicate on this one and maybe we can work it out."

"What's there to work out? I've already been barred from your
quarters, so I can't come back there, and you should be at home with
your kids instead of being here." I decided to shoot her a jab. "Actually, *I* should have stayed at home with my kids instead of being
here."

"What the hell is that supposed to mean?" Her eyes were slits. She
picked up her bra from the floor and turned it around backward before hooking the clasps and rotating the cups to her front.

"Just what I said. I should have stayed at home with my boys."

She pushed her breasts inside the bra cups and then snapped, "So
why the hell did you leave?"

"Beats me." I picked up her shirt from the floor and held it out to
her, hating the sight of her bare stomach. She snatched the shirt
from my hands and pulled it violently over her head. She thrust her
legs through her pink sweats and bent over to pick up her shoes.

"You know what, Rom? You're about a sorry somebody. Having a
little pity party this morning? Well, let me enlighten you: No great
tragedy befell you. You made your own decisions. You talk all that
yang about wanting to be with your boys, but it's all hot air. The fact
is, you enjoy being miserable. You like having a boulder on your
back, a cross to fucking bear. Makes you feel like you're the victim
here."

"I never said that."

"And what about your divorce? What ever happened to that? I
guess that was just another one of your lies."

I crossed my arms. I had not told her anything about the divorce. "I'm waiting to hear back from Lou," I lied. "She doesn't think the time is right yet. The boys just aren't ready."

"Bullshit." She tied her shoes, pulling on her laces so hard I thought they'd break. "We are people of action, in case you didn't know it," she continued. "When things bother us or we feel we've been wronged or we want something bad enough, we do something about it. All that lip service you give don't amount to shit. It's totally irrelevant. So, tell me something, Mistah Daddy of the Year." Her chest heaved with each word, and I could see how hard she was fighting to keep me from seeing her tears. She grabbed her purse from the chair and turned to face me, then she picked up her jacket from the floor and nailed me with a combination. "You're a king, right? So that makes your boys princes, ain't that right? So, King Romulus. After all that shit you've talked about how much you love your sons, how much you need to have them with you, what have you actually *done* to get them back?"

34

WHO STOLE THE COOKIES?

I struggled out of the commissary with two full bags of groceries and swore. Damn! I should have parked in a handicapped space! As big as I was I certainly qualified, because it was getting harder and harder for me to manage my ever-growing bulk. Although I was only seven and a half months pregnant, carrying twins was hard, hard work.

As I crossed the crowded parking lot, I spotted Rom's baby blue Saab pulling into the Class Six Liquor Store across the square. My heart pounded with something close to excitement. Although he lived nearby, over three months had passed since Rom had screwed me, humiliated me, then put me out of his barracks room, and I hadn't seen him since.

And I hadn't missed him either. At least that's what I told myself and everyone else. Rom had let our good thing turn into nothing, and I was still angry and confused. Although the remnants of my pride wouldn't allow me to call him, he made it a point to call Daddy and the kids whenever I was out of the house.

According to Daddy, Rom always asked about me, always wanted to know if there was anything I needed, but as far as I was concerned his polite inquiries didn't amount to a hill of beans. I wanted him to *see* me. To see my pain. See the damage he'd done.

Especially to my respectability. As soon as the word about my pregnancy and my single status got out, I was relegated to the status of persona non grata. Coupled with the fact that Rom had been barred from my quarters and strange cars sat watching my house at odd hours, I was doomed.

While Rom still walked around the post swinging both arms and looking like a man, most of the officers in the brigade avoided me like the plague. Forget about professional courtesy. Whenever I waddled past, their conversations would cease and snide titters, my-mammy jokes, and Aunt Jemima remarks flew my way. I ignored them. I may have looked like an ignorant breeding wench, but I still had my pride.

But now I pushed the last of my pride aside and found my voice.

"Rom! Rom!" I stood on my tiptoes as if that would make him see me better. He would have had to be blinder than Ray Charles in order to miss me in my bright yellow tent shirt and extra-large maternity jeans.

He kept right on walking.

I tried to speed up to catch him, but I dropped the bag of loose potatoes, and of course they rolled everywhere! Damn! I scrambled to pick them up, saying to hell with the two that rolled under the white Nissan Maxima. By the time I stood up, Rom had already entered the store, but I knew he'd heard me. And seen me. I pushed my bags into the trunk of my car and waddled across the square to the Class Six. Pausing to catch my breath, I leaned on Rom's Saab and hoped he wouldn't be inside too long because I had the sudden urge to go something fierce.

A minute later he stepped out of the store. He looked taller than I remembered. Skinnier, too. And dusty as *hell*. Like a dirty-ass Buck without the Preacher Man. He stared me up and down, then looked away.

"Hey," I said shyly.

"Hey to you, too."

"How's it going?"

"Slow."

He didn't even ask how I was doing. My stomach was filled to capacity with his kids, and he couldn't even bring himself to acknowledge them. "So, what have you been up to?"

"Same shit, different day." He ran his hand over his bald head and squinted into the sun. "Is there something you wanted to say to me, Sandie? I'm supposed to meet a few Frats to watch the game, and I'm holding up the brewskies." He glanced down at my belly, and at that moment the babies chose to kick. I clutched my middle.

His eyes softened. "You know what, San?" He nodded toward my bulging stomach. "You really oughtta think about putting those babies up for adoption."

"Oh yeah? And how would I explain that to my kids? Mommy lost your baby brothers on the way home from the hospital? Oh—I forgot. As long as you're not forced to explain anything to *your* kids, then it's all good. We wouldn't want them to know Daddy was having sex and living a normal life without them now, would we?"

"Whatever. It's just that I've been thinking about it, and I really think it would be the best move to make."

Right on cue I exploded.

After months of suffering at the hands of my command, ignoring their lewd comments, accepting their rude glances and embarrassing remarks, submitting to their sexist convictions, swallowing my pride, and wallowing in shame—four months of pent-up pain and fury spewed out of me like hot water.

"Best for *who*? I'm sick of you! Who are you to tell me what's best for me? Best for me would've been Sparkle *slamming your fucking head* in the car door the night I met you!"

Rom stared at me, then turned away. "So *ghetto*!" I thought I heard him murmur as he climbed into his car.

My heart cracked like an egg. I turned away, too.

Somehow I managed to speed-walk over to my car and climb in. I watched him pull away.

It ain't over, asshole, I promised silently.

Sniffling, I trailed behind his car like an amateur sleuth, the tracks of my tears wearing permanent grooves in my cheeks. He led me to the base's enlisted housing area and parked near a long row of three-bedroom houses. Unlike the officers' quarters where I lived, these houses were connected side to side, had no driveways, and lined both sides of the narrow street. I parked a half block away. Roughly ten cars separated us.

With a case of beer cradled in the arms that used to hold me, Rom entered the fourth house from the corner. He probably had some gullible little bitch in there, fooling her the same way he had fooled me! I'd played the fool, that much was certain. But Rom was going to get his. I swore right then and there that I'd make that bastard pay for the misery he had brought to my life.

One way or the other he was going to pay!

I reached in my purse and pulled out my switchblade. Because me and a knife were old buddies.

After all, I was a ghetto bitch from Brooklyn.

As soon as dusk fell, I crept from my car. I didn't give a damn about my meat or my milk as they sat growing warm in the trunk. The only thing I cared about was getting back at Rom. He'd been inside of that house for almost an hour, and I knew damned well that watching the game wasn't all he was doing.

He'd turned into a real lush. He probably didn't even run any-more, let alone sing, and I'd heard all kinds of stories about how the Military Police had to escort his drunk behind out of the club on Friday nights. Well, somebody was going to have to escort his black ass somewhere tonight, too. That much was for sure!

I inched up to the passenger side of his car and peered across to the house. I knew he'd be in there drinking for a while, so I felt relatively safe. The problem was, the babies were pressing down hard on my bladder, and I had to go so bad my front teeth hurt! Carefully, I flicked open the rusty blade and scraped it deeply across the baby blue finish until I reached his passenger door. Then I lowered my bulk and did a Korean-style kimchee squat next to the Saab's front tire.

I was too scared to risk cutting the tires on the driver's side—he might see me—but as long as nobody came out of any of the houses on the passenger side of the street, I figured I'd be okay. I had never before in my life slashed anybody's tires, but since people did it all the time, how difficult could it be? Balancing my considerable weight on my swollen ankles I chose a spot about two inches away from the air valve.

Shaking, I palmed the handle of the knife in my right fist, then wrapped the meaty fingers of my left hand around my knife hand. With my eyes squeezed shut I plunged the blade into the coarse surface of the rubber.

Nothing.

This was harder than it looked! I'd expected the knife to slice through the tire with style and ease, but it didn't, and now my ankles, knees, back, and babies were all protesting. I took a quick breath and raised my clenched fists above my head. I used all of my strength and brought the knife down in an arc, stabbing at the rubber with all of my might.

SWOOOOOOSH! The air rushed out of the tire with a deafening screech, scaring the holy shit out of me and causing me to lose my precarious balance. As I struggled to extract the blade from the spent rubber, I lost my footing, and the next thing I knew I was flat on my back with my legs in the air and my pride on the ground!

Well, wouldn't you know it, at that very moment a couple and their two brats came out of their house and saw me lying there in the street with my belly extended to the high heavens and panting like I'd just run the Boston Marathon!

"Look, Mommy, look!" the smaller brat said, ratting me out to his parents. "There's a big fat lady sleeping in the street right next to that car with the flat tire."

By the time I managed to roll my considerable girth over and pull myself up to my knees, they were standing over me staring down at me with concern.

"Are you okay, ma'am?" asked the husband, who was roughly twenty-five, skinny, and bespectacled. He extended his hand to help me up, and I gratefully took it.

Mistake!

The man was a flyweight. There was no way he could lift the heavyweight sistah off of her knees, although he gave it a helluva try!

"Move over, dear," said his wife, who looked like a lumberjack. It was easy to see who was eating in their house and who wasn't. She offered me her ample forearm, and I grasped it with both hands. Wifey pulled me up like a crane and never busted a sweat. Girlfriend looked like she could've blown Rom's tire back up with the same amount of ease.

As I stood up and looked at them sheepishly, I racked my brain for an explanation as to why I'd been on the ground. At that moment the older brat picked up the abandoned switchblade (which I'd forgotten all about) and held it up in the air.

"A knife! A knife!" he screamed like a total fool, scaring the hell out of his daddy, who was now looking at Rom's tire with great suspicion. I grabbed the knife away from him, being careful to avoid the blade, and folded it quickly. I stuck it down the front of my shirt in between my humongous hooters and then looked up at the couple with a stupid smile.

Who stole the cookies from the cookie jar?

"Did you cut that tire, ma'am?" the husband asked with an angry edge to his voice. I opened my mouth to tell a great big lie, and that's when my poor bladder finally let loose. A mighty gush of hot urine ran down not one, but both of my legs!

"Oh, dear. Look!" his wife cried frantically. "Her water broke!"

Yes!

"Oh, my Lawd," I played it off. "You're exactly right! My water done broke!" I backed away from them and toward my parked car. "Well, I gotta run, folks. I'd better get to the hospital before these five babies fall out!"

"Do you need a ride?" yelled the wife.

"No thanks." I duck-walked back to my car, leaving behind a trail of flowing urine. "I'll be fine!"

I burned rubber getting my wet tail out of there, and I didn't slow down until I reached Mel's house, twelve blocks away. I sat in the car before going in, wondering how the hell I could explain this to Charmel. I was tired, dirty, and as wet as a two-year-old, but for the first time in months I felt good. Really good. The funny thing was — as I sat there in that growing puddle with a stupid grin on my face — I was still peeing!

35

MAD AS HELL

I'd just finished making a security check of the post arms room when my CQ runner handed me a telephone message. It was from Sandie. Man, if crazy was a minute, that girl wouldn't last but a red-hot second!

She stabbed my tire!

I was on my way to my boy Teddy's house, where a bunch of Frats had gathered to watch the ball game. I'd just picked up the brew and surprise, surprise, surprise! She was leaning against my car when I came out of the Class Six store. Although I'd been secretly watching her for months, this was the first time I'd gotten a real close look at her. She was huge! I mean, it looked like she had two or three Shaquille O'Neals in the oven!

I'd wanted to take her in my arms and rub her back, her feet, her neck, and anything else that needed rubbing. I wanted to kiss her on that special spot, to give her a warm bath, to grease her scalp and brush her hair. To look deeply into her soul and say, "I'm sorry, baby. Please forgive me."

But I didn't.

I didn't know how to tell Sandie how I felt. I'd said a lot of foolish things that I really didn't mean, but I didn't know how to say I was sorry. I had dreams about her almost every night, and life without my baby was empty.

But I couldn't go back to her.

I felt some sort of evil stubbornness that prevented me from reaching out to her. From comforting her and being the man and father I knew she needed me to be. Knew I should be.

All of the anger and other fucked-up emotions I experienced were too wrapped around her for me to see straight. It was like I loved her, yet I hated her at the same time.

I was too ashamed to show my face to her Dads, so instead of going to her house, I parked near her job and watched her struggle to work. I followed her during lunch to see what she ate. What she fed my babies. I sat across from her house at night and peered into her windows. And as soon as she left for work in the morning I called her Dads and *checked on* my baby!

But I couldn't go back to her. My attitude was still too foul, too warped. My actions continuously belied my feelings. Seemed like everything I did was the complete opposite of how I really felt. So I stayed away from her.

And especially from her kids.

I didn't want to mess their heads up like I'd done my boys, who, to my surprise, were doing just fine without me. Sure, they missed me, but they weren't dying! That kinda pissed me off because, damn, weren't they supposed to be feeling just as bad as I was? I was just waiting for Lou to marry that asshole and change my sons' last names. Women did that type of shit all the time, and knowing how much it would hurt me, Lou would do it with a swiftness!

She hated me for leaving her and the boys.

I hated myself.

Somehow that was all Sandie's fault, too, and by the time I dialed her number, instead of feeling good I was mad as hell and not taking it anymore!

Fort Wood was in the midst of a severe thunderstorm. The great outdoors were unfit for both man and beast, and the howling winds rattled my windows in their panes. For the past month the babies had nestled high in my chest and given me severe indigestion. As part of my treatment plan my doctor had advised me to eat six small meals a day.

I opened a small can of tuna and mixed in a heaping spoonful of mayonnaise. Then I chopped a whole onion and threw that in there, too. A little relish and I was set. Grabbing a box of Ritz crackers from the pantry, I slipped out of my maternity pants and got comfortable in my shirt and underwear while sitting in front of the eleven o'clock news. The kids were asleep, and Daddy and Bunchie were upstairs talking.

Yes, Bunchie. She'd appeared on my doorstep like magic. It seems she and Charmel had been in deep cahoots, and they'd figured I could use some backup in my camp.

They were right.

"How'd you get away from Vernon?" I asked as Bunchie breezed in and kissed my cheek.

She shook her head. "Girl, he fell off the wagon. Went to work one day and drove his damned forklift off a dock. Didn't get so much as a scratch on him, but they told him if he wanted to keep his job he had to check into a thirty-day drug-and-alcohol treatment program."

"Damn." I hugged her. "Maybe it'll do him some good."

Bunchie had brought a large painting wrapped up in brown paper. "I'm just starting out, so my work isn't all that tight yet. But I wanted you to have this one 'cause I think it's one you'll enjoy."

"They let you check this bad boy on the airplane?" I eyed the huge package. It looked like it would cover half a wall.

"Yeah, but I had to pay extra. Go ahead, open it."

I tore the paper away to reveal the most stunning and vivid oil painting I'd ever seen in my life. My big sister had enough talent to open up her own gallery in Soho and make megabucks!

"Oh God, Bunchie," I whispered, tears springing to my eyes as I covered my mouth in awe. She had painted a masterpiece.

The painting depicted my entire family sitting around Mama's kitchen table playing a heated game of bid whist. Daddy and I were partners, and Mama Ceal and Bailey were paired up. Bunchie stood behind Bailey, while Ladelle, with her arm on my shoulder, leaned against my chair. Bailey was shown spanking Daddy's queen of clubs with his king and he wore a look of pure joy on his handsome face.

And he was healthy.

His face was full and his body muscular. Just as I liked to remember him. I vividly recalled the occasion that Bunchie managed to memorialize with her art. It was right before Bailey was diagnosed with HIV, a time when I'd still felt secure and protected.

In the painting, I stared in dismay at Bailey's trump card, and Bunchie had captured my wry expression to a tee. Daddy's eyes were on my face, and the love she painted seemed to jump off the paper.

Mama wore a satisfied smile, and somehow Bunchie had painted her presence brighter and larger. Her essence was that of a matri-arch, a formidable *mother*. She looked at her family with pure ado-ration, and her energy was electrifying.

Ladelle wore an eggshell-colored T-shirt and tight jeans. The fullness of her thrusting breasts and the curve of her hips were saucily prominent. Her thick, long hair looked windswept—and her smile was blindingly white. Her gaze rested upon the top of my head, and her eyes seemed protective. Safeguarding and secure.

Bunchie's self-portrait was unbelievable. She'd found and unrav-eled her true self. In the painting she wore an elegant, translucent magenta silk dress that seemed to flow forever. She'd exaggerated her every curve, and as a result her already abundant femininity was en-hanced. Her eyes rested on me with a sister-love that I knew would last me a lifetime.

She looked nothing like the abused Bunchie of that long-ago day, but rather like the serene, composed, and confident woman who had appeared on my doorstep with her hand on her hip, dressed to a T and looking to put her foot in Rom's ass.

Yes, Bunchie's work of art had captured the spirit of my family, but the love we felt for one another could never be bound to paper and seemed to seep through to my very soul. I knew I'd look at that paint-ing every day for the rest of my life, and it would always bring me comfort and joy.

I sat down to my tuna fish and crackers and dug in with gusto.

Above the noise of the wind and rain I heard Bunchie's high-pitched voice, laughing out loud at something Daddy said. I smiled. When I was finished eating, I'd go upstairs and join them, making more memories.

Thunder roared and the telephone rang, startling me so badly I dropped a cracker. It fell to the floor, where its thin splintered fragments scattered haphazardly across the linoleum. I reached across the end table and lifted the receiver, the traces of my smile still visible on my lips, never suspecting that this single telephone call would change the course of my entire life.

36

ALL CRIED OUT

Did you call me?"

"Damn." I sucked my teeth and twirled the phone cord between my fingers. Rom was forever calling *me* ghetto, but it was actually him who'd missed out on some basic lessons on class and etiquette. "You know, Rom," I told him, "I may have been raised in the projects, but my parents gave me a lot of home training and taught me how to cope with adversity. Can you say the same for yours?"

"I don't have time for this nonsense, Sandie. I'm on duty tonight, and I have work to do."

I cradled the receiver between my head and shoulder and massaged my belly with both hands. "Well, I just called to remind you that it's time to start my child-support allotment. I'm due in a few weeks, and, as you know, babies need cribs and diapers."

"How much am I supposed to pay you?"

"The same thing you're paying Lou. Plus half the child-care fees, of course."

"Dammit, Sandie!" Rom exploded along with a crack of thunder in my ear. "Are any of them other sorry suckers who knocked you up paying any child support? Or am I the only chump with a steady job?"

"Don't go there," I warned. "You don't do jack for my children, so leave them out of this!"

"Yeah, but I bet some of my money will go to take care of them and *those are not my fuckin' kids!*"

Fighting words!

"No, they're mine! Don't worry about what everybody else is doing—"

"You've got *three* kids with *three different daddies*, and now I'm supposed to take all the weight just because I'm number four but—"

I shook my head, trying to unclog my brain.

Was this asshole trying to shame me?

I lowered the receiver because I could no longer hear Rom. I was mortally wounded, but I had absolutely no tears.

I was all cried out.

My mind and body had gone numb, as if someone had suddenly flipped a light switch. Thrown a breaker. Blown a fuse. Outside, a low-hanging branch scraped against the sidewalls of the house, and the spitting wind seemed to beckon me with the promise of eternal relief.

Like I said, there wasn't a drop of shame in my game. There was no need. Although I'd made a lot of bad choices in life I'd always pulled my own weight. I had never been on welfare. I had never been without a job. I'd never had a man, other than my daddy, who supported me. Never. I was a self-made, self-supported woman, and whether I had three kids or thirty-three, *they were mine* and I took damned good care of them. On my own.

But Mama always said that what goes around comes around. I felt like the bottom of a dirty boot for what I'd done to Lou. I never should've given her husband the time of day. No matter what he promised me, how good he treated me, or how well he fucked me. I should have respected her boundaries enough to wait until he was divorced.

That's why I was having such bad luck.

I was being punished. I had to suffer for my sins.

And Rom had to suffer for his, too.

Hail brutally assaulted the roof. The harsh pittering pats unlocked the floodgate of emotions I'd thrust deeply inside of myself. I thought about Bailey, cold and in the wet ground; Mama Ceal, her poor heart weakened but fighting hard to hang on; Ladelle, desperately trying to make a difference yet fading fast; and Daddy, gasping upstairs, slowly dying.

The weight of my world suffocated me.

I exhaled and filled the entire room with grief.

I looked down at my bulging stomach and then at the telephone.

He won't give you more than you can bear!

He'd given me much more than I could bear.

Pushing away my partially eaten tuna fish, I pressed the receiver to my ear. "Rom," I said softly, interrupting his frenzied tirade. "I'm coming for your ass, Rom. I'm on my way."

I was mad enough to throw a piano!

I spit and spewed and cussed and screamed, and all the while I really wanted to cry. To cry out. To beg Sandie's forgiveness. Instead, I said some things that will haunt me to my grave. Every drop of my accumulated guilt and pain shot forth like greased lightning through that telephone line. My terrified CQ runner—a Private Benjamin if I'd ever seen one—sat chewing her nails as I screamed into the telephone. Suddenly I realized that Sandie had stopped yelling back. I knew she was still on the line because I could hear the TV in the background along with some strange wheezing noises that must have been coming from her.

Then she said quietly, "I'm coming for your ass, Rom. I'm on my way," and something in her voice told me she meant business. She sounded as if I'd finally pushed her way, way over the edge.

There niggah! Are you happy now?

"Sandie, please! Wait baby! I'm sorry, wait—"

The line went dead.

And so did my heart.

The wind blew a trash can past my window.

I scrambled to collect my thoughts.

What should I do? How did I handle this?

Although my judgment was totally askew, I knew the last thing I wanted was a screaming, pregnant officer swinging on me in the CQ office. Quickly, I ordered my runner to hold the fort down, then I grabbed my rain gear and rushed outside to head her off.

The Charge of Quarters office was located in the company barracks, a mere three blocks away from Sandie's house. I knew she wouldn't get far in this weather, so I drove quickly, hoping to catch a glimpse of her car as she drove up the cresting bluff that led out of her cul de sac. I turned down her street fully expecting to see her car struggling up the base of the hill, but instead I got the surprise of my life. Illuminated in the glare of my headlights was a small, heavy figure trudging up the hill at a breakneck pace.

It was Sandie!

And she was *moving*.

My baby was coatless and hatless. Her thighs were bare. The thin fabric of her maternity top was rain-plastered and molded to her swollen middle. It was all that protected her from the elements. All that protected my babies, because Lord knows I'd failed to.

As I drew nearer, all I saw was determination in her stride and hell in her heart. I jumped from the car and left it idling in the middle of the street, then I reached back inside to grab my military raincoat from the front seat, intending to shelter her. As I neared, Sandie's eyes seemed to widen and focus, and instead of the questioning pain I'd placed there nearly eight months ago, I saw rage.

Deep hatred. Loathing and contempt.

At that moment my own eyes were opened, too. Standing there with the wind and the rain angrily beating down upon us and the elements of the earth rocking her unsteady frame with each battering blow, I discovered my own truth.

I was a fraud.

I was a shit.

I was a fallen domino.

I was *definitely* not a king.

A king would've known how to treat his lady, his baby, his woman. His *friend*. A king would have maintained his castle. The castle that was most important, the castle he cherished. The castle he considered his home.

At that very moment, while absorbing the hatred pouring off her like the rivulets of water, I knew just how wrong I'd been. I was ashamed of myself. I loved this woman more than I loved my life. I loved her like a natural woman, not in the same way I loved my sons. I loved her like the queen she'd always been.

I reached out with the raincoat to take her into my arms, to comfort her and give her a small measure of protection from the storm, and that's when she caught me.

With a solid left hook.

Sheeiit, Tyson would have been proud of her!

Yeah, she had a fight in her, my girl did! By the time she finished with me, that right hook had turned into a left hook and then a right uppercut.

Did I mention her mean-assed jab?

I stood there and let her duke me up, and believe me, Sandie threw her weight around! When I finally managed to force her into my car, she was still swinging and muttering, "Motherfuckah! You trying to *shame* me? Huh?" Jab! "Huh?" Left hook! "HUH?" Uppercut!

Although I'd forced her inside the car, Sandie wasn't quite finished. Screeching, she leaned back in the seat and mule-kicked my dashboard like a maniac. I was worried. Her eyes were unfocused, and her breath was coming in short gasps. She could barely breathe, but she continued to scream, gasping for air and crazed with anger. Although she was inflicting some serious damage to my dash, I was glad it wasn't my balls, so I decided to let her kick and cuss away.

Suddenly, she stopped. She turned and leaned toward me like she wanted to jack me up again. I grabbed her arms. She opened her mouth to yell, and instead spewed hot projectile vomit all over me *and* the front seat of my precious ride!

Tuna fish! Yuck!

While I was busy wiping that funky mess out of my eyes, Sandie flung open her door, bolted from the car, and continued her manic journey up the hill. A moment later I jumped out, too, and even above the noise of the spitting rain I could hear her screaming and hollering, ranting and raving, not yet spent.

Surprisingly, she'd managed to get pretty far ahead of me. I jumped back in the car and made a U-turn—tearing up some lieutenant's lawn in the process. As I sped up the hill behind her, I glimpsed a moving shadow. A car. No, it was a Jeep. Blacker than the ace of spades, it slid backward out of a rain-drenched driveway. More silent than a serpent, it bore down on Sandie. On my babies— *Nooooo! Sandieeeee!*

I blasted the horn as I screamed out her name.

In a flash of lightning I watched the vehicle slam into Sandie's right side. Her swollen body went crashing to the wet pavement. I felt instead of heard the sickening crunch of metal on flesh and bone as the unknowing driver backed over my baby.

I know people who say that at the moment of death your life flashes before your eyes. Well, when Sandie's body disappeared beneath that Jeep Cherokee, my entire life flashed before my eyes. In an instant, I saw every single thing I had ever done, both good and bad. In a split second, I felt every possible human emotion I'd ever experienced.

I saw my life's scores as they tallied up, my virtues as well as my sins, and I knew one thing for sure. When I looked at my bottom line, the brothah came out wanting. I was *behind*. Not because I'd robbed, raped, or killed, but because I'd hurt.

I'd *hurt*.

I'd hurt myself by hating my daddy. Because of him, I set standards for myself that no mortal man could possibly live up to. Inevitably, I tumbled down off of my self-made pedestal and then I hated myself for being human. I'd hurt Lou by staying in a loveless relationship for ten years and ignoring her tipping and dipping for the sake of our children. I'd hurt my sons by mourning for them like they were dead—and expecting them to mourn for me, too.

But most of all, I'd hurt my baby.

My queen. Sanderella. The queen of my heart.

She wasn't responsible for my black feelings. She never asked me to leave my wife and kids. Instead of accepting responsibility for my decisions, I'd heaped my guilt on her slender shoulders at a time when she needed me most. Sandie was blameless. I had pursued this relationship. I'd chased *her*. I loved my baby real good until I made her believe in me. And then I turned my back on her and treated her worse than shit. It was my own guilt that had been sucking the life out of me, out of my woman, and now, perhaps, out of my babies.

My torturous thoughts took maybe two seconds, and by the time I bolted from my car and ran over to that Jeep, I had already sworn to God that if Sandie or my babies didn't survive, then neither would I.

37

BEGINNING OF MY END

I let them take her away from me when we reached the base hospital. I was covered in the bright blood that had seeped from a jagged gash in the back of her skull. After the Jeep rolled over her, Sandie lay motionless in the pouring rain. In a flash I ran over and lifted her in my arms, and to my horror, her body flopped limply like a lifeless rag doll.

Bright blood spurted from a huge break in her forearm, and the shoulder of her other arm was positioned at a weird angle. The driver of the Cherokee got us to the hospital no more than ten minutes after she'd been hit, and I held her still body in my arms and cried like I've never cried before. The driver insisted on staying with me and now we sat numbly, neither of us able to speak. Words were unnecessary. They could not possibly describe the pain.

It was the beginning of my end.

I'd always hated hospitals, and this one was no exception. This was the hospital where Sandie had planned to give birth to our babies. I cursed myself for not being there for a single one of her prenatal appointments. Mel had taken time off from work to stand in as her labor coach.

Poor Sandie. I'd done her so wrong.

There was nothing left for me to do.

"I'm sorry, man," the driver said for what had to be the one zillionth time. He was a young white captain, no more than twenty-seven. "I am so sorry. I just didn't see her . . . there was so much rain. I'm so sorry."

I nodded my understanding. What could I say?

I'd hurt her, too.

I'd given a nurse Sandie's home number and asked her to call Bunchie, who had called and cussed me out as soon as she hit Missouri. Sadly, I'd given her a few choice words, too. I knew it was just a matter of time before she came bursting through those doors, and I didn't know how to face her.

Here I was supposed to be a king.

Not only did I fail to protect my queen, it was me she was running away from! When my life got funky, I left my baby out there by herself, alone, in pain, and unmarried. And with her shame sticking out in front of her for the whole world to see. Then I helped the world grind her pride into the ground.

I put my head down in my hands and cried. Mortified. As long as I lived I would never forget how badly I had treated her. And how much she continued to love me.

There could never be another woman for me.

My heart would always belong to Sandie.

"Mr. Caesar?" someone called. "Which one of you gentlemen is Mr. Caesar?"

I raised my head and said, in tears, "That would be me."

The tall male nurse reached out his hand and said somberly, "Come with me, sir. Dr. Williams wants to counsel you."

"Can I see her?" I asked. "Is it okay if I just take one look at her?"

"You want to sit with your wife?" he asked.

I didn't bother to correct him. I nodded.

"Well, I don't see how that could hurt." He led me through a set of double doors on the right, then into a small room. There lay Sandie. Motionless, bloody, and on a hospital gurney. Fresh tears sprang to my eyes, and I didn't know if I could bear to look at her. Her stomach was still huge and distended, but somehow her body looked much smaller.

And so still.

I wanted to bolt from the chilly room, but my grief paralyzed me. I sank down to my knees and wailed until I felt a pair of strong arms helping me to my feet.

"She may still be able to hear you," the male nurse suggested gently. "Talk to her."

I staggered over to the gurney to get a good look at her face and to my surprise it was smooth and unmarred. With all the blood it had been hard to tell whether it had come from her head wound or if her face, too, had been injured.

I stared down at Sandie's quiet body and did something I had never done before. Gently, I placed both my hands upon the mound of her stomach, and I touched my babies. My lifelines. My blood. And then I did something that I had not done in a very long time. Something I should have done all along.

I prayed.

I prayed to high heaven for God's infinite mercy.

I opened my heart, spread wide my arms, and felt my soul leave my body with a mighty swooping roar. I promised my spiritual Father that no matter what happened in my life, from this day forward I'd be a better man. I would bear my own ills, shoulder the weight of my own decisions, and accept the consequences of my own actions. I would also call Solomon. My father. I'd accept his apology and forgive him so that I could also forgive myself.

Lightning flashed beneath my feet, and my spirit soared high above Sandie's body. I made a solemn vow that whatever my wrongs had been in the past, I would spend the rest of my life making them right if He would only spare my queen and our unborn children. Cymbals crashed and trumpets blared, and the ancient language of my ancestors spewed unbidden from my lips. I prayed to the God of Adam, Moses, Jesus, and Muhammad to forgive my sins, to forgive the sins of my queen, to forgive our every trespass, our every transgression. And in return I promised Him my life. I promised to live my life according to His commandments. The commandments He set forth in the Torah, the Bible, and in the Holy Quran.

Suddenly, I felt a protesting movement from within Sandie's womb. I snatched back my hands.

"They kicked me!" I yelled.

Sandie's lips parted and she whispered, "Good . . . they've been kicking me for months."

Thank you, God!

I reached down and planted light kisses on her lips, her cheeks, and her closed eyelids. "Baby, I'm so sorry. Please forgive me. I love you, Sandie, and I love our children—all seven of them. I'll make it up to you, I swear, I'll—"

"You smell"—she winced in pain and wrinkled her nose—"like tuna fish."

Just then a young but capable-looking doctor entered the room. He grabbed both my hands and shook them as one. "Hello sir, my name is Dr. Derrick Williams, and I'm going to be your wife's obstetrician. As you know, she suffered serious injuries in the accident, and her blood pressure has dropped dangerously low. As a result, the babies are in fetal distress."

Fear crumpled my face.

"Now don't worry," he soothed. "Although her injuries are severe"—he read from a clipboard—"a fractured pelvis, dislocated shoulder, several deep lacerations, and a possible concussion. If we act now, I can deliver the babies and turn her surgical care over to a highly competent orthopedic surgeon." The brother winked. "Who also happens to be one of *us*."

"Please, Doc, *please*." I grabbed his shoulders and begged, "You've got my future in your hands! Doc, help her. Do whatever you have to do for her and my babies!"

"Okay now. While she's probably experiencing some upper-body pain, we've given her a strong sedative and an epidural, so she should be numb from the waist down. Due to the extent of her injuries you won't be allowed inside of the operating room, but someone will come outside and get you as soon as the babies are delivered. They're premature, but there is a good chance that they'll survive. So," he said as he looked through a thick orange folder, "her O.B. records indicate that you two are having fraternal twins. Twin A, a baby girl, and twin B, a baby boy."

I looked down at Sandie.

A girl and a boy?

My whole body shook with joy, and suddenly I was certain of one thing. A love like ours was never, ever free. There had to be some agony.

For the ecstasy.

"What we . . . what we . . . name them?" Sandie whispered.

I had a lot of making up to do. A lifetime's worth. I bent over and kissed that spot on her forehead that I'd missed so much and answered, "You can name them Samson and Delilah, or you can name them Rumpelstiltskin and Thumbelina. Or," I said, and kissed my soon-to-be wife, "you can name them Romulus and Sanderella, two names that will go together forever."

She looked at me with a tired smile, and as they wheeled my queen into the operating room to bring forth the new princess and prince, I wiped my eyes and walked out of the room, then pushed through the double doors and stepped into my future.

Epilogue

LIVING JUST A LITTLE,
LAUGHING JUST A LITTLE . . .

That's my big girl! C'mon and let Granny check that diaper!" Mama clucked and fussed as she lifted a wriggling four-month-old Nandi from my arms. Nandi's dark curls were precious against her smooth brown skin, and a sweet baby smell clung to her clothing. "Here, Sandie." Mama passed me two thick oval-shaped pieces of gauze. "Don't pull that dress back up yet! Stick these breast shields inside your bra so you don't mess up that beautiful gown."

I sat at my spacious vanity with the soothing rays from the early-morning sun cascading across my bare breasts. The warmth of God's smile nourished my body just as I had nourished my child's. I fingered the front of my champagne-colored lace and chenille dress and obediently pressed the cottony material into my maternity bra. Nursing twins could be quite an ordeal, but with the help of an electric pump courtesy of their auntie Bunchie, and the bottled assistance of their father, my beasts had been tamed, and I loved every moment of it.

"Take her to her big sister," Mama instructed Bunchie. She secured the adhesive tabs to Nandi's diaper and gently placed her into Bunchie's outstretched arms.

I could tell Mama Ceal was nervous. She hadn't stopped fretting and flitting about since she'd arrived two days earlier. As promised, her heart surgery had given her a new lease on life. Instead of becoming tired and short of breath during the slightest activity, she moved about freely, energetically. Mama had always looked much younger than her actual age, but with the replacement of a simple heart valve she appeared more stylish and vibrant than ever.

"Baby girl," she said as she rearranged the fresh baby's breath in the small wreath attached to my veil, "Franklin would have been proud to witness this day."

I swallowed hard. Daddy had died while I was in the hospital recovering from my injuries. I hadn't been well enough to attend his funeral, and the thought of never seeing him again still made my heart shake with sorrow.

"I know, Mama. I know." I took her trembling hands in mine and kissed her slender fingers. I loved her so much it hurt. A single tear slipped from her eye, and she quickly brushed it away.

"But that's all right, sweetie!" Mama flashed me a brave grin. "He sent me in his place. That's the only reason I had strength enough to get on that airplane and fly way out here to Missouri. Your daddy's spirit gave me the power!"

I felt my own heart pumping the strength of my daddy's love through my veins. The day after I was hit, Daddy had forced Bunchie to bring him to the hospital to see me.

"Pook," he whispered, the small oxygen tank he carried barely adequate to support his needs. "Pook. I'm here, baby. Your daddy is right here." Although I was still tired and groggy from my surgery, I felt Daddy kissing me and holding my hands, smoothing the hair away from my damp forehead.

"Everything is going to be fine, my darling," he said. "Just fine. But you have got to carry on. Just remember that God is protecting you, baby. Remember how many people in this world love you and are praying for your recovery. And remember"—he held my hand just a little bit tighter—"remember, no matter what has happened, Romulus loves you, too." My daddy smiled down at me through tears. "He's a good man, Pook. But he's a man. He's just a man. Love him, forgive him, and build a new life with him. I love you, my darling daughter."

Three days later, Daddy was gone.

Hot salty tears crept down my cheeks and left a trail in the nutmeg-colored powder Bunchie had pressed onto my skin. I smiled up at Mama. "I've got him in my heart, Mama." I patted my breast. "He's right here in my heart."

Just then Sparkle and Charmel burst through the doors wearing dresses identical to Bunchie's. I tried not to laugh as they shot each other elbows, daggers, and dirty looks. I reached out to Mel and squeezed her hand. She'd been my truest friend, my staunchest supporter. After designating herself as my labor and delivery coach, Mel showed up regularly at my Lamaze classes, wearing neon-colored spandex shorts and a push-up bra. "Put some clothes on!" I told her when I saw a couple of husbands almost get pimp-slapped for staring at her trim midriff and those sister-girl hips.

Mel had looked around at the room full of expectant mothers stretched out on the floor like whales on a dry beach and grinned. "Sorry, hunny. I'm fresh out of pink muumuus!"

Sparkle had flown in from her new duty station in Puerto Rico, where, by her accounts, she was blazing a trail through a fraternity of Omegas. She bént over and kissed my cheek.

"It's time to *go*," Mel snapped, clearly pissed off by my good friend's presence.

Sparkle winked at me and giggled. "Yeah, baby." She wiggled her booty in her peach-colored dress as mischief danced in her emerald eyes. "It's time to go, because heffahs are jealous!"

"All right, you two," Mama said, and shooed them out of my sunroom. "Both of you best behave yourselves and let peace be still. Sandie, wait right here and I'll send someone in to help you down the stairs."

My hands were clammy as I sat at the end of the long hallway. The wine-colored carpet complemented both the iced-raspberry wallpaper and the mahogany veneer of the portraits scattered along the walls. We'd purchased this house only six weeks ago, and between the sheer size of it and its intricate layout, I was still reeling in awe. Soft organ chords drifted down to calm my nerves, and Mama's sharp voice barking out last-minute directions provided comfort to my soul.

"You ready?" I glanced up and found my sister standing beside me, dressed to the nines in a Liz Claiborne outfit that did a lot of justice to her slim figure. Ladelle had flown in with Tenea and her small family, and under the strict care and attention of her doctors and with the right medications and a proper diet, instead of the HIV dragging her down she was actually beginning to thrive.

The night before we'd thrown a sort of a bridal party. Mama had cooked a pan of lasagna, and Bunchie had recorded all of my favorite old jams. Along with Sparkle and Charmel, we'd planned to get our "eat" on and our "party" on to celebrate my last night as a single woman, but just as we were getting into a sistah-girl groove, Ladelle turned up missing in action.

"I saw her heading down the hall a few minutes ago," Mama piped up as we searched for my sister. "Missy must be laying down recharging her battery. G'on back there and wake her up."

I'd wheeled myself toward the back of the house where the guest rooms were located, with Bunchie following hot on my heels. We stopped before the closed door and gave each other a knowing look.

I flung open the door.

"Hot damn!" I clamped my hands over my eyes. "Call the police!"

"Lawd—*Jeezus*," Bunchie cried. "Cover that nasty cooch! Damn! I ain't *never* gonna have a drop of luck! And here I am trying my best to hit the damn number!"

Ladelle, her clothes neatly hung on a hook, lay sprawled on the bed like the Queen of Sheba. Her mouth agape, her legs cocked open spread-eagle style, her sleep shirt bunched up around her waist, her naked treasure glistening brilliantly for the world to behold.

Bunchie placed her hands on her perfect hips, livid. "Girl, *close your pocketbook!*"

I snickered. "Throw a sheet over her naked ass. I don't wanna look at nobody's ugly cat—not even my own!"

Bunchie pointed. "Well that there cat's got claws! You put a sheet on her, she's in your house!"

"I ain't!"

"Well, I ain't either! Anyway, Mama Ceal said to wake her up." She reached out one manicured finger and scratched the bottom of Ladelle's bare foot. "Get up and come join the party!"

"Both of y'all best leave me the hell alone!" Ladelle grumbled, then promised to join us in a few minutes.

"And put on some goddamned drawers!" Bunchie commanded.

"Yeah," I added, "some big white cotton bloomers that come up over your navel!"

We slammed the door, and Bunchie laughed. "Ain't that just like Ladelle? Forever showing her ass?"

And now my big sister stood smiling at me, waiting for my answer. "I said," she repeated, "are you ready for this?"

"As ready as I'm ever gonna get!" I giggled.

"Don't worry, San." Ladelle bent down at my side and put her arms around me. During my recovery she'd been a no-nonsense rock for me to lean on. "You're doing the right thing."

"Not according to Mel." I shook my head sadly. Charmel thought Rom was a dirty rat. Although she had promised to respect my decisions and stand by my side, she told me I should have turned my back on Rom the same way he'd turned his back on me.

"I told you about messing with those R's!" Mel reminded me. "Fool you once—shame on him. Fool you twice—shame on *you!*" And when she saw I was resolute, she said, "Okay, hunny. That dog may never bite you again, but don't you ever forget his black ass has teeth!"

Was she right? I don't think so. Yes, Rom had hurt me deeply, and his behavior was inexcusable. I was nobody's Mother Love, and there was no "forgive and forget" in my heart. Although our relationship needed work, Rom also had issues that did not involve me. His fear of following in his father's footsteps led him to experience a level of guilt beyond belief.

And he allowed that guilt to overshadow his love for me.

He came to me one rainy afternoon three weeks after my accident. "I'm going to talk to somebody, San." He'd already given me a marriage proposal and asked each of my kids not only if they'd accept him as a father, but also if they would honor him by taking his last name. "I've already called a counselor and I'm ready to heal, but I can't make any progress without you and the kids. Would you consider family therapy?"

Twice a week a family counselor came to our home where we received both family and individual counseling. Believe it or not, I'm actually learning a lot about myself and a lot about our unique family structure as well.

As I began to understand Rom's issues surrounding his father, I slowly began to forgive him. But would I ever forget? No. Never. I'd been through too much, and unfortunately his treatment of me said a lot about how he'd react if the chips were ever down far enough again. It would take years, if ever, for my level of trust to rise to its previous state. But when I looked past Rom's behavior and into his heart, there was no doubt that his love for me and for our children was strong. Besides, I was in need of forgiveness for my sins, too. Let the one among us who is without sin cast the first stone. Does love have to be perfect? Or should it simply be possible? Somehow I still had my doubts.

I sighed up at Ladelle. "Mel says it's stupid of me to marry him."

She spun my wheelchair around and glared. "Don't worry about Mel," my sister said firmly. "Worry about *Sandie*. Stupid is sitting by yourself in this big-ass house with five little kids and a man on the other side of post who loves you and wants to give you and your kids his heart and his name."

She ran her fingers through her hair, exasperation plastered all over her face. "Look, Sandie. You still have time to change your mind; you can call off the wedding and tell Rom to take a hike. You can cancel the DJ, pay off the caterer, and tell all these folks to let the doorknob hit them in the ass on the way out. But what the hell would that prove? That you're some kind of Superwoman who's so full of self-righteousness that you don't have room in your heart for forgiveness? Go ahead! Live the struggle! Stand on your pride and your worn-out principles if you think that'll make your girlfriends happy. Please!"

My sister stared at me incredulously. She placed her hands on the arms of my wheelchair and leaned down until her eyes were level with mine. When she spoke again, her tone was deliberate and controlled. "Go ahead and choose to be a single parent again, Sandie. This time with five kids. Be the poster child for the bitter black woman who doesn't need a man. Sisters in that boat come a dime a dozen, chilling on the welfare lines, full of pride with their noble attitudes tucked away in their empty purses. That's what's wrong with the black family today. Why we have the highest number of single-female-headed households in the nation. Nobody is willing to hang tough through the bad times as well as the good. As so-called liberated take-no-shit black women and successful got-it-going-on black men, we're too quick to throw in the towel when there's a crisis instead of sticking around to work our problems out. People go through changes, and sometimes they learn from them. You knew Rom had a heavy past when you met him."

"I know, but he hurt me so damn bad, Ladelle."

"So what?" She threw her hands in the air and backed off a few paces. "He fucked up! Haven't you? Besides, you knew how confused he was. Where his head was and where he was coming from. He was caught up in a bag, but Rom loves you and he's been good to you. There for you. For me. For Mama Ceal and for Daddy. Why should you deprive yourself of a good man and your kids of a good father just because he's not perfect? To satisfy some highfalutin bitch of a girlfriend who just loves to tell you what she will and won't accept from a man? Please!" She smirked and gave a short, harsh chuckle. "Believe that sanctimonious bullshit if you want to! She's probably jealous. None of us have perfect men. Perfect relationships. How could we when we're imperfect people? So just like the rest of us, Mel is putting up with some type of shit from her man, 'cause just like the rest of them, her man is putting up with some type of shit from her. Now if she says she ain't and you believe her, then she's a damn liar and you're a damn fool."

I nodded. So much of what she said rang true. I'd come into the relationship with my fair share of baggage as well, and Rom had not only accepted it, he was willing to deal with it.

"Listen, sister." Ladelle calmed herself and squeezed my hands. "Every now and then God gives us a second chance at life. Sometimes we deserve it and sometimes we don't. But whenever he sees fit to allow us another minute, another moment of happiness, we have to seize it. We have to take it and run like a thief without questioning it. If it feels right, then do it. This could be God's gift to you. And his gift to Rom. A second chance at happiness."

Her point was well taken. "Thank you, Ladelle. Thank you."

Suddenly my stomach curled, my heart quivered madly in my chest, and my breathing became shallow. My nerves were shot, plain old working overtime.

"How's that hip?" My brother-in-law strode down the hall in his black tuxedo. He looked trim and fit, dashing and debonair, much the same as he looked on the day Bunchie married him. Bunchie was on his arm and gazed at her lifelong partner with a satisfied smile. It was good to see her smiling so much these days. And even harder to believe that Vernon was responsible for her happiness. My brother-in-law had conquered his demons and done a complete turnaround with his life.

"I don't know if I'm ready to go popping and locking down the Soul Train line," I joked, reaching out to hug him, "but I'm sure game to do the Electric Slide!"

Vernon squeezed me tightly. "The slide? Ain't gonna be no sliding up in here tonight! More like y'all gonna be doing the bump and grind! Here you're having babies left and right, and I didn't even know you were having sex!"

I giggled and swatted at him.

To Bunchie's delight, Vernon had not only completed his treatment program, he'd quit drinking and gambling and enrolled himself in one of those anger-control programs where you go away and confront your demons in the hopes of totally purging them from your life. While Bunchie vowed to leave him for good if he ever got in her face again, after graduating from the program they agreed to enter long-term intensive marriage counseling. Without all of the old issues clouding their lives, they were able to pick up their shattered pieces and move on in their marriage. According to Bunchie, while things still weren't perfect, they were much better than before.

Ladelle and Bunchie walked beside me as Kharel held the door open and Vernon wheeled my chair along the plush carpet. We crossed the threshold of the arched white double doors, and paused. The view was spectacular. We'd come a long way from the projects of Brooklyn. Our formal dining room had been converted into a chapel with sparkling chandeliers dotting the ceiling and elegant velvet-backed chairs lining each side of the room. The area in the middle, reserved as the aisle, was littered with rose petals and tiny pink and white orchids.

Aunt Bessie and Uncle Boot sat up front with Mama Ceal and Solomon, Rom's father. Aunt Bessie's hat was broken down over her left eye, and she'd forgotten her teeth in New York, but a huge grin covered her face nevertheless. Uncle Boot licked his lips. He looked hungry.

Jamillah stood smiling with Nandi in her arms, while Hannibal and Mansa held on to Hanif and Kharim. A week ago we received the shock of our lives when Miss Lou, now known as Mrs. Louise Caesar-McDowell, called and dropped a bomb on us.

"I'm not sending the boys for the wedding, Sandie," she informed me without preamble or fanfare.

"W-what? Why?" I gasped.

A week after my accident Lou called me at the hospital with a message of condolence and goodwill. We had a long talk, Rom's ex-wife and I. A talk where I asked for her forgiveness and explained that I had never meant to hurt her.

"Girl, don't think you had anything to do with our breakup," she assured me. "We just weren't meant for each other. Hell, I was young, and I mistook his kindness as a weakness. I'm glad he has someone who will make him happy, because he deserves the best. He's a good man, Sandie," she told me wistfully. "A damned good black man. Don't make the same mistake I made. Hold on to him."

And now she was telling me that the boys couldn't come to share in our special day?

"Don't worry, Sandie," she quickly soothed me. "I'm not sending them for the wedding because I'm sending them for good."

My heart double-timed.

"Rom is always saying how much he wants them," she continued, "how much he misses them. Well, they miss him, too. And they need him. I figured since you two have what I hear is a bumping mansion and are rolling around in the loot, why not?"

Talk about the little old lady who lived in the shoe? Amazingly, from the mother of three I somehow became the mother of seven. It was all so unreal.

"Hey, baby," my soon-to-be husband said with a wink and a sexy smile. His arms overflowed with the dimpled brown bundle that was Askia, our son. Askia looked at me and flashed his perpetual grin. The more docile of the twins, he'd been blessed with an even temperament and a pleasant disposition. Although he was the smaller baby at birth and had sustained the bulk of the injuries during my accident, with the help of an infant orthopedic surgeon and intensive physical therapy, his prognosis for a normal childhood was excellent.

Rom cuddled Askia in his right arm and took my hand in his left. With the sound of Frankie Beverly's "We Are One" playing in the background, we made our way slowly toward the altar.

"She's beautiful," Rom's mother whispered as Vernon wheeled me down the aisle. Mr. and Mrs. "Big Daddy" Jenkins sat surrounded by Rom's four sisters and their children. As fine as Rom was, his mother and sisters were awfully gruesome, but of course I would never tell him that. I felt their smiles caress me as I rode by, but my eyes and my heart were locked on Rom.

As my wheelchair came to rest before the Good Reverend Morrison, Uncle Boot stood up from the front row of seats where he'd been sandwiched between Mama and Aunt Bessie. Mama Ceal beamed at me and mouthed *I love you* as Uncle Boot quickly traded places with Vernon.

"What man will stand up today and give this beautiful young bride away?"

"I will," Uncle Boot sounded off in a loud, clear voice. He squeezed my shoulder, sending me the power of his love. He had been the logical stand-in for Daddy. In fact, he said it was Daddy's dying wish that he stand up for me on this day. He and Aunt Bessie had flown to my bedside immediately after my accident. They'd been at my house with Bunchie and the children when Daddy had had his fatal heart attack and died. After everything my poor family had been forced to endure, my aunt and uncle proved to be blessed friends. They made all the funeral arrangements and had Daddy's body flown home to Brooklyn, where his funeral was held.

Droves of people turned out to put Daddy away, I was told. The old-timers of Brownsville had filed through Reverend Morrison's church for an entire day to show their respects to an old-fashioned black man who treated everyone as though they were blood family.

A sudden jolt of pain lanced through my back and settled in my injured hip, reminding me to rise from the wheelchair. I only used it when I was tired or when I had been on my feet for an extended period of time. All things considered, I had healed pretty well, although not well enough to stay in the Army. No problem. I'd been medically retired with a fifty percent service-connected disability, and that was all right with me! Between the sizable insurance settlement I was awarded from the accident, the *huge* insurance policy I'd received from Daddy, and the disability pension I collected each month from the Veterans Administration, I was set. I could finally afford to be an Army wife and stay home and raise my kids. I planned to devote all of my time and my energy to loving my children and my family.

"We are gathered here today to unite this man and woman in holy matrimony. Do you, Romulus Caesar, promise to love, cherish, nurture, and support this woman, for better or for worse, in sickness and

306 | Tracy Price-Thompson

in health, through good times and bad, for as long as you both shall live?"

"I do."

"Do you promise to be good to her? To be the landlord of her heart and the guardian of her dreams? To be a loving father to every child she has borne, whether that child be biologically linked to you or not, and to be a trustworthy husband in every sense of the word?"

"I do."

"Do you, Sanderella Daisy Vann Coffee, promise to love, cherish, nurture, and support this man, for better or for worse, in sickness and in health, through good times and bad, for as long as you both shall live?"

"I do."

"Do you promise to be good to him? To be the landlord of his heart and the guardian of his dreams? To be a loving mother to every child he has fathered, whether that child be biologically linked to you or not, and to be a trustworthy wife in every sense of the word?"

"I do."

"Then by the powers vested in me . . ."

The rest of the good reverend's speech was lost in the rumbling roar of laughter, music, and clapping hands. And then Rom's lips were upon mine.

"Life is a teacher," my granny used to say, and of course she was right. Over the past few years I've learned quite a few of life's lessons, but the one lesson that stands out above the rest is the lesson of love. Sometimes we have to suffer in order to become truly grateful. All throughout the pain and the heartache, the death and the darkness, I've been cloaked and blanketed in the strength of God's love. The love of my family, the love of my children, and the love of my spouse. My husband. My friend.

"Will the following children come up and stand next to this loving couple: Jamillah Caesar, Hannibal Caesar, Mansa Caesar, Hanif Caesar, Kharim Caesar, Nandi Caesar, and Askia Caesar." Reverend Morrison held one finger in the air. "Please join me in sealing this union with God's blessings and his eternal mercy on this lovely new family."

Family.

The most important thing in the world to me, and for the rest of my days on earth I will strive to keep mine strong. Because living just a little and laughing just a little ain't easy, but with a loving family by your side, your horizons are simply infinite.

A Conversation with
Tracy Price-Thompson,
Author of *Black Coffee*

Sanderella has such a wonderful and strong family in Black Coffee. *Can you tell us more about that?*

During periods of great hardship it is often the intimacy of family and the coping skills we garner from our upbringing that sustain us through the rough seas of our lives. In *Black Coffee*, I decided to portray a capable black woman who was obviously raised in a stable, loving environment surrounded by people who edified and encouraged her, but who was in no way exempt from the tribulations of life and the sorrows of failed relationships. As writers, we often rush to attribute the faults of our characters to some sort of dysfunction in their childhoods, but in Sandie's case I wanted the reader to become familiar with a flawed but dynamic character whose trying experiences were due not to being reared in an inferior environment but, like a lot of women, to her own inability to make wise, mature choices in love relationships. In order to properly portray Sandie's strength and fortitude during her periods of crisis, I felt it necessary to show the relationship between her familial interactions and her ability to cope with life on its own terms.

Were you ever in the military?

Yes, I began my military career as a Transportation Coordinator, MOS specialty 88N, and after ten years of traveling and deploying, I applied to and was accepted into Army Officer Candidate School. I was subsequently rebranched into the Engineer Corps, and served there until my retirement.

How much does Sanderella reflect your own personality? Is there a Rom in your life?

I get asked this question so often that it amazes me! Sanderella is actually a prototype of several women I had the pleasure of serving with. She has the spunk and sister-girl grit of a female drill sergeant I once worked with. She has the bad luck with relationships of a close friend who was an expert on rappelling out of aircrafts, but kept landing flat on her face when it came to spotting Mr. Right. She got her self-confidence and determination from a young private I once trained, who, no matter how many times she got hit with a brick, jumped right back up and rolled with the punches. And, of course, she got her coping skills and military expertise from me!

Quite often women want to know if I have a Romulus and where they can find one for themselves, but unfortunately I have to tell them, "Sorry, ladies! I made him up!"

What made you write this book?

While most readers know of someone who is either serving or who has served in the military, seldom are the unique challenges and triumphs of African-American soldiers portrayed in commercial fiction. Soldiers, sailors, airmen, and marines live and operate under constraints and within parameters that the average citizen may never fathom. After serving honorably and bearing witness to the boxes African-American service members must often force themselves to fit into, I decided to pay homage and tribute to my boot-wearing sisters and brothers. I wrote *Black Coffee* not only to give voice to the minority soldier, but also to examine, through literature, some of the realities and complexities of African-American military life, and in particular, the constraints and boundaries placed on military love.

Describe your writing process.

I do my best writing late at night or in the predawn hours of the morning. With so many children going in several different directions in our home, the atmosphere is usually pretty chaotic. I find myself mentally outlining plot sequences and practicing dialogue when in the shower or while shopping for groceries, then I have to rush back home to jot down notes. But my actual writing is done after my household has settled down. I require a peaceful spirit and minimal distractions to think creatively, so I usually have to sacrifice my sleep if I want my muse to take over.

Which authors have influenced you?

Oh, I have been influenced by several authors. I come from a family of readers and grew up in a home filled with books. My parents never restricted my reading materials; instead, they encouraged me to read as broadly as possible and to choose from a variety of genres. As a result, I am one of those strange readers who can read and find enjoyment in almost any type of book, but I must say I have been most influenced by awesome writers like Gloria Naylor, Pearl Cleage, Marita Golden, James Baldwin, Stephen King, Robert McCammeron, Maya Angelou, Jewell Parker Rhodes, J. California Cooper, Richard Wright, Sonya Sanchez, Walter Mosley, Alice Walker, Sandra Jackson Opoku, and newcomer Bernice McFadden.

What are you working on next?

Oftentimes the issues of intraracial prejudice between people of color are understated and minimized in contemporary fiction. While minorities may share common experiences, neighborhoods, and resources, the lines of demarcation can be quite distinct when it comes to matters of the heart. My next novel, *Chocolate Sangria*, explores the hearts of two lovers caught between the great cultural divide and the tribulations they face when lies are told, secrets are revealed, and black and Hispanic love spills across racial boundaries.

Reading Group Guide

The following reading group guide was created to enhance your group's discussion of *Black Coffee* by Tracy Price-Thompson.

1. Many people seem captivated and enthralled by men and women in uniform. What intrigued you about a romance in a military setting? What do you think about the amount of control the military has over someone's personal life? Could you operate comfortably in such an environment?

2. In the novel, Sandie came from a close-knit, loving family with strong ties. How did this help shape her character and bolster her ability to cope when times got rough? What do you think about the way the military forces its members to travel to far corners of the world, out of the immediate reach of their loved ones? How do you think she felt about leaving

To print out copies of this or other Strivers Row Reading Group Guides, visit us at www.atrandom.com/rgg

her children behind for extended periods of time while deploying to remote areas?

3. Based on your own experiences, how much could you identify with Sandie's choices in men? How does Sandie compare to you and the women you know in regard to how she handled her responsibilities to her children, her job, her family, and her love life? Do most women, much like Sandie, look for love, but often in the wrong places?

4. What do you think of a woman who has it all together professionally, but seems to have less success in her personal life? Does our society force women to choose between having a great career and being a good mother and a good mate?

5. Sandie was devastated when she learned of her sister's HIV status. Have you ever encountered a situation where someone you loved was diagnosed with an illness with a heavy social stigma attached, such as HIV? How do you think experiences like this change a person? How did it affect Sandie? What was Ladelle's reaction to her illness?

6. In the beginning of their relationship, Rom seemed to be the answer to Sandie's dreams. There was little doubt in her mind that he truly loved her. How did you feel about the fact that Sandie entered into a relationship with Rom while he was still married? Did she fall for him too readily? Or did she fight a good fight?

7. Despite the fact that Sandie did not want to have any more children, she stopped taking her birth control pills at Rom's suggestion. What do you think of her decision to follow his advice? What do you think of her decision to carry her pregnancy to term and to keep her babies?

8. Rom fancied himself a king. How much of Rom's inner conflict do you feel was a result of his father's leaving the family during his childhood? Did this have a direct bearing on the way Rom felt about leaving his own sons? How do you feel about the fact that Romulus pursued a relationship with Sandie while he was still married to Lou? Was his personal misery and desire for true love enough justification for leaving his wife and children?

9. Since it was Rom's idea for Sandie to stop taking the Pill, what do you think of his negative reaction when he discovered she was pregnant with his child? How did you feel when he blamed Sandie for his not being with his sons?

10. Is Rom a dog? Or is he simply a nice guy with conflict and issues? What about him appeals to you? Is there anything about him that makes you uncomfortable? What was your gut reaction when he called Sandie a bitch?

11. How do you think Sandie's accident reinforced Rom's feelings toward her and their children? Do you think he'd already realized the error of his ways before she was hit? Or was seeing her body crushed beneath the Jeep the true catalyst for his change?

12. How did you feel about Sandie's relationship with her mother and two sisters? What about her friendships with Sparkle and Charmel? Do you think women tend to nurture and support one another through rough times as fully as these women supported Sandie? Are there women in your life who will stick by you through thick and thin?

13. Sandie enjoyed a very close relationship with her father. Do most women use their fathers as measuring sticks for the men in their lives? Did Sandie expect Rom to love her children as

fully and unreservedly as her own father loved her half siblings? If you were a single mother, how would you have reacted if a man shouted to you, "Those are NOT my kids!"

14. Why do you think Sandie agreed to marry Rom at the end of the story? Was Ladelle right in her assessment of the growing single-parent crisis for black families in America? Do you think Sandie should have hoisted a "strong black woman" flag and raised her five children alone? Do we all have issues and enter into relationships with baggage from previous loves? What is the role of forgiveness in building and maintaining a strong, realistic black family? Does this story prove that true love conquers all?

ABOUT THE AUTHOR

TRACY PRICE-THOMPSON is a highly decorated Desert Storm veteran who graduated from Army Officer Candidate School after ten years as an enlisted soldier. A Brooklyn, New York, native and retired Army engineer officer, she holds degrees in business administration and social work, and is a Ralph Bunche Graduate Fellow. A member of the Athenaeum Honor Society of Rutgers University, Price-Thompson lives in New Jersey with her husband and children. *Black Coffee* is her first novel, and she would love to hear what you think of it. You can e-mail her at tracythomp@aol.com or write to her at P.O. Box 187, Fort Dix, NJ 08640.

Una B Hall
1349 Unity St
Fri 9.01